## TEMPTATION

Aileen had vowed to love, honor and obey the strange, almost savage man to whom she had been given as an untouched bride. She had promised to put her needs second to his, to humble herself to his purposes, his pleasures.

But now, in the presence of the handsome, elegant young man who was her husband's blood brother yet total opposite, Aileen felt the stirrings of a feeling she had never known before. She felt herself gripped by a power melting all resolve, all resistance to his eyes, his lips, his hands.

Now she knew what passion was and meant—and her marriage and her kingdom trembled on a kiss, hung suspended over a torrential floodtide of desire, delight and terrifying destruction. . . .

# DESIRES
# OF
# THY HEART

### ABOUT THE AUTHOR

Joan Carroll Cruz lives in New Orleans with her husband and their five children. She spent her high school years at a boarding school operated by the School Sisters of Notre Dame in Chatawa, Mississippi, where she was the editor of the school newspaper; she believes this was the beginning of her writing career.

Her major interests besides her family and writing are classical music and opera. Mrs. Cruz writes at night when her husband Louis, a truck driver, is on the road. She finds writing easiest "when I am doing the love scenes," and she is presently at work on her new novel, *Love Endures Forever*.

## Big Bestsellers from SIGNET

# DESIRES
# OF
# THY HEART

By

*Joan Carroll Cruz*

A SIGNET BOOK

NEW AMERICAN LIBRARY

TIMES MIRROR

*This book is dedicated to my brother*
*Daniel J. Carroll, Jr.*

THE FLARINGS of the fireplace and the flickering lights from listless candles cavorted about the mother's swollen abdomen. It was a difficult confinement. The pains had commenced during the thunderous storm of the previous night, but throughout the whole of the day, despite the gallant efforts of the mother to strain the child from her womb, the babe refused its birth. The delivery seemed ominously threatened now that darkness again shadowed Lauxburgh castle and the rains pattered ever so dismally against the glazed windows. The elderly physician and his assistant were fearfully aware of the atmosphere's increasing somberness. Already apprehensive for the mother's weakened condition and frustratingly helpless to relieve her agony, they could do naught but wrap themselves in fur-lined cloaks as defense against the damp drafts that swirled in the shadows like menacing spirits.

The vigil was long and lonely. The Anglo-Saxon women of the castle, who would normally have whispered tender encouragements to the sick of their own race, willfully avoided the chamber and retired with apparent disregard for the Viking mother's welfare. Perhaps their compassion was stirred when they passed her door and heard her moanings, but they refused to display concern: such would have contradicted the clannish prejudices that had always governed their unfriendly attitudes toward her. Furthermore, they had concurred, in many whispered conversations throughout the day, that the pains felt by the Viking inadequately compensated for the misery her people had inflicted on England in countless assaults of death, plunder, and destruction. Their interest in the expected child existed only in that he would someday become the ealdorman, and like his Anglo-Saxon father, would govern their district of Kent. If the mother was enduring pro-

1

longed pain, it was because justice was in small measure being deservedly meted out by a judicious power to this representative of a barbaric people.

Pity and concern for the Viking noblewoman were not entirely lacking. The father of the child sat in the adjoining chamber before a cavernous fireplace staring remorsefully into the quivering flames. Repeatedly he regretted his contribution to Marion's agony, sympathetically prayed for the welfare of his fragile wife, passionately condemned the pressures that had resulted in his diplomatically conspired marriage, and often damned the circumstances that had forced him to abandon the monastic life. It was unlike him to be so despondent. He was a patient man who had become accustomed to difficult trials during his administration of the district's affairs, but he was now pressed against the limits of his soul's endurance. He had never aspired to marriage and had from the beginning regretted his alliance with the Viking, more especially now when their union had resulted in such protracted misery. All the more discomforting was knowing that the mother dearly loved him and had anticipated their marriage and later the baby's birth with joyful, timid expectancy. His eyes, fixed steadily on the weak flames that sputtered on the glowing logs, bore traces of guilt and self-reproach that rebuked his conscience and pained his sensibilities. He did not love the mother and had no need or desire for the child.

Edmund was a man of many complexities. He was conscientious in the discharge of his duties as ealdorman of the district, in the protection of its people, in the governing of its many wealthy estates, in his loyalty to the monarch, and was as conspicuously dedicated to the fulfillment of his religious practices and ideals. His pleasures were few and simple. He enjoyed the company of learned men, the study of books, and was refreshed and fulfilled after hours of hunting in nearby forests. He was quick of mind, strong of body, placid of disposition, yet eager to arise to the defense of his people against terrorist intrusion. His hands, that now carelessly caressed the muted lion heads that sneered from the ends of the armrests, were huge, and his legs, languidly crossed at the ankles and laced from shoe to knee, were hard and thickly muscled. His shoulders were broad, and his arms, like those of the soldiers, were large from the practice of battlefield skills: in wielding battleaxes, in slashing and cutting with the sword, in the shooting of arrows from heavy battle bows, and in the dexterous use of the spear. His was a form that impressed the Vikings with its size and apparent strength and attracted the ladies with its robustness and virility.

He was thirty-three years of age, and although not a notably handsome man, his deep-blue eyes, his well-formed nose and mouth, and his wavy chestnut hair accented his face pleasantly. It was impossible to choose which of his parents he resembled. It could not be said that he bore a likeness to his mother, the Lady Wilfreda, whose extreme religious practices and prolonged fasts had not only displeased and repelled Edmund and his father, but had rendered her thin and sharp-featured; nor did he compare with his short, thickset father, whose questionable moral conduct was a cause of serious concern to his elder son. Edmund was as individual in his appearance as he was conspicuously distinguished in his religious ideals and moral strength—a grace for which he thanked God and especially the priests who were called to Lauxburgh to instruct him during his formative years.

As a cousin of King Alfred, whose name would later be appended with the tributive title "The Great," he was expected to pursue higher studies, which the king enthusiastically encouraged for all his people. It progressed that during his early adolescence he was permitted to leave Lauxburgh to join other boys of noble families at the Benedictine monastery of Tankenham for more formal studies. During those years he became progressively attracted to the life led by the monks and less interested in the mischievous adventures of his peers, whose respect and admiration he had steadfastly captured. Only when he lingered at the monastery beyond the required time allotted for studies did his father become agitated and demand his return. To placate his father, Edmund returned to the castle to train for the battles against the Vikings, whose threats were becoming increasingly serious and alarmingly numerous. When defenseless monasteries on the coastal regions were attacked and destroyed, the altar vessels stolen, treasured relics desecrated, and many monks brutally murdered, Edmund enthusiastically trained and dedicatedly arose to defend his people. Much to the satisfaction of his proud father, he fought with vigor and fury and inspired his troops to renewed energies. When the Vikings were put to flight and a temporary peace restored, Edmund was permitted to return to Tankenham for the rest his body sorely needed and the revival of peace his spirit craved.

There was one Viking, however, who was not so troublesome, who was of a gentle disposition, forgiving, considerate, soft-spoken, and retiring by nature. Suddenly irritated by the remembrance of the wife whose company he had avoided so often during their year of marriage, and who indeed was often far from his thoughts, he rose from the chair, arched the pain from his back, and walked toward the door that connected their rooms. It was a thick door that barred noises, yet he listened for some reassuring sound. Bowing his head, he closed his eyes as if to block out the grief that slashed cruelly at his soul. It was because of him that she suffered so, and at once the dampness that penetrated the darkened room enclosed him in a sinister embrace. Walking wearily toward the fireplace, he placed two timbers upon the blackened remnants of the previous ones and watched as they attracted hesitant flames.

Returning to the chair, he settled down, rested his head against the tall backrest, listened to the wind whistling against the window, and let his thoughts wander back to his bright, pleasant days among the monks, when his energies were spent plowing the fields, chopping wood for wintry fires, currying and feeding their horses, pasturing their cows, and shearing their sheep. Peaceful hours were spent with the scribes in learning the intricacies of lettering, in bee tending, and in candle making with the wax they so carefully harvested. There was pleasure in attending the early-morning mass in the semidark chapel, in participating in the two periods of recreation each day, but the exercise which provided the greatest source of peace was in the chanting of the Divine Office, when his pleasant voice blended with those that undulated in monotonously soothing melodies.

It was not surprising that he had repeatedly petitioned the abbot for admittance into the order—a privilege that was always denied him. Never was he told the hours the abbot spent in consideration of his requests, but he could vividly recall the times the slender priest entered his small room, paced about, and compassionately reviewed the reasons for the denial. As the elder of the two sons of the Ealdorman of Kent, he would someday succeed Sighelm to his seat of responsibility. His father's frequent exploits in minor border disputes with the neighboring Danelaw made that future the more imminent. The only hope offered for his acceptance into the order was his renunciation of the title in favor of his younger brother, Cestus, but Cestus was thirteen years younger than he and considered too young for the assumption of such authority. Even so, his younger brother's acceptance could not be assured, since Edmund was held in great esteem by the people. The reports of his generosity to the poor and elderly and his sympathetic concern for the working classes so endeared him to the populace that they anticipated a secure future under his supervision.

Cestus was not so well regarded. Since childhood the rumors of his escapades were exchanged in outraged groups, until he was known throughout the district as an annoying rascal who noisily raced through the hallways, who audaciously sought pleasure by taunting the clerics, and who, in order to avoid his lessons, hid not only his study books but frequently himself as well. His trickeries were well hidden from his father, and so frustrated were the castle's residents in being unable to report the child, for fear of falling into disfavor with his parents, that they satisfied themselves with proclaiming his only talents to be those of creating and executing irritating and constant turmoil. It was considered unlikely that such a mischievous child would change sufficiently with the years to assume a role of dignity—a prediction that proved to be amazingly accurate. The current rumors of Cestus' romantic conquests made conversations the more animated and were spread about until mothers of maidens were fearful lest he journey by. No, Cestus would not be accepted by the people, for their hearts were indisputably inclined to Edmund, and his predictable inheritance was ever extended as an impediment to his life in religion and the acceptance of his vows.

His arguments that the vows of poverty and obedience to the rules could be observed even while he was the ealdorman were often considered. He could dress simply, he reasoned, and could live frugally, with few if any trappings or luxuries in his chambers. As for the observance of the vow of chastity, his arguments were unacceptable and often debated.

"Your observance of this vow is impossible," the abbot had always maintained. "As the ealdorman, you will conduct business throughout the land and be presented to many marriageable young ladies. Someday you might weaken and desire to marry. Then you will find your vows more of an annoyance than you now experience at being unable to pronounce them. The people would want you to marry and bring forth heirs to succeed you—heirs they can love as they now love you. It is God's will for you," the abbot would continue. "He asks that you deny yourself the satisfactions and joys of the religious life and accept instead the commission of caring for his people. Try to accept this willingly, even cheerfully. Remember the Lord's admonition that we must take up our cross daily and follow him." But Edmund also recalled another biblical passage that many are called to the vineyard of the religious life but that few are chosen to remain in it.

Many would have considered him justified in dwelling on bitter thoughts that clutched at his mind at such stressing times, for then he recalled the many old monasteries throughout the land that truly and boastfully enumerated the many wealthy and prestigious men who had in days long past left wives and children, after providing for their care, to join their religious communities. Additionally, history duly recorded that in the days before England was unified under the leadership of one king, many kings of large districts similarly left their families, renounced their thrones of power for the simplicity of the monastic life, and exchanged their earthly crowns for heavenly diadems.*

* Notable among these is King Sigebert of the East Angles and King Sebbi, King of the East Saxons. See *Ecclesiastical History of the English Nation* by Beda Venerabilis (St. Bede the Venerable, 673–735), J. M. Dent & Sons, Ltd., London, 1910, pages 131 and 180, respectively. See also the account of Queen Etheldreda (the spelling of this name varies greatly), who is later mentioned in this book, on page 194 of the same work. This practice of leaving wealth and position in exchange for religious life was not uncommon in the days of early England, nor was the observance of continence. See also the life of St. Edward the Confessor. The annals of the saints likewise record many incidents when this was practiced. The Bible makes reference to this way of life in Matthew 19:12 and I Corinthians 7:29.

Edmund was permitted, nevertheless, to live among the monks and to wear the robes and sandals of the order. These were reluctantly laid aside for secular clothing when necessary visits were made to Lauxburgh, but were happily taken up again when he was able to flee the confusion of court life and escape to the tranquillity of Tankenham. Edmund's days were thus passed in prayer and peacefulness until his thirtieth year, when the will of God was made manifest in an indisputable manner.

Edmund remembered the details well. He had been awakened early one morning by the rapping on the door of his cell and by a whispered, "Edmund, arise." With the alertness he had acquired on the battlefield, he quickly rolled to the side of the pallet and would have sprung up had not the words of the abbot dispelled the first rush of alarm. "Dress, Edmund, and come with me. A courier from Lauxburgh is awaiting you."

It would be the usual summons to battle, he thought. The restless Vikings were again either attacking the coastal regions or scouring the countryside searching for adventure and seeking opportunities to forage and kill.

He threw the robe over his head and smoothed it and his hair into place as he joined the abbot in the moonlight that slanted weakly through a narrow window of the hallway. A lighted candle was handed him as they made their way quietly through the halls, past the cells of sleeping monks. Their shadows stretched eerily along the walls as they descended the stone steps to the office where the courier nervously awaited the delivery of his message.

The abbot motioned for Edmund to enter as they reached the room, where several stout candles flamed brightly. The courier arose quickly from the chair, and his escort of four soldiers sprang to alertness as Edmund entered. Their mail tunics and coned helmets shone mutely in the wavering lights, and their spears and shields seemed strangely misplaced in the house of prayer.

The courier fell to one knee and bowed his head respectfully. Edmund promptly waved a hand as though he wished the message to be delivered without ceremonial demonstration. In his eagerness to learn the cause of the unexpected visit, Edmund did not allow his glance to linger on the soldiers, whose astonishment was conveniently shadowed by the fixed nosepieces of their helmets. They had heard reports that Edmund dressed in monastic trappings during his stays at Tankenham, but it was the first time they had seen him so arrayed. It was one thing to see him on the fields of battle slashing his way in defense of his people, and quite another to see him monastically humbled.

The courier straightened, "My lord, your mother has sent us to summon you to Lauxburgh." His face was strained from the long ride and the gravity of the message he bore. He was reluctant to continue, and rubbed his spear nervously. "It grieves me, my lord," he continued haltingly, "to inform you of the death of your father."

The words lingered in the night dampness, but they were not the words Edmund had expected to hear. When he did not reply, the courier, with the introduction of the matter already broached, found courage to continue.

"It occurred while the Lord Sighelm and his party were hunting. They came upon a band of Vikings camped in the forest and were cruelly attacked by them. When the hunters were late in returning, they were sought. Most were found dead among the trees, but your father was found alive though near death from loss of blood. He died during the night, and we were dispatched here immediately."

Edmund was stunned by the report and stood silently for a moment. Then, rousing himself from his reflections, he placed his hand reassuringly upon the arm of the courier. "It will take me but a moment to change," he said, looking down upon his monastic garments. The words sounded strangely unreal, and without another word or glance toward the abbot, who stood nearby observing Edmund's reactions, he left. His steps sounded as though part of a dream until he halted at the top of the stairway and paused as a monk passed by, ringing a hand bell in his accustomed manner to awaken the others to prayer. In a singing tone the monk repeated: "Awaken in the name of the Lord. . . . Awaken in the name of the Lord. . . ."

Entering his cell, Edmund reached for the secular clothes packed so carefully in the chest beside his pallet and slowly changed. Carefully he folded the robe and placed it atop his small desk and arranged the sandals beneath it. One final glance was cast about the small room: at the crucifix that hung on the bare plaster wall, at the books on the small table, at the chair he had made in the carpenter's shop, at the high window through which he had often studied the passing clouds and through which he now saw the retreating darkness of night. Already the room seemed forbidden to him, and he left without closing the door behind him. Destiny had sought him out, found him unerringly, and was cruelly wrenching him from the life he cherished.

The abbot walked forward as Edmund returned to the office. Gently taking him by the arm, the abbot led him into the hall and out of the hearing of the soldiers, who slumped wearily in their chairs. "Accept God's holy will, Edmund," he whispered, "and he will bless you abundantly. I will ask your religious brothers to join me in praying that you will accept your future with holy resignation. Trust in the good God."

Edmund's eyes remained downcast, and he made no reply.

"You know, Edmund, you are always welcome here. Perhaps someday you will find time to visit us. We will set aside your books and robes. . . ."

Edmund smiled weakly, knowing that such days would never be, and knelt before the priest for a final blessing. Slowly the abbot raised his thin hand high in the air and traced the sign of the cross. "May the blessings of God almighty, his son, Jesus, and the Holy Spirit be with you, Edmund, all the days of your life."

Finishing the sign he had made so deliberately, he rested both hands on Edmund's head—the head that would soon be adorned with the golden crown of his royal office.

They clasped hands, and as Edmund turned to the outside door, he halted at the sound of sandals clapping against the flagstones. As mournful figures moving toward the judgment, the monks, with their heads inclined in sleepy recollection, filed by on the way to the chapel and morning mass. In spite of the shadows and their cowled heads, each of the monks was easily recognized: Brother Joseph, who had been Edmund's teacher of Latin; Brother Luke, who had the annoying habit of repeatedly sniffling; old Brother Abraham, the chief scribe; Brother Elias, the tailor, who held his cloth so closely to his weakened eyes when sewing. . . . Edmund

9

knew each of the twenty monks well and loved each with a brotherly affection. The sacredness of the early-morning hour, and the silence that was imposed on all, spared him the tender ordeal of bidding them farewell, and for that he was grateful.

The courier and guards joined him as he walked through the door into the dimness of predawn. He nodded a farewell to the abbot, mounted the horse the soldiers had brought for him, threw his mantle over a shoulder, and flipped the reins. The journey should be undertaken quickly to avoid a confrontation with the bands of Vikings who were always suspected of lurking about, yet Edmund was reluctant to leave, and permitted his horse to walk across the monastery lands and up the incline of the higher grounds.

In time the mass would be concluded and the kitchen workers would hurriedly prepare the cheese, bread, and milk that comprised the morning meal. When filled to contentment, the monks would begin the prayers and chores that would bring their day to satisfying fulfillment.

Drawing in the reins, Edmund turned in the saddle and looked back at the monastery, with its tall steeple reaching prayerfully to the sky, where birds were beginning their morning ritual of chirping and darting about. The morning star sparkled between wisps of clouds, while in the lush meadow, rounded sheep roamed about the dewy grasses and cows routinely swished their tails as they grazed.

Edmund and his escorts nudged their mounts along. Soon the sun would be thrusting forth its rays to signal the beginning of a new day, and for Edmund the dawning of a new life.

 II

THE ROOM was strangely quiet. The rain had stopped, and the whistling wind had spent itself. It was to be a dawn unlike the one three years before when Edmund left Tankenham. That day, the sun shone brilliantly and life went on unmindful of his heartbreak. This was a misty dawn, overcast, dreary, as though affording a sympathetic atmosphere for the mother's distressing condition.

There was a knock on the door connecting the two chambers, and Edmund glanced up, uncertain that he heard it. Once again it sounded, and he lunged forward to open the door, whose seldom activated hinges grated noisily.

Cedric, the physician, walked through. He was fatigued and worried, yet managed a stiffened bow of respect. "I have not come to report the birth of the child," he said, noting Edmund's concern. He walked closer to the fire and nervously adjusted the sleeves about his wrists. "It is a most difficult birth, my lord. The Lady Marion has been most cooperative, though the pains were severe, but the baby, even though it is small, cannot come of its own. Perhaps had the pains started later, when the babe was expected, it could be born without difficulty, but we now find we must take it from her. There is one method we must use, and for this we require your consent."

"My consent," Edmund hissed disbelievingly. "My God, why do you permit her to suffer so? If you must take the child, take it," he demanded.

"You misunderstand, my lord. We have attempted many times to take the child, but it produces only added pain, and the mother is now delirious from our efforts. Since the child is small, I thought it best that we permit it time, but we can wait no longer. We must use instruments, but this procedure has risks, of which you must be informed."

Edmund frowned at the words. Suddenly he remembered

the children he had known who were born simpletons because of the unskilled use of instruments; children who were kept hidden by their embarrassed parents; weak-limbed children who were constantly guarded from injury; and the many children who were spared lives of passiveness by their untimely deaths soon after their entrance into life. And the mothers! Had not Edreda, the guard's wife, died following the use of instruments? And there was Bedela, the crippled peasant woman who was carried about by her husband. She had given birth only when instruments had drawn the child from her, and had suffered paralysis as a result.

"There are certain risks . . ." Cedric repeated.

"Yes," Edmund said sullenly, "I know. There are risks."

Edmund turned and narrowed his eyes as he evaluated the physician's skills. Cedric was a capable physician, there was no denying it. He had lived in the castle as long as Edmund could remember. He had apprenticed many young physicians and had safeguarded Edmund's health and that of the other castle residents with admirable skill and diligence. He had delivered many, with few infant mortalities to mar his reputation. If Edmund was to entrust his child's life to any physician and feel secure in that trust, Cedric would be that physician. And if Cedric had determined that instruments had to be used—then it must be so.

Cedric read Edmund's thoughts and understood. "I have brought many infants into the world by this method. I will do all I can to ensure the continued health of the child and its mother," he said with compassion, "but I must have your consent before I continue."

Cedric seemed curiously interested in Edmund, who had joined him by the fire. He had heard rumors of Edmund's indifference to his wife, of his avoidance and suppressed annoyance with her, but Edmund was reacting as Cedric had seen all devoted husbands react in similar situations. He was sufficiently agitated and worried about mother and child to merit Cedric's opinion that he was, after all, a considerate husband and would be a grateful and loving father. All the rumors should be dismissed, Cedric thought. The ones he had heard about this troubled man and his fragile lady were undoubtedly incorrect. Would that all talebearers could see Edmund now.

They would see how wrong their wagging tongues had been.

Edmund sat down heavily in the chair before the hearth and leaned forward, with his elbows resting against his knees. Shielding his face with his hands, he asked, "You are certain this is the only way?"

"Yes, my lord. It is the only way."

"Then proceed," he said, leaning back in the chair. "Do all that you deem necessary."

Cedric stood for a moment looking down at the huge body suddenly made pathetic and rendered helpless by the seriousness of the crisis he was unable to alter. "You know I will do all I can," he said, placing his hand reassuringly on Edmund's shoulder. "If you wish to help, you might pray for the lady. She is very weak."

From the corner of his eye Edmund saw Cedric's white robe disappear behind the closing door that creaked and thudded into place. "God be with him," Edmund said aloud, "God be with him. In his care are the lives of two people and the conscience of another."

Edmund envisioned the preparations being made in the next chamber, and a frightening chill settled upon him. The embers were glowing red in the last blush of their existence, but there was no need to rekindle them. He could no longer endure being so near the pain he had caused to be inflicted on the innocent, trusting Marion. He rose from the chair, reached for his cloak, and walked into the hall. He covered the distance to the stairway in long strides and permitted his weight to fall wearily down each step. Perhaps he should have rapped on his mother's door to tell her of this crisis, but there was no need alarming her, if, indeed, any word concerning Marion would interest her at all. The baby might well be born in health, and perhaps Marion too would suffer no ill from the ordeal. He was correct, he reasoned, in not alerting anyone to dangers that might never occur.

Fortunately, no one was about except an occasional servant scurrying with basins of water for their mistresses, who were now awakening. He was too nervous, too irritable from worry, to converse with anyone. As he entered the quiet of the chapel, the sound of every movement seemed to crash against the rafters and disperse for the time the solemnity of its quiet. It was to this sanctuary of peace that Edmund often retreated when the demands of his office loomed menacingly or when the number and complexity of problems drained him of strength. Here he could absorb contentment and peace with his proximity to the body of Christ.

Edmund knelt on the step of the altar for some moments, alternately praying for Marion's safe deliverance and distract-edly studying the symmetry of the bronze candleholders. The faint odor of incense and the weak light of day that entered the lofty windows made the place as a world apart from the troubled one that lay beyond the double doors. Soon it would be time for the morning mass, but for now the chapel was his, and although he wanted earnestly to pray, the words were reluctant to come. Instead he was taunted with memories that were as fresh and vivid as if they had recently occurred. He was weary, and walking toward the bishop's chair that was always reserved beside the altar for his Excellency's in-frequent visits, Edmund sat down.

Before this very altar the bloodless body of his father had lain on black linen. Distinctly he remembered how his mother had stood stoically beside the body, endeavoring to appear as the faithful wife who disbelieved and discounted the tales of her husband's indiscretions. It was here that nobles, reeves, peasants, villagers, merchants, and priests from neighboring villages came to pay their final acts of homage and loyalty. It was here, the day following the funeral, that the archbishop, in simple ceremonies, invested him and placed the crown of Kent upon his head. The people were saddened by the loss of Sighelm but were, nevertheless, pleased to be gaining Edmund as their ealdorman, who, if the truth be acknowledged, was in every way more loved, admired, and worthy of their affections than had been his predecessor.

The year following Sighelm's death was a disturbing one, with small bands of Vikings from the settlement to the north making numerous raids on Kent in their greed for conquest of power and property. Many strategies for dispersing and re-pelling them were forwarded. Some were considered, most were disregarded, but there was a time when one plan was presented to Edmund which he could not ignore.

The Reverend Jerome, Edmund's confessor and the castle's chaplain, was troubled that day when he entered Edmund's office.

"You look as though a Viking had a spear poised at your back." Edmund had laughed.

"No, Edmund, but what I have to tell you might prove to be as troublesome."

Edmund placed the papers he had been studying on the table, folded his arms, leaned against the table, and smiled at the stout, waddling cleric, who toyed nervously with his prayer book. Edmund had become accustomed to such visits from his confessor and from the many clerics who came to plead for financial assistance or help of various kinds for the needy, and he had always been amused by the variety of the requests and by the petitioners' dependence on him, as though he alone had the solutions to all problems.

"What is it, Reverend? Does a poor farmer need an ox or plow? Does a church need new vestments? Come, tell me. What is it you desire?"

"My lord," he said, avoiding a meeting of the eyes. "I have been asked by the members of the council to speak with you concerning a delicate matter."

"Yes," Edmund said, relaxing his smile.

"The council has been meeting to discuss the matter of the Vikings, and we are certain we have reached a solution to most of the problems concerning them."

A solution to the problems! This indeed was worthy of thoughtful consideration. The Vikings—the Danes, or Norsemen, as they were called by some—had been the curse and scourge of the country for years. Their stealthy assaults on towns and villages had left much of the country devastated. The coastal farms and settlements were in constant danger of their attacks. These masters of the sea, who sailed about silently in long, low boats, their shields slung in sequence over the railings, their great sails billowing boldly above them, could capture ships at full sail or glide silently into ports or waterways during the night, attack swiftly, pillage, destroy, kill, and be off with the tide before the alerted militia could arrive from castle or garrison with soldiers to capture them or defend others from their terror. With the formation of the Danelaw, much had been accomplished in repelling their attacks, but it was not a complete solution to the problem.

Grasping at peace for the Anglo-Saxons, King Alfred had met in the year 886 with the Danish King Guthrum, whose baptism he had arranged and witnessed eight years before, and officially yielded to the Danes the lands that their troops had conquered and were then beginning to farm with the aid of kinsmen who emigrated from Denmark and Norway. By mutual agreement the boundaries of the two divisions were drawn. With the Tees River as the northern border, the Danes claimed the North Sea as the eastern border, and on the west the agreed dividing line touched the Irish Sea and slashed England diagonally to the Thames, where Guthrum had entrusted to King Fergus, Marion's uncle, the lands there which he had helped to invade and conquer. Alfred retained for England the inner portion of land between Wales and the Danelaw and all the southern territories from sea to sea.

With the proximity of the Danelaw across the Thames from Kent, the English district was located in a particularly vulnerable position, since attacks upon it could be made effectually from both land and sea. With the formation of the Danelaw, Guthrum and the minor Danish kings, who ruled small divisions of land under his jurisdiction, acknowledged no responsibility for the forays, which continued, and blamed them instead on renegade bands whose centuries-old restlessness for adventure spurred them to action against the official warning and directives of their nobles.

A solution that would curtail these tides of invasions would be welcome indeed.

"Continue," Edmund ordered. "What does the council propose?"

"You know, my lord, that the Danes are said to be loyal to their own folk. If a Dane of a royal or influential stature were to live here and participate in some manner with the government of this district, then the Danes might well respect our peace."

Edmund's eyes narrowed suspiciously.

The prelate cleared his throat and continued. "It has been brought to the council's attention that King Fergus, who, as you know, is King Guthrum's most trustworthy friend, has a niece, the Princess Marion, who would be willing to abide with us." The priest was reluctant to continue, and nervously rubbed his fat hands together. Then, summoning the courage he required, he continued quickly. "Since charters and treaties have been broken in the past, the council has recommended that a marriage would be a likely solution and that a child born of that marriage would surely guarantee peace for all time."

The voice that answered was controlled but gradually intensified until Reverend Jerome was grateful that his priestly robes prohibited too great a demonstration of anger.

"It is a serious matter for the council to meet without my knowledge or consent," Edmund calmly began. "It is doubly provoking that they should plot a marriage when they know my mind about this. By God, I will not have it," he shouted, raising his fist in the air.

Before the priest dared to interrupt, he studied Edmund, who stood defiantly with legs apart and fists resting on his hips, as though waiting on the battlefield for the signal to plunge into combat. Hastily begging the Almighty for divine assistance, he continued. "I beg my lord to consider that you are no longer in the monastery and that you are free to marry. It is even expected for a man in your office."

"I shall not marry. I shall not be bound to a woman. You know well that I await the day of my return to Tankenham."

"But, Edmund, you know it is impossible."

"Not impossible, Reverend," he replied cynically. "I am awaiting the day when Cestus has arrived at a more suitable age, or when his attitudes have matured sufficiently to assume this office."

"Then you shall have long to wait. He is still a boy, despite his age, and unwilling to abandon his frivolous and often shameful conduct. The people will not have him, and might rebel if you take such action."

"Nevertheless, Reverend, I await the day of my return to Tankenham."

"Can you not see, Edmund, that this is God's will for you? He did not desire that you remain with the Benedictines. He arranged that you would rule his people, and as I interpret the events of the past, and indeed the signs of the future, I believe it is his will that you marry and bring forth sons who would follow after you."

Edmund turned away. The words were reminiscent of those once spoken by the abbot, which had also fallen unwillingly upon his ears.

"Consider, my lord, that by your marriage, peace in a greater measure would be assured. It is not so great a sacrifice to ask that you marry, for thereby you will save the lives of countless countrymen and the virtue of many innocent womenfolk."

The priest's words pressed hard against his reasoning. All other efforts had been exhausted in attempting to establish peace with Fergus' subjects. This was yet another plan, and perhaps the final one. If only the proposal were directed at another, perhaps it would seem a most likely solution, but it was not directed at another, but at him, Edmund, the ealdorman and ruler of Kent. Yet his life was not his own. He had learned the lesson well in his early years. His desires were always dismissed in favor of the will of others, and contingent upon the demands of events and circumstances. His shoulders sagged at the inevitable. The peace of the country and the lives of his countrymen were dependent on his decision, and were he to ignore the responsibility, he would never justify his conscience if either were lost. Once again fate was directing the course of his life. No, not fate, but the pressures of conscience. Reverend Jerome knew well how to draw forth results. But he could not surrender easily. Numerous battlefield encounters had taught him to struggle to the end of the scuffle with what limited resources were available to him. Feebly he searched about for obstacles that might prove benevolently effectual.

"The Danes are pagans. Such a marriage could not be acceptable to the church."

"The Lady Marion is not pagan, my lord. When Guthrum was baptized, many of his countrymen likewise took the faith. King Fergus was baptized, together with many of his household, including the Lady Marion."

"What could possibly induce them to permit such a marriage? They detest us."

"No, my lord. It is known that they would welcome such a union in exchange for certain trade arrangements, for schooling in the trades, and for knowledge of our farming techniques. If you would but consider this proposal and agree with it, a delegation would be sent immediately to the Danes, and arrangements for the marriage could be promptly made."

It was useless to argue, futile to submit alternate proposals.

Fate had once again raised its vengeful and obstructive claws to rake and scatter his ambitions.

Edmund walked to where his father's battle gear stood propped against a corner of the room. The tattered flag with its snarling dragon head had seen many battles and had flown proudly over them. If it could fly less frequently over blood- ied and mutilated bodies . . . With a slumping of his shoul- ders that betrayed his feelings of defeat, he ran a hand over the scarred shield and spear of his father and said, "Mind you, I am not submitting to this. I pledge only that I will think on this matter."

Taking a deep, satisfying breath, the cleric moved with all haste on creaking sandals to inform the council of Edmund's impending decision and to instruct the delegation to prepare for its departure.

Edmund altered his position in the bishop's chair and won- dered about the time. Soon his mother, a few of the women and soldiers, and many of the servants would enter for morn- ing mass, but until then, solitude and silence were his. But he could not claim peace until the child was safely delivered and its gentle mother relieved of her sufferings. Edmund looked up prayerfully. How could an occasional association with this woman have brought her to such an ordeal?

Edmund distinctly remembered his shock when first he looked upon Marion. He had expected to see a woman of sturdy proportions with thick braids down her back, and had she worn a breastplate of metal and carried a sword and shield, he would have gazed unsurprisingly. The few Danish women he had seen were of slightly less than warrior propro- tions in conduct and physical dimensions, and it had been well known that they could fight effectively when their homes and goods were endangered.

He was not prepared for the short, fragile shadow of a woman whose frightened blue eyes dominated a delicate, blushing face. It had not been anticipated that the nobly born were of a more delicate constitution because for generations they had been spared the task of farming, of scratching out a meager existence in frigid northerly lands while the menfolk were pursuing glory on distant shores.

Marion did not resemble the women of her race in any respect. She was painfully timid, always gentle and understanding, and commendably forgiving toward everyone, especially Edmund's mother, the Lady Wilfreda, who showed in undeniable ways her superiority over the Danish intruder in her household. Marion was even more tolerant of Edmund's indifference of her, but then, an ealdorman with such prestige could not be expected to abandon the pressing demands on his time, to concern himself with the frivolous cares of a wife. Time and again she had smilingly, lovingly excused his brusque replies, no doubt certain that he would at length learn to turn to her for support and certain comforts. When their few brief physical unions introduced her to the joys of expected motherhood, all abuses and neglects were excused and forgotten. She had but to wait, for what father would not look lovingly upon a son, especially one who would someday inherit his title, and what father could not help but look favorably on the wife who brought such pride and happiness into his life? All would be overlooked, for on that day when her son would come forth, the district would rejoice with her, peace between the lands would be assured because of her, and love would certainly bloom in Edmund's heart as it had already blossomed in her own.

The bell roused Edmund as it pealed its summons to mass. After a moment the back door opened, and soft footfalls were heard scratching their way into the chapel. With long, hurried strides, a soldier crossed the length of the chapel, and with the excited impatience of a bearer of welcome news, announced in words poorly subdued, "Sir, the baby, it is here! The baby has come."

Servant women, catching the message, paused near the back door and hid their smiles in their shawls. As Edmund passed between them, they tittered and held their hands up to further shield their blushing cheeks. Quickly the news was shared with those just entering, and all turned their glances toward Edmund, who, without smiling, strode in his accustomed pace toward the steps.

The clanging of the bell continued to fill the hallway with its vibrations, but at once those who heard the news also seemed to hear pealing with it the soldier's joyful announcement: "The baby has come. The baby has come. The baby has come."

# III

THE PHYSICIAN was pacing the hallway when Edmund approached Marion's rooms. Quickly raising his hand to prevent questions, Cedric motioned for him to follow, and preceded him down the hall to the sitting room of Edmund's chamber. Edmund, noting his somber expression, followed apprehensively, removed his cloak, carelessly threw it over a stool, and faced the physician.

"The Lady Marion has asked me to speak with you," Cedric began, giving hint to the seriousness of the discussion. His brow furrowed deeply. "She does not wish you to be alarmed when first you see the child. I am grieved, Edmund, to tell you that the child has a deformity. The foot. It is malformed. It is not the worst I have seen, but it cannot be corrected, and I fear the child will limp on its right side throughout its life."

Edmund nervously rubbed his lower lip with a forefinger, thoughtfully adjusting himself to this unwelcome development.

"It is frail, my lord," Cedric continued. "It is not very strong, but it will live."

"And Marion?"

"She is weak and much troubled that you will be displeased."

"A father cannot feel other than displeasure that his child is so stricken. I am saddened indeed. Come with me," Edmund said, turning to the connecting door. "I desire to see this child."

"Not yet, my lord. I must speak with you further." Edmund turned and glared at the physician. "The Lady Marion is fearful you will be further displeased." Cedric was finding it difficult to formulate the words, but Edmund's impatient look forced him to relate the most difficult part of the message.

"The lady is fearful you will be unhappy that the child is not the son you expected. It is a female."

Edmund's frown deepened. "A female?"

The physician nodded.

As though a stunning blow had been struck, Edmund stood, silently comprehending the announcement. Never had it been expected that the child, the heir to his noble office, would be other than a male child. This was unreal, untrue. He, Edmund, ruler, judge, protector, supporter of the people, the strong governor upon whom everyone relied, could not possibly have fathered a female child. Had it been the second born, it would have been acceptable, but a female as the first born was disconcerting to his manhood, and one that was deformed was a double sorrow.

What was always said about deformities? That they were God's way of punishing the parents for the dreadful sins in their pasts? But no serious sin could possibly have been committed by the gentle, devout Marion, and as for himself, no dreadful sins had marred his record. But then, what serious sins could be committed when he had always been so closely allied with the Benedictines and had lived, worked, studied, and prayed with them for so long?

Then all became clear. The child's deformity was a punishment from God for the violation of his vow of chastity—a vow which, though not made formally, was nevertheless observed until a child was expected as a result of the marriage. Reverend Jerome and the abbot had been wrong. It was not God's will. The deformity and sex of the child were proof of that. His clenched fists showed white at the knuckles, and his nails dug deeply into the palms. He had foolishly accepted unsound advice. His confessor for once had incorrectly interpreted the will of God. The deformity would forever be a reminder of his transgression and would compound the guilt he already felt for having abused Marion's tender feelings toward him, though his own heart was devoid of any love or affection for her.

This child, with its sign of disapproval from an offended God, was, nevertheless, a child of that same almighty being, whom he should look upon with tolerance and, if possible, with some measure of fondness.

The child was unbelievably small. In a glance Edmund took in the fuzzy head, its red face with its swollen eyelids, the contours of its ribs, its thin arms and legs thrashing about in the incessant activity of a babe rudely cast into a cold and uncomfortable world.

Cedric reached into the cradle for one of its skeletal legs and flexed it with a deftness peculiar to physicians.

"You will see, Edmund, that the legs of a newborn are normally curved in this manner, and the feet are normally twisted inwardly, but the bones on the bottom of this right foot are much larger than those on the left one. As you see, the heel bone is drawn up higher than the other."

Edmund was oblivious of the other explanations as he stared at the foot, now jerking against Cedric's hold. It was obvious, to even the unskilled in such matters, that the child would never walk properly. It would be forced to walk on the front thickness of the foot, with the heel always remaining uselessly elevated.

Marion awakened, glanced toward the sound of voices, and mumbled weakly, "Edmund?"

Walking toward the huge bed whose curtains were tied back against the corner posts, Edmund quickly surveyed the linen coverlet that lay upon the small flat outline of Marion's body. Drawing closer, he stared at the dark recessed circles under her pain-weakened eyes. Her face, almost as white as her coverlet, was framed by once-golden hair now darkened and dulled by the moistness of frequent wipings that tangled it and made it drape in stringy trails about her pillow. Her face seemed longer and less full than before, and her mouth was strangely relaxed by exhaustion. Thin arms lay weakly beside her body, but as Edmund approached, she gathered the strength to raise one arm weakly to her face. Shiny moisture filled her eyes and fell lazily along her cheeks.

Edmund fumbled at the stool that was placed behind him, drew it closer to the bed, and sat near the whimpering woman. It was an awkward and embarrassing moment, but after a few minutes he spoke words that seemed too gentle to have been uttered by his own mouth: "Do not weep, Marion. Both you and the child are well. You should rejoice that your labors are over."

"Do not be ashamed of me," she said with effort. "I grieve

that it is not the son you expected." Sniffles replaced words as she dropped her hand and turned her face from Edmund, whose masculine proximity made a tender situation the more delicate.

Former reticences were forgotten as pity and compassion welled in his soul. Placing his hand against the small face, he gently turned it toward him until he could look into the blue eyes, now colored with delicate red tracings.

"There is nothing to be sorry for, and I am not ashamed of you. God gave us a daughter because that is what he wanted us to have. You are both alive, and for that we must be grateful. There is nothing to be sorry for—nothing." But in his eagerness to placate the mother, the words stung at his heart, for he *was* sorry—very sorry that his child would limp throughout its life, that it would be pitied and denied the normal activities of childhood, and that eventually her marriage and future might be altered because of her deformity.

Tears continued to glisten across streaked cheeks. "She is crippled, Edmund. She is crippled." The words were bitter, and she closed her eyes tightly against harsh reality.

Edmund withdrew his hand. What could be said? That it was a sign of God's disapproval—a curse to ever remind him of his transgression, his unloving intimacies with her?

The soft, kittenish cries of the infant gratefully barred further confidences. Suddenly alerted to the needs of her newborn, Marion wiped her eyes with the back of her hand, turned her head toward the cradle, and blinked at the woman who was bending over it solicitously. The cries grew so urgent and unaccountably strong for so frail an infant that Edmund curiously turned to watch the nurse as she picked up the bundled babe. Pushing the stool back to permit the nurse more freedom in moving about the bed, he watched the huge woman as she bent down to arrange the infant beside its mother. Almost numb from fatigue and the unreality of his new fatherhood, he waited while her torso completely blocked Marion and the baby from view. At last she moved aside, and Edmund suddenly found himself staring at a naked, blue-veined breast against which the infant was nuzzled, greedily snatching at the nipple that fell from its mouth with each of its struggles. Edmund's face turned crimson at the unexpected sight, but Marion, too exhausted and drained of modesty after so prolonged a birth, only grasped at the coverlet and cradled the infant closer to her.

Through tears that were once again clouding her vision, she whispered, "She may be crippled, Edmund, but because of it I love her all the more." Repeatedly she kissed the tiny head, while the fuzz about it became dampened with motherly tears.

Placing his hand reassuringly against hers, Edmund looked upon the small mite, who thrashed its arms about as it worked at drawing sustenance into its being.

The nurse who had placed the child upon the bed had been forgotten in the emotional proceedings, but had watched enthralled at the sympathetic developments. How kind and compassionate and loving Edmund was to feign acceptance of his crippled daughter. How considerate and sympathetic he was toward Marion. Cedric, too, had witnessed an impassioned moment that warmed his heart and convinced his reasonings that the talebearers had been incorrect. Edmund could never have felt aversion for this woman, as they had said. Why, Edmund had been by the bedside for some time now in personal communion with his wife, whispering assurances and lovingly caressing her hand. Edmund clearly loved this woman, Cedric reasoned, and no one, no matter how vehemently they might try, could convince him otherwise.

The baby, overcome by its unaccustomed exertion, fell asleep as Marion weakly pulled the coverlet about her chest. Edmund leaned forward to examine the tiny face more closely, while in the recesses of his troubled conscience he determined to overcome his natural indifference to Marion, for the child's sake. Somehow, with the help of God, he would become a considerate husband, and perhaps, too, a loving father. The woman who had repeatedly excused his shortcomings in anticipation of this resolve, gradually became radiant in spite of the strained signs of her recent trial, slowly turned her head in sleepy contentment until her ear rested against the generous fluff of her pillow. Having paid the price of physical pain and mental distress, she lapsed into deserved and benevolent oblivion.

Lauxburgh was an impressive castle, whether viewed from land or sea. It stood boldy atop a rocky cliff that rose from the watery depths of a bay whose waters were in constant exchange with the currents of the North Sea. On either side of the cliff, lower lands stretched their crescent arms around the bay, as if to protect the ships lying at anchor there. To the east, outside the walls that enclosed the castle's buildings, rainwater had collected from the night's deluge, creating a slushy expanse from the hill atop which the castle stood, to the forest beyond, and drained ever so slowly onto the beach that inclined to the bay. To the west of the castle walls huddled a village whose origins began when the Vikings first unleashed their stealthy attacks on outlying settlements. Farmers from the unprotected lands came to settle there with their families, as did tradesmen and craftsmen of every sort. Now grouped securely together so close to the citadel, easy access to its protective grounds was more conveniently and quickly attained in times of danger. Beyond the village was the wharf, where fishermen brought huge baskets with their catches and where kegs and crates of all sizes had been randomly stacked and abandoned because of the storm. Farmlands reached all about and stretched along the road leading from the castle, to connect with other roads and districts beyond.

The ships that lay at anchor in the bay rode the tranquil swells, their sails strapped and secured, save one, whose great sail, emblazoned with the dragon head of Lauxburgh, filled with wind and waited as one alert and ready to be off. A trailing red flag, slit at the end, as a serpent's tongue, flapped nervously at the height of the mast, while a skiff, let down from the deck, was gliding its way to the wharf. The rowers, with hooded mantles drawn against the cold breezes, waved and called greetings to the laborers onshore, who, similarly dressed against the cold, were rolling kegs of wine and carrying, shoving, and dragging crates toward the carts waiting to transport them into the village. The skiff was tied to the dock by a rower who leaped onto the wharf with the agility characteristic of a good seaman, as the others, remaining in their places, held their long-handled oars erect. They had not long to wait. At the top of a stairway that rose steeply against the cliff to the castle, a gate in the castle wall opened. Edmund emerged with Thane Godfrey, his trusted friend and overseer of many of Kent's royal shires. Stopping midway, they turned toward each other and clasped arms in farewell. Bounding down the steps with huge strides, Godfrey crossed the wooden wharf, his every step creating dull hollow sounds, and swung with graceful ease into the skiff. In a moment the oars were in their locks, and the men bent their backs against the strain.

Edmund remained standing astride two steps and leaned casually against the cliff while he watched as the oarsmen forced their craft across the restless water. As though impervious to the cold to which other men shivered in defense, Edmund continued squinting as the skiff neared the waiting vessel. At length Godfrey turned back to wave a vigorous farewell. Edmund straightened, returned the wave, and smiled faintly. He would miss Godfrey, though he would be gone but a few weeks.

They had known each other since childhood. As the son of a wealthy landowner, Godfrey was accepted in the castle as a lesser noble, had grown to become Edmund's steadfast friend, and except for the times when Edmund was at Tankenham, they hunted and hawked together. Godfrey had a ready wit, which Edmund gratefully welcomed at official functions, which normally bored him. Not the least of his talents was in caring for Edmund's shires, which spared him from many details and distractions so that his attentions could be more directed toward the broader matters of the district. In addition to assisting Edmund at times in the castle, he also served as occasional scribe, and for the present was Edmund's personal messenger to the Viking king Fergus.

Aware of the cold that made his eyes water, Edmund climbed the steps. It had been a difficult morning, and the absence of sleep during the stress-filled night made the prospect of living through the rest of the day most unwelcome. After latching the gate at the top of the steps and placing the horizontal bars in place, he hurried through the courtyard to the doors that opened into the castle. Glancing down the hallway toward the chapel at one end, he turned toward the great hall at the other end for the morning meal, which hopefully would restore his strength and invigorate his wilting spirits. But before he reached his destination, his mother's strident voice called to him. Turning abruptly, he waited for her approach. In her typical nunlike attitude, downcast eyes, blank if not somewhat stern set to her features, she walked with precise, almost gliding steps that barely caused her gown to sway. Her demeanor was irksome to many and had been particularly so to her husband, who was repulsed by the sanctimonious attitude she had assumed shortly after the birth of her second and last child.

Having made slow recuperative progress, she had visited her sister, the abbess, at the Benedictine convent of Chatham, which boasted of springs whose waters contained elements favorable for the convalescent. It was during this visit that she was attracted to the orderliness of activities and regular periods of prayer that she attempted to inaugurate at Lauxburgh on her return. Behind the short-lived introduction of such activities lay a reason known only to herself. Wishing to avoid the birth of another child and a repetition of a painful and long recuperation, she had anticipated that by enforcing prayer and the regulated reading of biblical passages, she would succeed in distracting her husband from the intimacies she considered repulsive and to attract him instead to the virtuous practice of restraint. Although a Christian, as were most of the people of Kent, Sighelm never shared his wife's religious fervor and was not above forsaking principles and the laws of his faith to seek companionship elsewhere. As a result of the rumors which developed, and her inability to reestablish his interest in her, she had grown into a bitter woman who turned all the more toward the satisfactions of her religion. In spite of the chaplain's admonitions, she soon twisted the church's teachings into the strictest of interpretations and fashioned its biblical quotations into meanings that suited her purposes. She had suffered no qualms of conscience when she turned her children's physical care more and more to others, so that most of her time could be spent in chapel and in her chambers in conventual pretenses. If ill was whispered of her husband, who could not but speak well of her when she prayed so fervently and encouraged the spiritual improvement of everyone in the castle?

As Edmund grew into manhood, she demanded more of his attentions and became more dependent on his kindly nature. But his love for her became strained as her faultfinding and complaining became habitual and intolerable. She had jealously watched the maidens' innocent flirtations with

Edmund and had stood guard at all social gatherings when, out of respect, he was forced to speak to all guests, be they maidens, beautiful married women, or eager widows. As could be expected, she objected strenuously to his eventual politically motivated marriage and sulked for days when her efforts could not bring about a cancellation of the plans.

"Son," she said in affected shock as she approached, "you have been out in the weather without a cloak?"

Edmund shrugged with annoyance. "I was seeing Godfrey embark for Wermouth. Fergus must be notified of Marion's safe delivery."

Wilfreda raised her eyebrows as she turned her head and cast a quizzically sideward glance at him. "And I wonder what his reaction will be to the announcement."

Edmund studied her sarcastic grin for a moment, then leaned against the wall and folded his arms. Experience with his mother's fluctuating disposition had taught him that she had much on her mind, which nothing, save outright rudeness, would prevent her from delivering. Caustic remarks would be forthcoming, and his attempts at vindication would follow. "And what, Mother, do you think his reaction will be?"

"I should think . . ." Wilfreda checked herself and quickly rearranged her expression. Turning a pleasanter, teasing expression to her son, she continued. "Let us not discuss Fergus for now. Tell me, son, why is it you did not notify me of the birth? But of course you had much on your mind," she said with feigned offense. "Cedric was kind enough to visit my chamber and tell me of the child's safe arrival."

"Have you been to see the child?"

"Yes, Cedric took me in. It is a pity, a pity."

A frown crept over Edmund's face at the words, and he watched as the light skipped about the tight braids of hair that became exposed as Wilfreda's veil began slipping on her nodding head. Quickly she reached for it and adjusted its folds over the hazel twists. "It is a pity the child is not all you expected."

With fleetness of thought Edmund envisioned the frail red mite of a child furiously kicking her misshapen foot. "It is what God desired for me," he said defensively.

"Do not blame the Lord, my son. It would appear the matter was not of his doing."

Edmund had mistimed the onslaught. Now it would be forthcoming. "Continue," he said resignedly.

"All of this could have been avoided, had you married acceptably—"

His frown deepened as he interrupted, "Married acceptably?"

There was no time to formulate her ideas into more gentle-sounding phrases. What was burning in her heart needed venting, and the words gushed forth as entrapped smoke belching free upon clear air. "You remember, Edmund, how I cautioned you when this alliance was being formulated? You must understand and accept the truth. You should not have married a Viking woman. Their blood is not compatible with ours."

The haughty tilt of his mother's head disturbed Edmund, but his silence was maintained, and his mother continued. "Not only is the race lacking in cultural advancement and social graces, but their very bodies are incapable of procreating suitably when their blood is mingled with that of a more superior nature."

The words that proceeded so venomously from his mother's mouth astonished him, but what horrified him the more was her self-satisfied attitude, as though she were actually pleased that Marion's supposed inferiority was confirmed by the child's deformity.

"Enough. I will hear no more of this." Edmund prepared to leave, but leaned toward his mother, and lowering his voice, added, "I know this for a certainty: the woman of whom you speak so cruelly would never have spoken in like manner of you, and I doubt that she would ever have harbored ill feelings toward you, as you obviously have done toward her, though heaven knows she had cause to." Edmund looked deeply into the startled face. "May I suggest, Mother, that you return to the chapel and pray for us all."

Never had he spoken to her in such a discourteous manner, and as he walked toward the great hall, she placed a hand against the wall for support. The emotional declarations of her son left her appalled. Had not the conversation ended so prematurely, she would perhaps have convinced him of the correctness of her opinions, but for the moment Wilfreda stood rebuked, experiencing both horror at her son's discourtesy and desolation at having fallen into his disfavor.

If Marion had gained his esteem, she was deserving of it, and Wilfreda grudgingly conceded that the recognition was late in coming. Marion had always possessed all the virtues she would have liked to claim. But the love which Marion thought to be inevitable, Wilfreda knew would never be in reality. Wilfreda fancied she knew her son well enough to know that he had no desire to fall in love with Marion or any woman, but if he could not bring himself to love her, the least he could do, the very least, would be to protect his wife from a slanderous tongue, even if that tongue belonged to his mother.

Edmund stopped in the archway of the great hall. Two quiet groups spoke in hushed tones while several servants rushed about setting up long planks of wood on trestles in preparation for the noonday meal. All turned and nodded in respect when they saw him enter. With a solemn inclination of his head as a polite sign of recognition, he walked to one side of the great hall to where his thronelike chair stood beside the huge fireplace.

One of the servants scurried about in the inner kitchen preparing a plate to set before him, while Edmund leaned back to enjoy the glow that emanated from the split logs. He had earned the privilege to indulge in a few moments of leisure, and he gazed lazily into the fireplace, which, during his boyhood, he often had considered to be large enough to accommodate several standing men in a fiery Gehenna. The steady sputtering and spitting of the fire would have eventually lulled him into sleep, had not the sudden, urgent running of feet startled him. Breathlessly a guard rushed up. "My lord, the physician. He wants you to hurry."

In an instant Edmund swung round in the chair and frowned deeply. "Tell me, man, what is it?"

"I do not know, my lord," he gasped as Edmund rose to follow him. "The doctor told me to hurry. He looked much worried." After taking in a breath, he added, "The physician sent the scribe for Reverend Jerome. He said the priest should bring the holy oils."

The full implication of the words took formation in

Edmund's troubled mind. He bounded forward, taking the stairway two steps at a time. The baby—it had to be the baby. Cedric had said it was frail. How could poor Marion accept the loss of her firstborn? What had Marion said: "She may be crippled, but because of it I love her all the more"?

Without rapping, Edmund opened Marion's door and entered the antechamber, where Cedric stood awaiting his arrival. "It is the lady, sir," Cedric announced before Edmund could ask.

Edmund was shocked into speechlessness as he looked past Cedric into the bedchamber, where the servant women stood mournfully about the large bed.

"The Lady Marion has suffered a most serious hemorrhage. The amount of the flux was so great that we fear her weakened body cannot replace its needs in time to reverse her declining condition. It occurred of a sudden. She is now in a profound sleep from which I do not expect her to awaken. I am grieved, my lord, to present you with this sorrow. Come. You will want to share her last moments."

Edmund did not move. It was unbelievable. This young woman could not be on the threshold of death just when she was to enjoy the arrival of the child she had so joyously anticipated.

Footsteps shuffled at the door. The Reverend Jerome quickly entered, wearing a long white linen surplice. He placed a vial of holy oil and a small book of prayers on Marion's desk in the antechamber and adjusted his gold-embroidered stole around his neck. After making certain the ends of the stole hung properly near each hip, he picked up the book and vial and motioned for Edmund to follow.

"*Clementissime Deus, Pater misericordiarum, et Deus totius consolationis . . .*" he entoned as he walked to Marion's side. Edmund stood at the foot of the bed as the priest made the sign of the cross countless times over the sick woman while reciting the prescribed prayers for the dying.

It seemed impossible that Marion could look worse than she had looked a few hours before, but now her pale complexion had turned a deathly grayish yellow, her cheeks were more deeply sunken, her nose seemed thinner, and dark shadows circled her eyes.

*"Misereatur tui omnipotens Deus, et dimissis peccatis tuis perducat te ad vitam aeternam."*

Cedric and the women attendants stood near with clasped hands and watched intently as the elderly priest dipped his finger in the vial of oil and traced the sign of the cross on Marion's mouth, nose, hands, and feet for the sanctification of the senses. The droning Latin prayers went on in the familiar strains that Edmund had heard repeated so often over bodies on the bloodied fields of conflict.

Desperation beat with Edmund's pounding heart. If only Marion would awaken so he could speak his apologies for the times he had deliberately avoided her, for the kind words that were never spoken. Oh, how he wished he could confess his sorrow for having married her when she could have been married in her own land to someone who could have made her happy. And, of course, there were promises to be made . . . if only she would awaken.

When the prayers ended, Cedric, in the almost deafening silence, approached the bed and touched his ear for many minutes against Marion's heart. After straightening, he looked toward Edmund with sadness.

No one moved, and only the sounds from the fireplace were heard. It had all been so sudden—so unbelievable.

Abruptly they were shocked into reality by the whimpering, kittenish sounds of the infant, who shook tiny wrinkled fists in the air. Its staccato gasping cries grew in intensity as its unfulfilled desire for food increased.

Edmund walked around the bed and knelt down beside the lifeless form. With the infant's wailings piercing the solemnity of the death chamber, he covered his face with his hands, bowed his head, and wept.

## ⤙ IV ⤚

THE PEALING of the funeral bells sounded over the country-side from the meadows and furrowed farmlands to the village and forests as the procession made its way toward the cathedral. The creaking and groaning of the wagon bearing the casket added additional dismal sounds as it rumbled along the road behind its team of plodding horses. Preceding the column rode a score of stern and formidably arrayed soldiers in their finest ceremonial armor: shiny coned helmets with fixed nosepieces, brilliant tunics of linked mail, and on their arms were proudly borne the ceremonial shields made of limewood and decorated with a covering of silver-studded leather.

Behind the wagon bearing the casket rode Edmund, his face sternly set, his eyes fixed firmly on the casket that strained at the ropes that secured it. He declined to look at the occasional groups of peasants who stood along the road: at the peasant men who watched, solemnly grateful that their wives had been spared a similar fate; at the women, who felt a sympathetic affinity for the noble widower, so sad in his new fatherhood, gained at the price of his young wife's untimely death.

A golden pectoral cross, partially hidden beneath a silver beard, caught the light of the sun and flashed its yellow splendor against the funereal black vestments of the archbishop, whose retinue of priestly acolytes rode with him behind Edmund. The gnarled, brown, callused hands of the peasants traced hasty blessings across drab linens as the ecclesiastic rode past with his hand held high in benediction.

Only a few of the castle's residents risked the threatening storm in the distance to witness the burial. Principally they were those who were surprised by Edmund's distress and sought to witness his grief to the end of the proceedings. There were few enough diversions in the castle, and this funeral, though morbid, was interesting in the study of human behavior. Many of the women who accompanied the casket to its ultimate destination had been those who sneaked quietly to view Edmund kneeling beside the casket in the sepulchral quiet of the chapel. All the women and men of the castle had been informed, through secretive discussions, of Edmund's grief, which had been greater than they ever expected. Perhaps there had been, after all, some love and tenderness in the intimacy of Marion's bedchamber. But if the castle women now expected to see some extraordinary display of emotion, they were grievously disappointed, for Edmund stood tall and composed beside the grave, as apparently cold emotionally as the frigid wind that blew about the casket.

The mass for the dead and the funeral prayers had been said, at Edmund's insistence, not in the cathedral, but in the privacy of the castle's chapel. There remained to be recited only the graveside prayers, which the rotund archbishop read from a book held by a vested acolyte. With the conclusion of the prayers, the blessing of the grave, and the sprinkling of dirt atop the casket, the ceremony was ended.

The mud-caked grave tenders, standing by with shovels held in readiness, watched as Edmund separated himself from the group and made his way around graves and between head stones that had sunk in the earth at awkward angles. At the side of the cathedral and within its dismal shadow, Edmund knelt by the grave of his father. The stone, with its runic letters, loomed tall and imposing, but the mud that covered the remains of his father's body had settled and was overgrown with dried tufts of grass. Such was the end of life on earth. After a moment Edmund arose and walked to where the procession solemnly awaited him. The skeletal branches of naked trees and the tall weeds that grew persistently upon the graves of peasants and nobles alike, swayed steadily in the breezes. Thunder rumbled in the distance, and the smell of rain-saturated vegetation wafted from distant parts across the graveyard. It was a desolate place, and he was entrusting to its forlorn isolation Marion's tender body.

The cleric was far from surprised when he was notified the next day that Edmund wished to speak with him. Edmund, of course, would require balm to soothe the soreness of soul which ached from his recent loss. He would need the assurances of his religion that Marion had been an exemplary Christian and was now experiencing the joys of the celestial world. All bereaved took heart and comfort in the knowledge of the ultimate resurrection of the body and their future reunion with loved ones in heaven, and the cleric was eager to relieve the burden of grief under which Edmund was suffering so resignedly.

Edmund was pacing restlessly when the priest entered his room.

"Reverend," Edmund said as soon as the cleric had been invited to sit, "have you the formula for the making of vows?"

The priest stopped arranging the thick folds of his floor-length habit and sat stunned by the directness of the question. "I must have it somewhere, but why would it be needed?"

"Because I wish to make a vow."

Turning to get a better view of Edmund, who had continued his pacing, the priest gazed with suspicion. "Indeed. What kind of vow?"

"The vow of chastity-continence." Waving his hand irritably, he added, "You know what of I speak."

It was incomprehensible. Only yesterday Edmund had returned from the grave of his wife, and was now thinking of vows—of all things. Edmund's grief ran deeper than he had supposed. His reasoning was drastically unsettled by the tragic loss, and his self-pity was accented by his desire to punish himself further by the making of a vow. "But, Edmund, that vow is reserved for monks, priests."

"Reverend Jerome, can you deny that Christians other than religious have made this vow and are still permitted to do so? Please do not hinder me. I wish to make this vow, whether I have your permission or not. If my memory is accurate, the vow would still be valid if I pronounced it without your sanction."

"It is true that in extraordinary cases the making of such a vow by a layman is permitted, but why would you desire to do this?"

"Because I believe—how did you say?—that it is the will of God for me," and he mimicked the words the priest had spoken to him a year before. "You may recall many months ago when you so successfully convinced me it was God's will that I marry? Do not be offended, but I see now that you were completely incorrect in your judgment. You once asked me why I could not recognize the signs of God's will. What did you say?—it was my duty to bring forth heirs?" He turned swiftly to continue his pacing. "I see now all too clearly that God was displeased with that interpretation of his supposed will. How often have we spoken about my eventual return to Tankenham? That is where I was meant to be. You know I accepted this office because it was my duty to do so. When the title can be transferred to Cestus, I will return to the monastery. This is my destiny."

"But would a vow now be necessary? . . ."

Edmund's attitude changed abruptly, and he continued bitterly. "Ah, you know the councillors and the king. Soon they will consider that the infant needs a mother, or they will devise other reasons to prevent my leaving. A vow of chastity would bar a future marriage and would leave the way free for my eventual departure."

Reverend Jerome rubbed his lips with a forefinger and asked, shaking his head disbelievingly, "Edmund, how do you reason your marriage was not the will of God?"

"It is so certain. If it had been God's holy desire that I marry, he would not have caused Marion's death—and such a dreadful death—hours of pain . . . And what of the child, Reverend? Not only was it a female, but its deformity will forever remind me of my sin."

"Your sin, Edmund?" he said, scoffing at the absurdity. "What sin?"

Edmund turned and glared at him. "What sin? The sin of marrying and using the woman's body only to beget an heir. I know, Reverend, that many men in similar situations have also married out of expediency, but that does not make it altogether pleasing in God's sight. To my consideration, when God is satisfied with a union, he blesses it with affection and love. I experienced neither of these, and besides, the child's affliction and its mother's death are proof of God's displeasure."

"Edmund, really, you are too overcome to be thinking clearly. Your reasoning is clouded by the events of the last few days. Take your rest. Cedric can give you sleeping herbs to aid you. If you want, I will seek him out when I leave. We can discuss this matter at another time, when you are less overwrought."

"No. You want only another opportunity to dissuade me. I desire to make this vow now, while I am determined to do so, and I would be most grateful if you would find the necessary formula."

"It is a mistake, Edmund. I earnestly ask that you wait until the archbishop is notified. You know that such a vow should be made with his approval. He must be notified."

"You are hopeful he will be more successful than you have been? Will you give me the prayer?"

The thick woolen robes fell heavily into place as the cleric stood up. Calmly and quietly he continued. "Edmund, I do not condone this. If you are determined to make this vow, I wish to have no part of it."

"Very well, then. Witnesses are required, are they not?"

The priest did not answer.

Edmund crossed the room and opened the door. Calling for a guard who was standing in the hallway speaking to one of his companions, Edmund instructed, "Notify my mother, my scribe Friswell, and whatever priests and councillors are visiting here, to meet me at once in the chapel."

With an immediate clatter of steel, the guard was off.

"Do not be anxious about me, Jerome. It is well that I formulate the vow in my own words." Noiselessly he closed the door behind him, leaving the cleric alone in the stillness.

Immediately after Marion's death, a woman was sought who would suckle the infant, and one had been found almost at once in the village. Bertha, wife of Ansgar, the cobbler, had given birth to a son the month before, and welcomed the opportunity and privilege to nurse the daughter of the Lord of Lauxburgh. Although the prospect of moving into the castle appealed to her, the move was impossible because of three other children in the family and the necessity of maintaining the home for her husband. Arrangements were therefore made for one of the castle servants to move into the cobbler's cottage with Edmund's child.

The cobbler's home was one of the many dwellings nestled against the western wall of the castle in the protective shadow of its battlements. Its thatched roof covered not only the living quarters but also the front portion of the cottage, which served as the cobbler's workroom. Such were the living and working arrangements for most tradesmen: weavers, bakers, cloth dyers, carpenters, and potters. Ansgar's cottage was situated at the end of the street near the warehouse by the docks. Cooling summer breezes sweeping in from the bay stroked the home comfortably, and during winter storms its occupants were grateful for the castle wall and the warehouse for shielding their home from most of the chilling fury.

The cobbler's workroom walls were cluttered with skins stretched on racks in various sizes and curious shapes. Straps, reins, and halters hung in disarray on nails and lay in the dust where they had fallen from their perches. On poorly constructed worktables about the room were cluttered curiously shaped cuts of leather. Half-finished slippers, purses, and gaiters lay in a heap, and finished shoes, awaiting their purchasers, were atop a mass of scraps. On the floor beneath the tables were snips and strings of leather mixed with the dust, and one must watch lest he trip upon saddles, leather bottles, and old dried hides. Sharp smells of acids and dyes filled the dim environs and were kept from penetrating to the living area by burlap draperies that hid the entrance to the back.

One large room served as the kitchen, play area, and bedroom for the children. A large fireplace built into one wall furnished needed warmth and adequate cooking facilities. Two beds were shoved against one wall; a small chest, tables, and a few chairs were the only other furnishings.

With the arrival of the honored guest and her nurse, the area curtained off for the parents' sleeping area was given over for their use, but when the nurse informed the castle of this inconvenience to Bertha and Ansgar, a crew of carpenters was sent immediately to construct another room to the modest dwelling.

The presence of Edmund's daughter in Bertha's home gave a substantial measure of prestige to the household, but when the workmen began their hammering and the added room began taking form, and when sacks of grain and sides of venison were delivered to the door, her neighbors, who had at first rejoiced with her in her good fortune, now cast envious

glances her way or avoided her altogether. It was a condition
that Bertha accepted with indifference. Edith, the nurse, was
a compatible guest. Born of the same peasant stock, she had
sought employment in the castle as a young girl and was
taught there many skills, of which the most pleasant was caring for the children of noble parentage. She was at least ten
years older than Bertha, and like Bertha, was satisfied with
her station in life. She proved to be a blessing to the household, for not only did she care for Edmund's child but also
assumed most of the care of Bertha's fair-haired male child,
whose pinkish plumpness sharply contrasted with the pale
thinness of his fragile companion. The neighbors could be envious if they wished to be—indeed, how could they be otherwise, for Bertha freely boasted of how ably her guest assisted
her with the cleaning, cooking, storytelling, and game-playing
with the children.

Relieved of the strain of child-caring, Bertha lost her
drawn look, and with the generous supplies of food furnished
by the castle, her body filled out to rounded, healthy proportions. Bertha was a woman of thirty-five years. Her face
resembled the full rounded features of the peasant stock, and
like her kinsmen, she possessed skills in weaving, cooking,
and sewing. Her arms were ready to caress any child who
happened her way, her laugh was quick, her hands ready to
assume any task, and her love of God was strong. Her genuine affection for Edmund's deformed babe, coupled with the
blessings she had brought to her adopted home, made Bertha
resolve that the weaning of her charge would be delayed as
long as possible.

The days passed uneventfully until the day one month after Marion's death, when a great clatter of metal and the
stomping of horses' hooves approached the shop. One of the
children, with curiosity demanding to be satisfied, rushed to
the window, peered out, and shrieked excitedly, "It is
Edmund. It is the Lord Edmund."

Looking furtively toward the door of his workshop, Ansgar
wished earnestly he had had the time to rearrange and clear
it of debris. With uncommon speed Bertha rushed into the
curtained area, cast off her patched dress, and hastily
changed into a clean linen one hanging there. Breathlessly she

emerged. Edmund must never see the suckler of his infant other than neatly clad.

"I have come to visit my daughter. May I enter your home?" Edmund asked Ansgar, who had rushed out to greet him.

With profound awe, Ansgar held the door for his distinguished guest. He had watched Edmund approach, but it was unbelievable that he was now speaking to him—a humble leather worker speaking to the great Lord of Lauxburgh. Before he knew it, Edmund was standing inside the shop. "Yes, yes, of course," Ansgar said quickly, "you are welcome to my poor shop. Please, my lord, do not be offended by the clutter. I have been most busily employed."

"There is no need for apology. A cobbler's shop is always so arranged."

Ansgar was pleased with the kindly words and the hint of a smile on Edmund's otherwise expressionless face. "Please, please, my lord, come this way," he said, leading the way around a cluttered worktable. "The child is asleep now, I think. At her age, that is all they do."

Edmund seemed reluctant to speak, and continued making his way to the back door, where Ansgar held the faded drapery aside for him to enter.

"My lord," Bertha said, bowing deeply. "This humble house is honored by your presence." Bertha was quick in noting how dwarfed Ansgar seemed beside Edmund, who instantly made the room seem smaller and poorly suited for the entertainment of nobility.

Edmund nodded approvingly. He surveyed the room and smiled at Bertha, about whom the children huddled, awestruck by their regal visitor. When his glance fell upon the two cradles beside the fireplace, he walked to the taller and more elaborate one and looked upon the sleeping daughter he had not seen since her mother's death.

One of Bertha's small children crossed the room, knelt down beside the cradle, leaned against it, and looked up in cherubic innocence at the visitor. Edmund's gaze wandered to the little boy's large brown eyes. "Do you play with her?" Edmund asked without smiling.

"No, she is too little," he said, reaching in and grabbing the infant's hand. Squeezing his finger into her small fist, he asked, "See this?" And he raised the little fist that held onto his finger so tightly. "She is quite strong for a girl," he said with studied seriousness.

Edmund smiled as the boy was quickly hurried away by his mother with whispered admonitions.

"Does she look well to you?" the servant woman asked after a time.

"Yes, very well, Edith. Very well indeed." Edmund seemed relieved, for the child had changed from a frail, thin newborn into a rosy fuller child who gave promise of additional health and well-being.

"In another month or two she will be so fat and pretty you will not know her," the nurse boasted, as Bertha, who had been standing nervously by, blushed crimson for her contribution to the child's improvement.

As though his thoughts were far away, Edmund stood by the cradle looking upon the sleeping child until gurgling noises and thrashing limbs in the next cradle demanded attention. The yellow-haired baby, his face red with rage, was trying desperately to swallow his fist. Edmund adjusted his cloak about his neck and considered it best that he depart before an embarrassing situation developed. "Is there anything you desire?" he asked, turning to Bertha.

"No, my lord, you have been most generous," she replied, nervously fingering a fold in her skirt.

"Edith," he said, returning his attention to the servant, "if there is anything they require, or anything that can be done for them, notify my steward without delay."

Edith nodded and quickly bowed deeply as he walked past.

Pausing briefly beside the children, who had stood quietly fidgeting, Edmund reached into his belt, extracted three silver coins, and pressed one into each hand. Amazed by their good fortune, they stared disbelievingly at the flashing metal until bright smiles broke upon their intense faces.

Ansgar, who had waited by the door, again held the curtain aside, and as Edmund walked into the shop, he stopped to examine the leather shoes Ansgar had been cutting. Picking up a leather vest, he examined its stitching and ran his hands against its smoothness. "I see you are skilled in all manner of leather work," he said, while studying the shapes of the skins hanging on the wall.

"Yes, my lord. I was taught the trade by my father, whose father also instructed him. I have had this shop for many years."

Edmund was satisfied, and turned his full attention to Ansgar. "I am grateful," he said, "for the hospitality you have shown my daughter."

Ansgar was flustered by the remark and knew not how to answer.

Edmund reached for the cobbler's rough hand and pressed it. "Thank you," he whispered, and was out the door with a draft of cool air.

Bertha and Edith watched Edmund's departure from a side window and giggled at the excitement of the unexpected visit, but there was one element of the visit they held most seriously. They knew with all the forcefulness of their womanly intuitions that Edmund dearly loved the babe but knew not how to express it.

If Ansgar had been surprised at Edmund's visit, it was as nothing compared to his amazement the next day when a servant from the castle came with instructions that he was to help the cobbler with all manner of work, cleaning the shop or running errands, and that he was not to leave each day until all was done to Ansgar's satisfaction. And if that were not enough of a blessing, orders from the castle began arriving for new bridles, saddles, chair covers, shoes, and belts, until Ansgar determined to look about for an apprentice.

Life was being good, and as he looked about his orderly shop, and at the stack of orders, he blessed himself and said a prayer of thanksgiving for his good wife and for the health-giving milk that flowed so abundantly from her ample breasts.

THANE GODFREY'S ship had been overtaken on the North Sea, and his message of the baby's birth was amended to include the news of Marion's tragic death. If King Fergus was expected to be greatly disappointed about the deformity of the child, outright rage was anticipated for the physician's inability to preserve the life of his niece. During the long hours at sea while following the shoreline of Kent and that of the Danelaw territories, Godfrey summoned his courage and all his diplomatic skills for this unpleasant confrontation with the Viking king.

Countless tales had been told of Fergus' fiery disposition and daring adventures. Although a minor king who governed a minor kingdom bordering Edmund's district of Kent, he was held liable to the great King Guthrum, who ruled the whole of the Danelaw, which boasted the occupation of other minor kings. Yet, in spite of his subjugation to Guthrum, Fergus had become a legendary figure. Many a storyteller who claimed to have known or seen him, enthralled relaxed audiences in the quiet of many evenings with reports of his boisterous and unexpected raids on Saxon soil, of his courage and phenomenal strength on the fields of battle. Youngsters too young to have lived through the attacks sat wide-eyed with interest while their elders relived the experiences and recalled how the frantic shouts of "The Vikings are coming, the Vikings are coming" had struck terror in the hearts of many as they fled their homes with hastily gathered belongings. Villagers, wearied of the raids and drained by the heathen thieves who plundered and stole grains and livestock, were relieved when his exploits were ended by the formation of the Danelaw and the declaration of peace.

If the creation of the Danelaw had managed to curb Fergus' appetite for adventure and conquest, his subsequent baptism, following Guthrum's example, and those of his family, closest friends, and advisers, did little to alter the Anglo-Saxons' opinions of him or his court. Many Saxons secretly concurred that his baptism was only a ruse, and though Fergus denied it, they believed that the outlaw bands of raiders who steadfastly clung to their pagan exploits were secretly sent by him to vent his anger at the pompous English, who claimed intellectual and cultural superiority. Only after Edmund's marriage to Fergus' niece were the raids across the border discontinued, but then many in Kent surmised that the raids had been discontinued to avert suspicion after Marion had been placed in their midst as a spy. For all her gentle and prayerful ways, few trusted her. The women firmly suspected that after she had gathered enough information against them, an overwhelming Danish invasion would result in their complete and final conquest. The Danes were not to be trusted, they reasoned, especially those who claimed reform by religious conversion.

The notoriety of the Danish king had indeed spread throughout many districts, but the man before whom Godfrey was presented bore little resemblance to the vigorous and virile Viking whose name had caused bitter hatred to surge through the veins of many Saxons. Slumped in his chair as if sapped of all vitality, his streaming golden hair in disarray about the fur collar of his tunic, he seemed an old man as he listened unemotionally to Godfrey's morbid messages.

Tirades were not forthcoming, and instead Fergus mulled over the words, apparently conjuring up the vision of the quiet, unassuming Marion, who had so joyously left his home to marry the English earl, unaware of the number of diplomatic maneuverings that had successfully entrapped Edmund into the matrimonial coalition.

Godfrey waited self-consciously until Fergus brought himself to reality. He rubbed his mouth and stroked his coarse beard before mumbling, "A pity . . . a pity. She died so young, so very young."

"The name of the child will be Lelia, sir," Godfrey added. "The Lady Marion had expressed a wish that the child be named after her own mother."

"Lelia? Yes, it pleases me." Fergus lapsed into far-reaching thoughts. "I do not know if I will ever look upon the babe's face, or even upon the earth of her mother's grave," he said forlornly.

"But surely, sir, you will someday visit our land," the thane graciously exclaimed, recalling, as he did, Fergus' previously disturbing visits.

"No, I do not see how it can be."

A soft rapping and a cheerful, "Father, may I enter?" caused both men to turn in the direction of the door, where a slender brown-eyed girl smiled radiantly.

"This is my daughter, Aleen." Thane Godfrey, who was standing before the king, straightened to a gallant posture. Aleen smiled coquettishly and swept into the room, her dark hair bouncing with her steps, the loose dangle of her gold-linked belt rattling musically with her every movement. An arm slipped around Fergus' neck as she bent down to kiss his forehead. "Our distinguished visitor has just arrived from Lauxburgh, and we have many matters to discuss. Can your business wait for now, my love?"

"Yes, Father, as you say," she said, while eyeing Godfrey cautiously.

"Aleen, please do me the kindness of fetching the steward. Thane Godfrey will stay with us. See, my dearest, if you can find him, and I promise to speak with you when you return." Fergus squeezed her arm affectionately, and she glided away, her silk skirts swaying fluidly above the tops of her red slippers.

"I do not know how I can tell her," Fergus said when their privacy was reestablished. "They grew to maidenhood together. Ah, well, heaven awaits us all, does it not? Marion was like a daughter to me. When her parents died, I took her to live in my household." He sighed deeply. "We shall miss her. Yes," he continued almost sleepily, "yes, we shall miss her. But then, I have the consolation of knowing she was happy the last year of her life. I have much for which to thank Edmund. Please convey my gratitude to him for his many kindnesses to her—for making her so happy. Her missives were a pleasure to read. She wrote so often of their mutual love and their joy concerning the child. Few marriages are so blessed. Edmund is a good man, a good husband. . . ." And he lapsed again into thoughts that obviously tormented his recollection.

Godfrey wondered about Fergus' preoccupation and his unexpected words. Marion happy? And Edmund responsible for that happiness? He could never tell Fergus the truth—it were better he retain pleasant thoughts about the marriage.

The steward appeared at the door and tapped lightly to gain Fergus' attention.

"Yes, Lothgar, our visitor will stay with us. See that he and his companions are furnished with all the comforts they require." And looking up at Godfrey, "Stay as long as you like. Rest, and perhaps before you leave, we can talk once more."

With a smile of gratitude, Godfrey walked behind Lothgar, but before he passed from view, he looked back at the king, who sat slumped in the chair as though asleep. His conduct had been entirely unexpected. "And to think," Godfrey said to himself, "that the dreaded Fergus, the fearful warrior, was too tired, too weak, or too sick to rise once from his chair."

Fergus was in the garden of the castle that in his younger days he had stormed and overtaken from the Saxons with such daring. Now tired and aged before his time, he relaxed in the glare of a sun that warmed the chilling edges of the swirling breezes. Bundled to his chin in a warm fur mantle, he watched a young couple who sat closely on a stone bench beneath the naked branches of a giant oak.

Fergus turned with a start. "Godfrey, I did not hear you approach. Here, sit here beside me," and he pushed to the side to provide room for his guest. Godfrey declined and sat instead on the ground near Fergus' feet and leaned against the trunk of a tree.

"Do you mind sitting here in the weather? This is one of the first really pleasant days we have had the whole of this season. I would like you to enjoy it with me. This is the kind of day that brings strength and health to a man's body," and he breathed deeply of the crisp air. "Yes, this is the sort of day that makes a man feel like a man," and he smiled down at Godfrey with a twinkle of jest sparkling his deep blue eyes. "Actually, I have much to discuss with you, and I know my attendants will not hear me here. Since the time I took ill, they have hovered about me. In the most unsuspecting places are a pair of ears ready to hear my every want. What I now say must be for your ears alone. I have watched you closely

47

these past days, and I feel you are dependable and trust-worthy."

Godfrey smiled and shrugged in embarrassment.

"Tell me, Godfrey, have you much influence with the Lord Edmund?"

"Edmund is a dear friend. We grew to manhood together, except for the times he was away at the monastery school. He has asked my opinion concerning many problems. Yes, I would say I have a small measure of influence with him."

"I see you are also modest." Fergus' attitude changed sharply. "I am a dying man, Godfrey. Ah, my physicians tell me it is a temporary illness, and they fill me with potions of roots, barks, berries, herbs—all sorts of bitter mixtures. But I am dying. The pains in my innards grow stronger and more numerous each day. It is strange when one knows he is dying. Suddenly all the truly important problems gnaw at you until they are resolved. For the present, I am concerned for her," and he tilted his chin in the direction of the couple sitting to the far side of the lonely garden.

"My daughter, Aleen. She came out here to keep me amused, but you see who has captured her attentions." He smiled with pleasure and pride at the thought of the dark-haired beauty, whose eyes danced mischievously at the young man who smiled blushingly at her words. "She has been the delight of my life. Full of spirit she is, and smart as well. Yes, she is intelligent concerning many things. Would you think she can train the wildest of stallions as well as any of my stable hands? She has a way with horses and young men. Tell me, Godfrey, do you think she is fair?"

Godfrey nodded his head affirmatively. "Indeed, sir. I find her most appealing."

"Do you think Edmund would find her favorable?"

Godfrey hesitated. "Yes, I am certain he would."

"Since you say you have some influence with Edmund, I wish to entrust you with a dying man's request. I wish you would do all you can to influence Edmund to marry my daughter."

"But, sir," Godfrey protested in bewilderment, "Edmund is a recent widower. He has just lost a wife. He could not . . ."

"The marriage could be formalized following the proper time of mourning," Fergus replied calmly.

"But, sir," Godfrey persisted as he rose from his place. "Why Edmund, when the lady seems to possess so much interest in the young man?"

Fergus shook his head. "That young man is not for her. He is still a boy. Aleen needs a man—a real man. One who could pull rein on her." Amusement brightened his face. "Yes, that is what she needs. Someone older to capture and tame her flighty nature." His pleasant thoughts changed to somber recollections. "One reason I took Marion to live with me was because she was older and wiser than her years. I thought she would have an effect on my daughter. My wife died when Aleen was but a baby. The child spent so much time with her brother and me that she preferred not the company of her own sex. When she grew to maidenhood, Marion taught her to dress and arrange herself becomingly, but she prefers the sporting life to studying the feminine arts. As you see, she is far from conducting herself as Marion did. She is not enticing the young man, as you may imagine, but is teasing the poor lad—making sport of him."

Godfrey's head snapped in the direction of a shrill squeal in time to see Aleen darting between trees and shrubs to escape the young man's grasp. Peals of laughter filled the dreary garden as the young man caught her beside the trunk of a tree and impulsively planted a kiss on her tugging hand.

"They forget we are here," Fergus said, squinting his eyes as he watched the giggling couple. "Yes, she requires an older man—a real man—to handle her properly. Godfrey, tell me, can you make this proposal to Edmund? I will pay whatever price you ask."

"Please, sir, do not speak of money. But tell me, if you will, why you chose Edmund? Surely you have many men of your blood who would make her an excellent mate. Surely someone—"

"No, there is no one here," he said emphatically, rising with some difficulty to his feet. "When I die, I am not certain what will transpire here, what upheavals there will be. I am not certain my son will care to assume my throne. I desire that my daughter be safely out of this country and happily married before I die."

Together they walked along the path, the dried bits of leaves crunching beneath their steps.

"Marion was happy at Lauxburgh. I wish the same for my daughter."

Godfrey envisioned Marion's sweet little face. She had been lonely at Lauxburgh, and if she experienced happiness with or without Edmund, Thane Godfrey was not aware of it. But then, she would write only pleasant things to her uncle, or perhaps even embellish the slightest of Edmund's attentions so as not to cause her uncle to concern himself about her welfare.

The wind shook Fergus' hair stiffly away from his face, and his eyes watered from the sting. "I have heard many favorable reports about the Lord Edmund. He is a good and wise ruler. I feel I know him, though we have never met. Call it a father's nonsense, but I know he is the man for my daughter. Please," he said, reaching for Godfrey's arm, "please do me this kindness. Please ask him before another woman captures his fancy and marries him. Please do this for a dying man."

They stopped and faced each other. The desperation of Fergus' request was disturbing. Never had Godfrey seen a man so thoroughly tormented.

Fergus was visibly relieved when Godfrey finally replied, "I will present your suggestion to Edmund. I do not know what I can accomplish, but I will see what I can do."

Fergus clasped Godfrey's hand with such emotion that Godfrey thought him close to tears.

"I do not promise success," Godfrey reminded him, "but I will see what I can do."

## ⤳ VI ⤲

THE PALL that had settled over Lauxburgh after the funeral
lifted for the most part, except where it shadowed the consciences of those who by snide remarks and flippant gestures
had succeeded, or at least thought they had succeeded, in
convincing Marion of her subordinate position in the community—a condition not altered by her marriage to Edmund.

Wilfreda had managed to dismiss the guilt created by the
cruel actions and biting words she had directed toward her
son's wife by placing them in the balance with the prayers
she had sped on high for the repose of Marion's soul. In the
twisted channels of her mind she indulged in the satisfaction
of knowing that it was indeed generous and charitable of her
to pray so fervently for the soul of a Viking. Following the
death, when she knelt in the gloomy half-light of the chapel,
her knees aching from their pressure against the stone floor,
her arms screaming to be dropped from their outstretched
position, no one suspected that there lurked behind her whispered words of intercession the selfish conviction that her
prayers were sufficient to release Marion's soul from the pains
she supposedly deserved in the depths of purgatorial fire.
Many fanciful moments were spent in the assumption that
not only had she gained bountiful merits for her charity, but
also that Marion would be pledged to thanking her for all
eternity for speedily releasing her from fiery punishment,
thereby opening for the Viking the entrance to a celestial
bliss that was undeserved.

The pensive moods that had characterized Edmund's behavior since he took reluctant leave of Tankenham were intensified since Marion's death, and it was with tender solicitude for his bereavement that all, from kitchen maid to his
councilmen, performed their assignments for him. If Edmund
indulged more in periods of self-reproach, he also sought relief for the burden by communion with his God. But he had

found prayer in the chapel impossible, since Wilfreda would invariably join him there. Kneeling before the altar, she would stretch out her arms in imitation of the crucified and tilt her head back as though rapt in ecstatic contemplation. It was not difficult to compare her extremes with the humble conduct of the monks or nuns he had known who bowed their heads unpretentiously in prayer. Wilfreda's religious extremes were intolerable, but never did Edmund confront her about them. It was far better to maintain their present peaceful status than to excite her, thereby risking the peacefulness of the entire castle. Edmund, therefore, took to praying in his room and embarked on a practice that was to edify and increase his esteem in the eyes of many.

Surrounded by a cordon of guards, Edmund journeyed to Marion's grave once each fortnight to pray beside the mound of soil before entering the cathedral to pray for her and the people of his district. Because of the attacks of Viking renegades, who were again appearing about the countryside, the guards about him became more numerous, until his pious visits were reduced to monthly observances.

Soon after Marion's death, when word of her passing had infiltrated to the renegade bands, their restless urge for battle sought release. Treaties were abstract matters, made only to be broken or ignored, but now that the substantial alliance with the Kentishman had been dissolved with the death of their Viking princess, their inborn craving for adventure and exploit were given relaxed rein. Their exuberance found freedom, and once again they reveled in renewed activities. Again their long boats, with sneering dragon heads peering from tall prows, sailed the horizon on cooperative winds.

At first their forays were of a less serious nature. Cattle were stolen, and livestock slaughtered for their consumption, but their forays for food contributed little to their thirst for the old days of adventure, and their plunderings soon assumed more serious proportions. Word began arriving at Lauxburgh of the murder of innocent folk whose only crime was their feeble attempt to protect the goods for which they had honestly labored.

Their senses dulled to the gravity of their actions, the Danes aimed for and attained more rewarding goals when they stealthily entered Wetson monastery on the coast and surprised the monks at prayer. While the religious were huddled together under the threat of sharpened battleaxes, the Danes removed the gleaming gold plate on the shrine of Saint Dunsley, taking with it an abundance of costly jewels that had been donated by the devout. After it was denuded of its treasure, the shrine was opened and the bones of the saint were cast about, to the horror of the religious and amusement and howling laughter of the trespassers. The monks crossed themselves devoutly at the sight and prayed for forgiveness of a sacrilege they were helpless to prevent.

After collecting the golden altar vessels, candleholders, and vestments made of valued fabrics, they killed, as lambs at slaughter, many monks, leaving, unbeknownst to themselves, the younger, more quick-thinking of the community, who feigned injury and death.

Following the desecration, Edmund dispatched many envoys to King Alfred seeking assistance and to King Fergus requesting his intercession in quelling the activities of the terrorizing Danes, who, it was believed, came from his kingdom.

Before effective measures could be enforced, the Danes struck a blow that was to cause the whole of Kent to gasp in disbelief. The chivalry in every man screamed to avenge the crime, and the heart of every woman was struck with fear of a similar fate at the hands of the dreaded Danes.

Lauxburgh was just arousing from a night of refreshing slumber. The cooks were busy lighting the fires under the grills, while the pleasant plop-plop of beating mixed pleasantly with the clattering of iron pots and the hurried scraping of feet. An occasional slamming of a door, the banging of boards and benches in the great hall, the distant moaning of a cow begging to be milked, the whinnying of the horses in the stable, and the shuffling of servants scurrying about on errands for their masters were customary sounds that were little heeded. But the urgent pounding on the main gate was not ordinary, and its persistent thuds made the guard rush toward it and lift the bars with deliberate haste.

Hardly had the gates separated when a breathless peasant lunged through, pulling his lathered horse after him. "Edmund, I must see Edmund," he panted, while struggling for air.

"Steady, man," the gateman cautioned, taking the reins

from him and turning them over to the stable hand who had rushed up. "Steady," and he grabbed the peasant by the shoulders to support him.

"The sisters—they sent me to fetch Edmund. The Danes. They pilfered the convent, killed some of the nuns. Edmund. I must see Edmund," and he struggled against the grip that tightened at the words.

"Come," the gateman said, and they bounded across the courtyard, past the stables and the inner grounds. There was no need to bring the visitor to the scribe for the customary permission before speaking with Edmund. The gateman had authority to act on matters of urgency. If anything were amiss at Chatham, Edmund would want to know of it without delay. Together they vaulted the steps to Edmund's chamber.

"Yes, enter," the voice replied to their urgent knockings. Edmund had been dressing and was adjusting his belt over a leather vest as the guard entered and presented the disheveled visitor.

"A messenger sent by the sisters of Chatham. I thought you had best hear his message directly," the gateman said by way of introduction.

The farmer awkwardly entered and fell on one knee in homage. Edmund strode forward. "Please rise," he said, bending down to assist his visitor. If there was one function that annoyed Edmund, it was the bowing and kneeling performed in respect for his position. Such should be reserved for the good God, he had always maintained, but his efforts in stopping the practice were futile.

"What could the good sisters be wanting so early in the day?" Edmund asked as he adjusted the strings that crossed his vest.

"Sister Walburga," he said, stammering nervously. "She came to my home while it was yet dark. She was shivering with fright." The little farmer's leathery hand slipped through his tousled hair as he struggled between rapid breaths to bridle his excitement. "Sister said the Danes surprised them a day ago. She said they pilfered the chapel and convent and killed some of the nuns. She said the Danes left this morning in the darkness. The abbess begs you to come directly."

Every muscle in Edmund's body stiffened at the announcement, and his eyes flashed with fury. "How did the Danes depart? Did the sister speak of that?"

"Yes, my lord. The nun followed them and watched as they boarded the ship that was anchored at sea. When their sail billowed and the ship moved away, she left for my cottage. I sometimes serve the sisters as carpenter and messenger, my lord."

"If they were far at sea, it would be impossible to apprehend them." Edmund frowned and rammed a fist into the palm of the other hand. "What else have you to tell me?"

"Nothing, my lord. The sister was disturbed and cried much."

"Come, then, we must go without delay."

As the morning sun gained altitude in the heavens, the shadows of the helmeted troops raced across the roads as the thunder of their horses' hooves preceded them. Farmers pulled rein on oxen and leaned against plowshares to watch their approach. Aproned women scurried from thatched cottages and shielded their eyes for distant viewing. Children danced about, anxiously awaiting their passage, but their childish excitement was quickly snapped into fright when the very ground beneath them shook as the horses pounded by in billowing clouds of dust. From behind the safety of their mothers' skirts they feared for their geese, who waddled away amid noisy honkings and frantic beatings of wings. Grazing cattle, flapping tails against swirls of buzzing insects, turned sleepy eyes in the direction of the galloping horses, and unconcerned with what they saw, continued chewing with low moans of protest for the brief disturbance in their contented existence.

Built upon the ancient ruins of a once important Roman fortification, the convent was ideally situated in a verdant surrounding that afforded privacy from inquisitive eyes. Its peaceful lands were of considerable size. Hares, unafraid of disturbance, lazily hopped upon the meadow that undulated from the rear of the convent buildings to the slope at whose feet lapped the shimmering waters of the North Sea. A Roman wall, now crumbling but still strong enough to restrain grazing cattle and sheep, encircled most of the farmlands, the gardens, cemetery, and orchard. Gentle hills ruffled rhythmically, lifting the lands to the west, where tall stands of hemlock and oak had encroached the land since the Roman occupation. The leafy curtain claimed the boundaries between the convent lands and the public farms and guarded the privacy of the convent by blocking the visibility between it and the settlement farther south.

Villagers who had stood by the gate in the Roman wall swung the portals open when Edmund and the soldiers approached, and those standing about in groups on the convent meadow quickly moved aside.

The main door to the convent opened, and the abbess, standing in the shadows, waited for Edmund to cross the green. Her calm, dignified appearance dissolved at the approach of her nephew, and by the time he was near, she fell against him with whimperings of relief.

"There, there," Edmund said consolingly as he held her thin face against his chest. Running his hand against the head whose veil lay upon his arm in rumpled folds, he whispered, "Cry, cry all you wish." But the words belied his impatience, for his being was in turmoil to know the nature and extent of the crimes committed. His kindly aunt, whom he had thought incapable of displaying such distress, continued sobbing uncontrollably in his arms. It grieved Edmund to see her so distraught. The abbess Grimbald was so kind in thought, so patient, so uncomplaining, so very much unlike her sister Wilfreda.

"Come, now, tell me all, so that I may know how to assist you."

Sniffing softly and wiping the tears from her face, she led the way to a room off the damp hallway. With her back to the door where Edmund remained, she stood, frail but erect, in the center of the room, where slits of light penetrated the bare room through long narrow windows. Privacy was soon secured by the thud of the closing door. "Now," Edmund implored, "tell me what happened here."

"During the early hours of yesterday morn," she began hesitantly in a high-pitched voice, "we were awakened by shouts—the harsh shouts of men. They had entered our cloister," she said in distress, her back still toward Edmund. "They crowded into the corridors and knocked on all our doors to awaken us. They made us leave our cells without permitting us to dress in our robes and veils." Her head shook from side to side in painful recollection. "They forced us to the assembly room . . . in our sleeping gowns and caps. They would not let us dress," she continued plaintively.

Edmund could not see her face, now flushed red with shame.

"While some of the men guarded us, we heard others throwing things about in other rooms. Later they came back with measures of cloth, candleholders, silver bowls, and the good dishes used by our guests."

Edmund was breathing heavily, and his face ill-concealed his frenzied desperation, but his voice was purposely rendered calm. "And then?"

"When they said they were going to the chapel to strip the altar . . . when they said they were going there, I asked if I might retain the consecrated hosts. I thought to spare them from sacrilege, but when I brought the key and opened the tabernacle, the man who was with me grabbed for the golden vessel. He . . . he put his dirty hand into it and picked up a quantity of hosts, and then, when another man laughed and said he had no use for them, the Dane threw them in the air and they fell like clumps of snow upon the floor. He threw all of them into the air. I knelt down to gather them up, but . . ."

"Yes, go on."

"He kicked me. I fell, and then he pulled me and pushed me toward the room where the nuns were." Her voice lowered. "After the Danes left this morning, I went back to the chapel and found the hosts where they had fallen. They had walked on them. The Danes walked on the very body of Christ. . . ." Her voice quivered with emotion. "I placed them on a linen cloth and locked them in the tabernacle. The bishop must be notified of this desecration."

"Yes, we will tell him later, but finish. What then happened?"

"They pilfered the kitchen and ate all we had there. They killed and cooked our fowl, and they killed many sheep, but they took the meat to their ship. They drank wine until . . ." Her voice trembled. "They drank until they began singing and making sport of us. They took Sister . . ." She could not continue, and abruptly stopped.

Edmund walked around the frail woman until he stood before her and looked upon the complete distress that wrinkled the drawn, thin face. "They harmed her?"

The little nun attempted to turn away, but Edmund restrained her and held her fast. "Tell me. Did they harm her?" He peered upon downcast eyes that refused to look into his. "Tell me," he demanded.

"They were terrible men," she whispered almost inaudibly. "They were boisterous, rough, crude, and their bodies stank sickeningly. Edmund"—and she buried her face in her hands—"Edmund, they ripped her gown . . ." A flow of tears interrupted. "They killed two of our nuns. They were young, and when they resisted too strenuously, the men thrust swords into them." She covered her mouth with a thin hand and closed her eyes tightly against the memory. "Blood was everywhere."

"Did they harm the others? Did they?"

The meaning of his words hung heavy in the cool stillness of the room, and her bowed head and red downcast eyes gave confirmation to his suspicions. Suddenly the small, slender figure became more delicate. "Come, sit down," he said, leading her by the arm.

Edmund stood preoccupied by the accumulation of the distressing events and watched the particles of dust swirling in the ray of sunlight, his thoughts racing about in similar unrest.

"They left before dawn," the small voice continued, but the words sounded unreal and strangely distant. "We dressed after they left, and Sister Walburga went immediately to seek assistance."

"Fergus!" Edmund said aloud, paying little heed to her final words. "Fergus was behind this," he added with bitter conviction.

"No."

Edmund turned toward the nun and watched as she nervously rubbed her small fists in her lap.

"No, Edmund, it was not King Fergus. One man said"— she quickly lowered her voice and her eyes—"they said since Fergus did not act against you for Marion's murder—they called her innocent death murder—they would mete out punishment in his stead. They said Fergus was too old to act wisely. They claimed Marion was poisoned. Fergus was un-aware of their actions."

"Mete out punishment?" asked Edmund with jaw set firmly. "They do not know what just punishment is." His flashing eyes narrowed in anticipation of judicial retaliation. "But that will be taken care of in due time."

Suddenly aware of the pressing needs of the community, he asked, "Where are the nuns?"

"They are eating. The village ladies were kind enough to bring mutton and bread. All of yesterday my poor daughters were not permitted to eat. They are weak and much bewildered."

Edmund threw his head back, studied the beamed ceiling, and remained silently gathering his thoughts. Finally, with a deep sigh he lowered his head. "Well, we have much to do. The bodies of the nuns. Where are they?"

"In the chapel. We dressed them and placed them before the altar."

"Take me to them. We must bury them before we leave."

"Then you have brought a priest with you?" the nun asked with relief, looking for the first time upon Edmund's face.

"No, there was no time . . . nor did we think to do so."

"Then how can we properly entomb them? Reverend Jacob will not be returning for several days. He is on his rounds of the country—"

"We will bury them as best we can before we take you and the sisters to Lauxburgh. The traditional prayers can be said later." Edmund looked upon her bewilderment. "Surely you realize you cannot remain here. We will take all of you to Lauxburgh, where physicians can care for you properly."

"But our enclosure. We must stay upon convent grounds."

"I am sorry, dear aunt, but we cannot allow this. The nuns must be cared for, and the convent and its lands must be secured from further attack. We cannot permit you to remain vulnerable. Come. Let us see to the sisters."

As they walked into the hallway, Edmund paused and asked, "Have you a cart? No? Well, then, we can secure some from the village. They will be honored for the sisters to use them. How many nuns have you now?"

"Ten, Edmund. We were twelve. . . ."

Hurried orders were given to soldiers standing alertly in

the hallway. The abbess listened, her thin body turned away in shame, her face hidden by her veil. It was good to relinquish authority to stronger, younger shoulders. So good to let others worry about carts, graves, caskets, rounding up the remaining livestock, if there were any. But as she stood apart listening, she knew another weight had been placed upon her, as it had been placed upon all the nuns: the painfully heavy cloak of shame and humiliation that might never be discarded during their lifetimes.

"I beg pardon for the delay," Edmund apologized. "Please be so kind as to show me to the chapel."

Together they walked silently through corridors that retained the dampness and much of the coolness of night, in spite of a warm sun at its zenith.

Two stunted candles burned steadily near the altar. The two bodies, neatly clothed in religious garb, stiffly lay on linen cloths that had been spread on the large stone platform upon which the altar rested. Edmund stood at their feet, his gaze sweeping their bloodless faces and the serene appearance of their bodies, which but a few hours before had endured such anguish. He knelt between them and dropped his head in prayer before the tabernacle that sheltered the crushed and soiled Eucharist.

The abbess remained behind Edmund and clasped her hands in fervent prayer.

Of a sudden Edmund began to pray aloud: "Though I should draw upon the last measure of my strength, or yet give up my life, the deaths of these two and the crimes committed here will be avenged. I accept from your hand, O Lord, whatsoever sacrifice may be asked of me in exchange for the peace of my country and the safety of its helpless women."

# ⌁ VII ⌁

THE RUMBLING of the ox-drawn carts and the dull thuds of horses' hooves on the hard-packed mud of the inner court-yard captured the attention of the curious of Lauxburgh, who hurried to windows and parapets to watch the latest diversion. What they saw caused questioning frowns to wrinkle many brows, for soldiers were gently assisting nuns from the carts—nuns whose black veils concealed their faces, nuns whose habits were pricked with bits of straw, bewildered nuns who were leaning against the thick wooden wheels of the carts, waiting for assistance.

Speculation ran rampant. Nuns had been occasional visitors to Lauxburgh, and their quiet, unassuming comings and goings produced little attention, but these nuns, who found it necessary to hide their faces, who were weak and ill, commanded the sympathy and complete solicitude of all. The curiosity of the onlookers would soon be satisfied, for the soldiers would relate the crime to their wives, who would in turn whisper it to the widows, maidens, and servants, until all of Lauxburgh, the district, and the whole of the isle would know of it.

Wilfreda rushed to the side of her sister, who clasped her as though attempting to absorb some of the strength of body and will that characterized Wilfreda's strong personality. Together they walked through the inner yard with arms entwined about each other. The others, helped by vigilant soldiers, were gently guided in the same direction, through corridors and into a sector of the castle where complete privacy was easily maintained.

The castle was immediately plunged into a state of emergency. Cedric was hastily summoned, and arrived promptly with his apprentice, who nervously carried a tray rattling with clay pots and jars of potions, herbs, and medicinal lotions. Servant girls flitted about with jugs of water, linens, and coverlets. Scullery maids, straining under the weight of large trays of food, cautiously made their way to where Wilfreda stood directing the proceedings in her usually efficient, domineering manner.

Once the physical needs of the nuns were attained, a tapestry was hung across the hall to establish a boundary for the temporary cloister. Wilfreda, fired by the importance of her position as guardian of the nuns, had her room temporarily changed to the one closest to the tapestry barrier, where she could more readily intercept all necessary transactions.

Reverend Jerome was the first to step within the enclosure when he was summoned to relieve tender consciences of their ill-founded guilt and to hear the confessions of those who stubbornly insisted on seeking peace through the spiritual graces of the sacraments for the evil done their bodies.

After assuring himself that the nuns were contented with their facilities, Edmund immediately dispatched envoys to King Alfred requesting reinforcements of troops to assist local soldiers in flushing the Danes from surrounding forests, and imploring both Alfred and Fergus to supply ships to patrol Kentish waters to seize the vagabonds or at least to prevent further invasions.

Reactions from both sources came swiftly. Alfred dispatched not only troops, but forwarded documents written in his own hand in which he expressed sympathy for the crimes reported and pledged assistance for whatsoever tasks Edmund deemed necessary to convert the convent to a secure situation. King Fergus conveyed profound apologies and entrusted to his emissary money to be used in the repair of the convent and the replenishment of its larder. In addition, he dispatched ships to seek out the pirates, and pledged appropriate punishment for the prisoners they would succeed in capturing. These delinquent Vikings would be denied the ultimate reward to which all Norsemen aspired. They would not be found worthy, by reason of a violent death on the field of battle, to ride the horse of a Valkyrie to Valhalla, the hall of the god Odin, where the souls of heroes abided. They would instead be subjected to the humiliating ordeal of a slow torture and a degrading execution.

The patrolling of Fergus' long boats in the North Sea produced vexations, for if one climbed the towers of the castle, the Viking ships with dragon-headed prows could be seen at anchor between the horizon and the entrance to the bay. It was an uncomfortable situation, for many supposed it a trap. If it suited their whimsey, the Danish ships, scattered at intervals along the coastline, could invade and perhaps conquer Lauxburgh. Suspicions were greatly increased by the number of couriers either coming to or departing Lauxburgh, creating a veritable whirlwind of messages between Fergus, Edmund, and Alfred. But those between Alfred and Fergus were far more numerous, for Fergus presented a plan for peace that, after careful reflection, met with King Alfred's approval. Following weeks of negotiations, King Alfred at last sent word that he would journey himself to Lauxburgh to introduce the latest strategy for peace.

A flurry of excitement swept through Lauxburgh at the announcement of Alfred's impending visit. The courtyards were cleared of debris, the stables tidied, while everywhere there was dusting and sweeping and polishing. Geese, lambs, and swine were butchered, and fruits and grains collected for the feasts that it was hoped would favorably impress the king. The cooks took delight in planning meals that would bring credit worthy of their talents. Nothing contributed more to the impression of a castle well administered than a table abounding with fine wines, varieties of fruits, and succulent meats.

Preparations of another sort were also in force, for servants and matrons were busy with needles and imported fabrics, making gowns for the unmarried maidens—gowns that might capture the eyes and interests of the unmarried envoys or soldiers who would accompany the king. In anticipation of loving attentions and flatteries, feminine hearts fluttered and the energies of nimble fingers increased as brilliantly dyed blue, scarlet, and lavender gowns took shape. Brooches, garnet rings, jeweled necklaces, silver and gold armbands were thoughtfully selected and set aside for the visit.

Other women besides the maidens were similarly distracted: widows seeking a second marriage and wives of soldiers who were not above enjoying the excitements of innocent flirtations while their husbands were absent.

The pomp that usually accompanied the travels of a king were absent when Alfred journeyed the distance from London to Lauxburgh. This was a time of caution, and such traditions must be relinquished for the sake of security. There was no need to tempt the roaming band of Vikings by extending the prospect of their killing or capturing the greatest of all prizes, the king of England. Consequently, Alfred was arrayed as the soldiers, and all who were attracted along the way by the din of clanking battle trappings thought them to be one of many detachments on patrol. Only when they approached the castle grounds did Alfred remove his helmet to permit recognition by the people.

The castle sentinels immediately notified Edmund and the people of his approach, and before he entered the castle gate the voices of many shouted his name. He was loved by his countrymen as sincerely and completely as the Kentishmen revered and honored Edmund. It was well known and appreciated how he labored to improve England's prestige. His efforts to enlarge England's naval strength, his establishment of monastic schools, his rebuilding of the city of London, and other achievements of cultural and military natures, made the people appreciate his visit all the more. Any king who would temporarily abandon such important matters to visit their land must certainly hold the people and their interests dearly to heart, and they demonstrated their love and appreciation all the more energetically.

Following the many rounds of greetings, introductions, and the evening banquet of welcome, Alfred visited the sisters of Chatham in private conferences. The next morning he asked to see Edmund, and Edmund, anxious to learn the strategy of the newest plans for a peaceful coexistence with the Vikings, hastened to the king's quarters.

Alfred sat relaxed before a tray of breakfast dishes that were in such disarray as to give ample testimony to the diner's satisfied appetite. Still clothed in his sleeping gown, Alfred warmly welcomed his caller. "Come, cousin, at last we can devote some time to each other. Here, have some mead," he said, filling a tankard with the honey brew. "I have nothing else to offer you. As you see, I have done justice to a tasty meal."

"I am pleased you found it to your liking," Edmund said, pulling at a chair. "I was delighted to learn you were able to leave your duties in London to visit with us."

"As you know, your difficulties here have haunted my thinking. But we will speak of that later," and he shrugged, as though warding off unpleasantness. "For now I must offer my sympathy to you on the death of your young wife." His voice became somber, as did the whole of his attitude. "I was very much grieved by the reports. And what of the child? Is she well?"

"Yes. The nurse informs me she is doing well indeed." Alfred seemed concerned by the statement until Edmund quickly explained. "I must rely on her reports, since she lives with the child in the village. The child does not abide in the castle, since it was necessary that we secure a woman to suckle her."

"Of course, of course," Alfred responded, a little flustered. "I had forgotten." A change of topic was needed, and Alfred continued, "You most certainly have been weighted with grief. First your wife, and then the tragedy at Chatham. I could not assist with the first sad event, but I can offer you aid with the second matter. Most of the troops I have brought with me can remain for your use. I will, of course, provide for their support, and my bursar will give you moneys which you can use as you will."

"You are most generous, Alfred, but—"

"Now, now, Edmund. You know I wish to help in any way I can. I did not tell you before, Edmund, that I visited Werborough on my journey here."

Instantly their eyes met in silent understanding. After his father's death, Cestus had moved there to his uncle's shire—a fact that evidently had not been brought previously to Alfred's attention.

"I was surprised to learn that your brother, Cestus, has abandoned his studies."

"Yes, perhaps you were," Edmund replied. He crossed his legs and shifted his position. "He always took little interest in his studies. He left the school to attend the funeral, and never returned."

Both of them knew the reason for the abrupt termination of studies. The monastic atmosphere necessarily interrupted Cestus' love for wagering, jesting, drinking, and the conquering of young maidens. With his father's death, his studies could no longer be forced upon him, and if he was indeed saddened by his loss, the iron hand that decisively fell upon all his frivolous plans was far from being missed, and his plans to continue his lessons were abandoned with total relief. But again his activities were stifled at Lauxburgh. Wilfreda's and Edmund's sharp glances and reproving remarks made him seek other arrangements, where his bent for relaxation and pleasure could be pursued with no interruptions of any consequence. The shire at Werborough was the perfect place for his operations, and he took full advantage of his uncle's preoccupation with managerial duties to clandestinely pursue his pleasures.

Alfred understood all of this, and there was no need to speak of the details involved. "I thought Cestus would have taken a wife by now," Alfred said, rising from his chair, obviously ill at ease with his thoughts.

"I doubt if the prospect ever crosses his mind," Edmund added, immediately regretting the implication of his thoughtless words. "Perhaps someday he will surprise us." The words hung in the air as Alfred stood with his thumbs hooked in the cincture around his waist.

"Alfred, you have more important matters to discuss than Cestus' nonexistent plans to marry. Would you rather we continue speaking of many unimportant things, or should we discuss the important issues for which you came here?"

Alfred was startled by Edmund's commandeering of the conversation. Edmund's attempt at turning the tide of words from the subject of his brother was effectively accomplished. "Yes, I do have more important issues. As you know, I promised to present plans for securing peace for this part of the land. I have corresponded frequently with the Vikings, Guthrum and Fergus, and certain plans have been formulated. You must understand, Edmund, that we must all make sacrifices to attain certain goals. But why should I speak of sacrifice to you who have drunk freely of its bitterness? Then, there are times, dear cousin, when our plans, our aims, are met with still more opposition."

Alfred deliberately avoided looking at Edmund as he walked to the side of the table. He picked up a book bound with leather and reinforced with tarnished bands of brass. "As we both know so well, the renegades little recognize the value of treaties or any written agreement. It would seem they respect human involvements, human commitments. I am speaking of marriages."

The air was suddenly permeated with tension.

"You must concur that peace was, for the greater part, secured during your marriage to Marion. You see, we could make countless agreements, which would mean naught to them. But a marriage is different. The human element is present—the physical joining of both bloods, both nations. That is real and binding to them. Since a marriage produced peaceful results in the past, we are prepared to guarantee similar results from still another marriage. No doubt Marion spoke to you of her cousin Aleen, Fergus' daughter?"

Alfred looked for recollection in Edmund's face but found none. Edmund's sprawling position in the chair belied his relaxed acceptance of the impending proposal. "Aleen is now of a marriageable age, and since Fergus is ill, he is anxious to see her properly married before he meets his end." Alfred pressed the book to his chest and crossed his arms over it.

Edmund's words came calmly. "I shall not marry, Alfred. Seek you another nobleman for this snare."

"I regret, Edmund, that Fergus specifically mentioned you, and Guthrum and I both concurred in this most logical of choices."

"No," Edmund stressed as he bolted from the chair. "I married the first time through duty, and see how it fared. The Lord punished me severely for the mistake. I cannot marry again. I have taken a vow. Reverend Jerome will tell you of it. The vow was properly made before the altar and before witnesses. Marriage is impossible for me." Satisfied that he had presented his most convincing and decisive argument, Edmund sat on the edge of the table, contented that he had affronted the presumptuous intentions of no less than three kings.

"Indeed? Before leaving London I spoke to Archbishop Helwig about this vow. You see, I was told of this unusual vow of yours some time ago. Marriage is indeed possible."

Edmund straightened his posture, and his face flushed in anger and incredulity.

"I was told that it need not be a physical marriage. The marriage ceremony can be performed, but the physical consummation need not occur. Such a marriage would not offend or nullify your vow. The Danes will recognize this marriage. I am told we can be certain they will disbelieve the factors concerning the vow. After all, how many men make such vows? Surely none are expected to continue its observance under the pressure of temptation. I am most sorry, Edmund. I know of your plans to reenter Tankenham, but consider this a temporary deterrent. It is the only means to gain peace for Kent. Please do not think me unmindful of your interests. How often I have thought of you! I had considered that perhaps Cestus might after all be acceptable for this assignment, but you and I know that he is still full of adventure and not ready for the restrictions of marriage. I am fearful that should he marry the Danish princess and consummate the marriage, and if his activities were still not curtailed, more troubles would develop—not just with the renegades, but with Guthrum and Fergus as well."

Edmund sat down heavily, leaned his head against the backrest, and closed his eyes as though asleep.

"It may well be that other satisfactory arrangements can be made in the future, and you will realize your dream. Archbishop Helwig informs me that the marriage, if not consummated, can be annulled. The Lady Aleen can remarry with the sanction of the church, and you will again be a free man. This is the only way, Edmund. Something must be done before other innocent persons are harmed . . . before other nuns are abused. Would that I were not already married. . . ."

Alfred's words produced haunting recollections for Edmund. Only weeks before, hadn't he knelt before the altar between the bodies of two young nuns and asked of God any sacrifice to ensure the peace of the country and the safety of innocent women? How directly and swiftly the prayer was answered. He was trapped on all sides. The archbishop was condoning the marriage, especially since the welfare of his religious flock was involved. Guthrum, king of all Danelaw, welcomed the marriage, and King Fergus, who obviously was the master force who devised the plan on behalf of his daughter, would no doubt gloat over the success of his plan. Added to this was Alfred, king of all England, who was endorsing the scheme and the indisputable sign from heaven— the sacrifice he had prayed for. How could one mortal man struggle against the wishes of an archbishop, three kings, and God?

"What think you of this, Edmund?"

"I have nothing to say."

"Do you consent to this?"

"How can I do otherwise? Tell me, Alfred, how can I do otherwise?" Visibly agitated, he rose from the chair, stroked his chin absently, and turned away to reflect. Then, after a long, tense pause, he continued, "There is one stipulation. It must be understood that an annulment will be immediately obtained when another plan for peace is drawn."

"I assure you this is understood by all. We will strive earnestly for that," Alfred reassured him. "At least Fergus will be happy with your consent. Poor man. He knows he has not much time left, and he is anxious to see his daughter as happily married to you as he knew Marion to be."

This was the first Edmund had heard of Marion's happiness, yet there was something about her whole attitude to their marriage, her sweet, long-suffering understanding, her timid mannerisms, her blushing encounters with him. Of course, she would have considered herself happily married.

"The Lady Aleen has consented to this arrangement?"

"Yes, she has, Edmund. Do I have your full consent? May I summon the lady?"

"Do what is necessary," Edmund said with a sigh.

With a final effort at easing their relationship, Alfred pushed the leather-bound book across the table toward Edmund. "In this holy book you can find solace. . . ."

Edmund looked momentarily at the etchings on the brass clasp before repeating defeatedly, "Do what is necessary, Alfred."

Grasping the back carvings of the chair Edmund had just vacated, Alfred watched as Edmund passed through the doorway without glancing back. Alfred lowered his head dejectedly. There were times when the unpleasant duties of his office were almost too cruel for his compassionate heart to endure.

The months following were pressing ones for Edmund, pressing enough to distract him at times from the knowledge that his intended wife would soon be arriving at Lauxburgh.

Edmund had spent much of the time at Chatham overseeing the installation of locks and bolts and the building of bell towers at strategic places so that alarms could be quickly sounded. The stand of hemlocks and oaks that had ensured the nuns' privacy from inquisitive glances was cut down and the land cleared with the help of troops Alfred supplied. Privacy must be sacrificed for the sake of security, for without the curtain of trees, the farmers who worked the fields nearby could maintain satisfactory surveillance.

Finally, after months of repairs, improvements, and redecoration of the chapel and damaged rooms, the day arrived for the return of the nuns to their beloved cloister. Almost as solemnly as they had arrived, they departed Lauxburgh, venturing out into cool breezes that comprised the dying traces of winter. Sitting regally upon their steeds, their veils flowing in the wind, they left in a double procession. Edmund accompanied the group, and about them rode an escort of soldiers, some of whom would camp on the convent grounds as long as the nuns felt the need for their protection. Wilfreda also joined the group. She, too, would remain at Chatham for a number of days or until she felt Lauxburgh could no longer function without her supervision. Behind them slowly plodded the draft horses that were strapped with bundles containing all manner of supplies.

Other wayfarers were also about with laden beasts and a soldier escort. On the road that diagonally intersected the one leading from Lauxburgh to Chatham, a curious group was approaching. Prominent was a young woman of perhaps eighteen, sitting tall in her saddle, her dark hair stirring in the breezes, as did the mane of her proud steed. Beside the young girl rode an older woman whose long golden braids of hair fell over rounded shoulders and ample bosom. The full features of her pleasant face bore traces of an uncultured, more common genealogy. The two groups of men who closely followed were easily identified. The Anglo-Saxon soldiers all carried metal-tipped spears and shields bearing the insignia of Kent and wore protective tunics of silver, with some wearing great furry mantles that covered sculptured breastplates. The other soldiers, unquestionably Danish, were less organized in their dress. Their clothing consisted of varicolored shirts and breeches of sundry shapes and designs. Their legs were concealed with a variety of coverings bound to the legs with leather straps. Their hair was longer and their beards straggly, giving their rugged features an appearance of general unkemptness. They, too, were adequately prepared for whatever difficulties they encountered, for their shields were either hanging from their arms or hung from the pommels of their saddles, ready for immediate use, as were their sturdy battleaxes, which were tucked carefully into the straps of their saddles.

"Who rides ahead?" the young girl asked with amusement. "Are they women?" And she almost laughed at the absurdity of the black-veiled figures riding in the distance.

"They are nuns, my lady," responded an Anglo-Saxon, "they are from the convent at Chatham."

"Oh, yes, the nuns of Chatham." She had recalled the name. Thereafter she scarcely took her eyes off the procession that crossed the road before her. Forgotten and overlooked were all the hints of spring that she had enjoyed so thoroughly along the way: the tender shoots of new grasses that peeped from between the winter-yellowed carpet on either side of the road, the tiny wildflowers whose buds pointed proudly at the sun, the trees that trembled gloriously with their emerald gems of early growth. The whole springtime beauty of an awakening countryside lost its interest for the girl as her eyes sadly followed the nuns until her own group turned onto the road the nuns had just traveled. With sure steps their steeds scattered the dust of the road, erasing the prints that had freshly settled, to replace them with the hoofmarks of horses traveling in the opposite direction.

With awakened courage and determination, the young girl faced the winding road that led to Lauxburgh and a future of uncertainties.

## ✦ VIII ✦

THE LONG, dusty skirt swayed forcefully as the incessant pacing came to an abrupt stop. "What could be detaining him?" the young woman asked angrily as she placed her hands defiantly on her hips. "It is an insult—yes, an insult," and she pointed her finger in the air to emphasize her words before commencing the pacing once again.

"Hester, go find that man. Tell him to announce my arrival to Edmund once more. If Edmund does not come soon to welcome me, I will leave this place. Do you hear? I will leave, and gladly, too."

"My lady, you distress yourself too greatly about this. The ealdorman has many responsibilities. He would not ignore greeting a guest, especially if that guest were soon to be his wife." A flash from large brown eyes signified disbelief in the words. "Now, now, my love, I will do as you say," and she reached for her mantle before venturing into the drafty hall.

It had been some time since they had ridden through the main gate. The sentry had walked with them on a brief tour of the castle grounds, pointing out the yards, granary, the smokehouse, and the kitchens, as they made their way to Edmund's office, where they were asked to wait beside their heap of bags and chests. For the most part, the time there had been profitably spent, for what better way was there to discover what sort of man Edmund was than to examine the contents of his workroom? She had strolled around it, examining the great maps on the walls, the decorated battle shields and tapestries, and although she dared not touch them, she had not missed one object on his desk and tables: the great sheets of paper written in a firm hand, the models of sailing vessels, the plumed pens, stone ink pots, jeweled daggers, ledger books, a small standing crucifix, a prayer book, and numerous candleholders with thick stunted candles. Mantles, swords, tunics, and leather pouches hung from pegs on one wall, and furniture seemed to be everywhere. Great carved

chairs were against the walls, and smaller chairs were clustered around a table on which a playing board was strewn
with chessmen. A scribe's table was near a huge desk, and
from behind the high-backed chair that was the most prominent in the room, Aleen surveyed the length of the room and
its cluttered contents.

It was an interesting room, but what had at first fascinated
her became unbearable with the passage of time. So long was
the wait, even after Hester returned from having delivered
Aleen's message, that Aleen's impatience grew to unbearable
proportions. It was so still and quiet, so deathlike in the
room, that when a masculine voice sounded, Hester and
Aleen looked at the tall slender figure as though he were a
spirit suddenly embodied. No sound had been made, no
grating of the door hinges.

Without smiling, the intruder introduced himself. "I am
Wulfric, Lord Edmund's chief scribe. The lord is late in returning from Chatham. You had best wait no longer. Come. I
will take you to your chambers." With a snap to the servants
he had brought with him and a point of his finger at the
chests and bags, he turned and preceded them all down long
corridors, up stairs, and down another hall, until he stood before a door that he opened for Aleen and Hester to enter.
When next they looked for him, he was gone.

"He said not a word of greeting, nor did he make any gesture of hospitality," Aleen remarked. "If he were a member
of my father's staff, he would be properly upbraided for his
lack of courtesy." He had, however, notified the kitchen, for
a tray of food had been promptly brought to them.

Aleen ate sparingly and was now nervously walking about
acquainting herself with her new surroundings. The sitting
room was sparsely furnished but was adequate for her needs,
and the bedchamber was larger than she had expected. The
accommodations were satisfactory indeed. There was ample
light, and the view from the windows was pleasing. She leaned
closer to the narrow opening and watched as the rising
tides of the bay burst in great sprays against the rocks on the
sandy beach. On the meadow that rose from the stretch of
beach, the naked trees cast spindly shadows, and already the
forest in the distance was consumed in a haunting dimness.
With a swirl of her skirt she turned quickly away and

looked upon the confusion. Chests and bags lay everywhere. Dresses and chains of jewelry were draped upon chairs and tables. An effort had been made throughout the afternoon to place her belongings in reasonable order, but she could not organize her thoughts or her things. The transfer from Wermouth and her beloved father, to Anglo-Saxon soil and a husband she had never met, had been difficult. She was too homesick, too confused with her new situation to worry about where to place anything. They could wait for now.

Flipping aside a tunic near at hand, she scowled. Was not Hester told hours ago that Edmund had returned to the castle? And hadn't she changed into her new crimson gown in anticipation of their meeting? Her patience was being sorely tried. Why was Edmund being so remiss in properly welcoming her? Turning her troubled thoughts to more carefree matters, she studied her appearance and was satisfied with it. The red gown emphasized the darkness of her hair and gave her cheeks a rosier glow. A golden chain that had belonged to her mother was wound twice about her waist, and crossed her chest, accenting the slimness of her figure. A similar golden chain, wound about her head, caught up her hair, permitting it to fall neatly down her back in a cascade of shiny brown. Aleen picked up her polished silver mirror and smiled into it. No one could deny that she was beautiful. Her lips and nose were well-formed, and her eyes—how effectively they could flash beguilingly, flirtatiously.

Aleen ran her finger under the chain that bound the fullness of the gown to her waist and adjusted the soft gathers that fell gently to the tops of her small slippers. I should not have changed, she thought. I do not care now if he had seen me with the dust of the road heavy upon my clothes. Nor should I have troubled Hester to arrange my hair. I no longer care what he will think of my appearance. But Aleen would not admit it, even to herself, that her curiosity about her future husband was boundless and must be satisfied and that she was most definitely concerned about his approval of her appearance.

"Aleen," Hester's voice whispered at the door of the bedroom, "the scribe is here."

He bowed when he saw Aleen and said crisply, "Follow me. The Lord Edmund desires to speak with you." Together they walked down the cool hall to the room at the end. It was a meeting room of some sort, judging from the great collection of chairs and the long table down the central part. There was one large fireplace, and Wulfric's poking and prodding into it captured her interest. The springlike temperatures that filled each day turned frigid each evening, especially so in homes and castles near the sea. Aleen rubbed her arms to dispel the cold and stood near the blackened grate as Wulfric fed it new timbers and coaxed the weakened flames into a crackling conflagration. At last, satisfied that his ministrations had produced satisfactory results, he straightened, and putting the poker aside, he glanced at Aleen and quickly lowered his eyes. "The lord will meet with you here," he said. But before she could reply, he was off, leaving her alone with the comforting glow of the fire and the sounds of the breaking surf outside.

If she had expected Edmund to appear momentarily, she was mistaken, and she waited somewhat apprehensively as the gloom of the room deepened and the furniture, the figures of the tapestries on the walls, and the great furs on the floors took on menacing dimensions.

Why did the castle seem so deserted? Only a few servants and women were noticed when first she arrived, and now only an occasional shuffling of feet and the muffled sounds of voices were heard at the far end of the hall.

Footsteps approached, but it was only a servant who lit the bracketed torch in the hall and then was gone again. At last, footsteps echoed in the distance—the sure footsteps of a heavy man—and her heart as quickly drummed in her breast, while a roaring in her ears all but dispelled the sounds that grew nearer.

I will take hold of myself. I shall meet him with dignity. It is not I who should be fearful, but he, for having kept me waiting half the day. Look at the darkness! Were it not for the fire, I would be in absolute darkness. He should be shamed. She rose from the depths of the large chair, drew herself to full height, and turned toward the door. He shall be on the defensive—that he shall. He has sorely tempted my patience, and he will know how offended I have been by this delay in meeting with me. She tilted her chin defiantly, and her blood flushed hot with annoyance.

The steps stopped at the archway. Edmund scanned the darkened room, but as he turned to leave, his eye caught sight of her figure silhouetted against the fire. "Lady Aleen?" he asked, turning his ear for her reply.

"Yes." Confusion surged through her body. In her anger, she had not fully reasoned how exciting it would be to meet the man she would soon marry, and as he walked toward her, she earnestly wished she had prepared herself for the flurry of emotions she was now experiencing. If only she could escape—to be consumed by the blazing appetite of the fire, to be absorbed by the darkness that claimed the other parts of the room.

"I thought you were perhaps in another room when I saw this one in darkness," he said, as though amused with the situation. "Did no one offer to light the tapers for you?"

As he reached for one of the candles, Aleen said with forced calmness, "When I was brought to this room, sir, it was still light."

"Ah, yes. You have waited some time for me. I regret I was delayed," he said. "Permit me to light this," and he walked back into the hall, stopped at the torch, and reentered, shielding the flickering flame with one hand. The bronze stand that supported several candles was brought to light as he touched each with the darting flame, but as each sputtered into activity, Aleen studied the features that became defined in the golden glow. So this is the warrior, the hunter, the would-be-monk, she mused.

"This has been a most busy day for me," he was saying as he moved the flame from wick to wick. "I journeyed to Chatham with guests who left this morning, and I was late in returning. I wish I had known you would arrive today. . . ." After lighting the last candle, he replaced the candle he had used into its former position and turned to look upon his guest. "Now there is time for us to speak," but as he looked upon Aleen, a deep frown momentarily crossed his face.

"Something offends you, sir?" Aleen asked, looking down on her gown and running her hand swiftly about her neck and along the chains that crossed her breasts.

"No, nothing," he said with a lowering of his voice.

"You do not speak truly, sir," she said with a saucy tilt of her head.

Edmund reluctantly admitted, "It is your age, Lady Aleen. It is your youth which surprises me."

"No one told you of my age?" she asked, frowning with disbelief.

"Yes, they did, but I had forgotten that eighteen was so young. Again I extend my apologies. I had no mind to offend you by my reaction."

"Perhaps it is not you who should apologize, but me. However, my age is something I cannot alter."

"Please be seated," he said as he settled comfortably in the chair opposite the one she had occupied.

"Thank you, sir, but I shall stand."

Quickly he removed the hand he had been using to rub his eyes and looked toward the slender girl standing before the fire with hands clasped casually behind her. "Tell me of your journey," he encouraged by way of introducing a different topic to their conversation.

"It was pleasant, sir. The inns along the way were comfortable, and because of our Anglo-Saxon escort, every convenience and courtesy were shown us. I thank you for providing us with soldiers for our safe passage. They were most courteous and helpful."

Edmund tilted his head as though waiting for her to continue, but she stood silently. "I am pleased your journey was a pleasant one. Your father, has his health improved? I was told he was ill."

"Yes, he is better now. His health improves each day."

He was staring at her—a steady stare that made her uneasy. If only he would stop.

"And your brother?"

"He is well. He is on a journey now, but he has vowed to be here for the marriage ceremony." The anger she had felt had long been forgotten. Who could remain offended by a man so obviously exhausted? But why is it difficult for me to think clearly, she thought as she checked her composure. He must not know that I am uneasy with him.

He shifted his position at the mention of the wedding. "Tomorrow we will confer about the plans. I have been requested to have the marriage as soon as it can be arranged." He was rubbing his hands nervously and repeatedly glancing toward the door.

"I have likewise been informed."

"Very well, we will see to the arrangements tomorrow." Again he glanced toward the door.

She knew not what to say, and turned her interest to the fire. He was staring again, and an unbearable silence developed, until the scribe Wulfric's voice mercifully intervened. "Pardon, sir. An urgent message awaits you."

Aleen's instincts were aroused as swiftly as those of a stalked prey. No sound had echoed in the hallway—there had been heard no approach of footsteps. Had the scribe been standing out of sight by prearrangement, and had he been told to interrupt when a lull developed in their conversation? Edmund had seemed relieved by the interruption, as though it had been expected but delayed. Anger flared within her. That is why he glanced so frequently toward the door. How dare he use tricks with me. Her eyes flashed arrows of indignation. We had only just begun our meeting. He had deliberately wanted it abbreviated. How dare he . . . She began to stalk away, but Edmund, surmising her thoughts, called to her.

"Aleen, we will meet again tomorrow. If there is anything you need or desire . . ." The rest of his words never found utterance.

"Your scribe awaits you, sir," she said in icy tones. Edmund moved toward her, but she walked through the room and into the hall with as much dignity as her anger allowed. Without acknowledging Wulfric's presence, she walked past. A man who would slink about, to appear and disappear, as it would seem his habit to do, deserved little respect. And as for Edmund: He would be stupid if he did not know that I am aware of his trick. I am not wrong about this, for the guilt on his face confirms my opinions.

Aleen slammed the door to her room, leaned against it and breathed deeply, rapidly, until the rush of fury abated. It had been a most difficult meeting, but she knew she had handled herself well. Perhaps next time she would participate in their conversation without the nervousness that assailed her this first time. But he knows now that I have been doubly offended by his actions, and no one desires to be thought ill of, especially by the daughter of a Danish king. I wonder what actions, what words, he will use to restore himself to my good graces? Tomorrow he will be different. I wager he will not use tricks again, nor will he keep me waiting for other meetings.

Aleen slipped out of her gown, threw it over a chair, reached for the nightgown Hester had carefully laid out for her, and drew it over her head. The candles beside her bed flickered comfortingly, and in the silence, reasoning settled upon her. *Perhaps I have been too harsh. He had much to do today, and many matters claimed his mind. Who knows but that I would have arranged a similar interruption, were I in his position. Nevertheless, tomorrow he will be more solicitous, more thoughtful and considerate. If he displays proper signs of amends, I will try to forget and forgive all the unpleasantness of today and show thereby how forgiving I can be. Tomorrow's meeting will be different. He will endeavor to repair my opinion of him by being winning and attentive toward me.*

Aleen sat comfortably upon her feather mattress as she unwrapped the golden chain from about her head and flipped the hair until it fell freely about her shoulders. Distractedly she twisted the chain around her hands. There were many thoughts crowding upon her. *Edmund was not as handsome as Marion had led everyone to believe, but it was always said that love saw beauty where others could not. In truth, one could say, provided she was generous, that he was pleasant of appearance. His figure was fuller, thicker than she had expected, but not offensively so. His chin was well shaven, his hair well combed, and his clothing properly arranged—good traits indeed.* Aleen smiled and twisted her mouth. Begrudgingly she conceded: *Yes, there is a certain charm about him. Who knows, someday I might just grow to like him.* And perhaps, she thought with a twinkle of her large eyes, perhaps he might regret having made that silly vow.

The challenge had been made. Even though it was understood that an annulment of their marriage might occur in the future to allow her remarriage and his entrance into religious life, would she dare to employ her feminine wiles to challenge his constancy? *Nothing will stand in my way, should I become interested in him. Nothing. There are ways of making him forget that vow.* She bent over to extinguish the bedside candles, and as she snuggled beneath the coverlet, she whispered aloud: "Yes, there are ways. . . ."

## ◄ IX ►

IT WAS a crisp morning. The kind that produced vitality for the body and well-being for the soul. It would be a glorious day for taking the tour of the castle, for meeting the people she would be living with. It was so thoughtful of Edmund to send word that he will take me about, Aleen reasoned. Of course, it is just an excuse to compensate for his glaring discourtesy of the night before, but it is thoughtful nonetheless. Perhaps life at Lauxburgh would be endurable after all, and she tingled with excitement at the prospect of spending part of the morning with Edmund. Perhaps now that the initial awkwardness of their first meeting had been met, their conversation this day would be more congenial and less strained.

Disappointment burst upon her when Thane Godfrey knocked and announced that he had been requested to escort her on the tour. Edmund had pressing affairs that needed his attention, so Thane Godfrey announced, but if he could not devote time to her now, she would after all meet with him later to discuss the wedding. At least it was thoughtful of Edmund to have selected someone she had met before.

Pleasantries were exchanged and inquiries made about her journey to Lauxburgh, but his questions concerning her father and his health made him uneasy. His sense of justice was goaded. He had given his word to Fergus that he would approach Edmund about the marriage Fergus proposed, but he had not, and he was now grateful that Edmund could not reproach him for taking part in the maneuverings that had culminated in the marriage agreement.

The tour began with Godfrey telling her of the occupants of the rooms that neighbored her own. Marion's empty chamber separated those of her own and Edmund's, and Wilfreda, whom she had yet to meet, was opposite and one door away.

"And the child's room?" Aleen asked when no mention was made of her.

"The child does not reside here. She is in the care of nurses in the village who are seeing to her physical care."

They made their way to the end of the hall to the room Aleen had visited previously. It was a meeting room, as she had surmised, and as she entered, she glanced at the fireplace, now devoid of light and as cold and silent as though she and Edmund had not visited within its warmth the night before. But the room was not empty. Two women sat comfortably, their feet resting on small padded footstools. In their laps were pieces of cloth, and wedged between their hips and their chairs were baskets with tangles of brightly colored threads. When they glanced up at the stranger being brought toward them by Godfrey, they smiled, put aside their sewing, and rose to greet and welcome the stranger in their midst.

"I am most honored to present to you the Lady Aleen, the Lady Marion's cousin," Godfrey began. "This is the Lady Aethelwynn and the Lady Hedby, cousins of Edmund's deceased father."

Smiles that had brightened their faces slowly disappeared at the mention of Marion's name, and although words of greeting were uttered, their averted glances and otherwise demure manner placed a frigid pall on their meeting.

The timidness Aleen had experienced at the introduction became tinged with confusion by their changed attitude. But, she thought, promptly excusing their reactions, I must remember that I disturbed their sewing. They are old women, gray-haired and thin with age, with fragile emotions that are fluctuating and unpredictable.

"Come, I have much to show you," Godfrey said, waiting to snatch her away from an awkward situation. He led her past the chambers to the opposite end of the long hall. On the left was a staircase leading upward, and to the right were columns, and between them were huge openings that, to Aleen's surprise, looked down upon a large room below. There were similar openings on the other side, and from these galleries spectators could observe all that was taking place below. A most interesting architectural feature, she thought.

"I have something of greater interest for you to inspect," and he preceded her up the stone stairs that wound in a spiral inside the cylindrical tower. At the top, Godfrey opened a door, through which Aleen passed into the light and wind. The circular floor was ringed with a crenellated wall, and as she walked from one narrow opening to the other, slices of the landscape came into view. There were the ocean and its horizon, the beach strewn with rocks and boulders around which foam swelled and retreated on each watery surge. The meadow was sprinkled with trees arousing from winter slumber, and in the distance was the forest that harbored the stag and boar that supplied the needs of many tables. Through another opening, soldiers were seen standing in the inner and outer courtyards, while fowl pecked in the dirt around them. To the front of the castle a road snaked to the horizon, dividing, along its progress, farmlands that rippled in verdant splendor.

Aleen darted from one opening to another. "It is beautiful . . . beautiful," she cried as Godfrey watched with amusement. "It is as though all of Kent—all the world—were at my feet."

It was exhilarating, and she closed her eyes and turned her face to the sun, while the wind blew capriciously through her hair and flapped between the folds of her gown. Looking once more between the openings in the stone, she remarked, "From my window I can see some of the ocean, the meadow, and the forest beyond, but up here, so much more comes to view. I shall never tire of looking upon this land." She blushed when she realized Godfrey's amusement at her conduct. "I forget myself, sir. Let us continue our tour," and she once more glanced upon the land before reluctantly walking toward the stairs, where their footsteps echoed in the entrapped coolness.

As they walked past rooms that Godfrey said were occupied by the officers, the chaplain, visiting priests, and Edmund's chief councillors, footsteps were heard shuffling up the steps from the first floor. A mixture of voices reached their ears, and as the sounds reached the top steps and down the hallway, they saw Edmund slamming his fist into his open palm to emphasize an opinion in a friendly argument. Aleen slowed her pace for the inevitable confrontation.

Edmund's eyes met Aleen's, but quickly his were lowered as he smiled weakly and nodded politely. Immediately his attention was diverted by one of the men with him, who resumed the discussion.

"Edmund, may I speak with you?" Godfrey interrupted. Turning to Aleen, he excused himself. "I must speak with him concerning matters of importance. I shall not take but a moment." Godfrey and Edmund walked to the side and spoke together in whispered confidence. After a few nods of agreement, they parted, Edmund to his companions and Godfrey to a slighted young lady. Suddenly remembering his lack of courtesy, Godfrey called to the men who accompanied Edmund and promptly introduced Aleen to them.

Pleasant greetings and generous compliments were made, but her attention was distracted by Edmund, who did not join the group, but stood idly aside, patiently awaiting the return of his friends.

Why, you would think it was customary for Edmund to meet me in the hallways, and why should he decline to present me to his comrades? One would think him ashamed of me, she thought as the formalities reached their conclusion.

The excitement, the anticipation that had accompanied the tour had vanished, and when Godfrey held out a hand to signal the resumption of their walk, his words of description and explanation were as so much humming in her ears.

Together they walked down other hallways, until Godfrey bade her look through a portal. Immediately below was the slope upon which the castle was built. At its depths gurgled the waters of the bay, which supported a dozen or more ships at anchor. A portion of the pier could be seen, with many skiffs and fishing vessels tied securely to it.

Godfrey was speaking of the village nestled on the other side of the castle wall and explaining about the rooms they were passing being those occupied by some of Edmund's soldiers, but his words held little interest. Edmund had claimed her thoughts, and she smarted painfully under the humiliation of his apathy toward her.

They walked past the chapel and then along a hall to the archway of a great room. Of a sudden, two great white dogs bounded toward them. Their sniffing and dull growls alarmed Aleen, until Godfrey bent down to pet them. Quieted by his familiar voice and reassuring strokes, they lazily returned to their places before the fireplace.

It was the great hall—the meeting place, the dining hall, and the recreational area of the castle. Aleen took in its vastness, then glanced upward at the second-floor balconies and the great beamed ceiling that was the collector of shadows. Walking around long tables and benches, they approached a group of women who were coyly smiling into the faces of soldiers, who seemed flattered and delighted by their attentions. Postures were shifted as Godfrey excused the interruption and presented Aleen to them. But again, feminine faces that were smiling moments before suddenly took on serious dimensions at the mention of her name, and although the customary civilities were observed, an icy aloofness prevailed until Aleen and Godfrey left them to the continuation of their conversation. Muffled giggles reached Aleen's ear as she followed Godfrey to another group, but shock at the unexpected aftermath of the introduction made her turn, until she faced them and glared at their jest that had her as its victim. The tittering promptly quieted under her irate stare. The soldiers and certainly the councillors she had met earlier were gracious and friendly, but the women were intolerable. It was a flagrant insult to be made sport of by those of a lower social position. They will regret this breach of good conduct, she vowed. Stunning resentment prevented her from voicing the angry words that broke upon her wrath.

"Godfrey," she said as she rejoined her guide, who had witnessed the interlude, "please be so kind as to take me to my chamber."

"But . . ." Godfrey began as he motioned toward the other group. If what preceded in the assembly room and here in the great hall were an indication of what awaited her, further introductions were unwelcome.

"I shall not endure further embarrassment such as I have been subjected to. Disregard these people and show me to my chamber." She stood tall, head held high, as though she already wore the gleaming crown of Kent. "In the future, present me only to members of the family and those persons it will be necessary for me to be acquainted with. I see that I shall possess few friends here," she said as she crossed the great hall with all the poise she could command.

Godfrey shared her indignation at the behavior of those who should have greeted their royal guest more properly, and he correctly judged that his words, however well-meaning and apologetic they might be, could do little in easing the strain. In respect to her desire for silence, he accompanied her down the cool hallway to her chamber. She hesitated at the door and turned to look into the cultured face that was contoured in distress. "Do not worry, Godfrey," she said as she placed her hand on his arm. "It is not your doing that I am unwelcome here," and she patted his arm and closed the door, leaving him to stare at the coarse designs in the wood.

How could I have expected to be welcomed and accepted here? Reasoning struggled against the inner turmoil as she nervously paced the little sitting room. How could they be expected to accept me—a Dane—after all they have endured at the hands of our renegades. But it was not I who was responsible. . . .

Her leather slippers continued brushing softly against the stone flooring as she tossed her thoughts about. Did Marion also endure such initial treatment? But she wrote that she was happy here. Perhaps they had become accustomed to Marion. Perhaps, too, they would become accustomed to her if she were patient. After what occurred at Chatham, such resentment could be anticipated. After all, I represent a race that includes those who acted unwisely and without my father's knowledge or approval. Aleen paused at the memory of her father. How delighted he had been when the arrangements for the marriage were completed, how happy he was, and, yes, even on the verge of tears when she departed for Lauxburgh. I cannot disappoint him. When he visits here, I must show him how I have been accepted. It will be a conflict between us, but the Saxons will see that I am not against them. I shall win them with friendliness and kindness, and I will take an interest in all that pertains to this castle and the people. It will take time, but it will be worth the effort, for I might very well be forced to stay here longer than I planned.

Aleen had taken pleasure and satisfaction in her resolves, and basked in the glow of her magnanimity: It is only what any good Christian should do.

If it were not for Edmund's impending visit, she would have joined the ladies in the assembly room. I would speak with them, whether it pleases them or not, and soon they will see they have little excuse to dislike me.

A change of dress accompanied her resolves. She repeatedly arranged the small veil she had placed over her carefully combed hair. The ruffles barely touched her ears, and curled around the head, favorably accenting the length and sheen of the hair. A gold-and-amethyst necklace encircled her slender neck, and she was satisfied that just the fashionable amount of skirt ruffled from beneath the smooth tunic that hugged her waist and flared to just below the knee. She was pretty, and she knew it, and pleasurable satisfaction was taken in knowing that Edmund, if he had sufficient sight in his eyes, would also take note of it. Perhaps that is why he seemed shocked when first he looked upon me. Perhaps it was not my youth, as he professed, but my appearance that surprised him. It was common knowledge that such prearranged marriages had been the occasion for marrying off the less physically blessed to hapless bridegrooms. Aleen dimpled coquettishly. Yes, that must have been the reason. I proved to be better than anticipated. And her smile deepened as she turned in a burst of exuberance. It was thrilling to know that one's physical appearance was pleasing to the masculine eye, and the challenge of winning the reluctant heart of an intended bridegroom was enough to bring an added twinkle to the eye of any maiden.

Edmund had been somewhat of a surprise, too, she considered. Although not truly a handsome man, he was nevertheless eye-catching and physically acceptable.

I know I could make him forget that monastery, and Marion, too, for that matter, but will I want to? Pleasant reflections were abruptly interrupted by a gentle knocking. The amethyst ring with its circle of pearls pressed uncomfortably into hands that clutched in exhilarating anticipation. I must calm myself. I shall conduct myself as though his visit means nothing to me, as though our wedding plans are of little consequence to me.

But Edmund was not standing in the doorway, only the scribe Wulfric, with his thin face and disdainful expression.

"I have been asked, Lady Aleen, to discuss certain matters with you and to secure your consent to these plans," he said, indicating notes on a piece of parchment. "May I enter?"

"It was my understanding that Edmund would come to confer with me."

"I know nothing of that. However, there is little to be arranged." He declined Aleen's offer of a chair and continued, "The ceremony itself will be conducted according to customary rituals, which will be explained to you later. We have only to select the day for the ceremony. The bishop has expressed a desire to conduct the ceremony as soon as possible, and this has met with the approval of King Alfred and the Lord Edmund. Is it correct that members of your family will be present?"

"Yes, my brother. He will arrive soon. My father is too ill to come now, but will visit later when he recovers."

"Very well. Will ten days hence be suitable? That will be a Sunday, in the morning. An afternoon of feasting will follow. Is that agreeable?"

"Yes, yes, anything you say." She was too disappointed to care. Why hadn't Edmund come himself? Did he not say last night by the fire, "We will make arrangements tomorrow"? Could it have been another unexpected matter that demanded his attention twice in the same day, or is it that he is deliberately avoiding me? Of course, that was it—that silly vow. He is afraid if he sees too much of me I may prove to be a temptation. Feminine vanity was satisfied with the latter reason, but she quickly scolded herself: I should not be thinking such sinful thoughts. But what if I am correct? Her disappointment dissolved into speculative delight.

"Your wedding garments have been prepared? . . . Lady Aleen," he repeated, "your wedding garments?"

"Yes, they are in readiness."

"Lord Edmund's mother, the Lady Wilfreda, will speak with you concerning the ceremony and its symbolism." His monotonous voice droned on and on.

And to think I dressed for nothing. Well, then, since Edmund is no longer expected, I shall seek other diversions. I shall visit the great hall, or perhaps I shall ride into the village to visit the child. Yes, it is a good day for visiting.

Wulfric had finished speaking much sooner than he had expected, but then, what was one to do with such divided attentions? "Then all is satisfactory?"

"Yes, yes, do as you wish. There is only one matter remaining. Thane Godfrey has told me that when I wished to visit the child Lelia in the village, I should ask for an escort to take me. Will you see that one is made available? I should like to leave quite soon."

The vertical lines between his eyes furrowed deeply.

"Can you see to this for me?"

"Yes," he said running his finger along the crease of paper. "I will see what can be done."

Aleen watched as he walked away. The slender legs, with their breeches strapped tightly to the knees and legs, seemed absurdly thin, and his narrow feet were so small that it was no wonder he was able to walk so noiselessly. It is well for him that he selected the work of a scribe. He seems too fragile to succeed at anything else. But never mind him—I shall visit today. I shall ride through the village, and I shall see Marion's child. The words seemed strange—"Marion's child." Marion? Sweet, timid, retiring Marion. Marion, who blushed so easily and who had never kissed a man in her life until her marriage. It was good for Marion that a diplomatic marriage had been arranged; otherwise she would never have married. Or was it good, after all? Marion would be alive today had it not been for her marriage to Edmund.

"I am the Lady Aleen. Is my horse saddled?" she asked of the first stableman she met.

Guttural sounds came from the man as he shuffled into the stable, motioning for her to follow. The man was oddly formed. His shoulders and head leaned too far ahead of the rest of his body, and he limped badly. His loud guttural noise drew the attention of the stableman, Thorkil, who was examining a horse's hoof.

"I am the Lady Aleen. My horse was to be saddled and an escort readied to accompany me into the village. Do you know of this?"

"No, m'lady. We had no such order," he replied in a slur that betrayed his peasantry.

"I told Wulfric to have all in readiness for me some time ago. It is nothing. I will find Wulfric and learn the reason for the delay." She smiled sweetly at the disheveled man as he wiped his hands against his leather apron. But as she turned to leave, she caught sight of the crippled stableman who was near the stable door stroking a horse's mane. "That man—he cannot speak?"

"Aethelwed? No, m'lady. His tongue was cut out years ago."

"But why?" Aleen asked in horror. "How could such a thing occur?"

"Some bandits in the woods, m'lady." He dropped his eyes and continued, "His father was a carpenter. He took Aethelwed into the forests to fell trees, and the bandits attacked. They killed his father, and when Aethelwed screamed, they cut out his tongue. They beat him, too. His legs were broken and his back was injured. Edmund brought him here and had him treated by the physician. He has been helping me since he recovered."

No reply was made to the narration. How could she speak when her heart seared with hate for the bandits, who were obviously Vikings, judging from the stableman's manner. Why would these men rebel against their rulers and continue to kill and maim helpless people?

Pieces of straw crunched under her feet as she walked to the stable door. The nodding heads of the horses in stalls on either side of her did not distract her attention from the muted man who was busy now in one of the stalls. She hesitated for a moment by its gate without turning to look upon his face. Quickly she walked out into the sunlight.

"The scribe Wulfric," she asked of the soldier who stood rigidly near the open door of Edmund's office.

The soldier nodded, disappeared into the room, and returned presently to his post with Thane Godfrey, who smiled broadly at her. "Lady Aleen, may I assist you?"

"Godfrey," she began in tones of confusion and disappointment, "I had asked Wulfric this morning to have an escort readied and my horse saddled for my ride into the village. I desire to visit the child Lelia. The order was not given the stablemen, and no escort was made available."

"Ah," he said, drawing the word slowly from his mouth.

"Would you kindly give the necessary orders for me?"

Godfrey moved uneasily and ran his hand nervously over his chin.

"Is there some difficulty involved?"

Godfrey hesitated. "I suppose I must ask once more for Edmund's permission," he said, like one who was unmindfully giving voice to inner thoughts.

From inside the office the muted sounds of voices grew louder, until Aleen looked past Godfrey and saw the figures of two priests and two men who had moved into view. They were asking questions and listening to Edmund's answers as though they were learning profound lessons.

"Edmund's permission?" She smiled and laughed inwardly at the absurdity. "I want only to look upon the child. I do not wish to carry her off. I am Lelia's cousin and will soon be her mother by marriage. I need permission? You jest with me."

But the look on Godfrey's face was not one of jest.

Edmund turned at the sound of her voice, recognized Aleen, and with the half-smile he had shown her earlier in the day, nodded and resumed the conversation before Aleen could acknowledge the apathetic gesture.

"Lady Aleen," Godfrey said as he led her by the elbow away from the door, "no one sees the child, my lady. It would seem that Edmund does not wish her to be visited."

"But why is that?" she asked sternly.

"I do not know. All I do know is that no one journeys there, and the Lord Edmund may become annoyed if informed of your intentions."

Aleen glanced back into the office, where Edmund was still speaking to his enraptured listeners.

"It is time she were visited by her kinfolk. Does he mean to hide the child?" she asked contemptuously.

"I do not know his thoughts concerning this. He will not confide in me about the child. I shall ask permission for you, if you still have a mind to do this."

Unaccustomed to having her desires thwarted or questioned, she countered, "Permission? Indeed you shall not ask for it. Twice today the lord neglected to meet with me as was prearranged, and now I require permission to do so simple a thing? Please be so kind as to inform the lord that I have departed for the cobbler's home to visit my kinsman. Do not bother to find an escort. I shall find the cottage myself."

Godfrey's words of caution were lost to her as she turned flippantly and stalked down the hall, anger emanating from her movements as an aura about her.

"Where is my horse?" she demanded of the stableman, who looked curiously at the angry woman who had earlier bestowed such a kindly smile on him.

"This way, m'lady," he said, easing around her and rushing past rows of stalls toward the back of the dusty stable. He fumbled at the lock with dirtied hands and finally unlatched it for her. Once inside the stall, Aleen glanced about for the pad and saddle. The horse stomped and raised his head high as she snatched for the pad and threw it across his back.

"I will do that for you," the stableman offered, while trying to reach for the saddle.

"Do not trouble," she replied sternly. "I can manage." But she struggled to lift it, and strained as she held it before throwing it into place. "Permission, humph," she mumbled as she reached under the horse for the cincture.

The stableman pushed back the hair from his forehead and watched as she deftly pulled and tightened the strap against the horse's belly. Satisfied that the lady knew what she was about, he retreated, leaving her alone with her anger.

With a flip of the hand, the straps with their stirrups fell on either side of the horse. Aleen reached for the bridle and with practiced movements eased the iron bit between the huge teeth and adjusted the straps about his head. Grasping the reins firmly, she led him along the hard-packed mud from the stall and into the open.

Permission to visit my own kinsman! she said to herself, not noticing the stableman and his mute helper, who, intimidated by her fury and the uncommon behavior of a distinguished lady, had receded into the shadows to await her departure.

Aleen stepped lightly upon a block of hay near the door, and placing one foot in the stirrup, neatly swung herself side-saddle atop the horse. Carefully she arranged the drape of skirt modestly over both legs, held her head high, sat tall, and with perfect riding form rode through the outer courtyard without condescending to acknowledge the presence of the people who paused to watch as she passed among them toward the main gate.

## X

THE CHILD's dimpled hands firmly clutched at the chair, both for stability in the newly acquired art of standing and in fear of the young woman bending over her. Large eyes shone from a full pink face, but even Aleen's most coaxing words could not inspire a smile. Aleen plucked delicately at the child's tight golden curls until, overwhelmed by the nearness of the stranger and the length of her hovering, tears welled in the child's eyes, and she began crying pitifully.

With tender words of reassurance, Edith picked her up and pressed her small head comfortingly against her broad shoulder. "Please do not be offended, but at this age it is natural for the child to be timid and frightened of unfamiliar faces," the nurse explained.

Aleen looked approvingly on the mutual affection that existed. The nurse seemed a pleasant and capable guardian for the child, and her spotless apron and the white scarf tied neatly about her head gave her an air of efficiency and motherliness.

"She blooms with health," Aleen said as she watched a thumb find a path to a tiny mouth. "I did not expect this, since I had been told she was sickly and weak as an infant. She has grown quite lovely under your care," and she nodded approval to the cobbler's wife, who blushingly smiled back.

"I cannot claim full merit for the excellence of her wellbeing. Her appetite is most satisfactory, and she eats well of all table foods."

An inquisitive frown crossed her face. "Are you telling me she is no longer on the breast? Are not babies fed in that manner for much longer a time?" Aleen's face took on a vague expression as she searched for recollection of the conversations of the new mothers of Wermouth, in which she had evinced little interest.

"They are, my lady, when they are weak and sickly, but as you see, Lelia is quite healthy and strong and has had no need of me for many months now. She has been standing by herself for days," Bertha said, looking proudly at her charge. "Soon she will be walking unassisted."

"Have you informed Edmund that the child is no longer in need of your services?"

"Oh, yes. We have mentioned it to him." Edith nodded agreement.

"Well, then, what does the Lord Edmund say?"

"Nothing, my lady. He says nothing."

"One would suppose the father would snatch at the opportunity to have the child near him," Aleen said disbelievingly.

The cobbler's wife and Edith looked uneasy and were reluctant to discuss the shortcomings of their lord, who had been so generous toward them.

Aleen was stunned. "What, then, does the Lady Wilfreda say of the child's removal to the castle?"

The women exchanged glances and lowered their eyes. "We have never seen her, nor were we instructed to contact her about any matter relating to the babe," Edith replied almost inaudibly.

Aleen's emotions were stirring uncomfortably. The delectable odors emanating from the pot of stew bubbling on the hearth fires suddenly dissipated, as though a storm brewed in its stead, replacing the wafting scents with tendrils of disturbances. "Does no one else but Edmund see to the child?"

"The physician comes when he is called, and a servant comes at times with grains and meats, but otherwise my husband, Ansgar, journeys to the castle with our requests and messages."

Aleen's face tensed skeptically as she nervously fingered the amethyst ring. Why would a child be so deliberately neglected by its family? she wondered. Perhaps Lelia reminds Edmund too much of Marion. That is it. He does not want the constant presence of the child to remind him of his dead wife. But something within Aleen rebelled at the thought that anyone could have loved Marion that dearly, especially a person as forceful and important as Edmund.

Lelia was snuggled in the softness of Edith's bosom. She

did not resemble her mother; indeed, Marion would have been greatly surprised that she had produced so beautiful a child. It must be something in addition to this. The nuns . . . Edmund and Wilfreda had been extremely preoccupied with the business of the nuns. That was it, Aleen thought with relief. That was the only explanation—it was not a deliberate rejection of the child, nor was it the remembrance of Marion. It was that more serious affairs held their attentions.

"You have done well with the child," Aleen was saying as she walked toward the cobbler's wife and took one hand in hers. "You have made the first months of her life happy ones, I offer my gratitude to you." Aleen pressed the plump red hand.

"There has been much business transacted at the castle in recent months," she said, turning to the nurse. "Perhaps that is why the transfer to the castle was temporarily delayed. Would you please be so kind as to notify the castle once more that the child is prepared to leave here? And please," she cautioned, lowering her voice, "do not mention that I suggested this."

Aleen leaned over and gently took up one of Lelia's tiny hands that held a fold of Edith's dress. "Farewell, Lelia," she said. "I will see you again soon," and she kissed the little hand before releasing it.

The horse's hooves clapped loudly against the cobbled street, but Aleen seemed unmindful of the noise as she pondered the situation at the cobbler's. Edmund and Wilfreda could not have been so busy as to overlook the child so completely. A necessity had existed when the child was placed in such humble surroundings, but for a child of royal parentage to remain there unnecessarily was a matter of concern, and perhaps people were already speculating about the cause for the delay. Another, more immediate matter presented itself. What would occur at the castle when she returned? Would Edmund reproach her for not securing his permission, for leaving without a proper escort? Nonsense—Edmund seemed not the kind to vent anger or to speak sternly, especially with a future bride. But then, she had taken it upon herself . . .

As though from nowhere a flock of squawking geese spilled into the street and surrounded her mount's legs, until it was difficult to guide him. Aleen reined in to permit the little boy with his long stick to nudge the waddling fowl quickly along the way.

It is a pleasant little village, Aleen thought as she surveyed the shops of every sort that faced the street. A bakery, with the delectable odors of newly baked bread riding the sweetened air, displayed golden loaves of bread and smaller sweet cakes near its open door. Stout ivory-yellow candles, which were destined to illuminate many a darkened cottage, hung from long wicks under the extended roof of the candle-maker's shop. The steady click-click of spinning wheels came from the shop of the weaver, and by his open door several folds of fabrics were neatly stacked on a table, ready for the inspection of prospective customers. There were shops of salt dealers, soap makers, wine merchants, and potters with clay jugs and bowls stacked against their storefronts. Near the blacksmith shop Aleen blinked repeatedly with each rhythmic hammering and watched with fascination as steam hissed from the bucket of water when a glowing iron was submerged in it. Along the way, a young merchant, hustled from a shop by its owner, timidly held up in both hands bottles of fine imported oil for Aleen's inspection and purchase, but his brisk steps alongside the horse were halted by a sweet smile of declination.

Hurrying women, carrying baskets weighted with their purchases, slowed their steps and watched as the royal lady passed. One large woman, holding her skirt aside, quickly emerged from a shop, holding a cackling hen for Aleen's consideration. The hen's wings fluttered furiously and its eyes blinked frighteningly as it tugged against the hold on its legs. The woman quickly lowered it as Aleen passed, and as though personally rebuffed by Aleen's quiet refusal to purchase, she returned to her shop.

Aleen nudged the horse along the street that was now becoming busy with other riders—soldiers on errands and groups of grand ladies who were out for an afternoon's ride. On reaching the end of the village road, Aleen turned onto the one that skirted the front wall of the castle and greeted the few riders who were traveling in the opposite direction.

Slowly she proceeded onward toward her new home . . . and Edmund.

Handing the reins to the mute stable hand, Aleen walked briskly across the courtyard. If a confrontation was to ensue between her and Edmund, it had best be quickly done with. But what words of explanation would suffice to explain away her actions and her deliberate failure to gain permission for her visit to his daughter? But then, why should an excuse be necessary? It was her right to visit her kinsman, and, yes, it was almost her duty to have done so. Perhaps it was best that he learn early in their relationship that she had a head of her own and would act in all matters as she saw best. No words are necessary, she thought. What had Edmund resorted to when his own actions toward her required some words of apology or explanation? All she had been offered was a sharp nod of his head and a cold, impersonal half-smile. Well, that is all he will get from me, she resolved as she made her way down the hallway. Perhaps even that will be unnecessary if he is busy and not about.

But on turning the corner, she was suddenly beset by guilt, not unlike a child caught in a prank who knew that the inevitable reprimand was imminent. For Edmund was leaning casually against the wall of his office, speaking with a manservant.

Panic flared as she momentarily slowed her step, but, no, she would react as though nothing were amiss, for indeed, if her actions be carefully considered, no transgression had been committed, and she drew herself tall and resumed her normal pace.

Edmund glanced down the hall when movement caught his eye, and the conversation was immediately halted when he recognized her. His forehead wrinkled, and he was about to speak, when, as she approached, she gave a quick nod and in perfect mimicry gave a polite but cool half-smile of recognition. She walked past, leaving him with his intended words unspoken and a quizzical squint in his eye. He watched her graceful passage toward the stairway until she turned and began her ascent and her subsequent retreat from his stare.

But as she climbed the steps, she could no longer refrain

from smiling in relief and in satisfaction with her conduct. Edmund could be handled, she reasoned, and he had better in the future deal with her more considerately. Her smile mischievously lingered, and she fairly glided along on winged feet down the hall to her room, the brown of her eyes accented with sparkles of excitement.

## ～ XI ～

THE DAYS preceding the wedding dawned and faded in rapid succession, and except for brief visits to the chapel for morning services, Aleen remained in her chamber reminiscing with Hester on the pleasant days at Wermouth and speculating on their future at Lauxburgh. But not all of Aleen's thoughts were shared, especially those titillating thoughts that dealt with Edmund.

During the chapel services, Aleen had made certain to remain behind the small group of devout worshipers, where she could study her future husband unobserved. What she saw impressed her but set her wondering what sort of man he truly was. Although the most masculine of men, Edmund was completely contemplative in chapel, frequently kneeling with eyes closed, and with his bowed head resting on folded hands. He seemed, but for the attire, a young Saint Cuthbert, or a Saint Wilfred.

Why would a man crave the monastery when he could have any of the young ladies who, like herself, frequently turned their heads ever so slightly away from the altar to where he knelt absorbed in prayer and totally unaware of their interest in him? The question fascinated Aleen, as did the identity of one young woman who was always near him. Kneeling behind Edmund and to his side, the woman could easily observe him and the activities at the altar beyond him at the same time without arousing suspicion. Aleen also noticed that this woman, very beautiful and provocative in her manner and appearance, was always near Edmund as he left the chapel and that she usually managed to capture his attention with brief whispered remarks. If it were not for this distraction, Edmund would leave not knowing or recognizing anyone, and indeed, he did not even know, nor would he have cared, that his future bride was present.

A strange, rather complex person, this Edmund, Aleen thought, and she resolved to learn more of this woman who took such an interest in him. Had she heard someone call her Judith? She must remember that name.

It was after one of these services that Godfrey called Aleen aside and presented her to Wilfreda, who had returned from her sister's convent the evening before to prepare for the impending wedding. Wilfreda had made an attempt to appear cordial, but behind the thin face and haughty manner, Aleen knew Wilfreda did not mean any of the pleasant comments she was making, and the smile was strained and forced, to say the least. But then, their first meeting had taken place early in the morning, when one could not be expected to be in the best of social form. Perhaps our next meeting will be more relaxed and pleasant, Aleen thought. I must make certain to please her in all things. It is important that we like each other.

The night before the wedding was a fitful one for Aleen. Brief periods of sleep were interrupted by the gusts of wind that whistled past the window, and the gentle staccato of showers. The breaking of the waves, which had always lulled her to sleep, seemed now to roar, and the occasionally slammed door and the distant shuffling of feet were as so many sacrileges against the sanctity of the night hours. But sleep would not come, even if it were as still as the hollows of the cathedral.

Taunting thoughts reached out from the darkness to entwine and constrict her wakefulness, until at last merciful sleep relaxed their grasp and sent them retreating into the shadows. But soon a new assault began. "The marriage is a mockery," she mumbled sleepily to herself, tossing the linen covering aside. Fright, panic, and resentment were her bedfellows. The annulment, which was her only escape if all did not go well, was months, years away, when and if a satisfactory alternate plan for peace could be devised. But what if the annulment came years from now, when her beauty was beginning to fade? Suppose she would not be able to attract another husband, and spent her maturity without realizing the joys of love and the comfort of a family of her own? But what if she fell in love with Edmund? What if he fell in love with her? That stupid vow would be in their way. Could it be dispensed? Would Edmund permit it to be dispensed?

"Enough of this," she said, turning on her side and burrowing her head in the downy pillow. But, oh, to be able to slip through the darkness to the stable, and to saddle Cenook in secret, and to fly with him across the countryside to the security of Wermouth. To put all this uncertainty behind and to let the procession of time progress to a more natural destiny instead of allowing nations, wars, and diplomats to dictate its course. Would the night never end?

The lonely call of a whippoorwill at length heralded the approaching sun, which remained hidden beneath the horizon but which gradually lightened the eastern sky, until its first cautious rays threw flashes of brilliance on the jeweled wings of the birds that flitted about in delirious abandon.

The room glowed with soft light, but the breeze that moved the window tapestries permitted errant shafts of sunlight to dart in with altered shapes, before disappearing just as quickly, with the plop-plop of the fabric against the stone sill.

Too tired to move, Aleen lay studying the silken folds of her blue wedding gown as Hester entered the room and walked to the bed with a breakfast tray. "Good morning, my lady," Hester said, making an effort at casualness. "The cooks tell me this is the customary food the brides in this district eat before their weddings," she continued. Aleen struggled to sit up, propped the pillows behind her, and waited as Hester placed the tray on her lap. The food, no matter how traditional it might be, did not appeal to her. Tiny cakes lay on a silver plate. A cup of honey, pieces of sweetmeats, and a glass of goat milk awaited her pleasure, but Aleen could not bring herself to touch them. "I am not a true bride," she reasoned, looking apathetically at the food. "It is not proper for me to partake of a bridal meal. Take it away."

"My lady," Hester protested, "eat just a little."

Aleen shook her head.

"Then just a little milk?"

Aleen grabbed for the goblet and took a few swallows before putting it down. That should please you, she thought, as she lapsed into daydreams.

"The guests from distant shires are beginning to arrive," Hester was saying from across the room. "I am told they will spend the night here."

Everything seemed unreal, even Hester's movements as she removed the tray. Before long, however, Hester was passing the ivory comb through Aleen's shiny hair, and eventually the wedding gown was being held high for her to slip into. The silk caressed her as it fell into place, and fluttered about her wrists and ankles. It was a beautiful gown. Tiny golden threads had been woven at intervals throughout the blue fabric that lapsed into deeper shades in the folds. The high, round neckline, the hemline, and the ends of the sleeves were accented with bands of gold woven in a repetitious pattern. A chain of gold encircled the slender waist and formed a slightly slanted Y in the front. The veil that fell about her face reached below the waist in the back and was of a similar fabric, with a matching golden band rippling about the edge. Tiny white leather slippers completed her apparel.

Hester took several steps backward to admire her charge. "You are most beautiful," she beamed with pride. "You are more beautiful than all these Saxons together."

"You are loyal, Hester." Aleen smiled back as she picked up a bit of skirt and watched as it shimmered back into place.

"Wait here, my lady, while I see if the others are ready." Aleen nervously paced the floor, but at length Hester returned, smiling excitedly. "They are in the great hall awaiting you," she said with a burst of uneasiness. "Come. We must go."

The inevitable moment had arrived, and Aleen was suddenly overwhelmed with dread. If only she had dressed earlier and had been in the great hall to greet the guests as they arrived, instead of having them wait for her.

"Hester," she pleaded, "please come with me." Together they walked down the halls, until the door of the great hall loomed ahead. Hester stopped, looked into Aleen's face, and kissed her gently on the cheek. "I wish you every blessing and happiness. Do not worry so, it will work out well," she said with a reassuring twinkle in her eye.

Those nearest the door interrupted their conversations and turned as Aleen entered. A smile broke across her face, and her eyes danced as she immediately recognized the back of a tall, broad-shouldered young man who, unlike the rest, had not turned to face her. But after a moment he turned and smiled as Aleen darted headlong into his outstretched arms. "I thought you were not coming," she said, looking up into his smiling face while tears streamed from her eyes.

"Aleen," he said teasingly, "did you truly think I would not attend the wedding of my dear little sister? What sort of heartless brother would I be?" and he bent down and kissed her forehead.

"Alcuin, when did you arrive? Oh, you are mean to have teased me so."

"I arrived only last night, too late for me to call on you. Dry your eyes, my sweet," he whispered urgently, glancing uneasily at the people standing around. "There are many guests here you must meet," and he turned to look for Edmund, who was already advancing.

Aleen dried her eyes with the backs of her hands, smoothed her veil, and glanced up in time to give Edmund a cursory inspection. Why, he looks handsome, she thought. A red tunic edged in golden braid fell over white breeches that were strapped neatly against his lower legs with the same ties that fastened his shoes. A golden crown was on his head, making his brown hair appear darker. The whole physical impact of his appearance was appealing.

"Good day," he was saying, while fingering the cross hanging upon his chest. "You are most lovely, my lady."

As though cold water had been splattered upon her, she knew his last remark was detached, certainly not well meant, and indeed must have been often repeated, for the words sounded as though he had in turn uttered them to all the women present. He had spoken them only because it was expected of him. It did not matter to him if she looked lovely or not. This was an unfortunate day, when many pleasantries must be voiced and customs observed, and he was obviously resigned to saying and observing all that was required.

If he could so easily recite words he did not mean, she, too, would likewise, with equal resignation, say and do what was expected, and she heard herself saying, "Thank you, sir, you are most kind."

"Come meet our guests," he urged, taking her by the arm with a courteousness that was performed for the benefit of the guests. But Aleen held fast to Alcuin's hand. Anything could be endured with her brother beside her.

The introductions proceeded routinely for Aleen as her thoughts centered chiefly on the impressive and beautiful people presented to her, and their relationships to one another. Not the least of her preoccupations as she glanced frequently toward him was the effective manner in which Edmund was hiding his true sentiments about this wedding, by graciously mingling among the influential and wealthy people as though he relished and truly enjoyed the proceedings.

Before long, two monks made their way through the crowd to Edmund and quietly reminded him, "My lord, the hour is drawing near when his Excellency, the archbishop, expects your arrival at the cathedral."

"Very well," Edmund said, raising his arms in the air and clapping loudly to attract everyone's attention. In a voice that resounded throughout the hall, he announced, "The archbishop awaits us. Let us be off. We will return later for amusements and feasting."

A cry of approval filled the room as everyone hurried for the door. When sunlight fell upon them, Aleen comprehended the magnitude of the occasion. The courtyard was filled with meticulously groomed and finely draped horses being held in place by equally well-groomed servants. The sounds of neighing and whinnying mounts, and the sharp commands of their riders, mingled with the banging of emblemed shields against the flagstaffs of the soldier escorts who were filing through the gate. The procession passed before groups of peasants, who had been standing along the road since dawn, waiting to view the beautifully dressed gentlefolk and to catch a glimpse of the ealdorman and his future bride.

Aleen, Edmund, and Wilfreda took their places at the top step before the assemblage and waited for the guests to mount and precede them to the cathedral. Of all those seeking places in the procession, Judith, whom Aleen remembered from the chapel, and Alcuin were the most prominent. Alcuin had apparently made an acquaintance with Judith while they had awaited Aleen's appearance in the great hall, for they talked with ease, and Alcuin helped her mount as though he had been accustomed to doing so. Judith knew she was being observed as she arranged her skirt about her, and she displayed her charms with flourishes, especially, it would seem, for Edmund's benefit, since she stole glances toward him whenever she was able.

There remained a solemn group standing before the main door to the castle. Aleen was contemplating the confusion wrought because of a marriage that could only be construed as a mockery; Edmund, with solemn detachment, was but a pathetic creature caught in an inescapable plot; and Wilfreda, her face drawn with fatigue from hours of planning and supervising, was as though seething inwardly for the inconvenience thrust upon her for a marriage of which she disapproved.

When the ceremonially garbed soldiers took their places before and after them, Aleen and Edmund began their ride to fulfill their destiny.

Deliriously joyful at the prospect of peace secured by the coalition, the peasants and villagers cheered as Aleen and Edmund passed before them. Flower petals were flung in the air before them, and daffodils and wildflowers plucked from the fields were pressed into Aleen's hands. Many in impulsive bursts of devotion grabbed and kissed Edmund's hands or were content to touch the horse or its drape. Edmund was delighted with the display and waved and called many by name. What kind of nobleman was this, Aleen wondered, who could pass with such familiarity among these dusty and drab people? It was clear that Edmund dearly loved them, and they in gratitude returned his affection in redoubled measures.

The gray church dominated the view before them, and nestled beside it could be seen the mournful rows of gravestones in the adjoining cemetery. At the church door, among the dismounting people and the horses being led away, were priests and monks waiting to accompany the couple to the high altar. In contrast to the happy attitude of the peasants, the priests seemed coldly severe as they stood silently in the dust that stirred about them.

Who it was that helped Aleen dismount, she did not know, but it was not Edmund. He had rushed forward to greet the clerics, many of whom he had known from the monastery. Religious decorum and reticence were abandoned as they were immediately caught up in the joviality of the reunion.

It seemed natural for Edmund to mingle with the black-robed men. It is a pity he cannot join them at Tankenham, she thought. Then I would be free to marry whomever I wished.

The clerics quickly reclaimed their composure and preceded the bridal pair into the dark, musty interior of the cathedral. Passing amid the common folk at the back, and the nobles assembled in the front, Aleen and Edmund approached the archbishop, who was standing amid his group of acolytes before the altar, where countless candelabra stood atop crisp linens.

King Solomon in his most glorious hour could not have looked more pretentious than did the archbishop, with his white beard resting upon the golden embroidered vestments, his pointed miter rising tall and imposing atop his head. His voice was all but silenced by the deafening pealing of the bells and the voices of the choir, which rose and fell in practiced chantings. At length the choir concluded its hymns, and the reverberations of the bells settled into silence, permitting the archbishop's voice to captivate the quiet that followed.

Never had Aleen been so self-conscious as she was then, with a crowded church behind her, Edmund standing motionless beside her, a sanctuary filled with solemn-faced clerics studying her, and the majestic, imposing figure of the archbishop praying before her. But she would not be intimidated, and she stood proudly—a credit to her race and breeding.

"Place your hands upon the Holy Book," the archbishop was saying in a whisper as Aleen and Edmund turned to the gold-embellished leather cover of a large book that was being carried toward them by two surpliced acolytes. After doing as they were directed, Aleen stared numbly at the muscled, hairy hand that was resting beside her own.

"Place your hand upon hers," the archbishop whispered, and Edmund at once obeyed.

Only the orders of the archbishop and the rubrics of the ceremony could entice Edmund to touch me, Aleen thought shrewdly as she glowed nonetheless under the warmth of his hand.

"Do you vow, Edmund, to wed Aleen and to live together in accordance with the teachings of Holy Mother Church, and the laws of God contained in this Holy Book?"

"I so vow," Edmund replied.

"Lady Aleen," the archbishop continued, looking over his prayer book at her, "do you consent to wed Edmund, to live with him according to the teachings of Holy Mother Church, and the laws of God contained in this Holy Book?" Bending nearer, he added with a deeper and almost inaudible tone, as if to safeguard it from the hearing of others, "And do you swear to honor all private and public vows previously made by your marriage partner?"

Aleen was struck silent for the moment at the thought of Edmund rendered so smug and complacent by this protection of his resolves. In outrage she wished to shout "No" at this addition to the standard rite, but the archbishop hovered above her, waiting for her reply. "I do so vow," she said begrudgingly.

Their hands were separated as the priests moved away with the Bible. Their places were taken by two other priests, one of whom held documents, and the other, great quills and small vials of ink. As Aleen and Edmund traced their names across the parchment, the scratching of the pens sounded throughout the church. The archbishop then turned slightly toward the sacristy, where a vested priest emerged, carrying before him a small golden crown similar to the one Edmund wore. He handed it over to the archbishop, who in turn handed it to Edmund. Standing beside his kneeling wife, Edmund held it high and then placed it gently atop her veiled head.

Many Latin prayers and blessings were recited before the archbishop looked into the crowd and spoke loudly for all to hear: "Before God and this assembly, I declare Edmund and Aleen to be man and wife by reason of the vows they have pronounced, and by the bestowal of this crown, I do affirm Aleen to be the lady of the district of Kent." The bells began pealing, and the choir intoned a spirited and joyous hymn as Edmund accompanied Aleen through the gathering to the door and into the pure springtime air.

The return to the castle seemed a great deal shorter than the ride earlier, and the peasants seemed even happier than before, and why not? Because of the ceremony just performed, the peace of their country was in greater measure assured. They had reason to trust that the silent, swift invasions of the past would be discontinued, that their young, handsome sons would no longer be slain in defense of their families' rights, that woodsmen and hunters would be less fearful of the prowling bands of outlaws. They could breed swine, oxen, and cattle without expecting them to be stolen, and could plow rows of vegetables, grain, and flax without having them overrun beneath the hooves of Danish horses. Yes, it was a day for rejoicing—at least, for some.

Aleen's hands instinctively reached for the crown that had shifted on her head as she seated herself at the table that had been set aside for the bridal pair, members of the family, and visiting clerics. At once the cold metal sent a chill down her back. Was this the same golden crown Marion had worn at her wedding? It was an eerie thought, and for the moment the roughness of the deeply engraved designs and the bumpy jewels felt as cool and rough as the stone that marked Marion's grave. Strange that she should think of that now, when she was surrounded by so many laughing people.

Edmund settled in the chair next to hers and nervously rubbed his arms as he looked about at the guests who were searching for their rightful places at the long tables that filled the center of the great hall.

With Edmund on Aleen's right side and the archbishop occupying the place to her left, Wilfreda claimed the place of honor to Edmund's right, and whether by invitation or her own choice, Judith claimed the chair beside Wilfreda. Alcuin immediately reached for the place beside Judith, while the other places at table were randomly picked by clerics and nobles.

Aleen did not notice those who claimed the other places at her table, for the laughing couples who sat at the long tables before her claimed her interest. They were in complete contrast to those at her table, who all sat, with the exception of Judith and Alcuin, with stoic regality.

"Ah, there you are," Edmund was saying, and Aleen quickly looked to the right, where Edmund was reaching back to pet the two sleek white dogs she had remembered seeing on her tour. Their tails waged happily, and they whimpered contentedly under his stroking hand. "There, now, sit still, sit still," and he turned, leaving them to search for a favorable resting place between and around the legs of his chair.

"We are to share the food from this dish," he said, indicating with a forefinger the golden dish a servant was carrying toward them. Edmund waited until it was placed between them on the table and the servant had left before adding, "It is the custom that we share the same plate. Will this offend you?"

"No," Aleen replied indifferently, and added with a proper degree of condescension, "not if it is the tradition."

The plate was filled with choice bits of sweetmeats carefully cut into small square morsels and surrounded with an amber butter sauce. Much to Aleen's relief, they were not expected to share the same drinking vessel, for another servant set before each of them gold-rimmed drinking horns.

The diners at the other tables had already plunged into their meal of roasted venison, haunches of mutton, baked mackerel, and larded boar's head. There were platters of cheese, jellied eggs, steaming corn, and freshly baked breads.

Neither knew how to begin, but at length Edmund placed a palm against the rim of the plate they were to share, and nudging it gently toward Aleen, offered her the first piece. With as much grace as the awkward intimacy permitted, Aleen reached for a glistening morsel and waited for Edmund to select his, but Edmund did not reach into the bowl, but stared at the doorway, where a man in a fur-trimmed tunic stood looking about uncertainly.

"The Lord Wulfmayer of Sussex," Edmund said. "I must greet him. With your leave . . ."

Aleen nodded graciously and watched as Edmund approached the latecomer, grasped his shoulders, shook him jovially, patted him on the back, and engaged in rollicking conversation. There was nothing for Aleen to do but wait for his return—a wait that would be a silent one, for the archbishop, to her left, was communicating with those to the other side of the table, and no conversation across the chasm of the empty chair seemed likely, for Wilfreda sat straight-backed, pretending no one sat on the other side of her son's empty chair. But perhaps Wilfreda was waiting for her to speak first. For want of something better to say, Aleen leaned toward Wilfreda and asked, "This wedding dish, Wilfreda, is of an elegant design. Is it of a great age?"

There was a deliberate avoidance of eyes as Wilfreda answered. "It was given to me by my mother for my wedding feast," she said without changing her expression.

"It is very generous of you to permit me to use it," Aleen replied. But Wilfreda took no heed of the words and continued cutting her meat as though no interruption to her repast had been made.

She is angry with me, Aleen thought in a flood of bewilderment. She is annoyed with me. Why? What has happened? Did I speak words that were offensive to her? It could not be. But for their brief meetings outside the chapel, no other words had been exchanged—only brief glances of recognition. Was some formality neglected, some courtesy overlooked? Aleen searched her mind frantically. But how can I be held accountable for customs of which I am unfamiliar? If any courtesy had been neglected, Wilfreda is to blame. She should have called upon me before our meeting at the chapel. She was expected to speak with me about the wedding customs, and she neglected to. Yes, I should be the one slighted. At least Edmund was beginning to be friendly, and the few words they had exchanged at table were promising. If only he would return. But the few steps he and his newly arrived guest made in the direction of the tables were halted as they continued their animated conversation, seemingly unmindful of the proceedings. As their dialogue lengthened, Aleen's flickers of impatience grew into a smoldering agitation that set her face into harsh lines.

Edmund finally seated the latecomer at table, but as he lingered to talk, and finally, as he motioned to a servant to care for his guest's needs, Aleen's eyes snapped in anger. *He does not care that he has abandoned his new wife. He cares more for the welfare of his guest. If there was a time he should be heedful of me, it would be now, when the ceremony was just completed. He has placed me behind these others in importance. How dare he!* Aleen's impatience reached unbearable limits when he lingered to speak with other guests who had turned and waved for his attention.

*I have waited long enough for him. Entirely too long.* And she looked into the bowl and the pool of melted butter that had collected and picked up a morsel. Her nose wrinkled in disdain. *I shall not partake of a wedding meal if there be no husband beside me.* The morsel was detestable, and she would have dropped it back into the dish had not a flick of a dog's tail caught her eye. Looking toward Wilfreda, whose interest was engaged by Judith and Alcuin, Aleen dropped the piece to the floor beside one of the dogs, who immediately awakened and snapped it up.

*I shall not share this meal, nor any other, with him,* she determined as she looked about to make certain she was unobserved. Drawing the plate closer, she reached for a handful, carefully let her hand down beside the chair, and released the meat to the dogs, who were patiently awaiting the dropping of another treat. *I would rather share my meal with dogs than with that . . . that discourteous, thoughtless rogue.* A smiling, placid countenance belied her thoughts as she carefully reached for another handful and cautiously deposited its contents between the legs of the chair.

When Edmund was at long last on his way toward her, the few morsels that had lain in the amber fluid were plucked up, and after a moment of deceptive hesitation, were dropped to the dogs. Aleen noticed with a downward glance, which did not require a movement of her head, that the dogs had swallowed the bits as though inhaling air, and by the time Edmund was settling into his chair, the fragments were long gone.

Aleen did not look at Edmund, but knew that the empty dish, now containing only glistening fluids, puzzled him, for it had been explained that the former contents were for the two of them to share, and certainly there had been too much there for one slender girl to have consumed by herself. She felt him suspiciously studying her and knew he was glancing at the two dogs, who roamed about and squeezed their way between the chairs, their noses close to the ground in anticipation of coming upon chunks that had been overlooked. Pretending to be unmindful of his perplexity, even under the scrutiny of his squinting eyes, Aleen gazed ahead at a minstrel who was singing softly while carelessly plucking the strings of his lyre.

Revenge was deliriously soothing. Just as the incoming waves overrrun the trampled sands of a beach, and retreat, leaving it smoothed, so her actions had washed her troubled emotions, replacing them with a contentment that shone in her eyes.

Edmund was dubiously watching her, but she cared not. The Blessed Madonna looking upon her newborn babe could not have looked more serenely radiant than Aleen, now gazing at the minstrel with beguiling innocence.

# ⤙ XII ⤚

THE GOLD filigree that encircled the rim of the ceremonial drinking horn provided a soothing sensation for Aleen's fingers as she rubbed the design and stroked the smooth ring of thick gold. Edmund had satisfied his appetite with fruit and baked goods, and except for an occasional accusatory glance at his new wife, all was formal and dignifiably courteous between them.

Utter contentment enlivened Aleen's face as she basked in the satisfaction produced by her retaliatory prank, and the sweetest of smiles were bestowed on those guests who glanced her way as they were leaving the long tables to accumulate in friendly groups.

A scraping of chairs at the head table signaled the official conclusion of the meal as all rose to form groups of their own. But Wilfreda, who had been attracted to the handsome Viking, turned toward him and, with Judith, formed an exclusive trio that was oblivious to all save the tales of exploration told by the adventurous male who was now feeling the joyous effects of sparkling wines.

Aleen gave a knowing sideward glance at Alcuin as he accented a point with a lift of his goblet. Judith's head was coquettishly tilted, her eyes aglow, and Wilfreda, tall and proud, was so engrossed in the tale as to be actually anticipating the surprising conclusion.

A surge of pride welled in Aleen's being. That rascal, she thought to herself. He does have a way of winning the ladies. Let him have his pleasure. He will have time enough for his little sister before he departs.

The archbishop was happily relating the experiences of his recent trip to Rome to the small group that had collected around Aleen and Edmund in anticipation of more interesting conversation. The men became increasingly nervous as the archbishop's voice droned on, and Aleen quickly surmised that at the speed with which each event was being related, it would take all of the evening to conclude the journey. But at least Edmund was dutifully beside her. Her satisfaction, however, was short-lived, for one of the guests begged pardon for intruding on the discourse, and taking hold of Edmund's arm, gently lured him to a group, who joyously welcomed him.

Aleen half-listened to the clerical narrator while the servants nearby assembled the remaining food to a side table and hurried to disassemble the tables and stack the planks and trestles in one corner of the hall. The moments passed slowly, monotonously, as the archbishop took his distracted, fidgety listeners through the interior of France. One by one his audience dwindled, until there remained only Aleen and an old man whose name she was never to learn. Reluctantly they were led by the cleric to a bench against the wall, where they sat on either side, politely entrapped by the prelate.

The hall was becoming noisier with drunken laughter, and minstrels added to the din with lively tunes. Red wine and mead flowed abundantly from the jugs of cup bearers as the familiar tendrils of discontentment and anger entwined about Aleen's heart. If her ears were claimed by the archbishop, her eyes were definitely at liberty, and there were darts of resentment aimed at Edmund, who laughingly found his way from one group to another, forgetful of the bride who should have been by his side.

I do not dislike Edmund, Aleen considered. I hate him. How could he consider himself to be righteous, so civil . . . the boor, the discourteous . . . Today of all days he should show concern and some measure of respect, instead of abandoning me to this cleric and his boring journey. If only I could escape this room. And with a flash of determination she resolved to do so. She glanced at her brother, who had added three more feminine listeners to his group, and knew they would certainly not be aware, nor would they care, if she departed.

Edmund had worked his way to the other side of the room, but then, what did it matter if he were aware of her leave-taking? In fact, it were better if he took heed of her justifiable displeasure.

Some of the landowners, prosperous shopkeepers, and lords of lesser castles and shires whose return home was necessitated by pressing matters were now beginning to leave, but those who could, would spend the night in the castle, and they merrily anticipated a long evening of more drinking and conviviality.

"Excellency," she said, interrupting his description of the Roman terrain, "I thank you for sharing the experiences of your journey, but I must speak with guests who are leaving," she said, while moving her arm away from the restraining hand that had been placed on her wrist. Before the cleric could speak a protest, she was standing, asking leave of the lone listener, and was off, wondering why she had not escaped the trap long before. With all due respect for his exalted episcopal position and the confidence and trust placed in him by other bishops, he was uninteresting and had bored her long enough.

"I am honored by your attendance here today," she heard herself saying to the nearest group, who immediately stopped speaking and turned toward her. "It pleases me that you are having an enjoyable time." She gradually made her way to the door and slipped through. After looking through the halls, she found Godfrey. "My brother for the moment is well cared for," she whispered confidentially. "Will you see to him later? I must return to my chamber."

Thane Godfrey was expected to participate in the reveling, but he preferred to concern himself with the problems that invariably arose at all such functions. There were the servants to supervise, food must always be in readiness, there were rooms to assign to guests, and there was the caring for those who succumbed to the effects of intoxicating drafts.

"Of course, my lady," he said, interpreting the cause of her concern. He had observed previously that before the celebration was half over, the wine-loving Dane would need support and assistance in reaching his bed.

She mounted the stairs quickly and hurried the length of the hall, which now seemed lonely and deathly still, except for the distant sounds of laughter. But as she opened the door to her chamber, she felt only relief. Hester, who had fallen asleep in a chair, started. "My lady," she said, making an effort to disperse the lingering wafts of sleepiness, "the feasting is over so soon?"

"No, Hester, it is not. I could endure the farce no longer. I will tell you of it another time." She took the crown from her head and carelessly placed it on a table. "Here, take this," she said, thrusting the blue silk veil into Hester's arms. "And this," she said, unwinding the golden chains about her waist. After slipping easily from under the gown, she flung it aside. "Take it and burn it. I wish never to see it again. Be off, Hester," she ordered, nudging her along. "You may retire to your room when you have fulfilled my order. I wish to sleep now."

Hester left with proper haste, but the instructions were not performed. Aleen was never to learn until many months later that Hester had carried the gold-embroidered dress to her room and tucked it lovingly beneath a Danish fur robe at the bottom of a chest.

With a sigh of resignation, Aleen sat on her bed and looked at the crown, leaning at an angle against a jewelry casket. It seemed a child's plaything, curiously devoid of its inherent prestige.

In spite of the two meals offered her that morning, she had eaten nothing, and was now dreadfully hungry. Quickly she slipped off the bed, walked into the sitting room, and looked around for some remnant of a meal Hester might have brought there for herself while waiting for her mistress to return. But in the corner on a table was her own breakfast tray, which she had refused earlier, except for the milk Hester had forced upon her. Why had Hester been so negligent in returning the tray to the kitchen? Regardless, here were the untouched honey cakes, and Aleen quickly lifted the linen napkin and reached for them.

Returning to her bed, she crossed her legs before her and indulged in hearty mouthfuls. The crown gleamed dully. It will become heavier as time passes, she reasoned. Would she ever be certain Fergus had used good judgment in arranging her marriage? But then, his decisions had always brought about satisfactory results in the past. We will see. But how can I be happy under these cruel circumstances with a man I dislike? Her face drew up in a sneer as she took another bite of the sweet cake.

Alcuin was still asleep and snoring softly when Aleen slipped into his room the next morning. His chest was uncovered, and she watched its gentle rising and falling. It was so good being near kin, even though he was unaware of her presence. Aleen walked to the chair where his sword and scabbard rested. Slowly and quietly she picked it up, withdrew the sword from its leather casing, and remembered the precious moment when her father had given it to him. Would that it would always serve him well, this gleaming silver strip of metal, but better, would that no occasion would arise which necessitated its use. Returning it to its place, she gently stroked his robes and picked up the mantle he had let fall beside the bed. How dearly she loved this drunken, handsome brother. How well he had developed into manhood—so strong of body and quick of mind. A moistness collected in her eyes as she remembered the skinny boy she had tumbled with so often in their childhood. The thin little boy who always challenged her to foot races, tree climbing, stone throwing; the little boy she found so detestable during arguments, but who had been so comforting during thunderstorms, when she had clung so tightly to him.

Drowsily he turned on his side to further enjoy the comforts of drunken slumber. Several more hours of oblivion would be required before the effects of his celebrating were dispelled, so for now her visit with him must be postponed.

Pleasant days followed. Aleen claimed, and was awarded almost exclusively, the full attentions of her brother. Together they went about the countryside, their horses once following the path leading to the cathedral, where Alcuin knelt in the dirt beside the grave of the young woman who, as a girl, came into his life as an adopted sister. Marion—the dignified, quiet girl who always excused his roguishness and patiently listened to his imaginary feats of valor and dreams of future adventures and conquests. Marion's child was not overlooked, and although their visit to her had been brief, Aleen was pleased that the child was less apprehensive of her than during her first visit. Excursions through the village, a visit to the wharf, and rides through country lanes were enjoyed, and languid moments of pleasant companionship were indulged in before time came to bid farewell.

Walking alongside the steed upon which Alcuin rode in such regal fashion, Aleen stopped at the gate, where he bent down to kiss his sister an affectionate farewell. As she stood looking after him, tears moistened her eyes. His escorts followed quickly in a whirl of dust and a scrunching of pebbles. A pall of oppression immediately fell upon her. She was alone. Of course, there was Hester, but she could hardly be relied upon to be a companion. She was too withdrawn, too occupied with her own thoughts of her secret past, too inept to help in alleviating Aleen's heartache and homesickness.

Tears slid down Aleen's face as she watched the riders being consumed by the distance. Perhaps years would pass before she would look upon Alcuin's face once more—indeed, if she ever would again. Struggling against the sobs that ached for release, she walked slowly through the courtyard toward the main entrance as though surrendering herself to imprisonment in a strange and unfriendly world.

## ⤙ XIII ⤚

BLUE, YELLOW, green, and red yarns lay tangled in the bottom of the circular basket that rested on Aleen's lap. Squeezing her fingers in the matted strings, she spread them apart and repeatedly glanced from them to the piece of unfinished needlework that was draped on the table by her side.

"You know, Hester, Marion tried many times to teach me to do this, but I held little interest in it. Perhaps I shall regret not having paid more attention to her instructions." After musing for a while, she picked up the cloth. "If I cannot execute this work with skill, at least I can pretend to be working on it." She stuffed the cloth into the basket and rose from the chair. "Hester, are you certain the maid will not speak to anyone of our purchase?"

"No, my lady," Hester said with a laugh. "The lass was too delighted with your golden bracelet to risk losing it by disclosing who bought her worthless threads. You can be certain she will not speak of the exchange."

Aleen was satisfied with the reply and began pacing briskly. "See if the ladies are coming," she said, nervously clasping and unfolding her fingers.

Hester walked to the door as softly as her bulk allowed, and ever so carefully eased the door ajar until she was able to peer down the hallway through a narrow slit. Quickly she leaned away from the door and waved for Aleen's attention. "They are coming now," she whispered excitedly, carefully closing the door so that its movement was unnoticed by the ladies.

Feminine voices and the flapping of skirts grew nearer and then lessened in volume as they made their way down the hall to the sitting room.

"Very well," Aleen said, picking up the basket and cradling it in her arms. "I am ready." But she hesitated as though un-

119

willing to move from the spot. She had strategically planne
for this afternoon. Companionship, she had decided, wa
what was needed so desperately to help her escape from th
self-pity that had descended on her after her brother's depar
ture. What better way was there to begin winning friend
than by joining the ladies during their sewing sessions? True
she had never been invited to join them. They had never sai
more to her than mumbled greetings, but perhaps it was expected that the lady of the castle, the wife of the ealdorman
would attend, and that, by her very failure to participate, she
had indicated her unwillingness to mingle with them in thi'
or any other function. This would be remedied, for Aleen
wanted desperately to win their confidence and join in their
whispered conversations and girlish giggling.

Aleen walked timidly down the hall and entered the room
where the dozen or so ladies had settled down to their sewing. But one by one the scattered babbling was quieted as she
looked about for the proper place to sit. Smilingly she surveyed the group and cautiously made her way to a chair that
was just the correct distance from one cozy group, but yet
not too far to discourage an invitation to move closer.

Several needles were poised in midair, and many eyes
critically assessed her every movement as she sat down and
made herself busy with the threads. But the conversations
were not resumed, and only a deathly, awkward silence prevailed. Aleen glanced up pleasantly at the group nearest her,
but only expressionless faces looked down on idle fingers. Un-
believingly Aleen looked around the room at each of the
ladies and read into their cold, haughty attitudes bitter accusations and stinging rejection. Aleen followed them with her
eyes as, one by one, the ladies noiselessly folded their fabrics,
placed them in sewing baskets, and glided from the room. But
as Aleen's eyes fell from them, they rested on the garments
they were carefully folding—not awkwardly embroidered
pictures such as she had, but altar vestments, stoles, maniples,
chalice covers, all intricately embroidered in golden threads.

My God, Aleen exclaimed to herself, looking from the
stitched crosses and golden clusters of grapes and shafts of
wheat to the roughly dyed woolen threads in her lap. How

careless of me not to have known that ladies of high birth, these cousins of Edmund, these wives of his officers, these wives of his councilmen, would find only altar garments worthy of their nimble fingers. But it was not this mistake in judgment for which she was being censured, but she herself, a Danish princess—a creature supposedly inferior to the lowest born Anglo-Saxon.

This is to be their conduct, she thought as the last of the ladies left. They would show a certain measure of politeness in the hallways, where Edmund or the priests and councilmen might chance upon the situation, but in closed, unobserved circumstances the clannish group would show their displeasure with flippant cruelty.

For a few moments Aleen sat motionless, with the rejection still smarting. Then, placing the basket on the floor, she rose, stood tall, her head held resolutely, although her face bore a despondent expression. I have been a fool, she thought, to have hoped they would accept me. With a tilt of her chin she continued: But why should I want to be approved and accepted by them? I always cared little for the company of women. And the revelation smoothed the lines between her eyes. Truly I do not desire the friendship of these gossipers, these vain, cruel women who spend so much time on themselves. She preferred the company of men, and in a flash she recalled her happy days at Wermouth, with her father and brother teaching her the proper rules for hawking and the proper posture for riding. Let the women have their exclusive friendships. She would not again trouble them, and neither would she again be hurt by them.

The room was silently forbidding. She must leave it. The embroidered cloth she had unknowingly clutched to her slipped from her fingers to the floor, to be crumpled beneath her slippers, and the reed basket, snagged on the hem of her gown, tumbled over, spilling forth tendrils of thread.

But she could not spend another afternoon in her chamber with her maidservant quietly cleaning as her mind reflected on past events, as was Hester's habit. What I need, Aleen reasoned, is to have the wind surging through my hair while Cenook carries me over the countryside. It was a beautiful day for riding, and with a smile she made her way briskly to the stable.

Cautiously Aleen pushed aside the stable door that hung precariously on loose hinges, and entered the dim interior, where trapped, stifling heat supported the repulsive odors of fresh manure. All was quiet except for the occasional snorting of the horses and the monotonous droning of flies.

"Cenook, my beauty," she said, pushing aside the gate of his stall. "I have neglected you," and she ran her hand along the length of his neck. "My beauty must not go hungry," she cooed. Picking up a small bucket, she walked to the grain bin and scooped up a measure. Returning, she poured the golden oats in the trough and waited as Cenook contentedly crushed and ground the grain between sturdy teeth. She was proud of this noble animal. He provided her with her greatest pleasure, for he galloped as fast as the wind, leaped the highest hedges, and responded eagerly to her every command.

Reaching down for his empty water bucket, she slung it over her shoulder and proceeded out to the well, but no sooner had she lifted the pail from its watery depths and transferred its contents to Cenook's bucket than she looked up and saw Edmund crossing the courtyard. Hurriedly she picked up the bucket and made her way back to the stable to avoid him.

She had thought of him often during the days following the wedding, and they were not kindly thoughts. Especially during the nights when sleep would not come, she had bitterly recalled their previous meetings and particularly his conduct at the wedding feast. She detested him, and if there was one person she wished to berate, it was he. Furthermore, his desire to evade her was no greater than her own desire to absent herself from anything in the least way relating to him. But when she reached Cenook's stall, she heard Edmund's voice greeting Aethelwed. She set the bucket down beside Cenook's stall and cautiously glanced toward him. He seemed different and amusingly unprotected without companions by his side. As he drew nearer, she turned away and busied herself with picking lint from Cenook's saddle blanket.

Edmund hesitated momentarily at Cenook's stall, nodded

his head, and with the formal weak smile she was accustomed to receiving from him, he greeted her, "Good day, Aleen," and continued walking to Boltar's stall.

The casualness of the greeting surprised her. If he thought his neglect of her could be forgotten so easily, he was mistaken. A warm flush of indignation surged through her, and she determined to ignore him in retaliation. Grasping at the blanket, she flipped it across Cenook's back and smoothed it into place.

Not seeing Boltar in his stall, Edmund turned to seek him out, but his eyes narrowed as he realized that his greeting had not been returned. Glancing in Aleen's direction, he repeated the words.

Picking up the bridle as though not hearing or perceiving that anyone was there, Aleen busily tucked the bit into Cenook's mouth.

"Aleen," he repeated as he approached her. It seemed impossible that his greeting had been deliberately ignored. But before he took many steps, she picked up the saddle and struggled against the strap that caught on a protruding board.

"Aleen," he repeated as he stood beside the stall, but Aleen continued to struggle against the saddle's weight and the restraining strap, until she replaced the saddle astride the fence that separated the stall from its neighbor.

Looking keenly at the face that was arrogantly aloof, he asked, "What troubles you, Aleen?"

She glared at him with deliberateness. He deserved to see her displeasure, and if the occasion developed, he merited to hear all the words of rebuke she had practiced for his behalf.

"Aleen," he said with a kindness she thought she would never receive from him, "what troubles you?"

"It surprises me, sir, that you remember my name," she said coolly, but as she again attempted to lift the saddle, his hand held it fast against the post.

"Please remove your hand, sir," she said, looking away from him, but his hand forcefully remained where it was.

"Tell me, Aleen," he coaxed, "what troubles you?"

Never, in all the time she had anticipated meeting with him, had she fancied it would occur in the stable, under such crude surroundings. "Tell you what, my lord?" she asked with subtle contempt. "Must I tell you that you have not spoken to me these past weeks? It might pain you to know that I think you notably lacking in the charity that our religion recommends that we exercise with one another."

She paused. She had said too much, too vehemently, yet his penetrating gaze was not altered. Obviously there was much venom that needed extracting, and he encouraged her to expel it. "Tell me more," he ordered.

It took courage for her to continue under his stern scrutiny and the hand that was uncomfortably close to her own, but she determined not to show cowardice. It was time that her thoughts be sounded, whether he liked their implications or not.

"Remove your hand," she demanded, and was surprised when he obeyed.

Edmund crossed his arms and waited patiently for her to continue, but his silent and alert manner unnerved her; yet he bade her continue. Bolstered by the unchallenged words already spoken, and stimulated to continue by a seething vexation, she added, "Three times, sir, I expected to meet with you to discuss matters that concerned me much, yet you found not the time to devote to me."

Edmund's frown deepened, as though recollection failed him.

"You were to show me about the castle, you were to consult with me concerning the wedding arrangements, and you were to approve my journey to the village to visit the child. . . ." Suddenly the remembrance of her unauthorized visit to the village and the rebuke Edmund could have awarded her made her hurry along. "It seems you and your vow must be guarded at all times, but I did not think it would prevent you from speaking to me. Or are you and your priestly friends fearful lest I attempt to seduce you? Please be assured, my lord, that if I was so inclined, and if I put my mind to it, I could win you in spite of your hovering guards. But do not be alarmed, I find nothing in you that appeals to me. Do not be fearful of speaking to me. I will not bother to tempt you."

The sound of plodding hooves interrupted the discourse, as the stable master entered with Boltar, who had been freshly curried. The sounds were halted when Thorkil looked up and saw the nobles. Bowing, he mumbled, not knowing whether to speak or not. The stale horse odors, the bland smells of oats and hay, seemed hardly the right air for nobles to be breathing, but matters of importance were being considered, for the lady looked agitated and the lord was tense and thoughtful. "Boltar is ready, my lord. Must I prepare him for your ride?"

"Put him in the stall for now, Thorkil," Edmund said with a hint of annoyance. "Wait outside for me, and close the door. Permit no one to enter."

Thorkil shuffled quickly to the stall, pushed Boltar in place, hurried out, and closed the creaking door behind him. Quiet snorts, and hooves scraping the well-pounded earth in the stalls, filled the vacuum created by the closed doors, and dust, newly aroused by Boltar's passage, swirled madly in the rays of light slanting from lofty windows.

Interminable minutes passed, in which Aleen fingered the smooth leather of Cenook's saddle, her back contemptuously turned to Edmund. At last she heard his steps as he walked to a bale of hay and sat upon it. "Please continue, Aleen. I wish to hear all you desire to say."

Aleen felt fully at an advantage. He was willing to receive the reprimand he fully deserved, and she was more than willing to deliver it with enthusiasm. "When I saw you here, I wondered why you would be needing Boltar. I had forgotten it is the observance of Marion's death. You were going to the cathedral again, were you not?" she asked, turning to catch his affirmative nod. "It is quite commendable, your devotion, your obsession with the dead, but it does my cousin little good. Have you thought, sir, to award at least a portion of that attention to your living wife? You forget that I am a stranger here, without kinfolk, yet you ignore me completely, as though I were sinful, as though I were eager to ensnare your precious virtue. I am not a devil, sir. I am a Christian, and I ask only that I be courteously considered, as are the other members of this place."

Edmund's eyes followed Aleen as she paced back and forth. Since no words were forthcoming from him, she continued to unburden her mind and heart.

"It is known that your people consider my kinsmen to be uncultured, crude, barbarous, but they would not think of being as discourteous as your people have been to me, and please recall that I am here at the request of your councilmen and your king."

"What are these discourtesies you speak of?" Edmund asked, straightening with interest. But Aleen checked herself. Enough had been said. It was unkind of her to criticize his people, and hopefully their attitude toward her might change.

"What is it they do?" he insisted.

"I prefer not to speak of it," she said, raising her head sarcastically.

Edmund arose and walked toward her. "What else troubles you?" he asked with kindliness.

Aleen had fully expected him to be vindictive, but instead he seemed sincerely sympathetic with what she had said. "I have spoken enough."

"No, I think not. Continue. I wish to hear it all."

The bitterness and resentment that had accumulated in her heart the past weeks screamed for release. The larger portion had already gushed forth, and Aleen struggled unsuccessfully to hold back the rest.

Edmund grasped her by the arm as though wishing to shake from her body the words that were left unsaid.

"You are rude, sir. If only my brother were still here. . . . You do not recall, I am certain, the manner in which you deserted me after our wedding for the companionship of your friends, leaving me to the mercy of the boring cleric and his monotonous narration of his journey to Rome. If my brother had known then how miserable you made me by your neglect, he would have plunged his sword through you without hesitation, and—"

"And you regret that he did not? Do you hate me so, Aleen?"

"No, my lord, I do not hate you. That is forbidden by our religion."

"But it is not against our religion that you wish me dead?"

Aleen lifted her head and averted his gaze. In her silence he would find his answer.

Edmund continued to look piercingly at her, studying her

features as he endeavored to read her mind, but what he found there only made his hold tighten against her arm. Now that her burden had been laid upon the deserving individual, she felt a relief that made her pleasantly helpless beside Edmund's forcefully attractive masculinity. Of course, she had lied about disliking him; in fact, with a little encouragement she might possibly grow to like him a great deal, in spite of his age, but he deserved to be hated, and she would try her best to persevere in that determination. For the present she had said all she had intended to, and she moved weakly against the pressure of his hold.

"Let me go," she ordered, but her eyes opened in disbelief as he disregarded her order and continued to hold her fast.

"It is now my time to speak. You must hear me," he said coldly, and Aleen was almost frightened by the intensity of his expression. "Part of what you have spoken is true. Perhaps I deserted you after the wedding, as you say, but I felt it my duty to spend time with the guests who traveled great distances to honor us. I rarely see them, and I noticed that you were busily occupied. I have not deliberately neglected you, as you claim. I have pressing matters troubling me, regarding the government of the district. I always expected to visit with you, but I seldom find additional time. I regret that my best intentions were never realized."

Aleen's eyebrows raised in suspicion, and with a voice louder than his, she interrupted, "I find your excuses lacking in truthfulness. In the weeks I have been here, your intentions could have been realized at least once, my lord. I do not wish to hear more. Release me."

As his hand fell from her, she looked toward him with brazen contempt. "Do not bother, my lord, to find time for me. If there are matters of importance I should discuss with you, I will consult with you when you hold court. I shall wait my turn beside the peasants." She moved away, patted Cenook on the flank, and was beginning to leave when her foot brushed against the pail of water she had set beside the stall. With a clatter it fell over, sending a spray of water into the air. With a swish it fell upon her gown, and to her horror, puddled the whole area around her. At another time she would have laughed at the occurrence, but she could not indulge in amusement. The moment called for poise, and with elegant grace she shook the droplets from her skirt and delicately stepped through the water onto dry bits of straw. With regal bearing she walked away.

"I will not need Cenook today," she said to Thorkil, who was brushing a colt in the cooling shadow of a great oak. The little filly pranced about as Thorkil snapped a hasty bow.

The warm, sweet air enveloped her pleasantly as she walked toward the castle, but she was discomforted by the sense of guilt and remorse she now felt. She had always imagined that relief would settle in her soul after she unburdened herself to Edmund, but she knew she had been too harsh, too bitter with him. How could she, who had never raised her voice to anyone, save Alcuin during childish competition, have said all she had said to Edmund? What could have made her . . . ? He would hate her for it, and curiously enough, she did not want him to hate her. During many fitful nights she would dwell on this meeting and regret all that transpired in the hot, smelly, fly-infested stable. The only satisfaction she could extract from the experience was that the words were deserved. She had spoken the truth.

Edmund leaned lazily against a post, reflecting on her impassioned remarks, and knew her observations to be correct. He had deliberately avoided her, but were not the women of the castle expected to provide all her needs and to keep her amused and genteelly occupied? He knew not that they had refused to perform these expected courtesies, though in truth he had suspected it. Perhaps they were reverting to the same behavior they had displayed to Marion. He would attempt to correct this. As for his neglect of her, had not the monks always cautioned him to avoid the company of women? Of course, his association with Marion was obligatory, he reasoned, by virtue of the country's insistence on an heir, but since his vow of celibacy had been made, he was directed to avoid those plotters of sin—women who scented themselves with costly perfumes, women who adorned their bodies with jewels and beautiful fabrics for the purpose of attracting the attentions of the menfolk. They must be ignored and avoided, as any other temptation.

Edmund walked around the irregular markings made by the spilled water, made his way down the passageway between the stalls and into the open. He shadowed his eyes with his hand as he watched Aleen walking casually in the sunlight, her gown and dark hair furling in the warm breezes.

She was a woman refreshingly different from those he had encountered before. Never would any of the ladies of his acquaintance, nor any female of the district, have spoken to him in that manner, but then Aleen had a rightful reason. Her words rang true. Indeed, she was lively, spirited, different, and appealingly charming. But more importantly, she was a woman whom he had best not neglect in the future.

Edmund ran his fingers through his hair and sighed deeply as he walked toward Thorkil, who was busy picking up a bucket and cloths. "I will not ride today," Edmund said while walking past.

Thorkil squinted into the sun and shook his head from side to side. "They both came for horses, then they say they will not ride." He shrugged his shoulders and continued picking up the rags. The conduct of nobles was at times confusing and unpredictable.

# ✒ XIV ✑

DEEP BOWS and slight twists of the little body accented each step the child took as she hobbled unsteadily across the kitchen to greet Aleen. It had taken twice-weekly visits to the cottage to earn Lelia's trust, and she now delighted fully in Aleen, for Aleen always had time to play with her and listen with raptured interest to her babblings.

Aleen bent low and quickly reached out to prevent the wobbly child from falling. Lifting her up, she pressed the little body to her. "You are so smart, Lelia, to begin walking. Such gallant efforts deserve a reward." She carried the child to the table, where she had placed her basket with its customary contents of sweet cakes.

"Here, Offa," she said, signaling to the oldest child after she had handed a cake to Lelia. Offa smiled, took the basket, and with a courteous bow of which he was quite proud, began the usual ritual of dividing the cakes among all in the house.

"She is smart, is she not?" Aleen was asking as she watched Lelia hobbling toward the children. "She grows more beautiful each day," she added, without waiting for the answer to her question. "Have you heard yet from the castle regarding the child's removal?"

"No, my lady. We have heard nothing."

Aleen mulled over the words and wrinkled her brow. It had been days since Ansgar had journeyed there to remind Edmund of the child's readiness to return to her family. Why would Edmund delay so very long in welcoming his only child back to his home? Aleen turned to Edith, who was toying with a corner of her white apron. "Tell me, Edith, when Edmund comes, what does he say? What is his conduct toward the child?"

Edith bowed her head, not knowing where her loyalty lay.

Should she keep silent about the lord's shortcomings, or should she tell all to the lady, who apparently held the child's interests to heart? Without moving her head, she looked up and bit her bottom lip. "I know not how to tell you," she said quietly.

"Please," Aleen coaxed. "I am endeavoring to learn why the child has not been brought back to the castle." Edith followed Aleen to two chairs that stood a distance from the children and sat down beside her. "Please," Aleen repeated persuasively, while laying a slender white hand atop Edith's stubby red one. "I will tell no one of your disclosure. You have nothing to fear."

Edith glanced at Aleen to assess the confidence she could place in Aleen's promise. At length she began speaking. "My lady, when the lord comes, he speaks to the cobbler before coming in this room. He inquires about the health of the child, and we tell him. He always asks if there is anything we need. He stays but a few moments looking at the child, then leaves. Each visit is the same. They are sad visits. He says only what he must."

"Does he play with the child or bring her things?"

Edith thought carefully for a moment. "The lord never brings things with him. The steward from the castle provides all we need. He never plays with Lelia. I have cared for the child since her birth, and it may sound strange, but I have never seen the lord even touch her."

"He has never held the child?" Aleen asked incredulously. Her thoughts went back to her own childhood and how frequently she had crawled upon her father's lap and how often he had picked her up and placed her on his broad shoulders.

"No," Edith continued, "he stands afar, and the child seems afraid to approach him."

"She is frightened of her father?"

"I know not how to tell you, my lady. If you will not be offended, I will tell you why I think this is so," and she looked up almost timidly, waiting for a signal to commence.

"How could you offend me?" Aleen asked, looking into the round face of the dedicated nurse, who had won her respect and friendship.

"My lady, you must know that we are aware of the circumstances of your marriage to Edmund. They were the same reasons for which Edmund married the Lady Marion, but you see, my lady, the lord did not care for Marion in the beginning, but it must have been during her pregnancy that he began to love her." Edith stopped to appraise the effects of her words. Aleen's expressionless face belied her true sentiments, for a strange feeling was now stirring within her.

Lowering her voice, Edith continued. "He was distraught at her death. I saw this myself, since I attended the lady during the delivery, and later, when she died. It was sad to see him weeping beside the body. It is for this reason that I believe he behaves thus with the child. She reminds him of the wife he loved so dearly. Do you think, my lady, that the child resembles the mother?"

Aleen shrugged, not knowing what to say for the words had come crashing upon her emotions. "I think the child resembles both parents," Aleen said hastily, in an effort to conceal her confusion.

"The lord always looks sadly upon the child. It is heart-rending to see him, for his thoughts seem far away. He cannot bring himself to approach the child." Turning to Aleen, she continued solicitously. "Please do not be offended. Since you do not love Edmund, I felt you would not be affected by hearing of his love for his first wife, but, my lady, you must remember that you asked for my opinion."

"Yes, I did. It is well you told me," and attempting a smile, she added, "I am not offended by what you have said, for you assumed truly. I have no tender feelings for the lord." But what Edith had said, Aleen felt to be true, and had placed emphasis on her own suspicions. "I must be going. I have much to do," and she stood up. But she would not even admit it to herself that she felt compelled to leave the cottage and rid herself of the strange, bewildering emotions she was experiencing there.

"Good day, Bertha," she said to the cobbler's wife, who was kneading dough on the far side of the room. "Good-bye Offa, Keeta, Leoba." And turning to the nurse: "I will see you again soon."

As Aleen turned to leave, Edith called after her, "Must I

inform the castle once more about Lelia's readiness to leave here?"

"No, Edith, the time has come for me to see to it."

She left quickly through a side door to avoid being detained by the cobbler in the workshop. She was too distracted to engage in sensible conversation with anyone.

Aleen had expected her emotions to abate after her retreat from the cottage, but she had been mistaken. The nurse's words echoed repeatedly in her ears during the ride to the castle. She was too engrossed with them, too numbed and dismayed, to take notice of the beauty of the countryside in which she had always delighted on these rides. Yellow dandelions and blue cornflowers growing in profusion along the gravel road nodded in the breezes as she passed, and the fruit trees that grew in a nearby orchard stood vainly frothed in pink-and-white blossoms. Bees were busy everywhere and darted from the trees to the splotches of clover that grew within their shade.

Cenook continued his plodding, while Aleen, deep in thought, was only vaguely aware of the sprays of petals the skittish breezes were detaching from the trees and capriciously strewing about her.

Dusty horses and donkeys, hitched to rickety wagons and crude carts, stood patiently in the outer yard, heads bowed dejectedly, while their tails lazily switched persistent flies. Only once each month was such regalia permitted in such disarray within the castle walls, that being the day each month when Edmund held court to settle disputes and to exempt from taxation those who suffered from recurring sieges of ill fortune. To the others who were inspired by their own needs or who were sent there by sympathetic churchmen, there were all manner of woes to be related, and varied assistances requested.

Aleen weaved her way around the assorted conveyances and handed the reins to the stable master, who had darted forward to help her.

So Edmund was holding court this day, she thought to herself. How fortunate. If I am to speak with him about Lelia, it had best be done today. Did I not tell him if I had need to speak with him I would consult with him on court days? With firm steps and forthright determination she made her way to his office, surveyed the groups of people gathered there, and sat upon one of the stools that lined both sides of the wall outside his office. *If my presence here is cause of embarrassment to him, so be it, for I have no other alternative if I wish to speak with him.*

Time passed slowly as individuals and groups left at intervals, following their interviews. All those who remained waiting were members of the farming class, dressed in ill-fitting, faded clothing that bore the coarse weave of primitive looms. But if they were ashamed of their raiment in contrast to Aleen's colorful attire, there was no visible indication, and only an occasional glance was directed toward her. One's identity was as carefully guarded as was one's problems, and all sat quietly, eyes for the most part downcast while they considered how best to present their needs.

Shocked by the dust on the slippers that peeped from beneath the cascading folds of her yellow skirt, Aleen drew them in and brushed off the accumulation as inconspicuously as she dared. She should perhaps change or inspect and rearrange her appearance more carefully, but her mission was of much importance and could not be delayed. After she settled back against the wall, the words of the nurse echoed disturbingly from the far reaches of her mind: "During her pregnancy, the lord must have grown to love her. . . ." *What should I care,* Aleen countered, *if he fell in love with her and every woman in the castle? The man is thoughtless.* But the echoes produced an uneasiness that Aleen did not like, for she somehow envied the quiet, withdrawn, blushing Marion, who, of all people, had found fulfillment and happiness, when she, the Princess Aleen, would be denied it forever.

Lelia, that living symbol of the love that existed between Marion and Edmund, was another matter. Lelia was not only her countryman, but, by law, her daughter as well. She had a responsibility to the child, for surely no one else seemed to care. But why the child should be rejected, Aleen knew not. Lelia was appealing, and a child Aleen had found easy to care for. It would be a pleasure to look after her in the castle. It would be a joy to amuse her, to play with her and teach her many things.

As wispy as ghosts in the night, three farmers passed before her on their way out, but she was awakened from her thoughts at the sound of her name. "Yes," she said with a start.

"Would you care to go in now?" the scribe asked, bending low for her reply. Aleen looked around at the people who had been waiting long before she had joined them. "No," she replied, "I would prefer to wait my turn."

With a nod of acceptance, he was off, and signaled for the next in line to enter the office.

A stiff-necked, uncommunicative Saxon he is, but at least he is sometimes considerate, she reasoned. Several men in turn entered the office. At last she rose from her place and sat beside an elderly woman and a young boy who had settled in the chairs beside the door. She would come after this woman, and already she was becoming uneasy about how best to present her request.

The old woman leaned over and spoke around the boy who sat between them. "The Lord Edmund is so kind that I thank God each day I live in his district," the old woman said in confidential tones, her smile revealing the loss of two teeth.

"Indeed?" Aleen said, looking into the leathery, sunburned face.

"Do you know the lord well?" the woman asked.

"No," Aleen replied indifferently.

"When I lived in Wessex," the woman continued, "the Earl of Crexburgh was guardian of my district. When he held court—ah, it was different from the way Edmund does." She threw her head back in amusement at her comparison. "He and the Lady Aethelah wore their regal robes and crowns, soldiers guarded their persons, anyone who lived in the castle was free to wander into the room to listen to our grievances, and more often than not our requests were not granted. Those were hard times," she said, shaking her head, "very hard times. Can you think of anyone more kind and generous than the Lord Edmund?" she asked with conviction.

Aleen shrugged her shoulders.

The old woman squinted under her bushy gray eyebrows. "You say you do not know Edmund?" It seemed unheard of that such a well-dressed lady would not know Edmund or immediately react favorably to her question.

"Yes, I know the lord, but not well."

Both women looked up as the door opened and a poorly clad man emerged bowing and repeatedly saying, "God bless you, God bless you."

Aleen was relieved that the chatter was terminated, and she breathed easier when the old woman lifted her faded shawl onto her head, took the boy by the hand, and hobbled into the room.

Aleen moved into the chair vacated by the woman as two latecomers took up places beside her. In the silence of the almost empty corridor, words came to her ears. It was the voice of the woman, and glancing to the door, Aleen saw that it was ajar. With no effort at all she could hear their remarks, but then, it would not be right for her to listen to such an intimate disclosure. Still, the words came. . . .

"You say the Reverend Cynric sent you?" Edmund said over the sound of crackling parchment. A moment's silence, and then: "How can I assist you?"

"My lord," the woman began, the words coming faintly, "my husband died many years ago, as the document states, and I have tried by myself to keep my daughter's boy. She and her husband were killed in the raid at the Bramham Moor two years ago, leaving me to care for this child and an infant who has since died. I had to sell my cattle and stock to buy grain and supplies, and, and . . ." The words dissolved into pitiful sobs.

A shuffling of feet, and Aleen recognized Edmund's consoling voice, "There, there, do not worry. I am here to help you. You have nothing to fear. Tell me what it is you wish."

Between pitiful sobs she added, "I have no money, my lord."

After a moment Edmund asked, "You have no one to help you?"

"No, I have no family left except this boy."

"Then I shall help you. Do you own your home and land?"

"Yes, my lord. I have a small cottage and a plot of land."

"Far from here?"

"No, my lord. I live in the village of Hertford, near the cathedral."

"Very well," Edmund said, and called for Wulfric. "Write down these orders. This woman is to be provided with sufficient grain to supply her needs for sixty days. She is to be given a horse, a decent one, mind you, a cow with a calf, several fowl and geese. She is to be given any seed she desires."

"Taxes, my lord?"

"Taxes?" Edmund shouted incredulously. "This woman is not to be taxed. Instead, refund the taxes paid by her husband during the last five years of his life." His voice softened. "How old are you, my boy?"

"I am ten, my lord."

"Are you in good health?"

"Yes, my lord."

"Would you care to work here in the castle? We are sorely in need of a boy to assist the steward. Would you be able to help him?"

"Yes, my lord," the boy answered enthusiastically.

"Could you ride here each morning except on the Lord's day? I will pay you well, and with your earnings you will be enabled to care for your grandmother."

"Yes, my lord. I will come every day."

In a different tone Edmund continued, "If there is anything more you need, or any service I can render, you will notify me, will you not?"

"Yes, my lord," the old woman sniffed.

There were steps, and then a whisper near the door: "Wulfric, see that they are fed well before they depart, and see to it that they are escorted back to their home. The woman seems too weak to travel alone."

Aleen was stunned by what she had heard, and like phantoms, the faces of the peasants who cheered them on their wedding day came to mind. There was no doubting why he was so dearly loved. How compassionate and generous he was with them.

The door swung open, and the old woman emerged holding a linen handkerchief against her mouth with a gnarled, thickly veined hand. The boy followed, wearing a look of pride and happiness that warmed the hearts and brightened the spirits of those who saw him.

Perhaps I have judged him too harshly, Aleen thought as she waited to be summoned. Wulfric returned from where he had taken the woman and boy and motioned for Aleen to enter. She followed him into the room and watched carefully as he closed the door behind her. No one must overhear them, and as she walked the length of the room she had inspected so carefully on the day of her arrival, she blushed furiously at the sight of Edmund and the remembrance of their last meeting in the stable. In a moment she had evaluated the situation. Edmund did not wear the royal garments she had almost expected, no guards were present, and no one was permitted to enter except the scribe, who was to write down Edmund's orders. Let me see how considerate and compassionate he will be concerning his daughter, she thought as she stopped before the desk where Edmund was writing.

Presently the scratching stopped, and he laid down the quill. "I am grateful for your patience," he said, blowing on the parchment, which glistened with wet ink. He smiled as he looked up, but his smile quickly changed to a quizzical grin. "Lady Aleen," he said with surprise.

"Yes, my lord," she said, trying not to sound sarcastic. Something about his attitude made her defensive, but she was not as nervous as she had expected to be. Catching him by surprise had placed neither of them at an advantage.

Wulfric climbed upon a high stool behind a tall writing desk, took quill in hand, dipped it into a jar of ink, and waited.

"If you have a problem, Aleen, I shall be most interested to hear it. What does it concern?" There was a hint of amusement in his voice as he leaned back, placed both elbows on the arms of the chair, and interlaced his fingers.

"It is not a problem, my lord," Aleen said, as though striking back. "I am here because of the child Lelia." Aleen avoided his stare and looked upon the battle shields hung on the wall behind his desk. This was no time for nervousness or timidity, and the ever-changing expression on his face was

138

both distracting and disconcerting, for even now his amusement had changed into one of almost predatory alertness.

"You may wait outside, Wulfric," Edmund said, turning slightly to the scribe's desk. "There will be no need for notes."

Wulfric climbed down from his stool and left the room noiselessly, as was his custom. "Continue," Edmund said after the scribe's departure.

Aleen gathered her thoughts, drew herself tall, and continued matter-of-factly. "Lelia is part Dane and is my kinsman. According to the laws of Kent, I am her new mother by reason of our marriage. Therefore, I feel it proper that I take interest in her well-being." She paused for Edmund to contradict, but no comment was made, and she continued. "It has been many months since the child has withdrawn her dependence on the services of Bertha, the cobbler's wife. It would seem time to remove her to the castle. I request your permission to do this."

No remark, no movement was made for interminable minutes. Presently Edmund rose from his place, slowly walked around his desk, and more slowly passed to her side and back.

What a disheveled sight I am, Aleen thought with a rush of self-consciousness. Her dress was wrinkled from her ride to and from the village, the hem was dusty in the back where she had not brushed it, and her hair was terribly windblown. She could feel his scrutinizing inspection. If only he would sit down.

"You have been to the cottage?" he asked, looking upon the pink petals that had become entangled in her hair.

"Yes, I have just returned."

"The child is well?"

"Yes, my lord, she is quite well. She is strong, and quite ready to be moved here."

"Would you agree that the child would be happier remaining there for a longer time with the cobbler's children? There will be few if any companions here of her own age."

"My lord," Aleen said, turning abruptly, "you mean to keep her there indefinitely and submit her and us to the criticism of the villagers and perhaps of all the people here as well? Already the villagers are whispering that because of her deformity she is not wanted here." Her flaring anger abated, and she was struck with shock at her own words and attitude. Turning back toward the desk, she continued in a more subdued manner. "I feel we must now stop these criticisms. I also feel that the child should leave the home before she becomes even more attached to the children. She is a good child, and should adjust nicely to the separation and the change. Besides, she needs the attentions of her family."

For a moment there was silence, until Edmund spoke. "You feel you know her well?"

"Yes. I have visited her often. We have become good friends."

"You are not repelled by her deformity?"

"I am not!" Aleen replied emphatically, and indignantly turned to face him.

"I merely ask," he said, raising a hand to quiet her. He seemed pleased with her reply. He walked to his desk, sat down, and leaned back in his former position. "You mean to supervise her care?"

"With your permission, of course. Edith will assist me and will stay in Lelia's chambers until the child is much older. I will help amuse her. When she is older, I will teach her to read and write. I have much time to devote to her." Aleen stopped. She did not intend to plead her case, merely to state it.

Edmund studied her through narrowed eyes. Silence beat against her ears, until finally he spoke. "Very well. I entrust her to your care."

It was difficult to hide her joy, but as far as she knew, her face remained expressionless. As she turned, she fairly skipped from the room, but before she had reached the door, Edmund called after her. "When do you mean to move her?"

"Tomorrow," Aleen replied. "Yes. Early tomorrow."

## ⌁ XV ⌁

IT WAS a difficult and hasty farewell. No advance notice had
been given. The cobbler's household had been startled in their
early-morning occupations by Aleen and her entourage of
servants, who drew by the side entrance with their creaking
carts. Bertha cried into her apron. Even though the departure
of the child had always been expected, and more so during
the past weeks, the inevitable separation was heartbreaking. It
was difficult losing a child one had suckled during infancy,
tenderly nursed during illness, played with, fed, and bathed as
carefully and lovingly as one's own. Ansgar stood by, patting
his wife's shoulder with dye-stained hands, but he too was
disheartened. Lelia had laid claim to a portion of his love.
Often he had held her on his lap while telling stories to the
children, who gathered each night around his chair before the
fire. Wintry winds had blown furiously outside, but near the
fire was contentment and love, and often were the evenings
when Lelia had fallen asleep with her fat cheeks resting
lightly against his heart. Often too were the times when she
had sought refuge in his arms.

Servants scurried around packing clothing into chests under Edith's directions, while Lelia's few pieces of little furniture, which Aleen felt would make familiar additions to her
new surroundings, were stacked high on the cart.

Bertha nodded her head at intervals as she forced back
tears during Aleen's whispered reassurances. "And you
know," Aleen said, grasping the cobbler's hand, "that we will
always expect you to make her little shoes. You alone know
best how to make them. We will come whenever a new pair
is needed, and please bring Bertha and the children to the
castle for visits whenever you like."

Aleen was tempted to cry at the sight of the cobbler picking up the child, who was dressed in her finest, and pressing

her against his leather work apron. His thin, snarly beard pressed for a moment against her small pink face. A kiss and much blinking on his part, and the child was released to Bertha, who kissed her and impulsively pressed the little cherub face into her expansive middle.

Aleen carried Lelia through the crowd that had gathered, to where two villagers stood, one man proudly holding Cenook, while the other had delegated himself to helping the royal lady mount. It was fortunate that her full gathered skirt permitted her to ride astride the horse. In that position, Lelia was placed on the saddle before her, where Aleen could support her with more safety.

A roar of mingled farewells and a waving of countless hands, and they were off, Cenook carrying his precious charges through the cobbled streets with high, prancing steps.

When the clusters of stores and homes were passed and the orchard and meadow lay before them, Aleen directed Lelia's attention to the fields, where curving rows were adorned with green-tinged wisps of wheat. "When it grows tall, we will see it waving in the wind, and we will watch as they cut it down and gather it. And I will take you to the miller, and we will watch as the great stone crushes the grain fine. And perhaps the miller will give us some to be made into bread or cakes for our dear Lelia. You have a great deal to see and learn, my sweet," and she continued with a rush of joy as her arm tightened about the child, "I will be happy to show and teach you all."

"Wave, Lelia," Aleen encouraged as they passed a farmer walking to the fields with his spade and hoe resting angularly against his shoulder. A short distance farther she was tempted to draw in and permit Lelia to watch another farmer and his oxen tilling the soil. "We cannot stop now, Lelia, we will watch another time. Your father awaits you, and little girls must not keep fathers waiting."

Edmund was in the great hall, languidly sitting in a huge chair reading the steward's accounts. Now that it was spring and the fireplace was no longer needed, his thronelike chair had been moved from before the blackened grate to a side wall, where thick red fabrics were draped behind it. The shield bearing the dragon-head insignia of Lauxburgh hung above the chair, and shields representing the other districts of southern England were hung in rows on either side. The room seemed larger by its rearrangement and was empty save for Edmund and the steward.

Aleen and Lelia waited to the side while Edmund examined the papers before him and repeatedly asked questions of the steward regarding them. The consultation assumed such length that Lelia became fidgety. "He will talk forever," Aleen finally said. She inspected the child she was carrying in her arms, arranged the small skirt, and pushed back the golden curls from her forehead. "We cannot wait forever," she said, walking forthrightly toward the dais. At once the steward stood tall and walked away, and Edmund, seeing who it was, sat motionless.

"Lelia has arrived, my lord," Aleen said happily as she stood the child down and held the little hand reassuringly. Lelia stared with large blue eyes at the unsmiling giant of a man before her, became intimidated, pulled her hand from Aleen's gentle hold, and reached into Aleen's skirts, peeping at Edmund from behind the folds.

"Lelia, greet your father," Aleen pleaded, but Lelia could not be made to loosen her hold, and Aleen found herself in an awkward stance, with the child pressing frantically against her, almost throwing her off balance.

"The castle is new to the child, and I fear she is displaying understandable fear at the vastness of her surroundings. Soon she will become adjusted to the change," Aleen offered by way of discounting the child's fear of her father.

"There is no need for apology," he said kindly, though visibly disturbed by the child's reaction to him. "Are her rooms prepared?"

"Yes." But Aleen paused. "There was only one chamber in the family's sector large enough for our purposes, my lord." The words came haltingly as she watched for his reaction. "I gave the child the rooms next to your own. Marion's former chamber. I desire that the child be near both of us, and it was the only chamber unoccupied."

Aleen saw with a degree of alarm how Edmund's penetrating gaze intensified at her words, until she felt he could see against the background of her soul all the tender and sad events that had transpired in that chamber. "No one said the rooms were prohibited," Aleen apologized, "but if you would prefer I place her elsewhere . . ."

"No," he said, shaking his head. "She may occupy the rooms if they are suitable to her needs."

"Yes, my lord."

The meeting had raced to a conclusion. Aleen looked from Edmund to the child. It had been weeks since his last visit to her. Were there to be no kindly words for Lelia? A fatherly touch or embrace? But Edmund made no motion.

"Good day, sir," Aleen said, while disengaging Lelia's hand and picking her up. As they turned to leave, Edmund's steady gaze saddened as memories came freshly to mind with the appearance of his deformed daughter. His self-accusations and guilt with regard to Marion, his cold impersonal relationship with her, and the painful end he had unwittingly brought upon her lashed at his conscience until his heart bled with remorse. The presence of the child within the castle was all that was needed for the painful wounds of recollection to continually burst asunder and fester.

Aleen and Lelia were midway through the room when Aleen stopped and again approached Edmund. Immediately on hearing her steps, he dropped his hand from before his eyes and looked wearily upon her.

"Sir, should I now bring the child to Wilfreda?"

"No," Edmund snapped, and then added sullenly, "She is quite busy for the moment. She will call upon the child later."

Aleen scarcely heard the words, so intent was she on Edmund's manner and expression, for she could not recall ever having seen such a distressful look on anyone's face.

My God, she thought, Edith spoke truly. The child stirs thoughts of Marion. He still loves her so.

Lelia beamed as Edith, Hester, and Aleen turned around her to view her clothing from all angles. Each nodded her head approvingly. The soft blue dress fitted the child nicely, and the delicate white embroidery around the neck was a dainty and lovely adornment.

"You do lovely work, Edith. Such fine stitches," Aleen said, passing her hand lightly over the geometric design.

"It is a pleasure sewing for the child, my lady. She makes all things appear better than what they are."

"How modest you are," Aleen replied teasingly. "She does look beautiful, does she not?"

"Yes, she gives honor to both parents."

A frown developed on Aleen's face at the words, but she promptly dispelled it and said cheerily, "Let us go, Lelia. We must be on time for the evening meal. There will be many people there who will want to see you. Come along."

It was nearing time for the evening social period, which would reach a peak during the evening meal and continue long after the plates were cleared away. It would be an excellent time for Lelia to become acquainted with the people she would live with until such time as her own marriage would remove her to another castle.

Aleen held back her steps and measured them to the still-unsteady, limping steps of the child.

Of course, the vain, highborn ladies would be there. They may reject me because I am Viking, she thought, but I should not fear that they would react in a similar fashion toward the child, since she is half Saxon. Yet, what if they ignore Lelia? No, they would not dare if Edmund is there. They would not wish to earn his displeasure.

The diners had not yet arrived. The servants were still setting up the tables, but the food had been brought in from the outside kitchen to warm on the inner stoves, and the savory odors filled the room.

Wilfreda was speaking with the steward at one end of the room and reading at times from a paper she held. When agreements were reached, Aleen grasped for Lelia's hand. "There is someone special you must meet, Lelia.

"Wilfreda," she said, causing the bowed head to rise, "this is Lelia," and Aleen smiled down at the child. But her pride in Lelia was not shared, for Wilfreda looked down as impersonally as though she were inspecting the slate floor. "We intended to visit you when Lelia first arrived, but were told you were occupied and would call on us later. I trust you were not offended by our failure to call on you immediately."

"I was not offended," Wilfreda replied indifferently.

Aleen was stunned as her thoughts raced on. Wilfreda had not been surprised by the child's appearance there. Perhaps Edmund had informed her of the child's arrival, but Wilfreda, it would seem, cared not if the child visited with her or not.

"She resembles the mother," Wilfreda said with detachment as she turned again to her paper.

Her whole attitude was disdainful, and Aleen's irritation was beginning to activate. Wilfreda must have instincts toward her grandchild as did all grandmothers, yet she was effectively suppressing them. This was no way to react to meeting the only child of one's favorite son. There should be loving words, hugs, a kiss or two, and perhaps even a tear. This utter detachment was too much to accept dispassionately.

Wilfreda's words further disturbed Aleen, and looking down on the child who was standing against her, Aleen remembered with clarity Marion's thin face and weak features. The child might bring Marion to mind, but she far from resembled her. She resembles Edmund, Aleen thought through a mist of confusion. Lelia has light hair, as her mother had, and blue eyes, but her face distinctly resembles her father's. Lelia's were well-rounded, well-defined features. . . .

"You observe the child too casually, Wilfreda," Aleen said with ill-concealed sarcasm. "The child clearly resembles your son."

No reply was made, but Wilfreda gave Aleen a long, sly look from the corner of her eye and walked away.

It cannot be so, Aleen thought bewilderingly as she led the child to a bench against a wall, where Edmund's dogs lay dozing. She sees not the Saxon, but the Dane. She wishes to ignore the child, and the father cannot find it within himself to approach her. Lelia could do without Wilfreda's interest, and perhaps it were better so, but Edmund? His love was essential. Little girls cannot mature properly without the love of their fathers.

As they sat waiting for the diners to collect, Aleen remembered her own pride in her father, how other fathers scurried about to obey his commands, how he ordered ships and warriors around with absolute surety, and above all, she remembered how he kissed her tenderly and the times he spent telling of his daring exploits. Lelia was also fortunate in having a father any child would be proud of, and she, Aleen, would see that their mutual respect and love flourished.

Groups of people began collecting in the room, but their comradely closeness prevented intrusion, and Aleen soon realized she would be unable to present the child to them. It would be more proper for Edmund to do so, she reasoned. When Edmund and the Reverend Jerome entered, walked to the head of the main table, and sat down together, Aleen reached for Lelia, who had been stroking the dogs, and led her to the table, but before they reached the bench beside Edmund, one of the noblewomen took the privileged place and sat tall with pride at her lucky acquisition. But Aleen was not to be so easily displaced. She had planned to place Lelia beside her father, and with Reverend Jerome on his other side, the lady would have to remove herself.

"Please be so kind as to make room for the child," Aleen said politely. The young lady, flustered by the request, looked to Edmund, who had started with surprise at Aleen's and Lelia's presence beside the table. But Aleen stood waiting, and the lady had no alternative but to begrudgingly move along the bench until there was sufficient room for both Aleen and Lelia.

"We are most grateful," Aleen said as she sat down and placed Lelia at the corner of the table next to Edmund. But she was not grateful. The woman had been one of those who had discourteously walked from the sewing room. She needed to know her place. I am Edmund's wife, Aleen thought disgruntledly, and I sit where it pleases me.

The meal began pleasantly enough. There were complimentary remarks for Lelia from the women who wished to flatter Edmund, but when Wilfreda joined the diners, interests were diverted to more general topics. Aleen was convinced as she watched their stealthy glances toward Lelia that many wished to amuse or be amused by Lelia, yet somehow knew Wilfreda's dispositions toward this child and perhaps toward most children as well.

Aleen did not know that youngsters, even those related to nobles, officers, or councilmen, were an annoyance to Wilfreda even though they were closely supervised and restricted in their areas of movement inside the castle. All parents, save a few, were pressured until they sought lodging elsewhere. Knowing this about the woman who so insidiously influenced their lives, and not wishing to lose favor in her sight, the women resolved to ignore Lelia, as they had so readily disregarded her mother.

Lelia had little interest in her food, and preferred to sit with her head turned toward Aleen, as though afraid to look in the direction of her father.

Two conversations soon progressed. Edmund and Reverend Jerome were engaged in their own discussion, while others at the table were busy with various topics over which Judith presided with fluttering eyelashes and frequent glances toward the head of the table.

At no time were Aleen's opinions asked for, nor was she included in the conversation, although she was sitting opposite Wilfreda. When the meal was completed, however, Judith directed her attentions to Aleen with such deliberateness that all at table listened carefully, except Edmund and the priest, who were arguing a point of ethics.

"That brooch, Aleen, is most interesting," Judith stated. "How came you by it?"

Aleen looked down to her bosom, where the golden brooch held the folds of her dress at a modest level. "It belonged to my mother," she said, running her fingers across the symbols in the metal. "It was given to her many years before her death by the queen of Brithweald, who was cousin to her. The designs have special significance," she continued, holding it at an angle for most to see, "but I do not know their meaning." All sat waiting for Aleen to continue. The embarrassment she felt at their unusual interest in her made her want to relieve it with more explanations. "I was told the queen drew the design and had it made at great expense with the purest gold. It has been my favorite ornament since my youth."

Judith folded her arms on the table and listened skeptically, as though waiting for Aleen to step unwarily into a trap, but neither noticed that Edmund had diverted his attention to the exchange.

"If you find the brooch pleasing, you may have it," Aleen offered, mistaking Judith's interest as a gesture of friendship.

"I would not accept it," Judith said with sneering aloofness. "It seems my sister lost a similar brooch during the invasion of Faversham."

Aleen did not know how she could survive such humiliation. Judith had meant to shame her by recalling the Danish foray and had implied that the brooch Aleen had loved as a relic of her dead mother was but a trinket collected in the raid, which, by devious means, had found its way into her hands.

The silence was intense until Edmund spoke. "May I see the brooch?"

Aleen fumbled with the clasp and then reached across Lelia to hand it to him. All eyes were watching, but only Judith seemed to take satisfaction in the situation.

"The name of the queen is inscribed on the back. Is this the same one lost by your sister?" And he held it for Judith to inspect.

Judith stared at the inscription, lowered her eyes, and made no reply.

"Judith," Edmund repeated, "is this the brooch belonging to your sister?"

"No," she replied contemptuously. "No, it is not," and she placed her hands demurely in her lap.

"Queen Aelfguar, was she not sent into exile on the death of her husband?" Edmund asked by way of alleviating the difficult situation. Aleen did not answer, and he continued. "It is my belief she traveled in secret to France. For all we know, she may still be living there. Has your family heard from her in recent years?"

"No," Aleen replied. "I know nothing of her." Making certain the meal was completed by everyone so that her departure would not be construed as a transgression of proper observances, Aleen stood up under the gaze of all and waited for the child. "Come, Lelia, we must go."

"Here, Aleen, your brooch," Edmund said, holding it up to her.

"Judith may have it," Aleen replied. "It can replace the one lost by her sister." Judith shrugged indifferently and turned her head away in declination. "Deposit it, then, in the treasury," Aleen said almost inaudibly. "Bid your father good evening, Lelia," she coaxed, but the child only looked timidly at him.

"Good evening, Lelia," Edmund said stiffly as Aleen promptly picked up the child and left the room. That Edmund had come to her defense, that Judith was in turn justifiably belittled, in no way assuaged her own pain, for this time she had been humiliated not just before the women in the sewing room, but before Edmund and all at table, and before the night would end, everyone would know of it. I shall never be shamed by them again. I shall see to that, she vowed. And I shall be certain no one offends Lelia, either.

Edmund defended me, she realized with a rush of excitement as the full implication of his actions settled upon her. He defended me. Perhaps I have judged him too harshly. He is indeed a protector, she thought, remembering the old woman in his office. A defender of the accused. And she knew she would forever be grateful that he had rescued her. Then, too, he had wished Lelia a good day, and she could not help smiling at both thoughts.

By the time the sun set behind the castle wall and darkness began closing in, Lelia was ready for bed. It had been an eventful day, and all Lelia needed was to be lifted into bed and covered. Like the cherubs she resembled, she succumbed quickly to the sleep of the innocent.

"Sleep well, my love," Aleen whispered as the child settled her head on the fluff of pillow. You are so good, Aleen thought, and so small. But of course it was the huge bed that made her appear so—Marion's bed, the bed on which Edmund had lain with Marion. But it was also the bed on which Marion had given birth and had died as a result. The room was so still now, and in the soft candlelight it was difficult to imagine that once this room contained worried physicians and priests reciting the prayers for the dying. So this is where it ended for you, Marion. And Aleen ran her fingers along the desks, chairs, and tables Marion had used during her brief marriage.

"You will be comfortable here?" Aleen whispered to Edith, who was tiptoeing about.

"Oh, yes, my lady. This is a most satisfactory arrangement," and she pointed to a corner of the room that had been curtained off for her.

"You remember, Edith, that Edmund's chamber is through that door, and that my chamber is beyond that one," Aleen said, indicating the opposite side of the room. "Call either of us if we can help you."

Aleen fell silent while standing beside the door that connected the room to Edmund's. It was strange how their friendship had taken such a pleasant turn. Edmund had defended her, and by so doing, had won not only her gratitude but a portion of respect as well. It is no wonder Marion loved him so.

Aleen had no way of knowing that in the next room Edmund's thoughts were on her, even as hers were occupied with him. Edmund had kept the brooch in his fist and was now examining it in the privacy of his chamber. An ornament that a daughter had treasured since childhood as a reminder of a mother she had never known could not be so easily cast into the treasury. The pin must be returned, Edmund thought, while placing it carefully in a drawer of his desk.

## ✤ XVI ✦

THE CASTLE had acquired an atmosphere of desertion.
Edmund had left several days before on an inspection tour of
two large shires, taking a cordon of soldiers and some of his
councilmen with him, and leaving Wulfric and Wilfreda in
charge of Lauxburgh's affairs. There was no way of estimat-
ing how long he would be gone, for the inspection of each
holding could take days to accomplish.

With Edmund gone, the increased responsibilities made
Wilfreda even more strained and stern than before, and when
Aleen received word she wished to see her, Aleen's mind
leaped about presumptuously. Wilfreda was not one to invite
her for an amicable discourse. She was too busy for that. Perhaps—and her mind toyed amusedly with the thought—perhaps there was a matter in which she could assist her. As
Edmund's wife, she could perform certain duties in his name.
It seemed unlikely, but yet, perhaps it could concern some
matters of state.

Wilfreda was one whose friendship Aleen was eager to fos-
ter. She was the dispenser of favors and privileges, the model
upon which the conduct and opinions of the castle were
based, and was the shrewd manipulator of people's affairs
and values. Wilfreda was clearly one to be wary of, and if
her friendship could be won, Aleen for one was eager to do
all, anything at all, to win her acceptance.

Rapping gently on the door of Wilfreda's chamber, Aleen
listened closely for the invitation to enter. Then, when it was
sounded, Aleen walked in as tremulously as though she were
treading sacred ground. Wilfreda, she saw, was sitting behind
a desk covered with small books and a neat collection of papers.

"Aleen," she said in serious tones as she put down the papers she had been studying. Picking up another paper, she

continued, "The scribe Wulfric has asked me to give you a message received this morning from Wermouth. It concerns your father." Wilfreda studied the pleasant face that suddenly tensed with curiosity.

"Yes?" Aleen responded as she stood before the desk.

"Your father had been ill for some time?" Wilfreda asked, unfolding the crackling parchment.

"Yes, he has," Aleen replied, her curiosity leaping into a wild surge of dread.

Wilfreda nodded and looked upon the paper. "This missive contains the official announcement of your father's death, which occurred a fortnight ago. He was afforded the sacraments of the church and was buried ceremoniously in the churchyard at Wermouth. Your brother was not present. It states further that your father died in his sleep of a serious malady. You knew of this fatal infirmity?"

Aleen was shocked by the words, yet there was the necessity of answering. "I knew my father was not well, but I was never told it was of a fatal nature."

It could not be true, she thought, as she was swept up in a fog of unreality. Fergus could not be dead, not the powerful man whose orders rumbled like thunder and were obeyed quickly, lest the lightning of his displeasure strike the unfortunate who dawdled with their enforcement. The handsome, virile man who laughed in the face of danger could not have succumbed to illness.

"They wished to spare you the truth." Wilfreda's voice came to her as she thrust the parchment toward Aleen.

It was the conclusion of the conference, and a signal to leave, but Aleen could not comprehend the reality of the situation. Her father had died, and she was told of it as easily as if Wilfreda were telling her of the late arrival of some ordered fabrics. No words of sympathy were uttered, and if Wilfreda would have given voice to her thoughts, she would have declared the country, all of England, fortunate to be rid of the despised Dane.

Seeing Aleen tarrying, Wilfreda added over the sound of flapping papers, "Aleen, at another time I wish to speak with you concerning a matter of some importance. It is necessary that you call on me when you can spare me time from your duties with the child."

The cynicism of the words was lost to Aleen. Her heart was heavy with grief, and she wished she could scream and shout her disbelief, to give vent to the pressure within her, but she held fast to the restraining controls of her emotions and fought back tears of sorrow. I will not show weakness before this woman, she pledged, and immediately corrected her posture and relaxed her frown. "Would you care to tell me of this matter now?" Aleen asked meekly.

"No, you will want to go to chapel to pray for your father. It can wait, but," she said with emphasis, "I feel I must tell you of it before Edmund returns."

Aleen's curiosity was now acutely aroused, in spite of having to concentrate on fighting back the tears of the heart. "I prefer that you speak of it now, Wilfreda."

Wilfreda looked hard at the slender figure before her. "I fear the discussion will be difficult for you to hear and accept." She paused, but Aleen added quickly, "It is kind of you to be so considerate, but I wish to hear of it now."

"Very well, then. You may sit down."

With hands folded neatly before her, Wilfreda began walking about as she arranged her thoughts, her face assuming harsher lines as she did so. Crossing behind the chair in which Aleen sat, she began. "I will speak plainly, for the matter requires forthright honesty. You will recall the conditions under which your marriage to my son was contracted. Had it not been for the murder of the monks at the Wetson monastery and the desecration of the Shrine of Saint Dunsley, and then the subsequent murder of two nuns and the attack on the others at Chatham, the marriage might not have been solemnized. Did you know that my sister is the abbess of that convent, and that she, too, along with the nuns, was brutally attacked? Holy nuns, these women were, and they were brutally attacked." The words were cold as steel and were lashed at Aleen with vengeance.

Wilfreda straightened, took a deep breath, and struggled to control the nervous twitching of her face. Continuing to pace behind Aleen's chair, she proceeded with the tirade. "The marriage is a temporary condition until such time as another means of maintaining a lasting peace is found. You know full well that my son has intentions of returning to the monastery. With all this considered, you would do well to dismiss any thought you may have of altering his plans from this commitment. It would be appreciated if you would refrain from contacting him directly concerning matters of small consequence."

Aleen sat tall, catching at intervals the swaying of Wilfreda's skirts as she turned to repeat her circuit.

"With regard to the child," Wilfreda said, "we would also be most thankful if you would not make her so conspicuous. The deformity is repulsive to many, and you would do well to discontinue calling attention to yourself at the expense of the child."

The words were wielded as a drawn sword, yet Aleen made no move to defend herself, and instead permitted Wilfreda to continue the disclosure of her thoughts, much as Edmund had once done to her in the arena of the stable.

"You maneuvered," the voice bitterly continued, "until my son gave his consent for the child's transfer here, but you neglected to consider that it would have been better for the child had she remained where she was."

Aleen could refrain no longer and interrupted with a quiet dignity that sharply contrasted Wilfreda's inelegant behavior. "You are ashamed of the child?" Aleen asked, turning to look into the eyes of her accuser.

Wilfreda seemed taken aback by the question, and stuttered the beginning of a reply.

"She is your son's child, Wilfreda. Have you no feeling for her?"

"She is not my son's child," Wilfreda snapped, her eyes glaring. "My son could not produce such a child. There are no deformities in our family. She is wholly Dane, and cursed by the Lord for the sins of her people."

The cruel words of rejection and accusation stabbed at Aleen's heart. "You speak thusly and yet claim to be Christian?" she asked quietly, and stood to face Wilfreda directly. "Listen well to me, Wilfreda. Your son readily gave me leave to bring the child here where she would be surrounded by her family. I see now she has no family. Since you renounce any relationship to her, and since Edmund gave her completely to my charge, I shall decide how best to oversee her well-being. Hear me well, Wilfreda. I will take her wherever I please, whether or not you are ashamed of her, or the others here are sensitive to her deformity. As for your son and his virtue—I assure you I do not desire to tempt him or lead him from the goals to which he aspires. However, if I should in time deviate from this resolve, I assure you I would not require a child to attract him to me. I desire to speak no further about this. Are there other matters that must be called to my attention?"

Wilfreda was glaring at her in impotent rage and made no reply.

"Very well, then," Aleen said, turning away. "Good day." And she glided from the room as though unaffected by their discourse.

Once in the hall, she leaned against the wall for support as trembling seized her. Suddenly she jumped at the sound of crockery crashing against the door beside her. The whole world has turned insane, she thought, while what seemed like suffocating air closed in around her. She lurched through the hall to escape it; then, as if propelled by unknown forces, she rushed down stairs and through halls and crossed the court-yard to the stables. Frantically she paced outside the stable while Cenook was being saddled. Then, snatching the reins from Thorkil, she mounted and spurred Cenook toward the gate. Turning to the left, they raced along the castle wall to the meadow, scaling bushes and thundering across the green. Back and forth she flew, the wind beating against her face and streaking through her hair, while her skirt and scarf beat wildly against her. From the castle wall, across the emerald turf, to the edge of the forest and back again, she rode, all the while unaware that on the road leading from the cathedral to Lauxburgh, a group of riders was watching her with interest. Edmund, in the lead, shielded his eyes from the sun, squinted into the distance, and recognized the rider. As they neared the castle, and the wall threatened to block his view, he fell back in the rank. Then, upon reaching the end of the file, he halted entirely and watched until Aleen drew in her steed and permitted him to walk along while he panted and snorted for breath.

Edmund nudged his horse forward and entered the castle gate. With his usually large lunging strides, he covered the distance to his chamber, and while unhooking his mantle, looked down on the papers neatly arranged on his desk. He was tired, and the papers were of no particular importance or interest. He walked to the line of hooks that held his belts, scabbard, and shirts, and hung his mantle beside them. But as he was untying his tunic, he passed the window, paused, and looked out upon the meadow. Not seeing the rider who had been there moments before, he walked nearer and looked out more intently.

Aleen was still upon her mount at the edge of the meadow, where the land gently inclined into the stirring waters of the bay. Slumped in the saddle, she looked out upon the waters that separated her from her home and the grave of her father. There were times for bravery and times for tears, and this was a time when she could justifiably surrender to self-pity. It was a sad day, an unfortunate day, when a dreadful enemy had been made and a beloved father had been lost forever.

The gentle waters swirled about the boulders that jutted from their sandy foundations, and the gulls that had been sitting upon them beat their wings, rose into the air, and swooped excitedly above a swarm of minnows. Beyond the bay, storm clouds were gathering, and lightning flashed against their darkness. But the rider could not be distracted, and sat motionless, while Edmund, from his vantage place, knew that she was crying bitterly.

The loss was acute, and for days Aleen remained in her chamber. her mind returning time and again to Wermouth, remembering the happy days of her youth when she thrived and flowered to her father's prideful approval. Lelia's entreaties for her attention provided only temporary distractions, and even while the child amused herself in the rooms, sometimes rather noisily, the face and form of Fergus returned in wispy form to haunt the mind that could not comprehend a world without his love and fatherly concern. If only Alcuin were here to provide consolation. There was Hester, but Fergus' death seemed to plunge her deeper into the thoughts that made her appear at times to be walking in a world of dreams. So great was Hester's withdrawal that Aleen wondered if Fergus' death had not stirred recollections of another's death, perhaps of someone Hester had loved dearly, someone who had returned that love. Many times Aleen believed Hester to be burdened with recollections even weightier and more haunting than her own.

What was it she had said not long ago concerning excessive devotion and prolonged grief for the dead? The stifling stables came to mind, and the afternoon when she had unexpectedly met Edmund there as he prepared to make his monthly pilgrimage to Marion's grave. What had she said about his obsession with the dead and his neglect of the living? She had upbraided him that day for his neglect of her, and now she was in need of a reprimand, for she too was guilty of a similar misjudgment. Another's happiness depended on her adjustment to her sorrow. She had indulged in self-pity long enough.

It was a beautiful, sunshiny day. A good day to shake away the bonds of grief, and the best place to loosen them was by the sea. The refreshing salty breezes were enough to renew and strengthen the spirit of any Viking. She would take the child, and together they would experience this renewal. Hand in hand they left their rooms and walked down the hall, but an open door that exposed a shelf of books caught Aleen's fancy, and she paused at the door. It was a library, and one filled with interesting objects and wall hangings. There were tables piled high with rolls of huge maps, and another was stacked with rolls of parchments wound about rods whose handles were elaborately carved. There were many books, and in a corner of the room were jeweled cups, golden daggers, gilded plates, ivory drinking horns on golden stands, models of sailing vessels, several lyres, and helmets of many shapes. A waist-high shelf that spanned three walls of the room supported huge volumes of books whose covers of wood were enclosed in skins painted in vivid colors. Some were jeweled to accent geometric designs, and others were inlaid with figures in silver and gold.

A table with thick legs stretched through the center of the room, and at its distant end stood a chair whose artistic aspects rendered it suitable for a king.

Aleen gazed in fascination at three hanging tapestries. Roman maps were on another wall, and around and between the fireplace and the windows on either side were hung battle shields and swords with jeweled scabbards. Interspersed among them were spears of various lengths and thicknesses. Hanging high on the walls were antlers and horns of animals unknown to the country, and on the back wall were skins, some striped, others spotted, of equally unfamiliar origins. The room was a veritable treasury, and Aleen's fascination with it was transformed to a flush of guilt for having entered its precincts uninvited.

"Let us return this," she said to Lelia, taking a quill from the small hand and placing it in a golden cylinder among others of its kind. "We should not be here." Aleen smiled and winked mischievously, but as they were about to leave, the sounds of a closing door and approaching footsteps made them stop. In a moment Edmund was there, blocking their path of retreat. His arms were filled with rolls of parchments and small books, but he stood holding his burden, while Aleen sensed his confusion and shame regarding his disorderly appearance. His hair was mussed, his rumpled tunic was in disarray and open above his waist, his legs were bare, and his sleeves were rolled high in carelessly formed circlets. He had apparently thought to cross the hall unnoticed, and was unfortunately caught in unseemly straits.

"I should not have entered, my lord. The door was open, and before I knew the seriousness of the intrusion, I found myself wandering about," Aleen offered apologetically. "I regret my actions." To distract him from her transgression and to ease his feelings of discomfort, she quickly added, "It is a most interesting room."

"No offense has been committed. Do not concern yourself. You are most welcome to visit here," and he walked toward the tables and placed the rolls and books on the appropriate stacks. "I have been transferring these from my desk. They accumulate so rapidly."

Relieved of his armload, he quickly adjusted his tunic and

ran his fingers through his hair. It was a friendly circumstance, yet both were ill at ease.

"Did you once say you can read?"

"Yes, my lord."

"Then you will want to come here often. So few people can read. It would please me to know these manuscripts are being used. Ask Wulfric for the key to this room whenever it pleases you."

"I am grateful, my lord. It would pleasure me greatly to read from such distinguished works. It is such a large collection," she said, looking around the room.

"Yes, it is a fine collection," he agreed. "My father began it, and for many years had monks engaged here in our scriptorium. King Alfred gave us other books. Some are in Latin. Do you know the language?"

"No," she answered, shaking her head.

"French?"

"A little. My tutor was a Frenchwoman."

"Then you may be interested in these," and he walked to the table on which small scrolls were carelessly heaped. "These are letters from the king of France, and these," he said, indicating three scrolls whose handles were longer and more intricately designed, "these are from the pope. Some of the larger ones are from the kings of England. You may find them of some interest. You admire this room?"

"Yes, I find it of great interest."

"Perhaps it is so, but I find it cluttered. It has one redeeming feature. On trying days, I can escape here to gain a few moments of quiet."

There was a long awkward silence, until Aleen asked, "These horns upon the walls—they cannot be from animals in this land?"

"No. My father gathered these from merchants who sailed here from distant lands. The skins were also purchased from them." He tilted his chin to indicate the tables in the corner, and added, "Those objects are from visiting dignitaries. I would prefer to dispose of them, but they form part of the treasury and are kept here for times of need, when they will be sold. There are others in the chests beneath the tables. Examine them if you so desire. They represent many nations and forms of art."

Silent awkardness again claimed the room, until once more Aleen felt compelled to relieve it. "We must go now. I see you have much to do," and she walked toward Lelia, who had been sitting beneath a table arranging in files the scrolls that had fallen off.

Edmund looked upon the limping child, who was supported by Aleen's hand. As they were nearing the door, he called after them and walked forward, rubbing one forearm absently.

Aleen stopped and turned.

His words came quietly, consolingly. "If I seemed startled to see you earlier, it is that I have not seen you since you received the message from Wermouth. I wished to express my regret for the death of your father, but I did not think it proper to intrude on your grief. Please know that I have prayed for him and that I regret his passing."

"I am most grateful," she replied, looking into gentle eyes. Suddenly rendered self-conscious by his attentions and genuine sentiments, she lowered her head and departed as he silently watched her passage.

## ~< XVII >~

TRUE TO her word, Aleen had exercised her intentions and had taken the child around at will. Lelia would not be denied the freedom of the castle to placate Wilfreda's eccentricities or to pamper the delicate sensibilities of a few. There was much to see and do, and Aleen was pleased that her objectives for Lelia to see and do all of interest around Lauxburgh also permitted her to wander into places and to visit with people she had not the courage to visit on her own.

There had been visits to the blacksmith, where Lelia sat entranced as the fire blazed and sparkled and the glowing metal was beaten into shape. In the bakery she delighted in pounding soft powdery clumps of dough in imitation of the bakers who kneaded and shaped small mounds for the brick ovens. Everywhere they visited, Lelia made friends—the candlemakers, the carpenters, the glass blowers, the cooks, the weavers. All were flattered at the interest shown in their trades and took time to explain their work to Aleen and to tweak the cheek and speak dulcetly with the child. The attentions they gave Lelia compensated enormously for the inconsiderate treatment in the castle. The poor and simple folk were sympathetic toward the child, and friendly toward her new guardian. The child's pitiful limp touched their hearts, and they showed a genuine affection and a deep attraction for her. Gradually, as their friendships grew, Aleen and the child could not walk but a few feet about the outer buildings without Lelia's name being called in greeting and Aleen given a polite bow of friendliness. It was delightful mingling among them, these honest and likable people, and it was not long before Aleen and Lelia had learned most of their names.

Lauxburgh contained such contrasts. Friendliness was to be found with those lowest in the social order, and only resentment and dislike among others on the higher levels. Wilfreda was not alone in her display of glaring snobbery. The other noblewomen, bored, and with much time and little to do, found it a pleasant diversion to find fault with Aleen, especially since they knew that by their condemnation of her they were finding favor with Wilfreda.

That she was the frequent topic of their conversations was no assumption on Aleen's part. Many times as she was passing by the whispering groups, their words grew intentionally louder, until she could not help but hear their disdainful words. "She and the child mingle with the peasants." "She exposes the child to their crudeness." "She wishes to gain Edmund's favor by her attentions to his daughter."

Their accusations distressed her. No one cares to be disliked, but Aleen had long ago pledged they would never again shame her, and if they did, she would never give them the satisfaction of knowing that they had. At such times, she walked blithely past them and pretended to be deaf to their words.

Aleen and Lelia rarely sat at the same table with Edmund, for fear of giving the least substance to the gossiping, but even as Aleen sat at other tables with those of less social stature, it was not uncommon to see two or three women standing by the gallery on the second floor looking down upon the diners and pointing and whispering and clucking that Aleen had no pride and associated with inferiors.

It was understandable that Aleen preferred to avoid the prejudices of the castle and to escape to the peace of the countryside. She and Lelia frequently mounted Cenook and rode out to meet the sunshine and stirring sea breezes. There was always much to interest them. There were days when the hunters emerged from the forest with their prizes—stags, hares, and boars. On those days Aleen and Lelia rode to the limits of the meadow to meet them, examine their game, and listen while the men told of the consummate skill they had employed to outwit the game.

There were days when the servants packed a basket with their lunch. There were days when they spent their time picking wildflowers and clover, or lounging and napping under the shade of great oaks. Other days were spent on the beach searching for shells and watching the silvery blurs of fish jumping above the waves and the sea gulls squawking and diving for the morsels of bread Lelia tossed upon the surf. If the winds were strong, they stood upon the cliff, arms outstretched, feet apart, laughing while the wind blew at their gowns as it did upon the sails of the ships that passed on the North Sea beyond the bay.

They were glorious days, Aleen delighting in Lelia's company as Lelia delighted in hers. What need had Aleen of anyone when Lelia was hers—precious, trusting, happy Lelia.

It was on one such pleasant day when Lelia was hobbling about from one clump of honeysuckle to another, trying in vain to snare flitting butterflies, that Aleen began feeling uneasy, as she often did when they were on the meadow. There was no one in the fields, near the forest or beach, on the parapets or turrets of the castle, yet Aleen had the eerie feeling, the disquieting conviction, that they were being closely watched.

It was the sabbath, and as on all days dedicated to the Lord, Aleen had helped Lelia into one of her finest gowns and had taken her to chapel for holy mass. According to their custom, they knelt behind the others and to the side, where Edmund could be watched with ease. Aleen found him most interesting. His appearance at first was imposing, yet as the mass progressed, he became less commanding and was as a biblical prophet, deep in communion with his God, with an aura of holiness about him. Perhaps he was meant to enter the religious life. . . .

Lelia, at least, was seeing more of him than she had while at the cobbler's, and his presence was becoming less awesome to her. Soon, no doubt, they would be friends, and perhaps a mutual affection would flower. God willing, Lelia would have pleasant recollections of at least a few years of fatherly love and attention before his return to Tankenham.

The morning passed slowly. There seemed less to do on the sabbath than on other days. There would be services in chapel at noon, and again in the evening, but Aleen had little attraction to these. The commandment to keep the Lord's day holy meant, in her estimation, attendance at holy mass and a hasty prayer before her bedside crucifix in the evening.

The chapel bell had ceased pealing the commencement of the noonday services when she and Lelia slipped into their chambers, changed their clothing, and crept down the halls, feeling pleasurably sinful for having successfully eluded entrapment in the musty chapel. The sunshine beckoned them, and they escaped with all haste to the fields, where falconers were engaged in their sport. One was in the scrubland near the forest, and others, at respectful distances, were in the grazing lands and fields, where thickets harbored their quarry.

Weeks before, the sportsmen had captured their peregrines and gyrfalcons in the nests before they were able to fly and had fed and kept them from distractions in darkened rooms, where they became easily accustomed to their masters' voices and handling. Once they were strong and able to take wing, they were fitted with tiny hoods. Thin straps were fitted around the bodies to prevent the fluttering of wings, and they were secured by the feet with other thin straps. Placed upon their trainers' gauntleted wrists, they were brought forth to await the sighting of prey and the exercise of instinctive urges.

The falcon that Aleen and Lelia now watched was already trained, and sat hooded and almost immobile on its master's arm. But once a desirable bird was on the wing and in sight, the hood and restraining straps were released, a whistle given, and it soared immediately, eager for conquest. With lightning speed the falcon spiraled its frantic victim, until, when above it, it swooped downward in a winged streak, darted at its victim, and struck it a fierce blow. Together the birds fell to the ground in a feathery struggle, the falcon's talons holding its victim in a death grip until the falconer rushed to retrieve his prize for deposit in his leather bag. Again and again the falcon was permitted to streak toward other prey, until the falconer's bag contained a sufficient number of delicacies to satisfy the epicurean cravings of his family.

When the falconer hooded and restrained his bird and galloped away proud and self-satisfied with his triumph over the wild, Aleen and Lelia wandered about collecting the feathers dislodged during the combat.

The air was exceptionally sweet, and wandering nearer the

forest, they came upon clumps of honeysuckle, their pale yellow trumpets emitting alluring perfumes. While Lelia hobbled about snapping the stems and collecting the blooms in a heap, Aleen gazed into the depths of the forest that rose cool and verdant before her. Once again her childhood yearnings were recalled—how she had repeatedly asked to join in her father's hunts. She had longed to watch the mysterious ways in which the hunters circled and stalked their prey. Why women were forbidden access to these adventures, she could not understand. It seemed a harmless enough place, with lovely ferns and flowery vines spanning tall pines and stately oaks. *This is not my own country, but another,* she cunningly reasoned, *and even if Father were alive, he could not refuse me admittance here. One way or another, I will enter this forest.* A crafty smile crept over her lips, and a gleam enlivened her eyes. *Yes, somehow I shall find the means to join in a hunt.*

In an instant Aleen turned and darted toward Lelia, who shrieked as she tripped over a stone and fell to the ground. Picking her up, Aleen held her close until the tears ceased to flow. Rubbing the aching knee, Aleen kissed the small wet cheek and set Lelia down again. "You have collected many flowers," Aleen said in exaggerated surprise as she looked upon the pile of crumpled blooms. Lelia, her mind once again drawn by the stems whose plucking caused such a delightful snapping sound, resumed her harvest.

Shielding her eyes, Aleen measured the time by the slant of the sun, clapped her hands, and whistled for Cenook, who cantered forward. "It is time for us to be returning, Lelia. Here, take some of the flowers, and we will leave." But Lelia would not be satisfied with a few, and instead tried to gather her collection in both arms. Aleen removed her mantle, laid it upon the ground, and together they placed Lelia's treasures upon it. Gathering up the corners, they tied it on the pommel of the saddle. The ride back to the castle was leisurely, their scented bundle bouncing on the side of the saddle, the feathers in Lelia's hand shuddering in the wind.

Upon arriving at the stable, Aleen reached into the mantle, extracted a bloom, and whispered for Lelia to hand it to Aethelwed, who stiffly bowed and offered a guttural response of gratitude. Thereafter it became a game for Lelia, and each person she met within the yard was handed a frayed and rumpled flower. Dusty and leathery hands reached for the stems and placed them inside weskits, belts, and aprons. Words of appreciation and a warming smile radiated from each recipient.

As they crossed the courtyard, a familiar voice was heard, and Edmund emerged from the main entrance accompanied by two prelates. Having met them directly, an introduction was unavoidable and inevitable, and much to her discomfort, Aleen heard Edmund's presentation. "Reverend Willehad, Reverend Stigand, the Lady Aleen and my daughter, Lelia."

As courteous smiles and nods were exchanged, without warning and before Aleen could react to stop her, Lelia plunged her hand into the bulging mantle Aleen had been carrying and gave a cluster of flowers to first one prelate and then the other. Both seemed amused and delighted by the innocent gesture but hurriedly bid farewell and rode off.

"My lord," Aleen hastened to apologize, "they did not leave because . . . ?"

"No, not at all," Edmund countered. "They were unfamiliar with the land and were concerned they would not reach Wetson monastery before nightfall. They were sent by Alfred to supervise the restoration of the buildings there. Well," he said with finality, "good day." But as he moved to leave, he caught sight of Lelia patiently holding a bloom toward him.

Pleasurably surprised, he knelt on one knee in the dust, peered intently into the timid face and large blue, expressionless eyes. Taking hold of the little fist that held the broken flower, he gently stroked it, accepted the flower, and smelled it. "I am most grateful for this, Lelia. And what have you here?" he asked, taking hold of the other fist that tightly held the feathers. "Most interesting," he said. He stood up and looked toward Aleen. The unspoken message was clearly understood. He was grateful for the pleasure the child enjoyed because of Aleen's interest and devotion.

"My mind falters," he said after a moment. "I have neglected to mention that you have guests waiting. The cobbler and his family have been waiting for some time for your return." With Edmund following close behind them, the remaining walk was silent and uneasy, but on approaching the door to the great hall, Aleen rushed forward and caressed both visitors. There was much hugging, kissing, and a few happy tears.

"Lelia," both visitors exclaimed, "you have grown so. The health of the sun is in your cheeks," Bertha was saying while tweaking Lelia's fat cheeks and pressing the little body against her pregnant middle.

The cobbler's children, all carefully dressed in their finest, were timidly smiling and accepting Aleen's hugs with good grace. "And you, Ansgar," Aleen was saying coquettishly, "you are so handsome today." He was beaming under the compliment, but shrugged it off as though accustomed to such praise. He was, in fact, neatly combed, his clothing was clean, his beard neatly trimmed, and Aleen realized that for once he did not smell of dyes.

Edmund had been forgotten in the rush of emotions and rounds of compliments. He had stood apart, near a drapery, where his presence was not obvious, studying the proceedings with his face set in serious lines. He left after a time, a man preoccupied with his thoughts.

Unknown to all, there had been another witness, whom nothing escaped. In a shadow of the kitchen door, Wilfreda, with a keen, perceptive eye, watched her son as he quietly left the room twirling between his fingers the stem of a yellow flower.

# ✦ XVIII ✦

THE YEARLY feast of Saint Etheldreda was rapidly approaching, and the atmosphere of the castle and neighboring villages was becoming increasingly festive. The plans for the annual fair in observance of the feast were formulated and excitedly anticipated. On that day the virtues of the revered saint who died centuries before would be extolled. It would be remembered that she had been coerced into marriage twice for diplomatic purposes, yet despite pressures put upon her, retained her virginity and ended her days in religious enclosure.* The pious would pilgrimage to her tomb and implore upon aching knees for miracles of health and temporal benefits that her reputation gave ample assurance of being bestowed on her faithful clients. The less piously inclined would be found that day either participating in or observing the various games of skill or chance that attracted crowds from miles around. There would be horse races and contests for wrestlers, javelin throwers, and archers. Falconers would demonstrate the skills of their birds, tradesmen would offer their most interesting articles for sale, bakers would have an ample supply of delicacies for purchase, and hopeful and ever-alert mothers would endeavor to present their eligible daughters to prospective suitors. Numerous silky kerchiefs would that day conceal demure smiles and blushing cheeks as the maidens appraised the prowess and physical excellence of each manly participant in the games.

It would be a gloriously happy day, when the cares and monotony of life would be cast aside for frivolity, the joy of family reunions, and the pleasure of renewed friendships.

As the feast drew near, the meadow that Aleen and Lelia had considered their own personal domain was more and

* Elisabeth Wilcocks, *St. Etheldreda* (Catholic Truth Society, London, 1961).

more invaded by carpenters noisily setting up booths for tradesmen to use in the display of their imported silks, golden vessels, and jewelry. Tables were set up for peasants who might bring embroidered homespun and whittled ornaments for sale. Judges of games wandered about setting up targets for the archers and staking out the courses for the horse races. As the festive day neared, travelers from great distances set up their tents on the perimeter of the field. The activity about the meadow increased until Aleen and Lelia felt themselves intruders and retreated to the tower, where they watched the bustling proceedings more advantageously.

The winds, which barely ruffled the leaves and grasses below, buffeted about them on their lofty perch—their private hideaway from which they peered between crenellated openings. Aleen had gloried in her occasional visits to this place since she was first shown it during her initial tour of the castle. Here the sky seemed so near as to be touchable, and the awesome world lay below for her condescending inspection and approval.

The excited anticipation of the feast mounted, until at last the feast day dawned and the visiting priests filed in procession to the chapel for the celebration of the mass of Saint Etheldreda, during which she was implored to mediate with the heavenly father on behalf of her faithful devotees. The litany of the martyrs and Anglo-Saxon saints followed, with the mingled voices of the responses reverberating in the crowded chapel. On and on the names were intoned and the petitions pleaded for, until, at the end, the name of the glorious Saint Etheldreda was emphasized in a louder, slower voice and a lingering *ora pro nobis*—pray for us— culminated the recitation.

A festive morning meal followed in the crowded hall, and then the visitors and residents of the castle proceeded to the still-dewy meadow, where horses were being walked about for the inspection of those who were considering placing wagers on their potential victories. The booths and tables were adorned and heaped with wares, and before long they were crowded with bustling inspectors and likely customers.

The flags that marked the racecourses snapped in the fresh breezes that swept the sunny field. Laughter was everywhere, especially, it seemed, among the visiting children, who darted around the booths and tables, around shrubs and trees to the distress of their distracted mothers and the irritation of those who unwittingly crossed their erratic paths.

Edmund mingled among the guests and watched the men of the castle as they coached the young athletes in the strategy of the competitions. The ladies gathered in groups and sat provocatively on the benches that had been brought from the great hall and placed conveniently on the fields. They made a glorious sight in brightly colored silk gowns that shimmered in the sunlight, their gold-embroidered sleeves, hems, and bodices flashing amber brillance. Jeweled brooches, bracelets, and necklaces sparkled as flamboyantly as the eyes of their owners, who peered enticingly at the athletes who proudly demonstrated their skills before their beautiful and appreciative audiences.

Aleen and the child wandered around observing most of the games and races, until they chanced upon the archery matches being held near the forest, where the misguided arrows of the unskilled would be safely diverted into the woody interior. The sloping ground provided a natural amphitheater for the match, and Aleen and the child sat at an inconspicuous distance upon the grass near a clump of shrubs.

The ladies were as fascinating to watch as the archers, for they gasped and squealed with each successful aim of their favorites. One after another, the bowstrings twanged and arrows whirred as they pierced the air, before thudding into the straw-packed targets. When at last a champion had been decided upon, a cry of approval sounded, but delicate sighs of regret escaped the lips of those who were disappointed at the early conclusion of the competition.

"You seek more matches?" the smiling champion asked his audience.

"Yes, yes," they echoed back.

"Then what think you of a game between our fair ladies?" and he looked to his defeated rivals for approval, which he immediately received. They nodded their heads and laughed encouragement to the ladies, who smiled with embarrassment at the absurdity of the invitation.

"You shall indeed compete," they teased. "What say you

we crown the winner?" Squeals and giggles rose as one of the men approached a sweet olive tree, broke off a branch with tiny fragrant white flowers, and twisted and entwined the leaves into a crown. "Now, who shall be first?" the champion asked, looking from one to the other.

All the ladies pursed their lips against any sound that might escape to indicate their acceptance of the challenge.

"The crown alone does not offer sufficient incentive? Then we shall offer an additional prize." He rubbed his chin, conferred with the other young men, and then proudly announced: "We have concurred that we, all of us, shall be at the winner's disposal for a day to perform any services the winner so desires. Now, which of you ladies can refuse the willing services of us all? A prize such as this will be greatly envied. Now, which of you will begin the contest?"

"But we know nothing of bowing." "We shan't be able to lift the bow." "Our arrows will never find their mark." Such was what they offered by way of excusing their attractively feminine weaknesses.

"We will assist you, and we shall move the targets nearer. No excuses will be honored. Now, who shall be the bravest and begin?"

A dainty hand rose timidly in the air, to the approving remarks of the men.

"Now, ladies, this is the way it is done," the champion said, standing near his blushing student. "Stand thusly, with feet apart, your left shoulder toward the target. Grasp the bow in the middle with your left hand, keep your arm straight, and place the bow down horizontally against you in this manner, with the string up," he continued as he moved his fragile pupil into position. "Reach for an arrow with your right hand, and place this little groove against the center of the string. Place your fingers about the string and arrow in this manner, raise your bow, making certain the shaft rests against the bow above your left hand, draw the string toward your chin thusly, take aim, and release the string. My dear ladies," he continued with a flourish of his hand toward the target, "if you discharge your arrows in this manner, they will do naught but find their way unerringly toward their mark."

Whispered remarks and stifled giggles climaxed the lesson as the first feminine archer fumbled through the positions and weakly shot her three arrows wide of their target. Aleen watched with disgust at the display of feminine flirtation as each blushing contestant daintily posed herself and either shot past the target or drew back so weakly as to make the arrows barely strike or often fall short of the mark. What more could be expected of such lovely ladies whose utter femininity prevented a more splendid showing? But even more repulsive to Aleen than their pretenses was the amusement and approving smiles the young men were bestowing on the fluttering, blushing ladies who could barely be expected to lift the five-foot longbow and draw back its taut string, much less strike with accuracy.

"Who else wishes to compete?" the champion called when the last willing contestant had finished. "Will no one else vie for the crown?" The young man looked about expectantly.

A clear, sarcastic voice broke the silence. "Should you not ask the Lady Aleen to take part? The Danes claim they are enabled to excel us in all manner of sport."

Aleen heard Judith's voice clearly—the woman the others were most influenced by, excepting Edmund's mother.

"Lady Aleen," the young man said, walking to where Aleen sat, appalled at being so brazenly drawn into the game. "You have been challenged, dear lady," he said, smiling kindly. "Come, try. You might well do better than they."

Aleen meant to decline, but all eyes turned toward her. She was in a perplexing situation, whether she accepted or not. "Very well," she said as she was helped to her feet. "I shall be back, Lelia. Wait for me here," and she walked through the hushed group to where the young man stood with the bow and quiver.

Aleen docilely followed his instructions and grasped the bow accordingly. He gently guided her through the positions. "Now, take careful aim," and as he backed away, she let go the arrow, which sped past the target until it lodged far behind the target in a knothole of a tree.

The laughter and snickers that resulted were not stifled, and remarks made among the ladies were intended to be heard by the archer. Aleen stoically watched as they laughed until tears were daintily patted from their eyes. "She performs more poorly than all of us combined." They laughed aloud as merriment was shared by all the women without exception.

Aleen held the bow down against her as she looked upon the ladies who were reputed to be cultured and intelligent yet were making sport so mercilessly of another woman who was their superior in rank. These were women who rejected her from their social life, women who refused to sit in the same room with her, women who spoke cruelly behind her back and made snide remarks for her embarrassment. They were unafraid to speak so sharply before the menfolk, for thereby they were confirming their own excellence by the contrast. She would permit this no longer.

Deliberately she reached into the quiver, plucked out an arrow, and moved to the line that marked the official place designated in the matches. Carefully and with easy movements borne of practice, she nocked the arrow and with a vengeful gleam in her eye drew back the string until the feathers of the arrow brushed her cheek, turned toward the group, and with deliberation aimed the arrow for a moment at each mocker.

Gasps and shrieks of horror rose as the frightened ladies watched the arrow's tip point directly from one heart to another. Aleen's thoughts were not difficult to discern as she gazed the length of the shaft, but when she had aimed her missile at all her detractors, she turned toward the target and in championship form drew the string even farther back and released it. Again it whizzed past the target and lodged beside the first arrow in the knothole of the same tree. A deathly silence settled upon the assemblage as the arrow vibrated in a blur.

"My third arrow," she asked of the young man who held the quiver. "My arrow," she repeated as she distracted him from his preoccupation with the missile that had thudded with a vengeance.

Quickly he walked toward her and with awed respect for the skill that equaled, if not bested the men, held the quiver for her convenience. Discriminatingly she moved the arrows with a flick of her finger until she found a suitable one. With a glance cast in the direction of the women, she stood defiantly, assumed the stance of a champion, aimed, and watched the arrow speed toward the tree until it took its position near the others.

"Would you name the winner, sir, or are there others wishing to compete?" she asked, turning to the men, who stood gaping at the unexpected demonstration of skill.

The self-appointed judge shrugged off his bewilderment, took the crown from the young man who had been holding it, and held it out for Aleen to take from him.

"I am most grateful," she said, placing it upon her head. She walked past the women, who sat in shocked silence. Halting, she turned again to the young men. "I must not forget to claim my prize." She smiled. "The service I wish of you all is a simple one."

"What is it," several voices said as they all walked toward her, their interest in her renewed and their questions concerning her abilities with the bow eager to find utterance. "You have but to tell us of it, my lady."

She tilted her chin, fully aware that their attentions had been wholly diverted from the ladies. "Since you have pledged yourselves to granting my most ardent wish, I am confident you will find no excuses to avoid fulfilling it."

"Nay, we shall willingly honor our pledge. Tell us what it is you wish."

"I desire to join you on your next hunt in the forest. I do not mean the simple hunts whereon you take the ladies. I wish to participate in the next serious hunt in the forest's depths. I will await it anxiously. I anticipate having you at my complete disposal, as you so generously offered."

With a sly smile she walked away, while the eyes of all followed her up the incline to where Lelia sat, obediently awaiting her return. "Come, my love," she said with hand extended. "We are finished here." Her smile was radiant. Her satisfaction was complete.

After a few steps she stopped abruptly beside the bushes, just barely avoiding walking into Edmund, who had been standing beside them, shielded from view. Aleen blushed crimson, for the twinkle in his eye and the proud look on his face signified he had witnessed all and had found pleasure and pride in her actions.

Confusion such as she had never known overwhelmed her. She had only moments before threatened the lives of the elite, was now the winner of a foolish contest and was wearing a ridiculous crown besides, and Edmund, instead of being offended by the display, was actually grinning foolishly at her.

"Pardon, my lord," she said, attempting to walk around him.

"A moment please, Aleen. May I walk beside you?" He placed his hand gently beside Lelia's upturned face and shared his continuing grin with her. "Your skill with the bow interests me."

"Does it, my lord?" she asked, not looking his way, but continuing to walk proudly across the clover. She had cast a measure of vengeance on her enemies and ceased their stupid remarks and laughter. There was nothing quite as satisfying as having placed one's detractors in their proper places, and if she came forth the conqueror of the situation, why be ashamed of it? And more importantly, if Edmund found her crown and her actions amusing, so much the better.

"How came you by this knowledge of the bow?" he continued.

"Do you forget, my lord, that my father was a Viking warrior? Our women are taught these skills as a means of protection while the men are absent from home. If I excel in the sport, it is only that I practiced diligently beside my father and brother, who were skillful hunters as well."

"Ah, I see," he said, studying her intently. "It had not occurred to me that your women of rank were trained in such crafts of war."

"We are not prepared for war. Bowing is also enjoyed as a sport, such as it is enjoyed here."

Edmund lapsed into silence and then continued quietly. "Marion had never mentioned that she possessed such skill."

"That is because she knew nothing of the bow. She was quiet and withdrawn, as you know, and disliked all outdoor sport. She preferred her books and embroidery," Aleen explained, trying not to make her words sound disdainful.

After another moment of reflective silence he asked, "Do you find our festival enjoyable?"

"Yes, very much so. However, I regret Cenook did not race, for he would surely have won. He performs best when I ride him, but unfortunately, I do not qualify as a rider."

"No, I should think not. Pardon me, Aleen," Edmund said on catching sight of a judge waving for his attention. "As you see, the attentions of an ealdorman are required for many diverse matters."

Aleen sighed with relief as he left. Her emotions had become jumbled within her, and without knowing why, she had been curiously excited by his interest in her accomplishment. With Lelia holding tightly to her hand, she walked toward a nearby bench and sat down. Looking between the people who strolled near her, she glimpsed Edmund laughing with two sweaty wrestlers who had just finished their contest. Dressed only in short breeches, they massaged their sore muscles, while their hairy chests expanded with each draft of air.

It is strange, she mused, how friendly he has come to be. But then, he is friendly with everyone. And she saw the easy manner in which he conversed and laughed with the wrestlers, patted them on the shoulder, and moved away to speak with others.

Strange, too, that he should bring Marion's name so often into their brief meetings. Marion, who had done nothing worthy of interest or value in her life, save to bring Lelia into the world, and then, even that was a partial success, since she had lost her life as a direct result. I must not think so of the dead, she reprimanded herself.

Edmund's back was to her, but it was not overlooked that his proportions were comparable to those of the wrestlers, who posed and flexed muscles for the approval of the older men who sat around the mat, eagerly awaiting the next contest.

Even more confusing than his continued interest in his long-dead wife was why a man of such physical appeal and vitality, a man who could capture with ease the affections of any lady he chose, would instead find life in a monastery more attractive and desirable.

Aleen would have denied it, had her attention been called

to the fact that she was studying the appearance of her husband with interest and satisfaction. She found amusement in the way the sun shone on his wavy chestnut hair, how the sheen of his leather jerkin covered thick muscular shoulders, how his knee-high boots caressed his thick, well-formed legs, how he moved with such self-assurance.

The games and contests and even the loud voices of the merchants extolling the merits of their wares seemed obliterated as Aleen's thoughts dwelt entirely on her husband. Time and again, when her eyes wandered away to the people passing around them, they soon returned to him with an irresistible attraction.

# XIX

THE ARCHERS were eager to honor their pledge, and in due time notified Aleen of a hunt two days hence. In humor and genuine friendship that her archery skills had promoted, they gallantly renewed their vow to be at her disposal, as they had offered on the day of the fair, and to be her slaves, her stepping-stones if need be. A change of men's clothing was provided; her gowns, they indicated, were totally unsuited for the forest. A tent would be set up for her at their main camp, and a servant could be brought if Aleen thought her services would be required. All had been planned with her comfort in mind, so they assured her.

The hunting lands were a world of their own, a terrain that Aleen had always yearned to explore, and at last its wonders and mysteries would unfold before her. It had never occurred to her that Hester would not share her excitement, but the always docile and cooperative companion was adamant at the prospect of having to accompany her mistress into the dark, forbidding woodlands. Her arguments were numerous and emotional for one who rarely opposed the wishes of her charge.

Ferocious animals of all sorts crawled and slunk about, waiting to devour hapless hunters, foolish women, or their servants who penetrated the breeding grounds for the purpose of slaughtering their kind, she argued. Such business had best be left to experienced hunters, and if Aleen would only reason clearly, she would forsake her foolish plans.

"Your dear father, if he were alive, would never give his consent to your plans. How can you do what you know he forbade?"

"Because, Hester," she whispered confidentially, "he is not alive." Raising her head defiantly, she continued, "Besides, I am older and married, and my husband does not forbid it."

"Perhaps your husband does not know of your plans. Already they are preparing for his journey to Wetson. He would certainly disapprove of your participating in such a hazardous venture during his absence."

Aleen's eyes opened in desperation. If only he does not hear of it, but then, the men must have told it to others, who would certainly report it to their lord. Perhaps they did not, she thought. "You must promise me," she said, turning to Hester, "you must swear not to speak of this." With a lift of an eyebrow, she added, "He cannot forbid plans of which he knows nothing."

"My lady," Hester gasped in disbelief, "an evil spirit has entranced you. What if harm should befall you? A dispute between our country and this one would take place, each surmising the accident to have been the devious plan of the other. Perhaps even war would develop."

"Ah"—Aleen laughed—"how well you dream in the light of day. No harm will befall me. Experienced hunters, and champion archers, and perhaps even soldiers will be with me."

"And what of the animals?"

"Hester, have we not traveled through timberlands on our journey here? Do you remember how the animals were frightened of us and scurried away?"

"Yes, my lady, but we rode along well-traveled paths. We were not there to kill them. Animals can sense the difference, and I hear tell they will gather together and attack hunting parties when the lives of their young are endangered."

"Hester," Aleen teased, casting a sideward glance of annoyance. "I have spent hours with my father and his huntsmen, and I never heard them tell of such a thing."

"Then consider, my lady, the opinions of the ladies of the castle. You, the Lady of Lauxburgh, doing such an unwomanly thing."

"It matters not to me what they think. Of that you can be assured. Please, Hester, do not argue with me further. You know quite well how I repeatedly begged my father to take me when he went on hunts. I loved my father dearly, but it was unfair of him to train me and spend much time in telling me of the sport, and then deny me the pleasure of accompanying him. 'Women do not do such things,' he would say. I am moved by your devotion and concern for my welfare,

Hester. You need not accompany me, but I will not be hindered. I will find another companion. I intend to join this hunt, and nothing will prevent me."

Sleep was impossible, and long before daybreak Aleen was dressed in the clothing the archers had provided. But even as she was pulling the belt tight, her suspicions were confirmed, for not only was an exceptional length of belt left dangling from the buckle, but the folds that it bound to her were numerous, and bulkier than were reasonably acceptable. There was no need to confirm her piteous appearance in her mirror. The breeches were bound well above her waist to prevent tripping, the tunic reached well below the knees, the sleeves were rolled many times to her wrist, and the leggings that were bound by cross garters were so thick with folds as to make her legs appear swollen with disease.

With a suspicious squint of the eye, a smile of realization lightened her face. If she was to appear ridiculous by her wearing of men's clothing, the archers had plotted that she should appear more so, and had deliberately supplied clothing of ample proportions. As she appraised the ill fit, she wondered, and correctly so, if the articles represented the combined contributions of the group. It had been a deliberate prank, well planned and thought out, and no doubt mischievously enjoyed. Instead of being offended, she smiled softly. They would not have dared to entertain such capriciousness had they not known it would be sportingly received. Her eyes lowered, and her smile vanished. At least the men had accepted and approved her. It was a most satisfying feeling, this being liked for oneself. A sharp contrast indeed to the other attitudes she had encountered.

With a glow of gratitude she surveyed her appearance in the first light of dawn. If they think I am equal to the trick, I shall be. I will join them as though nothing is amiss, and presently we will all burst into laughter. Hopefully the joviality will project to the end of the hunt. It was going to be a lovely experience, this hunt, and she was eager to commence it.

Quickly she walked into her antechamber and awakened the servant girl she had coerced and handsomely paid to join her. Drowsily the girl rolled to her side. "My lady, must I dress in that manner?" she said, shaking her head to dismiss lingering slumber as she assessed Aleen's apparel.

"No," Aleen answered irritably. "You will not hunt. Wear this," and she picked up the long tunic the girl had worn the day before and dropped it on her pallet. "You will stay in the camp. Hurry, now."

Returning to her room, she ran her ivory comb through her hair, pulled it to the back, and plaited it into one thick braid. It would not do to have one's hair obstructing one's aim.

Suddenly she froze, and her eyes widened. Edmund's journey was planned for this day. What if he should be tarrying in the yard and should see me like this? He must never see me so. And what of Wilfreda? Perhaps she would not be awake so early, and as for Edmund, Aleen would conceal herself until he was out of sight on the westerly road to Weston.

Something stirred uneasily within her. Edmund had witnessed her winning of the contest, but had not necessarily heard the manner of prize she had selected. Surely word had seeped to him, yet no restrictions from his office had been made concerning the hunt, and either he approved, or more likely took no interest in her activity. It was disconcerting knowing he did not care if she participated in such a potentially dangerous sport. He should care, and a bit of anger and disappointment sparked within her for his apparent neglect of her welfare.

With the maidservant behind her, Aleen carefully crept through the dim corridor until she was able to look down upon the yard through a window. She sighed with relief. Edmund's party was nowhere to be seen. He had a preference for leaving on such journeys before daybreak, and his horse and those of his escorts were not saddled and tethered, nor were his draft-horses in readiness, as they would normally be, had they been late in leaving. There were only the hunters and archers lounging in their saddles and sitting in groups on the turf. Some riders had already formed a haphazard rank that extended outside the gate Thankfully, the way was clear, and she quickly walked to join them.

Glancing toward the approaching figures, the group of archers sprang to their feet and stared in amusement. Some raised hands to their mouths; others immediately turned their heads to conceal their smiles. They held Cenook for her to mount, but kept their heads turned, bit their lips repeatedly, and gave her only stealthy glances as they greeted her. Presently they were all mounted, and with a signal to the leaders, they were off amid pounding of heavy hooves and the flapping of packs.

The air was clear and crisp, with just a slight invigorating chill. The fields and meadows that stretched on either side of the road still slumbered beneath a coverlet of glistening dew. Above them the noisily chirping birds flitted about in the weak morning light with an excitement that attempted, but failed, to exceed Aleen's.

The road arched gently as they neared the wood, and Aleen surveyed the party with ease. The experienced hunters were in the lead to direct the group to the most favorable place for a camp, and soldiers were interspersed among the archers and other men of the castle. Soldiers followed behind Aleen and the servant girl, and had joined the group, apparently as a defense against possible attack from vagabonds.

It was a slow, easy ride, and Aleen missed nothing in her inspection of the party: the bulging water skins flung across saddles, the sleeping mats rolled up tightly, the bows hanging from the sides of the saddles, the tightly filled quivers, the beasts laden with supplies.

The hunters in the lead were of particular interest, for they were relied upon to track the game and were perhaps the only ones who were not anticipating the venture with any degree of pleasure. Accustomed to entering the wood quietly lest they alert the animals, they were instead accompanied by an unusually large group of noisy intruders. It had been arranged, however, that the hunters, who were expected to fill the castle smokehouse, would camp with the rest but would penetrate deeper and would stay a day longer if necessary.

Aleen's eyes rested on the undulating double file of riders and upon the burly hunters on the inner curve of the arc, the ones on the outer fringe being partially blocked from view by their companions. She was still scanning the seven or so weathered huntsmen when a slight dropping back of one rider exposed to view his previously unobserved companion to the right. The rider, though dressed differently than was his custom, was unquestionably Edmund.

Somehow her first impulse to race back toward the castle was mastered, and she did nothing to break Cenook's steady pace, but the excursion suddenly lost its specter of excitement as thoroughly as if she had been drenched in a relentless cloudburst. The dread of having to inevitably face Edmund in her humorous clothing dominated her thoughts as they passed into the shadows of the wood.

The smell of decayed vegetation and the freshness of pine alternately swept about them as they ducked beneath low-hanging branches and made their way carefully around tangles of vines and clumps of verdant growth. The ride was slow, and after a time tedious, and when Edmund left the rank and waved vigorously toward a cluster of beeches, all eyes went to him. Suddenly, as if by magic, the thin figure of a hermit wrapped in skins stood in a clearing, waving back with a skeletal arm. As Edmund dismounted, the old man advanced, put down his basket of berries, and with a broad smile reached out toward Edmund. The rank did not slow its pace, but continued on, confident that Edmund would join them later. Edmund's sturdy arm was around the frail figure as the rank passed them by, and Aleen noted, as she rode past, how the old man's beard was so yellowed and streaked; how his knees stood out like small spheres from his thin, hairy legs; and how, from under thick brows, his eyes sparkled as he looked into Edmund's face.

At last the place of their encampment was reached, and amid the bustle of putting up tents, she was all but forgotten. But when she was approached and shown the tent she and the maidservant were to occupy, the young men who had snickered at her attire in the beginning of the journey graciously exchanged friendly comments, even though their eyes danced devilishly. If only they would dissolve into laughter and relieve the tension created by their trick, but no, they wished to overlook her garb and thereby prolong their pleasure.

In a flashing panic, Aleen's ears were alerted to a familiar voice, and before she knew it, she had spun around to face Edmund, and reddened furiously beneath his gaze.

"Lady Aleen?" she heard him ask. "Had I not noticed your

hair, I would never have known this to be you," he said with a twinkle.

He is not at all surprised at my presence here, she thought irritably. His amusement over her appearance was not appreciated, and she could not bring herself to look upon him, but submitted herself to inspection as would a naughty child caught unexpectedly arrayed in her father's clothing. Slowly and deliberately she felt his gaze wandering from her shirt to her shoes, which she was able to keep afoot only by careful shuffling.

Clearing his throat, he said in a diversionary tone, "I trust this tent will provide sufficient comfort for you. The journey here prevents us from burdening the animals needlessly, and we could supply you only with mats and furs for sleeping."

"It will be adequate," she replied, glancing at the tent and the stakes near her foot. If only he would go, she thought frantically, looking about at anything, everything, to avoid meeting his eyes.

"We will be leaving soon to find tracks. You may accompany us if you like." When Aleen nodded dissent, he walked away. Cautiously she looked up and had the suspicious feeling he was smiling broadly.

She pleaded exhaustion when the men assembled to leave, only too glad to employ any excuse to avoid Edmund. Stealthily she made her way to a fallen tree, sat down, drew her legs up onto it, and watched them from behind clumps of greenery. In the peacefulness of her hiding place she had time to sort and assemble her confused thoughts, the most prominent of which was Edmund's foreknowledge that she was to be a member of the party.

From behind fronds of ferns she watched Edmund speak to the members of his searching party before they set out on foot to survey the meandering streams nearby. He was a happy man this day, a man in his element, about to participate in one of his few pleasures.

The day passed rapidly, and before long the trackers returned as the sun was passing behind tall oaks and a penetrating dampness began settling After producing bread and cheese from their packs, they gathered around the fire and enjoyed their simple feast, with Aleen wedged into the circle. She was counted as one of the men, and ate heartily of the bread and cheese offered her, but in turn declined drafts from the wineskin. The men retired early, after eating and drinking their fill, and Aleen was grateful to do likewise. The chill of night was uncomfortably penetrating and made her chin quiver uncontrollably.

The maidservant had lain in the tent for some time, starting at every sound, fearful least any crawling thing should slither onto her pallet.

"You are too fearful," Aleen whispered with annoyance. She crawled onto her mat and arranged the furs about her. "There are many men here to protect us. Say your prayers and sleep well."

"But, my lady," she whispered anxiously, "what of tomorrow?"

"You will remain here, but do not fret. The soldiers are camped nearby and will attend you. Let us sleep." But after many restless moments, when sleep refused to come, in spite of her ardent desire for it, she turned toward the girl, who lay listening to the scratching animal sounds in the distance. The close quarters made for a confidential atmosphere, and the girl was more than willing to converse to ease her fears. After several incidental exchanges, Aleen directed the remarks to the subject foremost in her mind. Collecting her courage, she began, "Tell me, what think you of the Lord Edmund?"

"Ah. He is a man many women desire, even those much younger than he. My lady," she whispered, almost gasping, "I should not speak so to you."

"Do not worry. Tell me. I wish to hear what is spoken of him. You will please me much," she coaxed, while the maidservant squinted in the dimness to analyze her mistress's attitude.

Satisfied with her estimation, she began, "My lady, we servants speak little, and often the ladies talk in our presence as though we are unable to hear or are too ignorant to know what of they speak. At times they forget we are present as we go about our duties. We see more than they are aware."

"Yes," Aleen encouraged when the girl had stopped speaking. "What meaning do your words convey?"

"Only, my lady, that there are many who desire your position."

186

Aleen was grateful for the darkness, and she marveled that the girl, who only moments before was so fearful of speaking her mind, had now stated her opinions so succinctly. No further whispers were forthcoming, and Aleen rightly sensed that the girl recoiled from saying more.

The cold was intense, and Aleen longed to sit before the fire with the furs wrapped about her shoulders. The moment the maidservant began breathing deeply and she was certain she had drifted off to sleep, Aleen inched her way through the flap and sat alone before the fire, enjoying the comforting warmth and the coziness of the fur about her shoulders. She was alone but for the murmur of the trees and the moon that lighted the area in silvery softness. Huddled against the cold, she had naught to do but let her mind drift where it may, and the words of the servant girl repeated themselves vexingly.

Let their desires be cast in the dust to be trampled on, for I am his wife, and by law the only one he is to be concerned with, she thought with satisfaction.

The fire sputtered and snapped as Aleen placed some nearby logs on top the charred ones.

A thrilling gush of excitement burst upon her. What if he should fall in love with me? What if I should fall in love with him? The thought was almost humorous. But why is it I have become so uneasy when he is near, and why, she thought, yes, why should I have been unwilling to have him see me in these ill-fitting clothes when I cared not that the others did? And why did he not journey to Wetson as was planned, and instead join in the hunt? Could it be he heard of my plans and wished to overlook my safety himself? The thought was deliriously exciting. No, it is vain of me to think thusly. He enjoys hunting and postponed his journey to take part. But why should all this matter to me? she wondered. Cool comprehension settled upon her. She did like him, and she did find him most attractive, and, yes, with just a little effort, she could love him. And may the good Lord guard him diligently if I ever do, she surmised, for nothing would stop me from making him love me in return.

She looked at the thicket encompassed in an eerie darkness. Something beyond caught her eye. In the distance the moonlight sifted through the towering trees, and in a clearing, something was there, as if part of an apparition. She rose, and as though unable to prevent herself, cautiously crept nearer until she distinctly saw Edmund kneeling on a cushion of fallen leaves, his arms crossed against his chest, his head bowed contemplatively.

It was a momentous sight, for the trees around him rose and curved in architectural contours to cathedral height, while in the ethereal atmosphere the rustle of a leafy chorus seemed to accompany him in prayer.

Aleen gazed as though transfixed by the spectacle. "What manner of man is this?" she whispered aloud. "What manner of man is this?"

The crushing of dried vegetation underfoot awakened her, and her body immediately rebelled. Pain seemed to control every movement, and she listened carefully for other signs of activity before forcing herself to stir. It was time to be up, even though it seemed like hours before sunrise.

The previous day's activities—the early rising, the long hours of riding to the clearing, the tiring wait for the return of the men from their excursion, and a fitful night spent on a hard mat in a frigid tent—were not conducive to a refreshed and energetic body, and she was obliged to force her limbs to move. She had come to hunt, and hunt she would, or else risk being taunted by the archers, who would never cease extolling their masculine superiority.

The huntsmen had already left on their serious pursuits when the young men gathered, as eager as young boys, to be off on their adventure. Edmund had not left with the huntsmen, as Aleen had expected, but had waited for the archers and was testing the balance of a bow when Aleen joined them, attempting, as she did, to make herself more presentable by yanking her ill-fitting clothing into position.

The nods and greetings of the handsome young men were playfully exaggerated. "We are your servants this day, dear lady. You have but to make your wishes known, and we will hasten with all speed to fulfill them."

"Then prepare yourselves," she retorted, "for I shall demand much of you, and since you declare yourselves eager to oblige me in all things, you may begin by declaring me the greatest marksman among us."

The unexpected command brought roars of laughter and denials on all sides.

As Aleen acknowledged Edmund's presence, the excitement about him was contagious, and she was caught up instantly in his exuberance. He was no longer the serious, sometimes moody, often distracted Edmund whose mediocre interest she had learned to endure. This day he was happy, and if her evaluation was correct, he was looking down upon her with not only amusement, but pride and pleasure as well.

The pain that streaked throughout her body with the slightest movement was all but dispersed by the glow she now felt, and she could skip, yes, run, if need be. But her joy soon faded, and discomfort again claimed possession, for the walk, which seemed to meander endlessly, was tiring and the air was dank and chilling. Every stone pressed painfully into the soft shoes, whose improvised straps shifted and loosened, until at intervals she was obliged to stop and secure them once again. The belt, too, moved, distributing the folds uncomfortably, until soon it became a constant struggle to keep the clothing where it was originally intended to be. Added to these discomforts were the bushes and plants that beat against her legs and tugged at her pants. The overhead branches not only caught annoyingly in her hair, but threatened to slap against her face for her least inattentiveness.

The men were walking ahead in long easy strides, pointing out to one another the tracks they saw along the way. How dare they walk so tirelessly when they have burdened me so, she thought, and she frowned as she watched their proud heads and straight backs and the bows and quivers so casually slung about their shoulders. Her breathing was short and rapid, her tired body screamed for rest, and she pouted at the injustice of it all.

"Will we ever reach the place?" she asked, struggling on through thickets and clearings while the feeble rays of the sun seeped through the trees. There was one narrow stream to cross, they assured her, and they would be near the hunting grounds. A fallen tree was to be the bridge at one place, and as she stepped upon it, they extended their hands to assist her, but her ill-fitting shoes made her slip, causing her foot to plunge into the slimy mud. The cold ooze was repulsive, and she closed her eyes and tightened her lips to thwart any cry of shock. When the foot was plucked free, she knew her previous sufferings were as nothing in comparison to the new discomfort. With each step across the tree trunk, her foot slushed around in the damp shoe, a condition that was not relieved, as she had hoped it would be, by her contact with solid ground. The men could not refrain from smiling at her difficulty. Their most gallant efforts in removing the shoe and wiping it with dried leaves unfortunately did little in relieving its wetness. This was the final indignity, but she must bear it silently. She had asked to hunt, and would endure the consequences. Thankfully, she had to limp only a short distance.

Slowly and cautiously they approached a sluggish stream, and crouched quietly behind the trees and bushes nearby. A bow and quiver were silently handed to Aleen, and she was given to understand she would be the first to aim and shoot. The champion archer was beside her, and as they waited, he whispered softly, "This is an excellent position. The wind blows toward us and carries our scent away. There are many stags here, see, the tracks are everywhere. They water here, and if we are fortunate, and your aim accurate, we will have a prize. You had best prepare your bow," and Aleen slowly placed an arrow into position and held it ready.

The water gurgled as the branches and vines swayed in the breeze, until at last a snap of twigs was heard and then gentle snorts. Aleen looked ahead in amazement as a boar came into view. He was an ugly animal with formidable tusks protruding from his lower jaw and curving up over his long snout. His tough hide was covered with bristles of gray-black hair, and Aleen marveled that he could yet appear so harmless as he sniffed the ground and nuzzled randomly among the leaves.

"Wait until he comes nearer," she was cautioned. The suspense was acute. "Now," he whispered, "slowly take aim."

Carefully and ever so slowly Aleen raised her bow.

"He is in good positon," the archer whispered excitedly.

Aleen drew back the string and looked down the shaft of the arrow at the beast snuffling contentedly among the roots of a tree.

"Release your arrow," he repeated urgently, but Aleen held her position and watched as her hungry target started to move away when his search was unsuccessful.

The men, carefully hidden, and waiting nervously for her response, were near panic at her delay.

"Now. Quickly."

The arrow was not released, and when her arm became tight and painful from the strain, she relaxed the string. The boar caught the movement, raised his head, and froze momentarily. But before he could scurry off, an arrow thudded into his flesh above his foreleg. Falling to the ground, he snorted painfully, and struggled frantically to rise.

Aleen rose in her place. The archer who had claimed the prize she had refused ran forward. With a forceful swing of his small ax, he hit the boar a bone-crushing blow to the head that seemed to resound throughout the wood. Immediately the animal was quieted, and the archer, taking a dagger from a scabbard hanging from his belt, reached for the animal's foreleg, held it up, exposing its breast, and plunged the blade into its heart.

Horror-struck, Aleen watched as blood oozed forth and spilled upon the ground. An overwhelming sickness stirred in her stomach and grew in intensity until she knew it would rebel. Quickly she stumbled away and leaned weakly against a tree.

She wanted desperately to be left alone with her sickness, but someone was behind her. The words spoken were soothing, but their meaning was not comprehended, for Aleen struggled against both the forceful urge to vomit and the panic of knowing Edmund was witnessing her ordeal.

If I swallow and swallow, it cannot be dispelled, she repeated to herself frantically. I cannot vomit—not here before Edmund. Somehow, after moments of struggle and repeated swallowings, the calmness of his words fell softly on her ears, and with enveloping weakness the struggle with her innards was won.

"Here, sit down and rest," he urged. She could do nothing but obey, and as he sat down near her, she turned away until the rough bark of the tree gently scratched her cheek. "You will soon feel better."

"I shall never feel better," she retaliated.

"Yes, you will. This has been a frightening experience for you. I regret that you have witnessed such a bad kill, but do not think us cruel. We try to dispatch the animals as mercifully and swiftly as we can." Aleen drew up her legs as he continued. "Tell me, Aleen, why did you hesitate to release the arrow? You are an excellent marksman and could have claimed the animal with precision."

Her humiliation was complete. She had never looked more unsightly, she had failed miserably as a hunter and shown cowardice instead, and had gotten terribly ill before witnesses. Why hide anything when so much had been so cruelly divulged? "I have never hunted before," she said at last. "I have never killed a living thing. The beast looked so pitiful there, searching for bits of food in the mud."

"Then you have had quite enough of hunting?"

"Yes. I shall never hunt again," she replied vehemently, but then she added reflectively, "I always knew that such occurred on hunts, but to see it happen for the first time . . ."

"Tell me, Aleen. You say your father taught you to bow, but he never took you to hunt?"

"He would not take me, though I begged him many times. 'Hunting is not for women,' he said, and now I know the truth of his words. Women do not belong here. Look at me," and she straightened her legs. "I am covered with dirt, my foot is caked with mud, my clothes—that is, *their* clothes— are torn. See, my hands are scratched, my hair is mussed, and. . ." She stopped as she realized she had exposed her plight once again for his amusement. Quickly she flashed a stern glance to forbid laughter, but her glance was in vain. Edmund was smiling at her, and a twinkle enlivened his eyes. Her attitude softened as she looked at him. It was comforting to be with him and to have his complete and understanding attention.

Aleen smiled back as the familiar feeling of self-consciousness returned. She must divert his attention from her or else risk prolonged embarrassment. "I do not know how it is you take pleasure in hunting and killing."

"There is great skill involved. The animals have keen hearing and smelling, and do not forget, they can run faster." There was a moment's silence before he asked, "Are you feeling better?"

Aleen silently nodded.

"Would you prefer to return to camp? Yes? Then I shall

have someone guide you back. Perhaps when you are rested you will remember all of this with less horror."

After helping her to her feet, he called for one of the men, whispered instructions, and watched for a moment as Aleen walked somewhat tiredly beside him toward the camp. Instructions for the soldiers to guide Aleen and the maidservant back to the castle were delivered by her guide on their return. Both were grateful to be free of the forest and eager for the comfort of clean clothes and the genteel accommodations of the castle.

The sun was high when they reached the stable, and judging from the noise from the kitchen, everyone was eating, for no one but the stable hands were about. Borrowing a cloak from Thorkil, Aleen flung it around her and cautiously crept to her room.

"I shall never again speak of hunting," she declared to Hester as she willingly surrendered herself to being washed, combed, and perfumed. "It is repulsive, tiring, painful, and cold." She slipped between cool linen sheets for a rest and added, "It was strenuous, but at least one part of the exercise was pleasing," and she smiled wistfully. Laying her head on the downy pillow, she soon fell into restful sleep. Hester smiled and sighed deeply with relief as she watched her mistress succumb to pleasurable comfort.

It was the next day at noontime that Aleen had decided to make an appearance before Edmund and the archers. They would see her at her prettiest, and she spent some time before her mirror arranging her hair and entwining ribbons about her head. Her tunic was carefully selected, the pink silk one, and with perfume on the sleeves she made her way majestically to the great hall. They will forget my appearance of yesterday, she vowed as she made certain her silk gown drifted about in the most flattering manner.

The assembly seemed unusually noisy, voices were loud, knives clattered against plates, and benches seemed to scrape unnecessarily against the floor. But the women glared up as Aleen floated by as though unaware of their presence.

They are jealous that I have won the respect of their young men, she thought as she proudly raised her head. After sitting down as daintily as possible, she smiled sweetly and looked about for confirmation that Edmund and the archers had observed her improved appearance.

The archers were looking her way, but there was something about their expression . . . They nodded in greeting, whispered devilishly among themselves, and ate heartily, yet they shared a conspiratorial pleasure that was intriguing and mystifying.

Bowls of steaming beans, peas, and lentils, and platters of beef, venison, and mutton were passed around, but as Aleen's eyes drifted down the length of the table, there, at the end of the table, swimming in brown gravy, were haunches of meat that Aleen recognized instinctively to be those of the boar she had been unable to kill.

Stealthy glances were exchanged among the archers as Aleen dawdled with the vegetables on her plate, but her appetite had been ruined. When she cautiously looked toward Edmund, he was speaking with those at table, no doubt unaware of the circumstances or significance of the huge platter placed so prominently on the table.

The archers were not of a disposition to deliberately distress her by requesting that the boar be prepared specifically; however, they were not above taking advantage of the situation to observe the reactions of a lady who had exhibited her feminine weaknesses in a most charming and characteristic manner.

When the meal was completed and the diners began leaving the room, Aleen vanished, leaving the archers to enjoy the satisfying confirmation of their masculine hardiness.

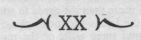

## XX

EDMUND WAS on another inspection tour of southern shires, and as was usual during his absences, the castle felt as though it were abandoned. Everyone was still in residence except Thane Godrey and a small escort of soldiers, yet the castle seemed as though life were somehow suspended, as though it existed somewhere between reality and the vagueness of a lonesome dream. At least it seemed so to Aleen, though she would not admit it if she had been fully aware of the underlying cause of her dejection.

The days since his departure had passed slowly, uneventfully, until one dreary afternoon when Lelia and Edith were deep into an afternoon nap. Aleen was bored. There had to be something different for her to do, and she opened the door and glanced down the hall for some hint of a suggestion, when, as though an invisible finger had pointed her attention to it, her eyes rested upon the library door. In the absence of something better to do, she would go there and read. Edmund had given her permission to use the room whenever she wished, and her mind flashed back to her first visit there, when Edmund had found her wandering about examining the books and wall hangings; how he had then offered his sympathy on the death of her father. Yes, she would go there and leisurely examine the room again. After looking back to where Edith slept on her mat and Lelia on the high bed, she noiselessly sneaked out.

She secured the key from Wulfric and entered the library, making certain the door was closed behind her. The room seemed smaller than she had remembered it. Its stillness was intense and invited relaxation. Had Edmund not said it was his retreat, his sanctuary of peace? The room was distinctly Edmund's, with its clusters of battle armaments upon the walls, its huge masculine furniture. It was as though a part of Edmund still lingered there, still haunted its precincts. She could feel him there as surely as she did that day when he had described the furnishings to her. But why should she feel so warmly, excitingly titillated if it were not that she was attracted to Edmund more than she cared to admit?

She glanced at the books propped against the long shelves that extended around three walls of the room, and the high stools placed before them. They were much too heavy and ponderous to entice her interest. Instead she selected a smaller book from the table and carried it to the end of the room to where the huge chair faced the fireplace against the back wall. The chair had been designed for Edmund's father, but it was now Edmund's, and she could almost envision him reclining in it. It was situated on a dais, on which Aleen sat and placed the book. She leaned against the carved arm and read with little interest until her eyes grew heavy from the sleepy atmosphere. Her head slipped onto the cushion of the seat, and she gradually fell into peaceful slumber.

How long she was there, she knew not, but approaching footsteps awakened her, and she desperately fought to dispel the resisting numbness of sleep.

"Do not disturb yourself," Edmund was saying. "Please remain. I am sorry to have awakened you. No, please stay where you are," he insisted as she attempted to gather up her skirt prior to standing. "I do not want you stumbling about."

The disrupted nap had left her numb, tired, and painfully sleepy. She remained sitting, as he directed.

"I came in only to deposit this book, which was given to me during my visit to Newbury. It is a lovely one," he said, holding it at an angle for her inspection. "The leather binding was tooled by a most gifted monk. It is lovely indeed." He sighed, his words bearing a hint of fatigue. "May I join you here?" he asked, looking upon the enticing cavity of the chair and its provision for a moment's relaxation. With an easy step or two he swung himself into the chair and sat down tiredly.

Was it a dream, or was Edmund actually sitting so close to her? "Your trip, sir—was it a pleasant one?" she asked, the words confirming the reality of the situation.

"Yes, but one always anticipates the return home."

His proximity unnerved her. Quickly she turned her head away. If only she could dash from the room, but he would only insist that she remain. Why, oh, why, did he have to find me in here? she thought, but she had no way of knowing he had heard from Wulfric of her presence there and had purposely entered.

Edmund leaned back in silence while Aleen waited patiently for the first opportunity to leave. Several minutes passed, with the silence drumming against her ears. Then Aleen's eyes opened in alarm. Wild tremors of excitement swelled through her being as Edmund began toying with the strands of her hair that had flown upon his leg with the sudden turning of her head. So still had she remained after that movement that the hair was not disturbed until he picked it up and began winding it upon a finger. Gradually his hand twisted and turned until her hair was wrapped around his hand. With firm but gentle pressure he turned her head toward him. She could not resist. The shivers of emotions rendered her helpless, and in a moment he was tilting her head until she was forced to look into his face. He was leaning toward her, but then a knock at the door disrupted the spell, and Wulfric's voice called to him.

Edmund did not take his eyes from her face as he acknowledged the scribe's presence. "Yes, Wulfric."

Reassured of his master's occupancy of the chair whose tall backrest shielded him from view, Wulfric announced the arrival of Thane Godfrey and his wish to confer with Edmund.

"Tell him I am coming," Edmund replied.

"Very well, my lord." The door closed.

Edmund tugged gently to release his hand, but the hair was knotted against it. Aleen would have to disentangle it, and as she pulled away strands of hair, he continued peering down at her until she thought she would faint under the scrutiny. Whether he moved his hand or she her head, she would never remember, but suddenly she was aware that his hand was softly touching her cheek, and to her amazement, she found her hand gently wrapped about his wrist. She lowered her head, and somehow his hand was free and hers had dropped to her lap.

He stood up and left without a word, leaving her to wonder how she would ever again be able to look upon him.

It was hot, but the breezes that always swept in from the bay were refreshing and made the weather tolerable. Healthy vegetation colored the farmlands that the bronzed peasants languidly tilled. Bees buzzed hurriedly about the wild roses that entwined the fences and around the daisies, violets, and cornflowers that grew in profusion in ditches and thickets. Clover had spread about the meadow, softly concealing the gouges and clumps of soil dislodged by the horse races and contests of the month before. So peaceful and beautiful was the meadow now that it was difficult to believe it had been thunderously pounded by the horses and trampled by hundreds of people. The land had been relinquished to them, and Aleen and Lelia eagerly claimed it again as their own.

Each day saw Cenook carrying them across the expanse to the beach, where Aleen waded in the surf up to her knees and Lelia thrashed happily in the gentle waves. These were busy days for Lelia, with seaweeds to be gathered and shaped into hills; there were shells to collect, pictures to draw in the sand, sea gulls to feed, and crabs to trap in sandy prisons. It was a blissful existence, this watching Lelia growing in health and happiness while enjoying the beauties of the world. It was a pleasure being with the child. She was affectionate and intelligent and loved Aleen as dearly as she might have loved her own mother, and Aleen gladly and copiously returned the affection. Lately Aleen was beginning to analyze the reasons for her own deep attachment to the child. She had never been attracted to children before. Why now should she be so strongly maternal? Was it the kindred element that attracted her Danish sensibilities, or was it pity for the child's loss of her mother? Was it her own lack of friends that made her depend on the child and made her so grateful for her company? Or was it because of the child's father? Whatever the reason, Aleen was certain of two things: that she dearly loved the child and that, were it not for Lelia, she could not have survived the former days of loneliness and painful rejection.

Lelia's treks to the beach were followed by a drying, a change of clothing if needed, a lunch beneath the cooling shade of a tree, and a nap beneath its leafy bowers, while Cenook contentedly grazed nearby. A folded cloth from the lunch basket served as a pillow for the child, who always lay nestled beside Aleen, who leaned against the trunk, as was her custom. There was always a smiling, "I love you, Lelia," to which the child would smile, relax, and drift into sleep. I know not how I could exist without you, Lelia, Aleen often thought to herself. You are a joy and a blessing.

For all its peacefulness and the pleasures involved, there was something uneasy about these daily outings. Aleen glanced about. It was as though someone were spying on her. No one was seen. The observer had to be in the castle. Perhaps Wilfreda was attempting to gain evidence to discredit her. Wilfreda was always lurking about. Perhaps the women were searching for an incident about which to gossip, or could it be that they still did not trust the Dane in their midst and were endeavoring to discover her in the act of signaling the Danish ships that sometimes crossed the horizon? Her suspicions were always dismissed: Let them gaze if they wish. Yet the feeling was persistent and annoying.

In spite of this uneasiness, the outings usually followed their accustomed order and climaxed with the same game—a frolic to catch Cenook. After his afternoon of grazing freely, he was refreshed, and his inborn vitality stirred his spirit to uncontrollable limits. With their every approach to snare him, he would give a start, raise his noble head high, and gallop a short distance, to await the next approach and his subsequent darting away. "You are so smart, my pretty," Aleen would say, "but you are a rascal to tease us so."

Lelia delighted in the game, and giggled excitedly as she hobbled near him, and her squeals of excitement echoed about the meadow each time he scurried away.

"Look, Lelia," Aleen would say, "you have but to whistle, and he will do the same." And her whistle, which, during more tranquil moments would signal for his immediate approach, now only sparked his nature to play. With each whistle he bolted, twisted, and galloped off, to await the next signal or approach.

Aleen had raised her arms in a futile attempt to corral him when she unmistakably felt the customary uneasiness of someone's gaze upon her. She hesitated while the wind tumbled through her hair and skirt. This would be one time when she would not dismiss the urge to confront the offender, and she turned toward the castle, dropped her hands to her hips, and glared defiantly. Fortunately, her eyes were keen.

One by one she examined each window until the sun reflected its light from a metal object. In an instant her eyes caught the flash, and in the dimness of the interior she could distinguish the familiar form of Edmund. He did not retreat from sight, as she expected, but kept his position and looked down steadfastly upon Aleen as she gazed steadily up at him.

Only Lelia's call and Cenook's nuzzling on her back broke the silent communication. She turned to grasp the elusive reins. They mounted, Lelia sitting before Aleen in the saddle, as was their custom. As the horse began its trek toward the castle, Aleen placed her arm securely around Lelia and looked up once more to find Edmund still looking upon them. A nudge in Cenook's flank, and they were riding with the breeze toward the castle gate.

It was bewildering, this sudden interest Edmund had in her. She required time to think about this, but a sudden flash of awareness struck at her heart with a chill. Could it be that Edmund saw in her a resemblance to the child's mother? A family resemblance would not be impossible to detect. Aleen was overcome with pulsating jealousy that a dead wife should cling so tenaciously and claim so completely the mind and heart of a husband who now belonged to another. Such a love as Marion claimed, in her letters, to have shared with Edmund could not have vanished so thoroughly with her passing, and if Edmund's love for Marion was as tender and fulfilling as she had claimed, Aleen was certain that Edmund was seeking, in her, Marion's resurrection.

By the time Cenook had arrived at the stable, Aleen was certain of her analysis, and with convulsive heartache she bitterly wished that the dead would bequeath such love to the living. Other thoughts caused pricks of resentment. Why should Edmund see in her a resemblance to the pale, quiet, timid, plain, unassuming Marion? If her mind was so tormented by Edmund's comparison, her heart suffered a similar fate, and her conscience rebuked her, for the young woman who had been her tutor, her girlish confidante, the woman for whom Aleen had once held a generous measure of filial love, was now remembered by her kinswoman with bitter, impassioned resentment.

# ~ XXI ~

THE TRADING ship lay quiescently anchored in the tranquil waters of the bay following its long ordeal at sea. It complained in woody creaks and rope strains, but nevertheless surrendered to its enforced idleness and submitted indulgently to the sleepy rocking of its watery bed. From the shore the ship appeared deserted but for an occasional mariner who from time to time tended to the needs of the bold but now somewhat humbled vessel.

The activity on the docks explained the ship's lack of industry, for its crew and its traders all seemed to be on shore. There was the haggling over the exchange of moneys, the supervising of the slaves as they rolled kegs of oil to the storage places, stacked chests, and carried covered baskets to less crowded areas. Shouts and orders filled the air that was already noisy with sounds of scraping, rolling, creaking cargo, the grunts of the workmen, and the rapid flow of foreign words. Above the turmoil were heard the excited arguing of local merchants in search of bargains and the dark-haired, flashing-eyed Venetians vehemently denouncing the ridiculously low prices offered for wares "garnered from distant lands and brought to this shore at great peril."

Seated on giant twists of hemp that were stacked away from the main routes of activity, Aleen and Lelia were able to see all, and they were awestruck by what passed before them. Shiny black men with little more than loincloths about their bodies struggled and sweated beneath their burdens, while casually walking around were the proud Italians and men of other nations who had joined the trading ship on its route. There were few women, but these were equally interesting, and as they passed before the hemp, they completely captivated Aleen's attentions. They were dancing girls from a far and mysterious land, and nothing was lost to Aleen as she watched their undulating, rhythmic movements, from the sensuous eyes that peered above fluttering veils, the rings and chains that jangled noisily, the shimmering, almost transparent cloths that draped their bodies, down to their bare feet, which seemed to caress the planks of the wharf with their every step.

Had not Aleen been preoccupied with her surveillance, she would have heard Thane Godfrey approaching. Startled by the mention of her name and the group of men standing beside him, she slid from her perch and smiled through the introductions of the captain, navigators, and officers of the Venetian ship. They were all handsome, weather-toughened, and courteous men, but they were as anxious to be off on their business as was Thane Godfrey. They left after a respectable time, while Lelia desperately clung to Aleen's hand.

They crossed the dock, weaving between the clay jugs and the crates in their path, and boarded a long skiff, but as the oarsmen settled into position and prepared to place their oars in the locks, the captain ordered a halt and whispered to one of the men. Immediately he leaped out and made his way toward Aleen.

"My dear lady," he said, carefully pronouncing his words with a pleasant accent, "the captain invites you and the child to inspect our ship. We have treasures on board which a lady of your distinction would find of interest. You would honor us by your visit. Have you ever boarded a Venetian ship, little child?" He asked, directing his words to Lelia.

"No. She has never been aboard a ship of any nation," Aleen answered for her.

"Then it would be our privilege to escort her about our humble vessel. You and the child would do us great honor by your inspection."

Aleen was thrilled at the prospect of boarding the foreign vessel, especially since it had plied the waters of many foreign lands and had, as was indicated, alluring treasures that only the discriminating would appreciate. The prospect, however, created a dilemma. It would be proper to secure the permission of Edmund or Thane Godfrey, but Edmund was somewhere in the castle, and Thane Godfrey, paper and pen in hand, was in the midst of settling an argument between red-faced merchants. He could not be reached, for the crush of men about him prevented penetration, and there was no time to seek out Edmund. A delay in her decision or a declination of the gracious invitation would indicate distrust and cause keen embarrassment to the visitors. Their kind offer must be accepted, and as Aleen walked to the skiff with Lelia, her thoughts tumbled about. These seamen had been here many times before, or they would not be permitted to walk around so freely, and Thane Godfrey's attitude toward them had been easy and friendly. What harm could ensue from a visit to a vessel anchored in Lauxburgh's waters? Besides, their proposal had been presented as though they had been accustomed to entertaining visitors and were themselves fearful lest they offend her by their failure to invite her aboard.

The captain himself escorted them about the vessel, pointing out with pride the quarters of the officers, the galley, the hold, but his geniality was discarded in a surprising manner when they reached the lower deck of the ship. There they came upon sailors lounging about in the doorways, where the drafts of air offered respite from the heat. Verbal attacks in their native tongue were cast upon the sailors, who looked up in a drunken stupor as though not comprehending the words of their captain, or if they were comprehended, it was beyond their power to enforce them. There was something curious about the glazed look in their eyes. Aleen had seen drunken men before, but the intensely intoxicating effects they were experiencing could only have resulted from a potent beverage of which the men of England were as yet unfamiliar.

Aleen watched as one of the men weakly reached toward a gourd, plunged it into a bucket, and drank gustily from its depths. What he did not consume he deliberately splashed upon his head, and while the captain berated his lack of proper behavior before a lady of such noble stature, she continued watching as the water ran over the man's dirty hair and face, onto his shoulders, until small droplets of moisture trickled down his bare, hairy chest. The captain, appalled by the man's conduct before a distinguished guest, hurried Aleen away, but Lelia, who had been tarrying behind, stared longingly at the water. With the swiftness characteristic of a child engaged in mischievous activity, she reached inside the bucket for the gourd and drank her fill, as water dripped from the side of her mouth and onto her dress.

"Lelia," Aleen cried as she turned to look for her charge,

who was then holding the gourd to her mouth. Rushing back to where Lelia stood, she snatched the gourd from the child's hand and quickly dropped it into the bucket. Bending closely to the child, she wiped the droplets from her dress and rebuked her in gentle tones. "Lelia, you must tell me when you wish refreshment," she said, glancing with poorly suppressed disgust in the direction of the dirty men, whose eyes were vaguely following her movement. "You should not have tasted of this water, for surely it is tainted."

With a light hand on the child's shoulder, Aleen steered her back to where the guide was awaiting her return. But before they left the quarters, the sound of the gourd plunking into the bucket was heard again. A slight turn of her head toward the noise, and a sudden thought jarred her recollection. It seemed unusual for drunken men to crave the satisfaction of water, but with a shrug she dismissed all interest in them. Stepping into the sunlight, she cast her attention immediately on a seaman nimbly climbing the mast to secure the end of a sail whose securing strap had worked itself loose, permitting it to sway untidily with each roll of the ship.

The inspection of the ship continued, but Aleen's interest had been spent. The heavy accent of her guide taxed her mind, and his detailed explanations, she thought, could interest only a builder of ships. She was not sorry when the tour was over and she was once again in the skiff crossing the water.

During the small voyage back to Lauxburgh, Aleen sat on the back seat of the skiff, her gaze fixed upon the castle, with its majestic towers reaching toward the heavens. It was a lovely sight, for it stood so proudly, so elegantly, dominating the bay and the lands encircling it. With a rush of pride she looked down upon Lelia, whose head leaned tiredly against her. There were many prejudices and difficulties existing there for both of them, but together they could meet and conquer all. Nuzzling her chin against the softness of Lelia's golden hair, Aleen smiled wistfully as the oars plopped into the water and the waves gurgled swiftly against their shanks.

A wayfarer, newly arrived at Lauxburgh, would have thought the Venetians in command of the castle, for no one except an occasional Saxon soldier was in sight; only black slaves and broad-chested, hard-muscled, flashing-eyed Venetians were there, laboring under the weight of carved chests and willow baskets as they carried them up the stone steps from the dock to the side entrance in the castle wall. One by one they crossed the courtyard on their way to the great hall, where they were relieved of their burdens, only to make their way back down to the dock for the next consignment.

The battlement near the side entrance afforded an excellent view for Aleen and Lelia to observe both the activities of the dock and the industrious men who mounted the steep stairs with their articles representing crafts of many distant and alluring lands.

Later in the day the goods and treasures would be carefully displayed in the great hall for the inspection and procurement of the discriminating nobles of Lauxburgh and the wealthy landowners and merchants of nearby villages. It was for this reason that the display was scheduled for the day after the ship's arrival. Messengers had been sent to interested parties immediately after the anchoring, and time was needed for the purchasers to journey to Lauxburgh. This was the usual procedure when merchant ships arrived, but if Edith had not reported this to her, Aleen would not have known. Wilfreda would never have informed her. Since the time of Aleen's visit to Wilfreda's chamber when acidly bitter words were exchanged, Wilfreda had avoided her, and when contact was mandatory, Wilfreda conducted the business with contemptuous aloofness.

Thane Godfrey and Scribe Wulfric were likewise undependable for information. Thane Godfrey, as Edmund's chief envoy, was usually on the roads of the country on business for the ealdorman, and the scribe was often too preoccupied with the multitudinous chores of his office. Neither could Aleen look to the women for information concerning the activities of the visitors. They still ridiculed the Viking in deliberately audible conversations, and waved as banners of superiority their Anglo-Saxon breeding. Their evaluation of her, even from the beginning, had been correct, they reasoned. What well-bred Saxon woman, trained in the ways of gracious living and accustomed to the comforts and privileges of noble stature, would dare to take bow in hand and threaten to plunge arrows into their hearts, as she had done the day of the fair? She was as crude and barbaric as others of her lowly race, and therefore not deserving of their friendship or company, even if she was the lawful wife of Edmund, the Lady of Lauxburgh, and, therefore, preeminent in rank. They would not be so considerate as to inform her of any activity or codes of conduct relating to visitors.

Aleen was dependent entirely on the servants for whatever information she could garner, but at times this too was insufficient, as it was on this occasion. Somehow Hester and Edith had failed to learn or to relay to her that it was customary for the castle's occupants to avoid the great hall during the time of the arrival and arrangement of goods. The merchants were born exhibitionists and wished to amaze their potential buyers with a surprisingly grand display of their merchandise.

Innocently unaware of the restriction, Aleen found herself near the great hall the morning after the Venetians' arrival, and when Lelia expressed interest in the high-pitched wailing of a flute, Aleen saw no reason to deny the child's curiosity. Together they entered, and were immediately struck with its contents. Tables seemed to be everywhere, and upon them were objects that dazzled the eye and benumbed the senses.

Venetian merchants were everywhere, nervously arranging their wares. The items were placed first one way and then another in what they hoped would be the most eye-catching display. Each table, it seemed, was reserved for a particular group of items. One was laden with gold and silver drinking vessels and plates, another with jewels of every color and size, including pearls and ambers, which were in great demand. Another bore every manner of jewelry—belt buckles and golden wrist bands of exquisite designs and inlays. There were jeweled brooches and rings, some etched, and others displaying gems of enormous size. Waist chains and necklaces were beaded, jeweled, and enameled in every conceivable design. Other tables were strewn with articles of ivory, jewel caskets, horns for the blowing of signals, silks from distant lands, fine linens, furs, pelts, jugs of wine, spices, and veils whose blue, purple, yellow, and crimson transparency boasted a comparison to celestial tissue. Strange bottles and vials were elegantly displayed on another table, but when Aleen approached it, the very air betrayed their contents. The mingled odors of perfumes assailed her nostrils, producing a sensuous tide of euphoria. With eyes gently closed, she breathed deeply of the scent produced from the exotic flowers of mysterious lands.

Her preoccupation had distracted her momentarily from Lelia, and when Aleen looked for her, Lelia was near the only group of people in the room. Flutists sat cross-legged on the floor near her, blowing softly into their instruments. Standing near them were harpists and other musicians, whose flutes, embossed in fragile figures of gleaming metals, were of various lengths and thicknesses. When they moved to take up places beside the other musicians on the floor, Aleen stared in disbelief. Two of the women she had seen the day before on the dock, the two whose forms had been properly swathed in layers of silky fabrics, whose faces were discreetly hidden behind veils, were now standing there less modestly arrayed. Red silk skirts hung from their hips, the transparency of the fabric revealing the slender outline of their legs. Twists of silk scarves scarcely covered the upper parts of their feminine forms, leaving their slender waists bare. Clicking bracelets, gaudy collections of rings, and neck chains with dangling amulets decorated their bodies, as did a draped string of small golden disks that rimmed the forehead.

They were beautiful. Their dark skin was smooth and flawless, and their faces, seen through the transparent veils that partially hid the lower part of their faces, were nearly spellbinding. Black eyebrows arched gently over long thick eyelashes. Their lips were red, their hair long and glossy black, and their bodies sleek, well-formed, and temptingly appealing. And as Aleen drew nearer and heard their soft voices, she understood their language to be different from that of the Venetians.

Lelia limped toward a chair that had been earlier moved aside, and as if in imitation, one of the dancing girls also sat down and watched the other, who began undulating her bare arms to the enticing voices of the flutes. Her movements were slow and fluid, and the transparent veil she held in her hands softly rippled with the gentle turns of her body.

The harpists began plucking their strings, giving a richer, fuller body to the strains of the flutes, which ranged from thin weak wails of the long slender instruments to the deeper, louder, thicker tones of the larger horns. The music was beguiling, and the dancer's movements expertly interpreted it with her smooth, easy movements.

Aleen was captivated by the dance, but wondered how and why the staid Saxons permitted such blatantly impassioned antics. If this were the dancer's native dance, and the Saxons accepted it as such, and further permitted its performance, they were to be commended for their intelligent appreciation of the art and their tolerance of their guests' lack of clothing. Perhaps, though, the dancers were to array themselves more modestly when performing before their hosts.

There was no doubting but that they were practicing for a later performance. The area reserved was larger than was needed for musicians and dancers. A standing audience, or an audience of squatters on the floor, was obviously expected. Whether or not the two unexpected and uninvited guests displeased them, they did not indicate, and Aleen remained sitting on the floor beside Lelia's chair, watching as if enchanted.

The music alternately developed from subdued strains to mounting, frenzied melodies enhanced with sweeps of graceful hands against strings and the precision movements of fingers along the golden throats of the flutes.

The gentle swayings and turns of the dancer picked up momentum, her slender arms stretching at times above her head, with the silk veil trailing and twisting about her.

No movement was lost on the enraptured Aleen, from the tilting turns of the head to the shrugs of the shoulders, to the swaying of the hips, the bending of the knees, to the movements of the bare feet as they stroked the floor with each swishing movement.

A smile and a prankish gleam lit up the face that had been so studiously absorbed moments before, and when the mad, whirling music returned to melodious waves of tones, Aleen removed her shoes and made certain she was carefully concealed from the vision of the musicians and at a discreet distance from the dancer. Timidly she turned about in rhythm with the music, first looking over one shoulder and turning around, then looking over the other and turning in that direction. Gradually gathering confidence, she moved to the side of Lelia's chair and whispered, "Lelia, see, I can dance too," and the child's face lit up with gaiety.

"Dance, 'Leen ... dance, 'Leen," she pleaded, and she bounced excitedly in the chair.

"It is quite easy, my love," but she knew there was a vast difference between her hesitant, stiff movements and the sweeping, flowing gyrations of the dancer. Nevertheless, it was pleasant having music dictate one's actions, and the secret, she soon learned, was to permit the melodies to possess the body and permit it full sway.

The idle dancer had watched the mimicry with interest, and after a moment she smiled, rose from her place, and walked toward Aleen. Aleen abruptly stopped, fully expecting the girl to be offended by the sad imitation, but she was pleasantly smiling, to Aleen's complete relief. Untying a small filmy silk veil that had been loosely draped about her hips, she waved it, showing Aleen the proper positions for the arms. Gently handing it to Aleen, she placed her hands on Aleen's arms and slowly turned her around. Aleen understood the wordless lesson and began moving to the music, watching her tutor's approving look as she did so. The girl raised her skirt to show the correct position of the feet, and when satisfied with her student's reaction, passed to another lesson. With her hands steadily against her shoulders, she indicated with a rolling of her hips the manner in which Aleen was to move this way and then that. Then there was the raising of each shoulder in a rolling action not unlike the movement of waves. There were twists and trailings of the veil, bends and turns with the head held backward. With her teacher joining in the dance and suggesting movements to coincide with the music, Aleen gained confidence and permitted her emotions full expression.

It was delightfully exhilarating, and as the music intensified, her heart beat furiously, until it seemed the melody itself was throbbing in her veins. Tossing her head back, she twirled around and around, until the columns of the balconies above her revolved in dizzying spirals. Dancing toward Lelia, she swayed around the chair and teasingly trailed the veil around the child.

Lelia burst into giggles and snatched at the veil, which barely eluded her grasp. Again and again Aleen teasingly shook the veil about the child, snapping it back just in time to make Lelia chuckle with delight.

Closing her eyes, Aleen swayed with the music as though she were one with the ever-restless rocking, rippling sea and the vacillating winds. Instinctively she knew she was doing better than what could be expected of one who was just introduced to the art, and she delighted in her newfound freedom, and spun freely. Her skirt billowed with each turn, and the scarf fluttered softly about her face.

The teacher was pleased with her pupil and guided her near the other dancer, who nodded approvingly. Together they danced, communicating, with quick glances and smiles, an unspoken language that required naught but friendly acceptance.

Again Aleen danced toward the clapping child, until she playfully struggled against the veil that wound about her. The music was swelling with rapid waves of glorious warmth, as the sun, which blazes in magnificence after clearing obstructing clouds. Frantically the nimble fingers flew up and down the pipes, until she thought the excitement of their wailing would take away the little air she was able to capture in quick, gasping breaths.

Throwing her head back, she twirled around in unison with the frenzied melody and watched the columns above her revolve in a maddening blur, but the blur consisted not only of the columns, but faces, many faces, stony faces, disapproving faces.

She stopped with a start and looked up. The balconies were crowded with women—Judith, her cohorts, and Wilfreda—all looking down upon her in judicial sternness.

The music stopped, with trailing notes from flutes that were deprived an impassioned ending. An awkwardly painful silence claimed the room as Aleen realized the inelegant situation in which she had so innocently placed herself. She stood abased before her accusers. She struggled desperately for breath, her heart beating madly in her breast from the exertion of the dance until she thought it would burst forth from her body. But her discomforts were as nothing compared to the depth of shame into which she was so forcefully plunged.

Their thoughts were easily discerned. It was undignified of her, the lady of the castle, to behave so frivolously before anyone, much less visitors from another land. Instead of concerning herself with the Venetian men of wealth and position, she had instead improperly cavorted with half-clad dancers.

No one could gauge the searing pain of her public degradation, but suddenly all was intensified when Edmund's voice filled the room. "A beautiful dance, an excellent performance. You must all join me in giving gratitude to the musicians and the skillful dancers."

Aleen had spun around at the sound of his voice, and watched in near-panic as he walked across the room from a side door. Edmund motioned to the people who were crowded about each door, and to the ladies on the galleries. "Please, all of you, join me in a drink of friendship with our talented visitors."

Why is it he is always there when I least wish him to be? she moaned. Why, oh, why did I forget myself? But in a moment Edmund had taken her by the arm and was leading her to a table, where the cupbearers were hurriedly setting up goblets and jugs of wine. He was smiling pleasantly as he placed tankards into reluctant Saxon hands, and taking a jug from the servant, he began pouring wine into the vessels already held by the Venetians.

"Linguist, you may convey to our honored guests our welcome and gratitude for the treasures they have brought here, and to the dancers and musicians our appreciation for the dance they have just performed." The turbaned, dark-faced linguist, who had listened with diligence to each word, turned to the performers and began in a low, rapid voice to translate Edmund's words.

"To the visitors," Edmund intoned, raising his goblet, but only a faint flutter of response greeted his toast.

Aleen sipped cautiously of the bitter brew, but Edmund, she noticed, had gulped his down with relish. He was convivial—too convivial—in his efforts to relieve the awkward coolness of the group. The Saxons would not succumb to his efforts, and continued to glare disapprovingly at Aleen, yet he continued his constant chatter through the interpreter, as though he was oblivious of their attitudes.

The visitors were speaking of Aleen's dancing and the ease with which she had so quickly learned to perform the movements. It was the kind of attention that made Aleen think only of flight.

"Yes," Edmund agreed pridefully. "The Lady Aleen has many talents."

Shivers of total abasement seized her mortified being, shivers as cold as the stone floor beneath her naked feet. "My shoes," she gasped, quickly raising her fingers to her mouth.

Edmund turned toward her and surmised her dilemma. Their eyes met, and he smiled. "Where are they?" he was saying as casually as if inquiring about the weather. Aleen experienced boundless gratitude for his conduct in endeavoring to make what had transpired earlier appear as an acceptable occurrence which he, for one, regarded as proper and normal. In response to his question, she hesitantly made her way toward the chair, the Saxons stepping aside as she passed among them. Edmund bent down and held one of the shoes for Aleen's convenience. Raising her foot delicately, he slipped it on with ease. Aleen looked down on the dark hair of the gallant man before her and glanced cautiously about to catch the reaction of the silent observers. They were as coolly condescending as before, but no one's expression matched that of Wilfreda, who was standing at a distance, staring toward Aleen with insidious hatred.

What had Wilfreda told her that day in her chamber? "You will avoid the company of my son. . . ." And now, here she was before an assembly of witnesses, with Edmund kneeling at her feet.

"Are the merchants present?" Edmund began asking around. Several men made themselves prominent. "Very well, then, may we begin to examine your articles?"

The men, dark-skinned from hours on sun-streaked oceans, nodded assent and eagerly walked toward the tables to assist and encourage their potential buyers. Cinctures of shiny fabrics encircled their girth, and this they rubbed repeatedly. Their eyes twinkled greedily as they placed their hands satisfactorily about their persons, as though eagerly anticipating an increase to their corpulence. They were almost piratical in appearance, with golden rings glistening from their hands and white rows of teeth grinning slyly under thick mustaches.

Whispers grew in volume as the people turned toward the display and exclaimed over their excellence and rarity. Aleen looked down at the forgotten veil she had been holding on to so desperately. One corner was hopelessly rumpled. Walking toward the dancing girls, who were sharing a conversation over their half-filled goblets, Aleen motioned for the linguist and handed the veil to her tutor and newly acquired friend.

"Please convey to the lady my appreciation for the attention she so graciously awarded me, and for her kindly instruction." She paused to allow time for the translation. Looking from one beautiful face to the other, she continued, "Please tell them I shall never forget their kindness, the beauty of their music, or their company, which pleasured me greatly."

The modulated rippling of the translation fell strokingly upon her ears as she fought back tears of self-pity. *Why do I succeed so completely in alienating myself from these Saxons, when with ease I can encourage friendship in others?*

Her teacher spoke in soft fluctuations. The linguist turned toward Aleen. "The dancer wishes you to keep her veil as a token of esteem." Aleen looked upon the smiling face and the proffered veil, whose heavenly transparency seemed to quiver of its own volition.

"No, she must keep it," Aleen said, while laying her slender white hand gently against the dancer's arm. "Please tell her she must keep it. I am grateful, but she will have more need of it than I, for I shall never dance again."

Aleen looked into the large, sensuous eyes as the linguist rattled the translation, but she lowered her eyes quickly to avoid the dancer's sympathetic understanding. She turned, and to her surprise found Edmund standing behind her. "I thought you had left," she said quickly in excuse for having ignored his presence.

"There are many things displayed here which might interest you," he was saying in dismissing her apology. "There are books written in many languages, which you may wish to examine. Please look about at your leisure. You may have whatever you desire."

"I desire nothing," she replied, her words tinged with despondency. "Should I procure anything, they would adjudge me unworthy to possess it. With your permission, sir, I shall retire to my chamber."

"No," he snapped with an intense frown. "You must stay

and mingle. If you conduct yourself as though you are guilty of an indiscretion, you will augment the fallacy of their opinions. Pretend you are unaware of them," he whispered. "Mingle among them and speak kindly," and he stared into the large brown eyes as though transmitting into her being fortitude of spirit and strength of determination. "Go, now, and be as though nothing is amiss."

Under his forceful stare and with his admonitions sounding in her ears, she moved away. Her smile was vague but her attitude amicable as she approached a table to examine jeweled rings and pearls in which she had no interest whatsoever. She was examining a casket of small pearls when a group of ladies joined her at the table. They continued their conversation as though unaware of Aleen standing beside them.

"Perhaps pearls would be more suitable than rubies," Aleen heard Judith saying. "See if there are some of the proper size," another voice suggested.

Judith looked about the table, on which a great variety of gems was displayed. "May I see these?" Judith asked, and without waiting for a reply, she took the casket containing the pearls from Aleen's hands as easily as if Aleen had been holding them for her. No recognition of Aleen was made; no mention of Aleen's name. They were boldly enforcing their ostracism of her by being coldly indifferent to her presence.

Smitten by their cruel conduct, Aleen moved to the next table, where another group of ladies was excitedly examining a great variety of cloths. There were fabrics of every known fiber—silks from China, cottons from Egypt, linens, woolens—each boasting unique designs in its weave. The colors rivaled those of the rainbow, and the wide selection presented difficulties to the ladies, who found it challenging to choose among them.

Aleen selected a length of purple silk and held it before her. Her thoughts, however, were busy, not with the sheen and softness of the cloth, but on a voice that somehow reached her ear in spite of louder voices nearby. "How can she claim to be a suitable guardian for the child when she has not the discretion to avoid the company of immoral women?" "She wished to draw attention to herself by entering the hall before the others," another voice added. "She may be the lady of the castle, but this does not give her license to disregard our traditional observances." "It is my opinion she has proved herself unworthy of our respect and the child's affections." Yet another voice continued the theme: "She has proved herself to be as common as *those* women." Aleen immediately knew by the accentuation that the performers were considered only a little lower in social rank than the Danes. Perhaps, Aleen reasoned, because we do not expose our bodies. "I knew it to be a serious error in judgment for Edmund to have married her," the voice continued. "It would have been proper had he chosen from among his own race, instead of a barbarian who so readily displays her true worth. She will no doubt continue her supervision of the child and attempt to convince us that what she has done is not worthy of reproach." "Poor Edmund," another voice added, but Aleen did not wait to hear. As though propelled by the urgings of a somnambulistic voice, she walked away. The purple cloth she had held so tightly against her slithered to the floor.

The door was her only salvation, and as she walked toward it, she felt an overriding indignation that the Saxon women had so boldly shown their disapproval of her. It was not only unchristian of them, but brazen that these—her subordinates—should dare to judge her actions so cruelly. But the reasoning that smote her most was her own disappointment with herself for allowing their opinions to attack and conquer her natural tendency to boldly confront and dominate any opposition. Why had she yielded so easily to their criticism when she knew she should have remained to stare unwaveringly at them with a challenge to confrontation that they would dare not accept? There was no hope of ever winning their friendship. It was sad knowing she had succeeded only in further alienating herself, when she had always before been so successful in charming and winning. Their consistent denunciation of her had drained her spirit more completely than she had realized, and as she walked through the halls, the stone walls likewise seemed to rebuke her with their coldness.

Aleen stopped. Blocking the way to her room were two maidservants sharing engrossing comments. She could not bring herself to pass them. If there were only some hole, some crack in the walls she could hide in to await the ending of this painful trial. There was a hole, of sorts—the shadowed stairway leading to the tower. With carefully placed steps she reached the safety of its shadow and quietly climbed the height. Carefully opening the creaky wooden door at the top, she stepped into the elements. Immediately her hair was disturbed by winds spawned by an approaching storm. The air smelled of its moisture, and the swiftness of the moving clouds attested to its imminence. Looking down from her place, Aleen numbly watched the swaying trees of the meadow and forest. On the bay, the tide, as though unimpressed with the magnificence of the Venetian ship, rocked it about on noisy waves with careless indignity.

In spite of the turmoil of the elements, she sensed a presence, and spun around to see Edmund mounting the top step, holding a purple cloth that was abruptly caught up by the wind. Quickly she turned away, as if expecting him to disappear with the immediate diversion of attention, but he approached, stood beside her, and looked down upon the restless bay.

Her thoughts flashed about. How strange it is, she thought, that he ignored and neglected me for so long, and that he is now so persistent in his interest of me.

"I entered this place unobserved, sir. How did you know where to find me?" she asked, not taking her eyes away from the watery horizon.

"The door here was left open, and the draft in the hall alerted me, especially since the maidservants said they had not seen you pass. You left too soon, Aleen. There were many articles you did not examine. Even the child was saddened that you left so quickly."

"Lelia," Aleen gasped, and moved as though ready to dash toward her.

"Do not concern yourself," Edmund said, placing a restraining hand on her arm. "Edith has her amused."

"How thoughtless of me," she said in distress, looking up into the heavens. "I was too concerned with my own affairs to remember the child." Wearily she turned toward the crenellated wall.

"You worry yourself needlessly about the child," Edmund continued. "She is being adequately cared for. I did not wish to alarm you by mention of her name. I merely stated it to prove that we regretted your premature departure."

"*We*, sir? You exaggerate. There is no one there, save the child, who has interest in me. I am certain the assembly was even relieved by my early departure."

Edmund knew not how to answer, but before he could reply, she spoke quietly, "My lord, tell me. Is dancing so very wrong?"

"Indeed it is not." There was a hesitation before he added, "They are envious of you, Aleen. Why is it you cannot perceive that?" He turned toward her, but she was suddenly oblivious of all but the words that seemed to have been incorrectly borne to her ears by the vacillating wind. It all seemed unreal. Edmund, who only a few weeks ago had seemed to despise and dislike her, was now professing his awareness of her problems, was admitting to having analyzed them, and was now rendering his judgment by calling it envy, of all things.

"Envy, sir?"

"Yes, envy. They resent your freedom of spirit, your love and enjoyment of life. They have been shackled long with the restrictions of conduct that have evolved here. They are envious of those who are not similarly restrained. Unfortunately, their rules of proper behavior have developed in such a manner as to render them overly critical of the smallest infractions. I sincerely regret that they are stifled in their pleasures, Aleen. Pity them."

I will not, Aleen thought bitterly. But why, Edmund, why is it you do not see that it is your mother who is responsible for their attitudes and their unfavorable view on life? But then, perhaps you are aware, she thought, and you are unable to alter and correct them. It was a legitimate observation that she could not bring herself to voice.

The silent moments passed slowly, awkwardly. When Aleen again spoke, the words were cold and forthright. "All our problems can be resolved simply, Edmund. Send me from this country."

"What is that?" he asked, turning toward her again.

"Permit me to leave, sir. Send me away, if you will."

"But why, Aleen? Where do you wish to go?"

"I wish to be sent to Wermouth. I do naught but cause you shame here. I shall never be accepted by the women, no matter how hard I try or wish to be. I succeed only in scandalizing them. When I am at Wermouth, the marriage would still be honored by my people."

Edmund had suddenly become disturbingly alert. "Surely you know that Wermouth was captured and is now controlled by Ecfrith. Had you forgotten?" She had not forgotten, for after the death of her father, when her brother did not return in time to claim the inheritance of the kingdom, the neighboring king overran and took the territory by force. Even now, Aleen feared Alcuin would never return from his journey of exploration.

"Do you think you would still be welcomed there?" Edmund was visibly relieved with the introduction of this hindrance to her plan.

"Then send me to Gruntvig. My father's people will accept me there."

"But what of Lelia? Would you not miss her?"

"I would hope, sir, that you would give me leave to take her with me. I will send her to visit here whenever you like."

"You have given this careful thought?" Before she could answer, he added emphatically, "No, I will not permit it. Speak no more of this! Here," he said, changing the course of their conversation. "See what I have brought you."

Aleen did not move.

"Here, see what it is," he coaxed.

Aleen reluctantly turned, her eyes falling upon a length of purple cloth Edmund was proudly holding up for her approval. "Is not this the cloth you were admiring?"

Aleen could not bring herself to confirm the correctness of his selection, so pleased and surprised was she that he had so carefully watched her and wished to please her with an unexpected gift.

The darkness, brought on by thick gray clouds, softly fell about them, erasing the iridescence she had briefly noticed before on the cloth.

"What shall you make of this?" he asked while draping it around her shoulders.

No answer came forth as Aleen stared up into his face.

"The color becomes you," he said looking tenderly into her eyes as he continued clutching the fabric.

He is a man of contradictions, she thought, while staring upon his intense features. He professes to be inclined toward the religious life, yet a man with such intentions would not be spending so much time in comforting and reassuring me and pleasing me with gifts, and ... and looking upon me so tenderly.

"You know, Aleen, you dance well," he said with gentle conviction. Immediately Aleen turned her head at the painful recollection. His hand went swiftly to her face, and with tenderness he turned her head until their gaze once again met. She stood as though transfixed as she watched him bending low over her, until, with surges of excitement, she felt the softness of his lips upon hers. The transition from a world of gusty winds, crashing waves, and grumbling clouds was easily made as she entered a pleasanter world of overwhelming emotions she had never before experienced—a world composed of the pleasure and satisfaction, of the mingled emotions of two lovers, an all-encompassing world of gentleness, fulfillment, the culmination of unconscious desires, of complete and willing surrender.

His lips were pressing harder, more earnestly, until their combined emotions were as the winds spiraling about them, as deafening in their ears as the thunder roaring above them, as violent as the lightening that sparkled and crackled nearby. It was a moment that she earnestly wished would extend into eternity. When at last he held her tightly, with her ear pressed against his heart, she was conscious of nothing except the thunder of his heartbeat and the rhythm of his rapid breathing. The embrace was a protection against any unpleasant intrusion, even the fury of the threatening weather. Here was warmth against the chilling breezes, satisfying healing for all injuries, comfort, and a proof of his loving interest in her. The disappointments of the past months were forgotten in one grand moment, and nothing mattered except their closeness and their continued love, for in a flash she realized the deep love she had always nurtured for him.

I love him, I love him, she thought repeatedly as she rubbed her cheek against the linen that covered his heart. It was a relief, this emergence of the subconscious.

Gently he was maneuvering his hand around her head and lifting her face up toward him. There was an intensity about his gaze as he stroked her chin with his thumb that at the same time pleasured and frightened her. The hold of his arm about her waist tightened until she thought she could no longer endure the emotion of it.

Each attempted to understand the thoughts of the other, but a cooling wetness broke the spell. Droplets of rain fell upon Aleen's upturned face and ran in shimmering lines down her face and neck. A smile spread slowly across her face at the humorous development, until Edmund caught its contagion and smiled back. They stood for a moment, sharing their joy, until, when they were about to break into laughter, the gentle rainfall became a downpour and they were forced to hurry for shelter.

Once inside the stairway, Edmund closed the door against the elements. Their closeness was deliriously exciting, and when Edmund reached for her hand and raised it to his lips, the chills that ran down her back were even more exhilarating than the wetness of the rain.

At once the noises from the great hall reached their hearing, and Edmund reluctantly released her hand. Together they walked slowly down the stairs as though trying with each step to prolong the sweetness of their company. On reaching the landing, Edmund turned to her and reached once more for her hand. Again he kissed it, caressingly, lovingly, but the noises from the hall grew in intensity, and duty demanded his attention. "Join me, Aleen," he said pleadingly. "I must leave here. I regret I must return to the hall."

"But my lord, my tunic is quite wet," she said, looking down upon her sad condition, and in an effort to improve her appearance, she removed the purple cloth that had become limp with wetness.

"I must go, Aleen. If it were not that I must oversee the activities there, I would not now leave, but I must." And he released her hand and hesitated as though reluctant to leave her.

"Good day, Aleen," he said with such tenderness that Aleen for an instant thought herself incapable of enduring separation from him, but the moistness of her clothing soon dispelled the thought.

"Good day to you, my lord," Aleen replied, lowering her eyes demurely. As he walked away, she called after him, and he turned. "I am most grateful for the cloth." With only a hint of a smile, he turned again and was off.

Aleen glided in the opposite direction, to her chamber, with a lightness of step that betrayed her sweet happiness. But Edmund was deprived of a similarly pleasant experience, for in the safety of a shadowed recess Judith and her friend were standing, their mouths gaping. They had seen Edmund and Aleen emerging from the darkened stairway, had seen the kissing of the hand, had witnessed the ease and gentleness of their leavetaking.

Edmund was surprised by their presence in the passageway, but gave a cordial nod of greeting and continued on his way, knowing full well that what the women had witnessed would be embellished, that it would be reported to Wilfreda without delay, and that she in turn would lose no time in demanding an explanation of his conduct.

## ⤙ XXII ⤛

EDMUND WAS the Lord of Lauxburgh, but he was Wilfreda's son nonetheless, and not above being advised and reproached. With the swiftness of a distressed mother arising to the protection of a threatened child, Wilfreda called upon Edmund for a denial of the rumors that had circulated since the night before. But an explanation of his presence with Aleen in the tower stairway was not forthcoming. That he was seen in friendly exchange with Aleen was not wrong and could only be construed as such by evil minds. What had transpired in the tower, however, was thankfully not witnessed and not of anyone's concern save his and Aleen's.

Many years' experience in observing his mother in such rantings had taught him a valued lesson. If he were to exert patience and to exercise the charity his religion recommended, he must remain silent and let her give full voice to her discontented thoughts. Instead of replying, Edmund leaned back in his chair and braced himself for the impending tirade that would be delivered whether his explanations were given or not.

Wilfreda's usually stony continence became contracted with hatred and suspicion as her serpentine mind coiled and flexed on the far-reaching effects wrought by the circumstances that had been so eagerly reported to her. Bitter accusations and denunciations were made, impending doom for his soul and Lauxburgh was predicted, and a pledge to avoid a repetition of such scandalous conduct was pleaded for.

Edmund's stern gaze followed the thin, erect figure as she walked to and fro. Wringing her slender hands, she sermonized on the avoidance of evil influences and the merit to be gained by the avoidance of temptation and the consistent practice of one's principles and commitments.

Edmund was bitterly aware that it was such extreme conduct that had driven his father from her side and into the peace of a separate chamber. It was Wilfreda's warped and scrupulous opinions that had driven his brother, Cestus, to seek release and freedom by passing in swift succession from one monastic school to another, with brief but infrequent visits home. Edmund was grateful that he had been separated from her influence, at least during his youth, by his attendance at monastic school and his brief entrances into religious life.

Edmund sighed deeply, repeatedly rearranged his position, and tried to relax as best he could while waiting for Wilfreda to conclude her admonitions. When at last her energies were spent she turned to him and pleaded compassionately, "You have not spoken, Edmund. Do you agree with what I have said? Have you nothing to say to me in your defense?"

Edmund pressed his lips together, squinted his eyes, and gave due reflection to her questions. Then, relaxing his face, he spoke. "Yes, Mother. I have but one thing to ask of you. When you leave here, would you kindly inform Reverend Hewald that I should like to speak with him?"

An all-encompassing flood of relief softened Wilfreda's face, and she stood as though weakened by the ordeal, but grateful that her efforts had brought about the desired result. He had heard her words well, had seen the errors to which he was exposing his soul, and wished as a result to confess his weakness to a priest, who would in turn pray with him for strength and determination to continue living righteously.

Tears of gratification almost flooded her eyes, but then she frowned and asked, "My son, would you not instead wish to speak with your confessor? The Reverend Hewald is newly ordained and I fear too inexperienced to counsel properly."

"Nevertheless, Mother, I should like to speak with him."

A weak smile crept across her face. "Very well, then." It was of little consequence to whom he would confess and seek counsel so long as he desired to do so.

As she turned to leave, her pleasant expression at once turned into a subtle sneer. She had won out over Aleen. Henceforth her son would view the wench as a sinful influence to be diligently avoided.

With his long woolen robes beating against his lanky legs, Reverend Hewald eagerly hurried down halls to keep his appointment with Edmund. And when Edmund motioned him to a chair and spoke of a secret mission, the new cleric's ministerial zeal knew no limits. He had been resurrected in one brief moment, from the boring assignments usually relegated to the newly ordained, to the excitement and intrigue of a secret assignment.

"No, my lord, I have never been to Rome," he replied in answer to Edmund's question.

"Then you shall see it."

The priest's bright eyes opened in disbelief and anticipation.

"Not only will you see Rome, but you are to speak to the pope on my behalf."

The young cleric was nearly struck dumb by the prospect, but he was dutifully attentive when Edmund continued. "Many months ago, Reverend Hewald," Edmund began, while nervously pacing about, "I made a vow against the advice of my confessor. It was a vow to observe continence—celibacy. I intended to become a religious and thought this would prove a hindrance should I be asked to marry again for diplomatic reasons." The cleric's head nodded in comprehension as Edmund detailed the circumstances surrounding his second marriage. "The vow was made immediately after the funeral of my first wife, when I was tormented with grief and the thought that I was responsible for her death, since it occurred as a direct result of childbearing. It is for this reason I feel the vow could be annulled. I wish you to speak with the pope, tell him of the circumstances, and plead on my behalf for a dispensation."

"But, my lord," Hewald stammered, "have you spoken of this with the archbishop?"

"I have not. I know his Excellency well. We have had many disagreements in the past, and I wish not to trust this matter to his discretion. He might be influenced by his desire to retaliate for decisions of mine which he opposed."

"Nevertheless, my lord, the archbishop should be informed."

"I should find it uncomfortable dealing with him," Edmund continued. "You perhaps have not heard of our frequent disputes."

Reverend Hewald hesitated. He had indeed heard the reports concerning Edmund's criticism of the archbishop's spending of church moneys for personal comforts. Though to all outward appearances the archbishop and Edmund enjoyed a mutual respect, the undercurrents of opposition were known full well to members of the clergy.

"This matter requires the understanding and compassion of the pope. I cannot risk asking the archbishop for this annulment. Then, too, I should not like for him to know of these plans, should the pope refuse nullification. Such would make our relationship more strained than what it is. However, should I receive a dispensation, I should care not what he thinks. Are you willing to intercede for me?"

The priest's head hung as though weighted by what had been told him. At last, looking up, he answered, "Yes, my lord. I shall."

"Very well. You must notify your superiors that you have been entrusted by me with a mission. You are to leave as soon as you can prepare yourself. A ship already awaits to take you to France. Two of my most trusted guards will accompany you. They have been sworn to secrecy and know only that you are going to Rome, but are unaware of your mission. You are not to inform them or anyone of its nature. If you are asked in this country, you are to say your assignment takes you to France. It will not be an untruth, since you will journey the length of that country and into Italy. The soldier Gruftwin has made the journey before, and is familiar with the locations of the monasteries along the way which will supply you with fresh horses, food, and lodging. I expect you to press hard and to return without unnecessary delay. You are young. The journey should prove no hardship for you. Here," he said, reaching toward a small bag on his desk. "In this pouch is more than a sufficient number of coins for your expenses. Are you still willing?"

"Yes, my lord." And he arose from his chair. "Pray, my lord, for the safety of your envoys."

"I shall. Now, will you do me the kindness of bestowing on me your priestly blessing?" Edmund asked as he knelt down.

The priest beamed proudly at Edmund's recognition of his newly acquired faculties. Closing his eyes and lifting his face heavenward, he carefully enunciated the Latin prayer, lifted his hand high to trace the sign of the cross, and placed his hand on Edmund's head.

From the door which the cleric had been negligent in closing properly and which had been ever so carefully opened to permit a narrow view of the room, Wilfreda could see, at the far end, the priest bestowing what she assumed to be the blessing of absolution. A sly smile of victory lightened her face. There was no satisfaction quite like that of knowing one's son had received advice concerning his temptation, had received forgiveness for his weakness, and was now fortified with renewed vigor and steadfast determination to continue his virtuously celibate life.

Aleen turned on her side, snuggled into her pillow, and smiled as she looked upon the purple cloth draped carelessly upon the back of her bedside chair. It was the one tangible proof that the events of the night before had not been a dream, but a reality—a pleasant one that made her spirit soar and her eyes dance with merriment. The impossible had occurred. Edmund had held her close against his body and had kissed her. The very thought made her tingle excitedly. But drifts of foggy doubts clouded her recollection. Was it Aleen he had kissed, or the ever-hovering memory of Marion?

Oh, she moaned annoyingly to herself as she reached for the coverlet and pulled it about her, I shall not be tormented so. It was me he kissed. He must have tender feelings for me, or he would not have given in to weakness and indulged so in the forbidden. Her conscience was assailed with misgivings. It was wrong to tempt a man such as Edmund, but then, I did not really tempt. It was he who sought me out. If the matter must rest on anyone's conscience, let it lean hard on Edmund's.

Now, what shall I do about the cloth? She rose, sat on the side of the bed, and reached for the silky fabric. She stood up and draped it about her. It is too transparent for a tunic. Shall it be fashioned into a veil? I shall ask the seamstress—the one they call "the Greek." She will know exactly what to do with it. Aleen wrapped it around her shoulders and rubbed her cheek against the softness. It was thoughtful of Edmund to have taken notice of the cloth she had examined in the hall and to have purchased it for her. Her heart was about to burst with happiness. Softly she began humming the melody the flutes had wailed the night before, and she swayed and turned to its rhythm.

The world was glorious this day ... and the future? Aleen closed her eyes to enjoy the delicious sensations to the fullest. She stopped abruptly. The Greek! Yes, she must see the girl, and quickly, too. Many lengths of cloth had been purchased, and before many hours had passed, the girl would be besieged with orders for tunics and mantles. If I hurry, I might place my order before the others. Feverishly she rushed and fumbled about for clothes and shoes.

Where is Hester? Why is she not here? After running the comb through the length of tousled hair, she folded the cloth neatly.

What if I should meet Edmund? The thought made her blush furiously and her eyes dance mischievously. There is no situation concerning Edmund that I cannot handle, she said to herself, and with a jaunty tilt of her head she rushed off.

The Greek was not to be found, but her sewing table was cluttered with cloths, threads, bronze needles, and stone spindle whorls. Her iron shears were at an angle in her bronze workbox, as though recently placed, yet there hovered a strange atmosphere of abandonment.

"The Greek is not here, my lady," the weaver announced as she entered the room. "Nor will she ever be again," she added as she climbed upon her stool before the loom.

Aleen's perplexity invited further information, which the aproned girl was eager to share. Lowering her voice to a whisper, and glancing about cautiously, the girl continued. "Last night I heard the steward speaking to her. He said Edmund had made arrangements for her to leave with the Venetians, who would make further arrangements to reunite her with her people. Edmund must have paid handsomely for her passage. She was given a large settlement besides. I heard them discussing it. She is on the ship now, awaiting departure."

Aleen walked toward the table and fingered the cloths that would never be plied with the Greek's flashing needles. One could never become friends with her, Aleen thought forlornly as she recalled the times she had visited the sewing room with Lelia. The Greek's reluctance to speak, her quiet diligence to work, and her always saddened attitude forbade a friendly approach. Yet, though we never spoke together, I know I hall miss her.

The image of the Greek's pretty face came to mind. It was an unhappy face, a brooding face, an unreadable face, one that drew compassion and sympathy. At once the reason for Aleen's feeling of kinship with the girl unfolded as clearly as the sun bursting forth from a veil of clouds. They were both exiles in a strange land. One of them, at least, would retrace her steps and be reunited with her people and loved ones. Aleen would envy her a little for her successful escape. I know I shall never pass this room without feeling the loss, she thought sadly.

"Wilfreda must be pleased that she is at last free of her," the weaver added as an afterthought while she nimbly adjusted the loom weights.

Aleen turned. "Why should Wilfreda be concerned with such a quiet, withdrawn sewing girl?"

The weaver's eyes opened incredulously. "You mean, my lady, that you do not know why Edmund's father detained her here?" As soon as the question was uttered, it was immediately regretted, and the girl dropped her eyes in confused embarrassment, but not before Aleen had read in the words and reactions the partial reason for Wilfreda's bitterness.

"I should not have said that, my lady," the girl mumbled. "The subject is never mentioned, although everyone seems to know of it. Please, my lady, do not report to anyone that I thoughtlessly told you of it. If word of this reached Wilfreda, I would be punished severely in many dreadful ways."

"I shall say nothing. Do not be fretful."

So that was why the Greek seemed to brood and to be ostracized even by the servants. It is no wonder she seemed so sad. Whether her sinful acts were by force or consent, the girl had many uncomfortable recollections to bear with her, to what Aleen hoped would be a better life in her native land.

The purple cloth draped on her left arm had lost her interest. She would concern herself with it at another time. Slowly and carefully Aleen picked up the scattered needles, adjusted the iron shears inside the Greek's sewing box, almost meditatively closed the lid, and snapped the catch into place.

When Aleen returned to her chamber, Lelia was not waiting for her, as she had expected, nor was she in her own room being prepared for their daily round of activities. Perhaps Edith was bringing Lelia in search of her, and she in turn determined to do likewise and to intercept them on their way. But Aleen was not prepared for the sight that met her when she passed the door of the great hall. Wilfreda, Judith, and three of their constant companions were seated in an intimate huddle, and before them, sitting on a stool, was Lelia, her face timidly averted. Wilfreda wore her customarily cool expression, but the others were apparently attempting to win the child's favor by extolling her lovely features, which they claimed duplicated those of her father. Wilfreda completely dominated the situation, and Aleen dared not interfere. No one had observed her presence, save Edith, who was sitting to the side of the group in dutiful readiness. Her eyes darted from Aleen to Wilfreda, until she lowered them, lest Wilfreda sense the silent communication.

Aleen retreated. Perhaps Hester knew the explanation of this sudden interest in the child by the women who previously had looked down their noses at her deformity.

Hester was smoothing the bed linens when Aleen confronted her with the question. The sudden agitation, the averted eyes, denoted her complete knowledge of the situation, and her continued absorption with the exact placement of the coverlet displayed her reluctance to share the answer that would satisfy Aleen's burning interest.

"You must tell me, Hester. I shall not leave this room, nor will I permit you to leave it, until you tell me what I wish to know."

Hester paused, straightened, and carefully guarded her eyes.

"Tell me," Aleen demanded.

"Wilfreda was here," Hester responded hoarsely. "She waited for you, but when you did not return, she told me to deliver a message."

"Yes, yes, continue."

Hester nervously entwined and squeezed her fingers. "She was quite annoyed, Aleen. She said from henceforth she will have complete custody of the child."

"But why?" Aleen asked in distress.

It was a painful experience for the faithful servant as she reluctantly continued. "Wilfreda said your conduct of last evening proved you unworthy to supervise the education and the moral formation of the child. She made many unkind comments about you, my lady." She paused before continuing. "She said you have already exposed the child to an immoral and shameful situation by dancing in pagan fashion before the castle's gentility, and as a consequence, she claims you have lost the respect and esteem of everyone. She will assume guardianship of the child, a trust she said you betrayed by your questionable conduct in the darkened hallway. She said further that you are not to interfere, nor should you confront Edmund with this matter." Hester raised her eyes to Aleen. "Had I not been a servant, my lady, and she not the mother of Edmund, I should have struck her."

"Tell me, Hester. Did she say she had Edmund's permission?"

"She did not mention it. Perhaps she has his approval. I do not know."

With an air of experiencing the unreal, Aleen walked to a chair, sat down, and stared vacantly ahead. Why was it that each time her spirits soared with happiness, they were so quickly and effectively battered down? Perhaps there was some truth to Wilfreda's reasoning. Surely she should not have let youthful exuberance replace noble dignity, but her dancing was innocently performed, and she had been unaware that the musical rhythm that came so naturally to the visitors was regarded as immoral by the Saxons. Or perhaps it was not the music, but the garments of the performers that offended Wilfreda. As for the darkened stairway, how could any witnesses question their conduct, since they had merely exchanged a few harmless words? Whatever intimacies had been shared had taken place beyond the view of anyone. There was no escaping the knowledge that her most innocent actions would always be misconstrued in the minds of the Saxons.

And what of Edmund? Had the tumultuous elements the evening before influenced his loving actions with her, and did he now regret them in the calmness and reality of the morning light? Had he denounced his thoughtlessness by giving Wilfreda permission to supervise the guidance of the child?

It was a confusing world—an unpredictable and cruel existence, one that always lashed at her when she least expected it.

There was only one course of action. She would avoid contact with Edmund and Lelia. Her heart constricted with the decision, but she was firm in her resolve, and for days she listened at the wall that separated her from the child for any sound that indicated Lelia's happiness and well-being. The few times she had cautiously observed the child with the ladies, Lelia seemed still unaccustomed to their company. She was sullen and bored and sat to one side, as though punished and ignored.

Aleen missed their outings, and when she needed escape and a rejuvenation of spirit, which came only with the salty sea air in her nostrils and its breezes whipping about her, she would take a book, cross the meadow, and sit on the grassy slope by the beach. Many afternoons passed in such lonely segregation, until one day, when the wind was unusually strong and hissed noisily in her ears. She did not hear the approach, but when a jerking shadow startled her and she turned in fright to see who was intruding on her peace, Lelia seemed to come out of nowhere. So happy was the child to see Aleen that she threw herself into Aleen's arms. The unexpected weight caught Aleen off balance, and she fell back upon the clover and rolled from side to side, hugging the child and kissing the little head she held so closely. "Lelia, Lelia, I missed you so." The child's silent but beaming face echoed the sentiments. As she lay on her back, with Lelia sitting upon her abdomen, she tickled the child and laughed through her blurring tears, until yet another movement caught her attention and a shadow crossed her. Looking to its source, she saw Edmund astride Boltar, looking down on her with a penetrating gaze that read her soul. She struggled to right herself. In his regally silent bearing she quickly knew the answers to all her confusions, until his stares brought blushing recollections. He nudged his steed and made off, while Aleen's heart beat strongly in rhythm with his cantering mount.

"So you surprised me and jumped upon me," she said, turning at last to Lelia. "Well, you shall not be able to do so again, and for that matter, you shall not be able to hug me again," and she rose and dashed from the child, who quickly darted after her in limping strides. Giggles echoed across the meadow as Aleen's skirt repeatedly eluded the tiny extended hand. But then in a moment Aleen turned, swooped up the child, and pressed her close. "Did you miss me, Lelia?"

The child nodded assent.

"Well," Aleen said smiling at the round little face, "from henceforth you need not wonder where I am, for I shall always be near you."

Contented days followed. Busy days that were filled with journeys to the fields, observing the frolicking newborn sheep, the gathering and winnowing of grain, the milking of cows, the grinding of corn. . . . But the happiness they enjoyed would again terminate, as it always did for Aleen, with crushing blows against her heart; and fate would again appear with cruel interference.

# ~ XXIII ~

A DAMP cloth covered Lelia's forehead as she lay asleep, and the coverlet was pulled away from the little body. The white gown that ended at the knees permitted the legs and the fragile white feet, one perfectly formed, the other grotesquely twisted, to lay pitifully exposed.

"It is a fever, Aleen," Edith whispered while dipping a cloth into a bowl of water. The physician had examined her and left to report the illness to Edmund. She raised the cloth, and then, with a swishing rush of water, wrung out the excess.

Aleen sat on the stool that had been placed near the bed and studied the small face and the shadows that had already formed beneath the eyes. Lelia had been unusually warm and listless the day before, Aleen recalled, but it seemed then to have been the effects of a busy day in the sun.

"She is young and strong. In a few days she will be dashing about the meadow," she predicted emphatically. It was a vain attempt to reassure herself, but the words did not bear conviction. Lelia was clearly possessed by a fearful illness. With each slumbering breath, the little chest rose and fell, but no sign of awakening was evident, except when Edith turned the damp cloth or exchanged it for a fresh one. Then the eyes, languored by fever, opened, gazed aimlessly, and then closed again. There was something about the glassy look of the eyes, the seeing yet unseeing quality, that made Aleen wonder.

Warm breezes, sweetened by their passage over blooming jasmine, roses, and clover, blew gently through the narrow windows that permitted little penetration of light. It was no wonder Lelia was sleeping so soundly, Aleen thought. The somberness of the room, the constant rippling of warm air, the stillness that reigned, were enough to stir drowsiness in anyone. She stifled a yawn and blinked herself awake, but her lethargy was abruptly dismissed when the door opened with a loud creak that ripped rudely through the peacefulness of the sickroom.

Edmund strode through. His attitude was one of urgency, and his grave frown deepened as he studied the small, slender body that lay so weakly prostrate. "You must leave at once," he said emphatically to Aleen.

"But, my lord . . .

"Have you had the fever?"

"No, I think not."

"Then you must leave. The fever spreads quickly, and I desire all who have not had it to remain within their chambers until it subsides. . . . Edith," Edmund said, turning his attentions from Aleen.

Anticipating his question, Edith began, "I have never suffered from the illness, my lord, but I will not leave. The child needs one of us, and if the Lady Aleen cannot remain, I will."

Edmund began an objection, but Edith interrupted. "I was in this very room when the child was born, and have been with her each day of her life. I will not leave her now when she needs me most."

The room was restored to somberness for a moment as Edmund considerd Edith's argument. "Very well, then, but, Edith, are you aware of what may transpire?"

"Yes, my lord. I have lived many years upon this earth. I prefer to do my duty than to hide myself in the hope of adding more to their number."

Edmund walked to Edith, took her by both shoulders, looked tenderly at her, and whispered close to her ear.

"I am most grateful," Edith replied when he had finished.

"Let us leave, Aleen. You have been here too long already."

Aleen paid no attention to his instructions, so taken was she with Lelia, who had awakened at the sound of the voices and was looking around with vague awareness. Her eyes wandered, but comprehension of what she saw was distorted.

"Thirsty," Lelia said weakly. "Thirsty."

Edith hastened forward with a horn of cool water, placed a hand beneath the child's shoulder, lifted her up, and pressed the rim to her lips.

*Those eyes. Where have I seen them?* Aleen demanded of

herself as her senses poised with apprehension. And Edith. Did she truly speak of dying from the illness? A stifling dread encompassed her, and her skin crawled with fear. It was all unreal. Lelia ill, and Edith speaking of dying. Well, Edith was old and could die if she wished, but not Lelia. Lelia must grow to be old before death could be considered; besides, children do not die so easily. But something made Aleen tense and restless.

Cedric, the physician, bent over the little form and spoke softly, but the eyes continued to wander aimlessly.

Those eyes! I shall die myself if the thought of those eyes does not stop haunting me.

"Come, Aleen," Edmund said, taking her by the arm and leading her across the room. It was an unsteady floor, which rocked like ... like the deck of a ship. Yes, and men, unsteady on their feet, were sitting about in a drunken stupor, looking up with eyes dull from drink. The memory of the men appeared as a vision, until it seemed they languored about the room, pleadingly looking up at her in their search for help. But they were not drunk—no, not drunk, but sick. Men sick and sweaty from fever. The same fever that made Lelia's eyes as glassy as their own. With a wrench of her arm Aleen freed herself from Edmund's grasp and turned toward the bed.

Lelia's little form seemed dwarfed by the bed, which was much too large for her. There was no questioning why. It was an adult's bed, her mother's bed, a bed that Marion had shared intimately at times with another, the bed whereon Marion had given birth and had lain ill, the bed on which she had died.

Recollections of Viking superstitious beliefs came rushing upon her, until the fury and force of them beat thunderingly in her ears. Yet another vision came to mind, a vision wherein bearded physicians and candle-bearing priests shook their heads sorrowfully over Marion's dead body. "My God," Aleen said aloud as she lunged toward the bed, but Edmund quickly restrained her. "Edmund, please remove her from that bed. It is cursed with death. Please. She must be moved elsewhere," Aleen pleaded, her face traced with panic.

"I will do as you say. Come, you must leave before you too fall victim to this illness."

"I wish to stay, Edmund. I cannot abandon her."

"Aleen, you must leave her. You are not abandoning her. Please understand. Edith will be with her. Come. I will not permit you to expose yourself needlessly."

She could no longer resist, for the strain had rendered her helpless.

"You must pray for her," Edmund was saying as he closed the door behind them. "I will not disillusion you about this fever. It is a most serious one." His tone changed as he continued. "There are many others already stricken. The dock workers were the first to feel its effects. We did not know the Venetian ship was diseased when we permitted them to board it to assist in the transfer of the cargo. The ship left in apparent health but later returned to report the illness. They requested medicinals and reported the death of three seamen before leaving once more."

Aleen turned away and covered her face with both hands. My God, she said to herself. If he knew I took the child aboard and exposed her to the illness, he will hate me for it. It is I who am responsible for this. I can never tell him. No, never.

"Come, now, Aleen. The Lord is more apt to answer prayers when the welfare of children are concerned. Do not worry so. A physician will be in constant attendance. Consider, too, that she is quite strong."

"Edmund. You will not forget to have the bed exchanged for another? It is a death bed. It would be a bad omen, should she remain on it. Edmund," she said, the crease between her eyes deepening, "Edmund, what of your health? Have you had the fever?"

Pleased with her concern, he replied with a slight smile. "Indeed, I suffered from it when I was in attendance at the monastery school." Then, as his face became grave at the thought, he continued, "I remember it well. Many of the monks died. Many villagers suffered greatly, and many also died, but somehow I survived. You see, Aleen, I survived, and I was a child at the time. Lelia will survive as well. I must go now. There are arrangements to be made, and I must warn the others. Remember, it is important that you remain in your chamber. There will be difficult and lengthy days ahead, but with the help of God, they will be shortened. Will you help me pray for Lauxburgh, Aleen?"

"Yes. I shall pray for Lelia and you. I will pray for Edith, Hester, the priests, Thane Godfrey, the scribe, and the servants. The others must pray for themselves." The implication was obvious.

"Aleen," Edmund said, feigning shock, "you must pray for all."

She looked into his eyes, turned crisply, and strode away. Before she knew how she had gotten there, she found herself on her knees before her bedside crucifix, with a voice sounding in her ears the words once spoken on a sunny mountainside in Palestine long ago. "When you pray," it suggested kindly, "pray thusly: 'Our Father, who art in heaven . . .'"

The prayer was said repeatedly to quell the accusations that tormented her, the only way to hinder the surges of dread and the vision of those sick eyes that peered at her from all sides. Her knees ached, and her muscles screamed in their strained misery, until she was forced to change position. Adjusting the chair until it faced the cross, she remained praying for some time. Wearily she leaned against the leather backrest.

"Ask the Father in my name, and he will give it to you," the voice continued. The words, so carefully lettered by monks in labored devotion, came easily to mind, until, at last, when the darkness exchanged places with light, she experienced some relief from her ordeal. The good God might hesitate before answering her prayers, but he would not refuse to answer Edmund's. It was fortunate Edmund was so close to God. It was a relief, a blessing. Thus consoled, she lay across her bed and wandered into peaceful oblivion.

As Edmund had predicted, the days were difficult and painfully long, and since no one except Edith was permitted in Lelia's room, few words were circulated about her condition. Somehow gossip concerning the others was still exchanged, but it concentrated chiefly on the conditions of the ill, those who recently showed symptoms of the disease, those who died or nearly died of its ravages, and those who thankfully survived.

Servants avoided contact with the nobles, and their services were limited by Edmund's orders. They prepared trays of food, which were left at the doorways of their masters and mistresses. Pails of water were provided each morning, and this for drinking, washing, or cleaning. A rap at the door signaled the deposit of tray or pail, but before the signal was answered, the bearer was off on other duties, except those few who lingered momentarily for a hasty exchange of rumors.

As the number of the ill increased, the servants were pressed into ministering to them, and the trays evidencing the limited time spent in food preparation. Little by little the choice of foods dwindled, until the fare settled into a daily ration of bread, a wedge of cheese, occasionally a goblet of goat's milk, and a portion of meat so quickly and carelessly prepared as to cause the diner to hesitate before partaking of it, if, indeed, he did at all.

There was little to do to amuse oneself during the long, hot days, and Aleen suffered much from loneliness and boredom, what with Edith caring for Lelia and Hester serving as a tray bearer. There was more time to be tormented by guilt than she liked, and there was little diversion to discourage its persistence. Time and again she wondered about the disease and its choice of victims. The scourge respected neither king nor earl, merchant nor peasant, but selected its victims carelessly. Why she had not fallen victim instead of the child, she could not reason, for both she and the child had boarded the stricken ship. If she dies, it will rest heavily on my mind till the last day of my life. If she lives, the memory of this illness and my implication in it will be mercifully softened by the accumulation of time. If only we had not visited the docks that day, if only we had refused the invitation of the Venetian captain, if only . . .

Day after day Aleen listened with ear pressed against the connecting door for any sound that would indicate Lelia's return to health. But except for the sounds of leather shoes, the dull thud of clay water vessels against the floor, an occasional cough or mumbled words, no definite opinion could be formed.

The days passed with uninterrupted boredom until the day when Hester rapped at the door and stood at a cautious distance as she spoke to Aleen through the narrow opening. "I bring your tray, Aleen." Raising a hand of warning, she continued, "Wait until I leave before reaching for it."

"One would think you a leper, Hester. Come in and speak with me. I miss you greatly."

Hester did not advance as invited, but kept her distance.

"What is it, Hester? Surely you could stay a moment."

"I have been asked to serve the sick, my lady," Hester said, eager to conduct the business for which she came. "The Lord Edmund has sent me to seek your permission to do this." But before Aleen could object, Hester rushed on with her request. "I am sorely needed to assist the physicians. Those who knew of the gathering of herbs and the preparation of medicinal potions have taken ill, and only I remain. I must assist them, my lady."

Aleen's sullen voice replied after a moment, "Should I lose you, I would grieve much. You have been my companion since my childhood. How shall I endure life without you? If you can reassure me that you have already suffered from this fever, I will grant you leave."

"My lady, it would mean nothing had I suffered it before, for it is said the disease strikes many times."

"Who said this?"

"Many of those now sick have had the fever before. They have complained of this repetition."

"My God," Aleen said, clutching at her heart. Edmund was still vulnerable. What if he should get sick and die? Then indeed there would be no reason for me to live. Even though the child should survive, I shall die if Edmund does. "What of the Lord Edmund. Is he well?"

"He is well, but very tired. He is the father of all now, the protector and consoler of the sick."

"And Lelia?"

"She is no better, yet no worse. She drinks the potions we offer, and Edith has never left her side."

Edmund is not yet ill, and Lelia still lives. "Thank God," Aleen said, "thank God."

"Have I your permission?" came the small voice.

Aleen looked upon the round face and examined once again the full features she loved and knew so well. A braid of hair fell on each breast, and Aleen remembered with affection how often she had sat on Hester's lap and toyed with the long plaited hair so many years ago. "If you feel you must do this thing, I give my permission, but, Hester, in God's name, take care."

"I have no wish to die, my love, but I am needed, and it is my duty to help where I can. Aleen," she said with greater seriousness, "should you become ill, I will be by your side to aid you. You must never fret that I shall neglect you."

Their eyes met, but the tears that began to seep into Hester's were not seen, so quickly did she leave. Aleen stepped into the hall and watched the retreating figure. The full skirt, held into place about the thick waist by a strap of leather, swayed from side to side with each step, and her rounded shoulders seemed to droop with fatigue. "I shall never see her again," Aleen said aloud, her eyes becoming moist. "I know I shall never see her again."

The hammering sounds the carpenters made traveled swiftly toward the forest and then slammed back to the castle with even greater volume. From dawn to dusk they worked to construct coffins to accommodate the dead of both the castle and the village.

It was strange how one became acutely aware of sounds. With no one to speak to and little to do, one soon began to interpret each sound: the long slow strides of the physicians, the hurrying steps of the servants, the heavy, uneven steps of the water carriers, the soft steps of the nurses. Each cough echoed and reverberated through the halls, but the sound that was most dreaded was the ringing of the small hand bell that alerted everyone to the presence of the sacred host as it was reverently carried by the priest on the way to the chambers of the dying. Somehow the ringing traveled around hallways and up and down stairways until its origins on one side of the castle were heard faintly, but surely, on the other side.

The rumbling of the funeral carts were likewise magnified with each revolution of its solid wooden wheels, until each creak, each strain over obstructing pebbles resounded as though their destination lay within the halls of the castle.

Aleen had leaned out the window to watch the first carts as they carried their shifting, swaying coffins to the cathedral cemetery, but it was depressing, and she cringed from viewing other processions. At such times, the faces of happy villagers came to mind: dusty farmers, disheveled shepherds, and goat tenders, hurrying women with babies, fat traders and plump bakers, kindly but smelly tanners. Which of them were enclosed in the yellow, splintery coffins that were arranged so unceremoniously on the backs of the carts?

The elements were peacefully and deceptively encompassing the castle, with its interior turmoil of pain and fear, in much the same way as the carefully carved and decorated rune stones and whitened stone markers decorated and concealed the graves whose interiors contained morbid matter. Deep blue skies embellished with fluffs of gray-white clouds hung peacefully above, while clear, fresh air stirred around crenellated walls and towers and in their passage brushed the whiskered heads of wheat and disturbed the leafy stretches of trees. The sun shone brightly on fruited fields and verdant meadows, on clumps of thistle and wild roses. Its glorious brightness sparkled the curling edges of waves and lighted the dark interiors of freshly opened graves.

The sea, yes, the sea and the Venetian conveyors of treasures, disease, and death. Perhaps most on board were victims of the illness. By now the sea had accepted their dead, and the ship might well have been left to the mercy of currents and tides. The Grecian seamstress, if she were still alive, would now hold little hope of rejoining her people. If she had boarded the vessel visibly relieved of her burden of courteous enslavement, if her face betrayed the joy she must have felt at her leave-taking, Aleen could not envision it. The eyes, which must have once flashed enticingly in her youth, were now dulled with disillusionment. The full, beautiful mouth had long ago lost its eagerness to smile, and seemed frozen in malcontent. If only she would live and be happy once more . . .

A faint ringing of a bell disturbed Aleen's thoughts. One of the dying was awaiting the reception of the Lord. Its delicate ringing continued as Aleen left the window, where she had been searching the horizon for the Venetian trading ship, and sat down. How tired one becomes with little to do. She slumped against the hardness of the wooden backrest and let her arms droop over the sides as she traced the course of the bell ringer and the priest.

They were not headed for the rooms of the servants, nor the soldiers' quarters. They were climbing the stairs and were turning toward the hall by the nobles' rooms. Perhaps one of the women was sick, perhaps Wilfreda. If only they would minister to Wilfreda and she would die. . . . No, Lord, forgive me. I should not indulge in such thoughts, though they be pleasant ones. . . .

With a start, Aleen sat up and tilted her head attentively. A frown crossed her face. They were not headed for Wilfreda's room; they were approaching Lelia's. With a bound and a flip of skirts and hair, Aleen reached the door and ran to where they stood at Lelia's door.

"Stop," she shouted, her voice vibrating through the silent halls. Her eyes were ablaze as she looked from one to the other. One priest, his body draped in a heavy liturgical cape, clutched to his chest the sacred species that was covered with a silk-embroidered cloth. He stood reverently, his head bowed in respect to the sacred treasure he carried. The priest who preceded him wore his black woolly robes and held a fat yellow candle in one hand, a small bronze bell in the other. "You have made an error," Aleen said tersely. "This is the room of the child Lelia."

"It is to this room we were summoned," the priest said respectfully.

"You were incorrectly informed. No one is dying here. Please leave, lest the child be disturbed."

The door opened, and Aleen turned to face Edith, in whose drawn face she read the morbid fear that had tormented her dreams. "No," she said, shaking her head. "No," and she turned again to the priest. "No one is dying here, leave, leave." With a desperate sweep of her arm, the candle and bell went crashing to the floor. The bell rolled about in a noisy circle on the stone floor as Aleen passed it and entered the room.

At the sight of the child, color drained from Aleen's face. Her mouth opened automatically in dismay and shock, and a hand lifted to stifle what uncontrollable sounds might escape.

The child was unbelievably gaunt. Circles below the eyes had darkened and expanded, until the upper part of her face seemed in shadows. Yellow-gray skin stretched across the face and nose, giving the unmistakable appearance that was peculiar to the dying. The gown was clinging from the repeated spongings, and emphasized the thinness that had resulted from the disease.

The thick, stuffy odor of burning candles reached her nostrils, drawing her attention momentarily from the sickbed, making her aware of the surroundings. Edmund, who had been sitting to one side of the bed, straightened tiredly and looked in her direction. He was too weary to rise. Vacant eyes bore witness to inadequate sleep and the desolation at the child's precarious condition.

Several candles on a nearby table were lazily burning and sending tendrils of smoke into a gathering haze. Their golden holders were those from the chapel's altar, and Aleen recognized with dread the vials of holy oils and the small cross needed in the priest's bestowal of the last blessings.

Partially hidden by the table and the candles knelt a figure reminiscent of a biblical prophet, whom Aleen recognized instantly as the hermit she had seen in the forest the day of the hunt. Momentarily distracted by the noise of the bell clanging to the floor and her approaching steps, he had hesitated, then resumed his recollection with his head inclined, his gray beard partially concealing his folded hands. His long hair fell against thin flabby arms, and his deerskin drape covered a body frail from age, deprivation, and deliberately inflicted mortifications. When he had arrived, Aleen knew not, but if Edmund had requested his prayers, the child's condition must indeed be critical.

"You were to inform me," Aleen said harshly, looking toward Edith, who had closed the door and had joined her near the foot of the bed.

"Aleen," she said, smoothing her hair, "we knew you would want to be near her, and we did not wish you to risk your health once again. Understand our concern for you." While Edith pleaded for understanding, Aleen noticed that her eyes were finely streaked with red. She was exhausted from her constant vigilance, and she looked rebuked and humbled as Aleen added gloomily, "Nevertheless, you should have informed me."

Aleen walked near the side of the bed opposite to where Edmund sat. Apparently knowing that an interference on his part was futile, Edmund sat slumped, looking at her with eyes dulled by fatigue.

A thin layer of perspiration covered the child's arms and neck, and small droplets of moisture from the forehead and face held streaks of hair flatly against her skin. Aleen closely inspected the sleeping child. The arms were pathetically thin; the little hands that had so eagerly snatched at shellfish and wildflowers now lay idled by a weakness that threatened to claim her very life.

Aleen reached for a damp cloth and began applying it to the fevered forehead with delicate strokes, when the child, revived by the cooling moistness, opened her eyes and stared numbly at Aleen, who quickly relaxed her look of concern.

"Lelia, my love. Lelia. Do you hear me? It is Aleen, my sweet."

The child blinked slowly and resumed her stare.

"You will be getting well soon, my sweet. Very soon."

The child opened her mouth slowly and said hoarsely, " 'Leen?"

Startled by the unexpected sound, Aleen stood still, as though made of stone.

" 'Leen," the child repeated with effort, "I scared."

Aleen's heart beat violently. Could the child possibly sense what was feared by all? Rage mingled with panic. If such was the case, it was the fault of those present for making the room a death chamber, with a long-faced hermit mumbling prayers, candles burning near a crucifix. . . . My God, Aleen shouted to herself. My God, the child still lies on her mother's deathbed. Edmund promised. He promised to replace it with another. She cannot remain upon it. To do so would mean certain death. "Come, Lelia," Aleen said, bending over the child. "There is nothing to fear. I will hold you." She slipped her hands under the warm body and lifted her up. Carefully she carried the limp form to a chair, sat down, and arranged the child comfortably on her lap.

She was not aware of Edmund's approach, and she looked up with a trace of annoyance as he spoke. "You should not be so near the child. It is foolish to risk your health."

Aleen looked rebukingly at him. "You promised to substitute another bed," she snapped scoldingly. Her impatience with his lack of trust made him less deserving of her attention, and she diverted her concern to offering Lelia a goblet of water that Edith had held out to her.

The little head with its dark mass of knotted hair fell limply against her arm. Signaling Edith for a cloth, Aleen continued to wipe the thin body in loving strokes.

"I scared," the child repeated weakly without opening her eyes.

"I am holding you now, my love. You are safe. Here, let me hold you closer." She reclined the little body until it rested fully against her. The sticky hair and the dampness made contact uncomfortable, and Aleen wondered with sorrow how it was that a human body could contain such heat.

Aleen stroked the hair and cooed softly in the child's ear. "You will begin to feel better now, my love. You must try hard to get well. There is so much for us to do. We must visit Ansgar and Bertha and play with the children. Cenook is eager to take us to the beach once more. It will be good to wade again in the surf. Yes, very soon you will be well, and we will play once more on the meadow. I will force you to eat many honey cakes, and you will become as fat as Bertha." Aleen kissed the sunken little cheek that had once dimpled in its rosy plumpness. "You must hurry and get well."

The muscles in the little body relaxed. There was no further need of encouragement.

Aleen continued to stroke the head she held tenderly against her breast. It was a dream—a very bad, frightening dream. The stuffy dreariness of the room and the brightness outside where squawking birds darted across the azure sky made all seem unreal, a dream of sorts.

Edmund bent down, took the child tenderly from Aleen's arms, and placed the body carefully on the bed. Aleen stared uncomprehendingly as he arranged the arms and straightened the legs.

Edith was weeping quietly, and the hermit, his eyes closed tightly, was reciting fervent prayers in low, monotonous tones.

Strangely numbed, Aleen sat quietly staring at the thin body. Her vision slowly fell from the child to Edmund, who was standing by the bed looking down sadly upon his daughter. Her eyes wandered down Edmund's tunic, down his thick calf muscles, his bare ankles, his soft shoes, to the shadow beneath the bed. There, near his feet, lay the small shoes of his daughter. Rising from the chair, Aleen walked toward them, reached under, and lifted only the shoe that was oddly formed to accommodate the deformity. Squeezing it gently in her hand, she walked across the room. Thoroughly exhausted from the gamut of emotions she had endured since the first day of Lelia's illness, she left the room as though benumbed.

## ∽( XXIV )∼

LELIA WAS but one day in the grave when the weakness Aleen had first experienced during the funeral service intensified its hold upon her. It was the journey to the cathedral burial grounds in the heat of the sun, she reassured herself. When it persisted throughout the day, her outpouring of grief was held to blame. But when the weakness was at last accompanied by a lightness of mind, uncertain equilibrium, and distorted vision, she surrendered completely and willingly to her bed.

Overwhelming sickness and pain assaulted her. The hours of sleep, which in the beginning were welcome refuges from her grief, began to take on sinister effects, which proved more disturbing than the ailment itself. Frightening vertigos bore down upon her, and taunting, unhappy faces appeared in dizzying sequences. Unpleasantries from the past presented themselves, until her more recent tragedy plagued her frighteningly.

The procession to the cathedral graveyard once again wended its way down pebbled roads. Edmund seemed to be beside her once more as she rode behind the cart bearing two rough coffins—one belonging to a villager whose family followed at the rear; the other, identical in size and construction, belonging to Lelia. Edmund had refused to permit the carpenters to employ more time and effort on his daughter's coffin. It was a trying time, and Edmund meant to show his affinity for all those who sorrowed by burying his own in the common manner. The lids of both coffins were splintery and ill-fitting, but Lelia's bore a small opening where two boards met improperly due to the gouging of an inexperienced woodsman, whose error in judgment had not been corrected by the hard-pressed carpenters. It was this opening that had held Aleen's attention throughout the journey to the churchyard.

Dirt will surely seep through, she had repeatedly bewailed to herself during the journey. Even now the opening incessantly appeared before her delirious mind, until she felt herself

246

becoming disembodied and taking on a ghostly form that glided and slid like smoke through the opening and into the darkness within. "Awaken, Lelia. Awaken. They will bury you, Lelia. Awaken. They will heap mud upon you, and you shall never escape. No, never, never, never . . ." she cried deliriously. "Hurry, Lelia, we must leave this place. Hurry, hurry. . . ." Each entrance into the morbid darkness was followed by her slow recession back to her mount, with the sun burning against her face and the wheels of the cart crunching gravel with each persistent revolution of the wobbly wheels. It was a sickening experience, but at times she emerged from the delusions, to find Edith speaking consolingly to her. There were times when she imagined she saw Edmund beside her bed, at times standing, at other times sitting. What was vision, what was reality, could not be distinguished.

Again and again she returned to the churchyard, and saw once more the grave tenders placing Lelia's coffin beside the gaping hole that patiently awaited its consignment. Once again hallucinations exerted themselves, until she thought she envisioned Marion's arms writhing up from the adjacent grave as if to claim and embrace her child. Aleen seemed to glide in long, hard strides toward the phantom arms, to desperately kick and stomp them, but the skeletal arms, undisturbed by Aleen's frantic efforts, continued their unseeing search. Perhaps Lelia could be saved if she prevented this contact, and she continued kicking with a frenzy, until her breathing became too rapid to endure and her lungs threatened to burst asunder. A nausea, and then she felt herself turn at the sound of sobbing, to see Judith, Wilfreda, and the women standing beside Lelia's coffin, dabbing at their eyes. Such hypocrisy could not be tolerated. These women, who were offended by the sight of the child's deformity, who considered her accursed by God, these women who ignored Lelia for many months, were now standing there before Edmund, mournfully weeping for the child. While in reality Aleen and Edmund had ignored the hypocritical display and remained stoically controlled, reserving their grief for private moments, Aleen, now in the grip of delusions, envisioned herself flying toward the women, chasing them from the churchyard with contemptuous anger. They were not permitted to mount their horses as Aleen followed them in hot pursuit, and they seemed to run inelegantly down the dusty road, shrieking crazily, while their skirts and veils beat wildly about them.

Then, somehow, the delirious visions seemed to transport her once again to Edmund's office, where he had guided her following the funeral. She was crying while Edmund comfortingly embraced her. Words were spoken—words that made her agitated and then regretful, until the recollection of the funeral made her writhe on her sickbed. With long, gliding steps she seemed to leave Edmund and to pass through haunted corridors until, safe within the privacy of her chamber, her sick fantasies concluded with her fists pounding on the walls in frustration.

Days of physical and mental torment passed in rapid order, until the sickness gradually subsided and the flights of delirium diminished. It was then that Edmund wearily quit the bedside and made his way to the chapel, where he fell to his knees on the cold stone floor before the altar.

"How can I thank you, Edith?" Aleen asked when she drew strength enough to speak. "You are tired. Take your rest. I shall sleep peacefully now."

"Nay, my lady," came the gentle reply. "I have been in constant attendance since you took the fever. I shall not leave you until I am certain you are recovered."

Aleen's eyes were closed as she spoke. "Then I shall properly scold Hester for not relieving you." The words were meant lightly, but when Edith did not arise to defend her comrade, Aleen, even through her weakness, sensed the sadness Edith experienced.

She was later told in gentle, apologetic tones how Hester had taken the fever from those she tended, had died as peacefully as the illness permitted, and was already buried.

It seemed impossible that Hester, who had cared for her since her birth, who had soothed her rumpled feelings and wiped away the tears of the heart, was gone, never to be seen again. How could she endure life without the happiness Lelia provided and the security and comfort of Hester's brooding companionship? She was tired in body and spirit, and to her bewildered mind all seemed akin to a dream. "They are not dead," she said aloud as a wave of drowsiness swept over her.

"They are lurking about in some darkened hiding place waiting to be happily discovered."

A lingering weakness forced Aleen to lie abed for many lonely days—days when the sad illusions developed from foggy unreality to veracious clarity. Of all the unhappy memories, one in particular struggled to emerge until she could no longer prevent it from dominating her thoughts.

It had occurred following the funeral, when Edmund had guided her into his office. She was standing before the very desk where once she had pleaded for the guardianship of the child when dismal reality beset her. Never again would small arms entwine about her neck, nor would pink blossom lips kiss her, nor limping steps follow her. The emotions she had suppressed throughout the brief graveside ceremony could no longer be contained, and in spite of Edmund's imposing nearness, she had covered her face with both hands and dissolved into a consuming grief.

Edmund had placed his arms comfortingly around her shoulders, but their mutual sorrow encouraged a closer contact. With ease she slipped into his arms, until her face rested upon his leather tunic. Thus embraced so tenderly, she cried full measure until her whimperings and sniffles subsided. Yet, even then he did not move to release her, and she, comforted by his nearness and the easy patting of his hand upon her back, remained with her head sweetly inclined against the man she loved so dearly.

"God is cruel," she said as she at last straightened.

Kindly words fell consolingly upon her. "It is only now that you think so."

Edmund was still so near that she could have leaned once more upon him, had she felt so disposed, but she remained erect, though she kept her head inclined to conceal her puffy face and reddened eyes. His hands had found their way to her shoulders, and he held her fast, as though unwilling to let her go.

"He has taken away everyone I dearly loved," she said sadly, and although she wished to add, "except for you," the words could not be sounded.

"Do not pity yourself, Aleen," Edmund said, "for you have much for which to be grateful, nor should you be saddened for those you have lost, for they now exult with their creator."

"It is unfair that they rejoice, for they have left me sorrowing. And I do pity myself, for I know I shall never be happy."

"Aleen," Edmund said in cajoling fluctuations, "you know full well that with the passage of time your sorrow will be lessened."

"I know that it should, yet I know that for me I shall never know happiness."

"Indeed you shall, Aleen, for I am prepared to give you whatever will console you. Tell me what it is you desire," and he bent closer toward her face.

"I should desire that Lelia and my father be resurrected," she said heart-rendingly. "I should desire that my brother return from distant waters, I should desire Hester by my side . . ."

"But, Aleen, it is impossible. Name for me something truly attainable."

There was a pause; then: "I should desire good friends to converse with, the acceptance of those living here, the affection of someone, perhaps another child, to brighten the days. . . ." The words were immediately regretted. Edmund could not secure for her the acceptance of the people, nor could he make of these people good friends, but another child to substitute for the one lost was quite attainable. Although the words had been spoken easily, with little thought to their tenor, the implication of her request hovered between them, and the words echoed upon their ears. Were it not for the helplessness she felt and the initial stirrings of the fever, she would have felt total shame for having spoken so candidly, and her humiliation would have been complete for the allusion thus created.

Edmund did not reply, but the inner sensations he experienced seemed to convey themselves through hands that still gripped her shoulders. Then, as though the proposal had created a barrier between them, he let go his hold and turned aside.

His reaction disturbed her momentarily, but then a debility swept upon her. It was all too much to think of then. She was tired and hot, and no longer cared what he thought. Let him consider the words if he wished, she thought, and feeling a twinge of contempt for his too virtuous life and commendable self-control, she looked at him from the corner of her eye with something of a sneer. It is not I he is married to, she thought, but Holy Mother Church.

The recalling of this incident disquieted her, and she fidgeted with the bed linens she had pulled about her. How could I have implied that I desired a child? I meant only that I wished an orphan, or some homeless waif to care for. The words did not convey my true thoughts. Yet in her heart she knew that the words did indeed convey subconscious desires. How shall I ever face Edmund again? I shall die of shame for the proposal I unwittingly voiced. But then, Edmund will exercise charity—he will overlook and will give me no cause to feel abased in his sight.

The thought consoled her, yet she blushed furiously as she turned on her side.

"How capricious it has been," Aleen said aloud as she watched Edith's head bobbing this way and that as she poked a broom beneath the bed. Her gray twists of hair were held atop her head with thin golden rods, and Aleen marveled that they did not become loosened from such energetic movements.

"Capricious, my lady?" she asked without stopping her activity.

"The fever. How is it I did not die, yet it took the lives of Hester and Lelia? Why is it you did not become ill? It was selective, capricious."

Edith finished her probing, stood up, and leaned against the broom she held before her. "It is the Creator's will, my lady. There were some he wanted beside him. There are others who must wait longer. I shall go when it pleases the heavenly father. Until then I shall serve as best I can." With her loyal declaration voiced, she again busily activated her long-tassled broom.

Aleen longed to inquire about Edmund, but discretion prevented her. Edith was undoubtedly aware of the rumors that had spread since the night in the tower, and Aleen wished to avoid a reference to the embellished tales and a subsequent outpouring of her heart concerning their untruth. But when Edmund did not visit her chamber during her convalescence,

Aleen became fearful lest he too was bedded with the contagion.

"No, my lady," Edith replied when Aleen at last drew courage to inquire about his health. "He is not ill, though I wonder that he is not. He has visited the sick repeatedly against all caution, and has been most generous both personally and monetarily to those who grieved. It has been said that he is most assuredly a saint."

"But why, Edith, is it that he visits the sick, yet could not visit his wife?" she asked, feeling resentment for his glaring omission.

"My lady," Edith said, turning her bulk around with amazing agility, "the lord spent days by your side. You were not aware of his presence, but I myself saw him praying often for your recovery. He would leave for short times to conduct business, and would return forthwith to resume his vigil. It was only when you were safely past the crisis that he left you. He was most admirably loyal." The attack upon the Lord Edmund made Edith defensive, until the satisfied look on Aleen's face allowed her to relax, knowing she had arisen with admirable zeal to defend the man whom all revered.

Aleen was comforted by the words, and the smile she felt inwardly sparkled her eyes, but then the cool voice of rationality sounded. Edmund had recently lost a daughter, and not long ago, a wife. What would the Vikings surmise, should he lose another Viking wife? What would his own people think? It could not have been love or devotion that prompted him to pray by her bedside, but concern lest he lose the esteem of his own people and be perhaps thought of as accursed, and fear that the Vikings would retaliate for the loss of the second Viking noblewoman.

But of course he loves me, she countered. There was the evening in the tower, there was the day in the library when his hand became entangled in my hair. . . .

Hester's possessions had to be removed from the room she had occupied in the servants' quarters, or so Aleen conjectured, for she cared not to admit that it was the contents of a personal chest that drew her to Hester's room. The remembrance of Hester's brooding journeys into the past, the mystery of her early life, her loves if there were any, the reason for her ready acceptance into the confidence of the Danish royal family, had always vexed Aleen, and now that she was free to investigate the chest which might hold the answers to her questions, her curiosity demanded gratification.

The walk to Hester's room would be her first excursion since her illness, and she dressed with care. A blue linen dress constructed of a fine, delicate weave was her choice. It hung loosely about her shoulders, and her chain girdle had to be latched two links tighter than had been comfortable before her illness. Wide sleeves concealed her thin arms, but nothing could disguise the remnants of illness still lingering on her face. Her image reflected harshly in her mirror. Her dark eyes, underscored by shadows, appeared sunken, with a wide-awake quality that startled her. And in spite of the ample helpings of food Edith had forced upon her, her cheeks were depressed and sallow. Aleen experimented with various arrangements of her hair, but neither pulling it back from the face nor arranging it atop the head served to alleviate the vague look of her eyes, and golden ornaments around the hair only emphasized her pathetic condition. There was only one person she wished would not see her so, and that person was too occupied with restoring the castle to normalcy and attending to affairs postponed by the epidemic to trouble himself with her.

She stared at her reflection, placed the silver-framed mirror on the table, and shrugged her shoulders. She could do nothing to improve herself. At least she could be grateful that the hallways were dim for the most part, and would offer an unfavorable atmosphere for a close inspection. She would remember to remain in shadowed areas if a meeting with Edmund was unavoidable.

It was one matter to walk about the enclosure of her chamber, and quite another to traverse the long musty hallways. More quickly than she had suspected, her strength drained from her and she was forced to hurry along in spite of it, to arrive at her destination before the limits of its capacity were reached.

Entering the room pointed out to her, Aleen quickly sat down and waited while fatigue passed and tides of strength returned.

Hester's haunting presence seemed to fill the room, and

Aleen felt as though Hester saw each movement and condemned Aleen's intentions.

It was a simple room, with no wall ornaments. A bed, table, chair, and chest were the only furnishings. Tunics and aprons were hung on nails, and two pairs of worn shoes were sitting forlornly beneath them. There were few articles on the table—a piece of parchment, an inkwell and quill.

Soon Edith would help her dispose of Hester's belongings or to select those articles which would be of use to her. Hester, she felt, would have wanted her friend to have them. There was little to dispose of, however, except the contents of the chest.

A tabernacle being sacrilegiously violated could not have produced more ominous assaults of conscience than Aleen experienced as she placed both hands against the lid before opening it. Hester, Aleen felt, was peering over her shoulder, futilely attempting to protect her property from possible defilement.

There was a protesting crack of wood and the grinding of rusty hinges as the lid was lifted. The contents at first seemed inconsequential, but when the undergarments, veils, crudely embroidered cloths were put aside, Aleen frowned, for a collection of curious items was uncovered. A man's golden wrist band claimed her attention. She picked it up and ran fingers over the coolness of its embossed designs. A small sword, a drinking horn rimmed with plain gold, a bag of coins, a silver-edged ivory comb, a keylike girdle hanger, a beaded necklace, and packets of scented herbs were all carefully removed, some replaced in the chest, others placed on the table.

Squares of linen concealed other articles. Aleen unfolded the first packet as though it contained the most fragile of substances. A dagger, dulled by time, reflected a muted bronze gleam as she uncovered it. Careful fingers unfolded a piece of parchment that contained a locket of hair. A garnet and a golden brooch were closely examined before Aleen rewrapped them. Another packet contained three infant dresses, yellowed by time and made of linen in a common weave and design.

Carefully placed beneath the linen parcels was a familiar blue silk fabric, and on moving it, Aleen immediately recognized the golden border of her wedding gown. The silk veil was quickly cast aside as Aleen slipped the gown from the bottom of the chest. What memories it evoked as she shook it free of its folds. She had thought it in ashes long ago, having ordered Hester to dispose of it following the wedding. How angry she had been at the time. How certain she was then that she hated Edmund, and how certain she was now that she did not. It was sentimental of Hester to have kept it, she thought as she held it up against her.

Edith entered, and Aleen quickly rolled the silk into an unrecognizable bundle, not knowing why she should need to conceal it, and dropped it into the chest.

"Please, Edith, have this chest removed to my room. I find I must examine the contents at my leisure. And, Edith, you may have what is on the table, and these things hanging here."

While Edith placed the articles in the droop of her apron, Aleen's thoughts returned to Hester's mementos. It was an odd assortment, and true to the anonymity Hester would have applauded, the articles cast no solution on the mystery of her past.

Edith was carrying her newly acquired articles to her room a few doors away as Aleen set out on her circuit of hallways. She had not gone far when the heavy sound of urgent footsteps approached, footsteps Aleen instinctively knew were not those of Edmund. Looking back, Aleen watched as a young priest hurried by as though bearing a message of grave importance. At the far end of the hall she saw him knock on the door of Edmund's office, wait, then knock again. The door opened, and for a moment Aleen caught sight of Edmund as he recognized his caller, planted a friendly hand on his arm, and drew him in.

As Aleen passed the office, she strained to hear words that would allude to the message the cleric bore with such importance, but no sound was heard. One would think him the courier of King Alfred, she thought. And with a smile of amusement: Or perhaps even an envoy of the pope.

"One would judge from the speed with which you arrived here from the harbor that you lost no time on the journey," Edmund said as he poured a tankard of mead and handed it to the priest.

The vessel was refused with a shake of the head and a resisting hand. "I find it too warm for mead, my lord. I require no refreshment."

Edmund leaned against the edge of his desk and studied the unsmiling cleric. Then, crossing his muscular arms, he patiently listened as the traveler related the details of the journey: the speed of the sea voyage, the heat of the plains of France, the hospitality of the numerous monasteries along the way, the speed with which they pressed forward, anything, it would seem, to stall the results of the errand. With each change of topic, Edmund's face set in harsher lines, his eyes tensed, and his muscles hardened, but no interruption was made.

Eventually Edmund stood up, leisurely circled the desk, then nervously sat down. Resting his elbows on the chair's arms, he touched the fingertips of both hands together and pressed them against his lips. The priest's babbling soon ceased under Edmund's steady gaze, and a formidable silence developed.

The priest nervously entwined his fingers and rubbed the palms hard against each other. "I did not see the pope, sir," he said softly, his words causing a squinting of Edmund's eyes. "He is ill. Some say he is dead, others say he is dying. Most assuredly it is a fatal illness, a lingering one. Perhaps by now he is truly dead. During the illness the affairs of the church are executed by his staff of respected churchmen. Arrangements were made for me to present your plea to them. They listened most attentively to my arguments, and after discussions of the matter, which they conducted in my absence, they called me before them two days later and gave me their judgment."

The priest rearranged his position, wiped a forefinger against his mouth, cleared his throat, and continued hesitantly. "They said, sir, that . . ." He glanced at Edmund and continued more determinedly, "They said, sir, they could not grant a dispensation of your vow."

An outburst was expected, some thunderous denouncement, but Edmund remained admirably silent, almost virtuously so.

"They enumerated very carefully the conditions under which the vow was made, namely, that it was made of your free will and over the objections of Reverend Jerome. It was properly witnessed, and the pledge understood by all the attendants. They declared it a legitimate vow. They explained that you, as the ealdorman of this district, are not only the temporal leader of the people entrusted to your care and supervision, but that as a baptized Christian you are also, in a manner of speaking, a spiritual leader, a model whereby they may fashion the elements of their much simpler lives. They stressed, sir, that if you are permitted to make vows, and then, when convenience suits you, to dispense with them, then the people could in fairness expect similar considerations. They further indicated that the taking of vows, whether private or solemn, especially one of this nature, to observe continence, are serious pledges to be considered carefully and to be pronounced only under the direction of competent counsel. Edmund, they wish to make of you an example. They declared that the church has been endeavoring to discourage the making of private vows, and they wish to prove, by your folly, the detriments which may result. I pleaded with them that you pronounced the vow immediately following the funeral of your wife, when you were experiencing extreme mental anguish. They listened, but when I concluded, they each in turn signed two copies of their pronouncement. I have here a copy they said should be given to you." And he fumbled with the pouch hanging from his leather belt. Extracting the folded parchment, he placed it on the desk before Edmund.

Edmund's arms dropped against the chair, and his fingers tightly grasped the carved ends of the armrests, where lion heads, jaws opened, fangs exposed, posed in silent roars. The parchment, freed from the restraining confines of the pouch, moved as though relaxing its uncomfortable fold.

"My lord, I pleaded your cause as best I knew how." Edmund leaned his head against the back of the chair as his eyes roamed among the beams of the ceiling. "I am most grieved, my lord, that I am unable to bring you a more favorable decision."

Silence again claimed the room, until the priest, realizing Edmund had no intention of speaking, rose from his place. "I shall go now, sir." But as his sandals scraped across the floor, Edmund rose, walked toward a window, looked out, and called to the priest. His voice was cold and forthright. "The soldiers who accompanied you," he began, "have been forewarned that they were to mention the destination of your journey to no one, under penalty of death. You are similarly cautioned. You may not disclose the nature of your journey or its destination to anyone, including the bishop or your superiors. Should you do so, I shall be forced to forget you are a priest."

The young clergyman stood as still as a child being reprimanded by one he fears. Edmund continued scanning the countryside, as the priest, though unobserved, nodded courteously before departing the room.

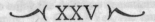 

HE WAS splendid of body, fair of face, and proud of spirit. The haughty air with which he rode toward the castle was enough to spark the romantic interests of the maidens clustered about the windows that overlooked the courtyard and the road. The casual manner with which one hand rested on his hip, the flippant tilt of his head, the light but confident hold of the reins, bespoke convincingly of a lusty appetite that caused the unmarried ladies to flutter excitedly, young married women to consider the untimeliness and wisdom of their marriages, and older women to bemoan the maturity of their years.

He was decidedly a young man of some wealth, judging from his manservant, who drove a cart laden with leather bags and sturdy chests of wood that contained, no doubt, costly clothing and articles of luxury and convenience. Two strong, high-stepping horses of selected breeding pulled the cart, while a young golden-haired boy of seven or eight sat on the back, dangling his naked feet in the billowing dust.

It was Edith who excitedly informed Aleen of the arrival of Edmund's brother, and it was she who urged Aleen to join the others in the feast of welcome. Aleen's reluctance evoked gentle persuasions on Edith's part. It was the courteous thing to do, she argued. Indeed, it would be unseemly for her not to dine with Edmund's brother on his return to Lauxburgh. Edith's cajoling eventually weakened Aleen's resistance. If she had no interest at all in the feast, occurring, as it did, several weeks from the time of the plague, she had even less interest in what she wore, and she surrendered willingly to Edith's busy attentions. A yellow tunic was selected, a gold link girdle was draped at just the correct angle about the hips, and her hair was combed and arranged neatly down her back, its sheen emphasizing the delicate yellow of the linen gown. A short white silk veil was secured in place by a thin golden rod, and its ruffles, falling about the ears, softly flattered the face that had reclaimed its former comeliness. When Edith had suggested wearing jewels, or at least a golden necklace to fill the scoop of the neckline, Aleen steadfastly refused, until Edith was convinced that no amount of inveigling would result in compliance. Aleen had refused to wear jewelry of any nature since the time Judith had made a spectacle of questioning Aleen's acquisition of a brooch and intimated before a long table of diners that it was part of the booty of Danish raids. If the amount and quality of jewelry a woman wore attested to her social position and importance, then, Aleen reasoned, she must be considered of common lineage in spite of her Danish nobility. Subsequently she refused to wear the jewels bequeathed to her by her mother, for she cringed from having them critically analyzed and their procurement boorishly conjectured.

A cursory glance confirmed the neatness of her appearance. At least they will have no cause to accuse me of being pretentious. "Well," she said, "the sooner I begin my ordeal, the sooner will I return."

The hallways resounded with the noise of the festivities, which matched, if not exceeded, those that had taken place before the plague, this in consideration that many of the most enthusiastic revelers had succumbed to illness.

The second-floor gallery loomed enticingly before her, and she paused beside one of the pillars, hid herself carefully within its shadow, and stealthily looked down upon the assembly. The hall was crowded with the castle residents and the most prosperous and influential village merchants, shire lords, and their wives. The masters of King Alfred's ships, now docked in the bay, were present, as were many monks of Tankenham.

Edith had misjudged the importance of the social gathering. Everyone there was dressed elaborately. Even Edmund was dressed fashionably. His dark blue, hip-length tunic was embroidered with small golden emblems, his linen breeches were strapped with care against his legs, his shoes gleamed in their newness, a gold wrist band shone from one arm, and a golden pendant hung from a heavy chain around his neck. It would take an event of extreme importance to induce Edmund to suspend his period of mourning and to adorn himself so uncharacteristically, and it would seem that the return of this prodigal brother was of such substance.

Edmund is indeed handsome, she thought, looking longingly at him. One could be proud of being wife to him if she had been his choice and if the threat of annulment did not hover over their marriage. Aleen watched as Edmund took a flagon of ale from a cupbearer and began himself to pour from it into the empty horns and goblets of his guests. Her eyes followed his every movement, but the touch of her cheek against the cool marble of the column terminated her reflections, and she allowed her attention to fall on others.

Wilfreda was happier than Aleen could ever remember. Indeed, Aleen had never before seen her smiling as willingly as she was now doing. And her gown. It was not in the modest design she customarily wore. No. This one was low about the chest and revealed subtly the breasts Aleen thought Wilfreda did not possess. Narrow bands of rabbit fur accented the neckline and the edges of the sleeves that fell softly about the wrists and dipped in long points. If Aleen's instincts were correct, the dress was an old one, although it did not appear to be of great age, and must have been designed when Wilfreda's days were happier and more fulfilling.

Wilfreda conferred briefly with a cupbearer and then approached several monks who were gathered about a young man with yellow hair. Smiling radiantly, Wilfreda took the young man by the arm, and after a number of polite comments to the religious, led the young man away in the manner of a good hostess who desired to share her honored guest equally with all present.

So this is Edmund's brother, Aleen thought as the young man was being led to another group. His physical assets were plainly evident. Under his short scarlet tunic, which gleamed with a border of interwoven golden threads, was a body thick with hard muscles. He was broad of shoulder, narrow of hip, tall of body, and remarkably fair of face. He was likewise unbearably nonchalant and disgustingly proud. The young ladies could not but help being keenly aware of his sexual attractiveness, his innate talent to charm and conquer, and if they honestly appraised him, they would know that without the slightest twinge of conscience he would casually discard his willing victims for other challenges. He was a willful man accustomed to having life bend according to his whims and to having his appetites promptly satisfied.

Wilfreda and Cestus had joined a happy group who were delighted at the intrusion, but Aleen soon noticed that while Cestus sipped casually from his goblet and pretended interest in their conversation, he was in fact interested in the young ladies who coyly smiled toward him.

A noise in the hallway startled Aleen, and she quickly and easily slipped back into a shadowed recess to await the passage of two women, who were giggling as they made their way to the feast. When Aleen was again free to continue her clandestine surveillance, her eyes fell on Judith, who was extremely comely, with her hair twisted about her head in shiny braids. Her slender white neck was flattered by the low V of her gown, and she wore only the most delicate of jewelry to emphasize her fragile features. She was older than Cestus, else she, like the maidens, would be vying for his attentions.

All the women were elegantly dressed and wore a display of jewelry such as Aleen had never before seen. The men too were carefully attired, and even the monks were impeccably neat in their carefully brushed robes.

Before long, servants appeared with huge platters of mutton and venison, bowls of beans, corn, and squash, and plates of cheeses and breads. There were wooden bowls of figs, apples, and nuts, and numerous jugs of wine and mead. All were carefully arranged on the tables that were adorned with candleholders supporting tall new tapers for use when the feast and merrymaking extended far into the night.

When the guests evinced interest in the savory aromas and began to mill around the tables in search of a suitable place on the long benches, Aleen was suddenly frantic with the realization of the speed she must exert to reach the gathering, to be properly presented to Cestus, and to greet the guests before taking her place at table. But then, how could she do so when she was dressed so simply in comparison to their finery? They will think me a servant, and I would not blame them. I cannot attend like this, she thought, holding her skirt out with both hands and wrinkling her nose. Edmund would surely be shamed by my appearance, and there is not sufficient time to change.

She glanced again at the glittering assemblage and Wilfreda

smiling so proudly beside her younger son. I wonder, Aleen thought, transfixed by the sight of Wilfreda's unusual gaiety, should I join them, would she continue to smile? I shall not vex her by my attendance.

Immediately despondent by her decision, she looked again upon the carefree group before returning to her rooms.

"Edith," Aleen said to the startled maid, "you must go to Edmund in the great hall and inform him that I am ill and cannot attend the feast."

"But, my lady," Edith stammered as she watched wide-eyed as Aleen unlatched the links of her girdle, "you *must* attend. Why—"

"Perhaps I should, but how can one who is ill in bed?"

"You are not ill, my lady," she said accusingly. "Do not ask me to lie."

"Well, then," Aleen said, slipping out of her gown and kicking off her shoes, "tell him I have taken to my bed and cannot come. He will think I am ill, and you will be spared a lie. See, I am truly upon my bed. Now, hurry."

In due time Edith returned with a tray. "The lord asked me if your illness was of a serious nature, and when I told him it was not, he instructed me to bring this to you. He regrets you cannot join them."

I could be boundlessly pleased by this consideration, she thought as she examined the contents of the tray, if he were not as equally solicitous of all the sick who are brought to his attention.

The grapes alone held interest for her, and she nibbled a few before sprawling across the bed. Laughing voices and squeals of laughter rode the breezes of dusk and the cold drafts of musty halls. Perhaps I should have attended, she thought reprovingly. At least I could have sat near Edmund, or at least have been able to look upon him. She smiled, and her face colored at the recollection of their gentle intimacy in the tower and their more recent closeness in his office following Lelia's funeral. But her smile relaxed at the remembrance of Judith basking under Edmund's attentions. Were Judith married to Edmund, she would not have permitted such foolishness to exist between them for long and would have no qualms of conscience in blatantly tempting him until he abandoned his resolves.

It seemed inappropriate for laughter and merrymaking to resound where only weeks ago the groans of the plague-stricken and the whimperings of the bereaved were heard. But mourning could not retrieve the dead from the lonely exile of the grave, and the challenge of life without them must be faced. A little merrymaking was as a balm, affording a soothing respite for souls burdened by the hardships of the recent ordeal. From the increasing noisiness, it would seem they were applying the balm generously.

Before the sun cleared the watery horizon of the North Sea, a sleepy stable hand, yawning and stroking sleep from his eyes, indolently managed to bridle and saddle the horses ordered for use that morning. Before long the hunters, eager for sport, claimed their tethered mounts, and the noise of hooves on hard-packed mud were quickly exchanged for the distant crunching and clicking of the graveled road. Heading for the forest on the tangent cross of grazing lands, the sound of hooves soon became muffled by the thick dewy grasses. Thus quieted, their excited voices were permitted to speed across the coolness, with auditory precision, back to the castle, to fall upon ears dulled by sleep.

One set of ears, however, alertly strained to hear the dying echoes until they ceased altogether in the entrapment of the forest greenery. Bright eyes opened wide and peered out the window at the pink fluffs of clouds suspended serenely in the azure sky. With Edmund and the male guests off on a hunt, it would be the perfect day for the journey to the cobbler's cottage that had been planned, but reluctantly postponed, for days. It would be a sad visit, for it related to Hester's iron-bound chest that stood in a somber, shadowy corner of Aleen's outer room. The sight of it caused chills of depression whenever Aleen's glance fell upon it, until she pledged to settle the disposition of the contents straightaway and to store the emptied coffer elsewhere.

The treasured relics within were linked somehow to the faraway look Aleen recalled seeing so often in Hester's eyes. Since Hester had no family or loved ones—at least that Aleen knew of—it fell to her to dispose of the articles Hester had treasured so dearly. At first Aleen had meant to keep them secure, as her servant had done for so long, but their presence unnerved her, and since they produced no explanation as to the happy or unhappy elements of Hester's life, she resolved to dispose of them, and no more grateful recipients could be envisioned than the cobbler and his wife.

How proud Ansgar would be to wear the gleaming armband and the bronze dagger. How proud he would be to display the small Viking sword. And Bertha. Bertha would be intolerably proud of her acquisition of the gold-rimmed drinking horn and the garnet brooch. How gratefully would she accept the garments Edith had found too large. They would fit Bertha nicely, but if they did not, Aleen could well imagine the friendly pomposity with which Bertha would disburse them among her village friends.

It was a good day, and Aleen determined to venture forth, especially since she was certain Edmund had taken his brother hunting. She had yet to be formally presented to Cestus, and she had surreptitiously avoided him—not so much that she was reluctant to meet him as she was reluctant to face Edmund, who was always with him.

During many fretful nights when the memory of Lelia haunted her grieving heart, she recalled painfully how Edmund had stiffened so at her mention of another child to fill the lonely void Lelia's death had produced. Because of the weariness that day, she had felt no shame that her words had conveyed more meaning than she had intended, but now that Edmund had had time to reflect on them, she blushed at the mere thought of facing him. Since he was hunting this day and she held no fear of meeting him, she felt as liberated as a gyrfalcon, unhooded and free to fly at will.

The contents of the chest were stuffed into two leather pouches Edith produced. The emptied chest was to be removed before her return. Picking up the folded parchment that contained the slip of hair, Aleen touched it to a flaming candle, dropped it into a bowl, and watched contemplatively as it burned, sending repulsive fumes to her nose as it reduced itself steadily into blackened ashes. Father, brother, lover— from whose head was the lock so sentimentally clipped? The mystery of Hester's past was unsolved and sealed forever.

Together Edith and Aleen carried the pouches to the stable,

where Thorkil tied the straps together and slung them on either side of a donkey. At the mounting block, Aleen lifed herself lightly upon Cenook, reached for the rope tied to the donkey's neck, and set out for the village.

Tears came to Bertha's eyes when she saw Aleen at the door. She was pleased to see Aleen, but their reunion was saddened not only by the absence of Lelia, who had always been with Aleen on their visits, but also by the condition of the cobbler, who, it seemed, had suffered from the plague and had since endured lingering symptoms. A weakness still invaded his body, so much so that when he stood, a dizziness blurred his vision and muscles tightened in his neck, while a loud drumming noise sounded discomfortingly in his ears.

Bridles, shoes, harnesses, saddles—all lay abandoned on his worktables. Unfortunately, no skilled craftsman, nor even an unskilled workman, could be persuaded to maintain the trade for him. Since the onset of his illness he had been forsaken by his apprentice, who likewise became ill and now feared further contagion from the cobbler's peculiar condition, as did all the people in the village. For weeks now Ansgar had lain disconsolately on his bed in the room once occupied by Lelia and Edith, praying to regain his health, yearning to complete his unfinished work, now covered with dust, and desiring most earnestly to be of some use to his burdened family. He drank faithfully of the concocted herbs the physician brought, but no improvement was noticed. Such were the grievances illness had thrust upon him. He did not neglect, however, to be grateful for his sturdy wife, his healthy children, and the ealdorman's beneficences.

"I have gifts for you Ansgar," Aleen said, anxiously trying to relieve the strain of speaking about his ailment, yet attempting to hide her reaction to his pitifully gaunt appearance. "Here," she said after locating the cold metal deep within the pouch. "This armband you can wear proudly when you are well. And this dagger, too," she added, placing it in his skeletal hand. She had meant to cheer him, but he only clutched his gifts sadly. A sick man had no need of such. "The rest is for you, Bertha. Please give them to whomever you wish, if you have no need of them."

"My lady," Bertha repeatedly said in astonishment as she

pulled out the drinking horn, linen undergarments, tunics, and at last the garnet brooch. "Where came you by these things?"

"My maidservant, Hester, died of the fever. It would grieve me to have these things reminding me of her. She cared for me since my infancy," Aleen continued despondently, "and was a most faithful and loving companion. I do not wish to offend you by offering you her things—she being Danish—"

"God rest her soul," Bertha interrupted. "I am honored. You speak well of her, and thus will we think of her."

Always sensitive to the moods of others, Bertha easily noted the change that had taken place in Aleen. Talk of sickness had brought back the unpleasant memories that had so often assaulted her young friend. Aleen craved the company of the limping child whose confidence and friendship she had won in the very room in which she now stood. Looking lovingly at the playing children, and noting the ever-plump child whose birthdate almost coincided with Lelia's, she keenly felt her irreplaceable loss. Her face became solemn as she glanced about the room that recalled so many memories.

Bertha, feeling pressed to alleviate the distress of her noble friend, quickly began to remove her newly acquired articles from the bed. Straightening the coverlet about her stricken husband, she asked, "Would you walk with me, Aleen? I must journey to the wharf for fresh mackerel. Ansgar loves it so." Picking up the newest addition to her family, she cradled the infant in one arm and slipped the other arm through the handle of her basket. "Come, Aleen," she urged, "it will be a pleasant walk. Our old fish dealer died of the plague, and our new one has asked so much for his smelly wares that we have all taken to journeying to the wharf ourselves for fish that is fresher and less costly." The children scampered happily behind them, chanting verses that had become popular among their playmates.

It was a leisurely walk along the cobbled street that separated rows of thatched-roof dwellings and stores. Before long the road ended, and they were obliged to walk across a small tract of land. The children ran ahead down the slope to the wharf, and bounced upon the loosened boards that slammed noisily against the supports. Deftly their little hands grabbed at a railing to which boats were sometimes secured, and with fluid movements of their little bodies they swung themselves to a sitting position, plopped their feet in the gurgling water, and sent up sprays of water.

Bertha and Aleen settled themselves on the grassy slope and watched the laughing children. "Our wait will not be lengthy, Aleen. See, they are taking in their nets." She raised her chin, indicating by its movement the boats anchored within the bay.

How placid it was. The fishing boats rocked listlessly on quiet waters, gentle breezes rearranged blotches of clouds, and the sun alternately peeked from behind their thick whiteness. It was good to enjoy it all with Bertha. She had thought Edith was her only remaining friend, but she was wrong. Thank God she could also claim Bertha as well.

"Aleen," Bertha said, glancing warily at the young lady she had grown to cherish, "if it distresses you not, will you tell me of the child? When the courier you sent gave us word of Lelia's death, I believed him not. Did she suffer much?"

"Yes, she suffered, but she was spared much by stupors brought on by the illness and the medicinals. She was awake at the end, and died in my arms. Press me not for further details. It pains me to think of it," and she turned her head to hide her struggle against the tears that rushed for release. They would stop only if her mind and heart were distracted by other matters, and without turning her head, and struggling hard to control the quavering of her voice, she asked dispiritedly, "Tell me, Bertha, were you or the children stricken?"

"Nay, my lady. When my Ansgar took sick, I kept him in the room. The children I kept away from everyone. I once suffered a fever as a child, and I feared little that I would suffer again. My mother vowed then to pilgrimage to the shrine of Saint Cuthbert if I recovered. As you see, I did. I, in turn, vowed likewise. I pledged to go on a pilgrimage if my little ones were spared. Thank the good God I have a religious debt to pay." Lowering her voice, she added, "But I think it was the prayers of my Ansgar that did it. Did I tell you he prayed that he be stricken instead of the children? His prayers were also answered. He is a good man, Ansgar."

Two of the three fishing boats had turned their bows homeward and were slicing the waters as their oars were plucked in and out of the sparkling waves they created.

"I hear tell, Aleen, that Cestus has returned home. Is this true?"

"Yes, it is so," Aleen answered, running fingers through hair the shifting breezes had disturbed.

"The rumors hereabouts have been numerous. Do you think they speak rightly—that Edmund intends to return to Tankenham?"

Aleen turned sharply to her companion. "What say you?" she demanded so sternly that Bertha felt immediately apologetic.

"My lady, surely it is known that Edmund would someday return to the monastery."

"What else do they say?" Aleen demanded again.

Bertha fumbled for words that would soothe the agitation so suddenly aroused, but on finding none, she continued her report. "They say that the Lord Edmund sent for Cestus, since he is now of age to accept the responsibilities of the ealdorman." She leaned closer and confided, "They say Edmund thinks Cestus is old enough to discontinue his frivolous life and to settle himself to serious matters. With Cestus assuming the burden of the office, Edmund would be free to return to Tankenham, as he always planned to do. Since you once said there was no love between you and the lord, I thought mention of this would not trouble you." Bertha looked curiously at her friend as she placed the infant in her arms. "I see, Aleen, that I have distressed you."

The words reached Aleen as did the distant voices of the hunters at dawn. After adjusting the babe in her arms, Aleen looked toward Bertha, who was carrying her basket toward the wharf, where the children were supervising the docking of the boats. As she looked down on the sleeping infant, the words seemed to wound her heart. *But Edmund has no mind to return to Tankenham. He loves me. A woman's instincts do not go awry in such matters.* Though she would not let it reach the level of clear and unbiased consideration, she knew there existed the possibility that their brief and tender moments together were the result of weaknesses on Edmund's part—he being of flesh and blood, as are all men. *Yes, too much weakness,* Aleen thought. *Why could he not tell me of these plans himself, instead of permitting me to hear of it from the villagers? Why could not someone in the castle have informed me of this?* Then, with a presage of the desolation she would feel at his departure, she summarized her random thoughts: Why else would Cestus have returned home? It must be as Bertha told me.

Wet, silvery fish slipped and thrashed inside the basket Bertha held out to her in exchange for the whimpering babe. As if on signal, the children, accustomed to the procedure, started for home and began rolling and tumbling in the soft grasses as they made their way. Soothing words had calmed the infant, and the women trudged to the village in silence. Their thoughts were their own, and so absorbed was Aleen that she was unaware that slimy water from the fish basket was running along the reeds and dripping steadily down her skirt.

The sun was high when they reached the cobbler's shop. Walking around to the side door, where Cenook and the donkey stood in fly-infested warmth, Aleen gave the basket to Bertha, who promptly consigned it to the oldest child with a nudge and a gentle order to deposit it and the smaller children inside. With a light touch on Aleen's elbow, Bertha made a courteous pretext at helping her mount. Then, with a firmer grip she gained Aleen's attention. With womanly intuition she read Aleen's heart, and in the dulcet tones she had practiced so often on her children, she said, "Pay no heed to my words, Aleen, 'twas only rumor."

Aleen turned Cenook around and pulled on the rope tied to the donkey. The monotonous clopping of the two animals lulled Aleen into a stupor that dulled the mind but left the heart aching from the vicious possibilities that had clawed at it. Then, as Aleen guided Cenook to the path along the castle wall, a voice called out, "Maiden, wait. I shall escort you."

Startled by the unexpected words, she looked back in quick reflex and saw Cestus astride a noble beast. I thought him hunting, Aleen thought with a flush of perplexity. He drew up to her side, and as she studied the smirk on his face, she knew she resented him completely.

"Aye maiden, one as fair as you needs escort. A service I am most delighted to render," and he bowed in his saddle with a flourish.

Aleen ignored the gesture and continued to look ahead as she flapped the reins for a quicker gait.

"You wish to ride faster to be rid of me? I cannot believe this," and he reached for Cenook's reins and held him back. "Let us be friends, maid. Tell me your name."

The look Aleen gave him was meant to unseat him, but he only dropped his head back and laughed heartily. He is arrogant, detestable, she thought in frustration as she tried to yank the reins from his unyielding hand. 'Tis no wonder he does not hunt. Such would soil his hands and weary him. He prefers to annoy maidens instead.

"Aha," he said as a sly look crept across his face. "Your mother warned you about strange young men. You need have no fear, I am Cestus, brother of the ealdorman Edmund."

The pompous . . . Aleen searched her mind for a word sufficiently evil enough to describe him. Why, he thinks I am privileged to ride beside him, she thought angrily. He thinks I should be awed that he speaks to me. Her frown deepened with annoyance. So he takes refuge in the shadow of Edmund's good name. Perhaps I should tell him who I am, order him to quit me, and report to Edmund how his brother accosts maidens on the road. But no. I shall let him hang himself in a noose fashioned of his own words and actions.

"I have revealed my name," he said; and then added pleadingly, "Tell me yours. You do not wish to speak? Nay, you *cannot* speak! That is it. Well, then, I shall learn of you just the same. Let me see," he said, appraising her attire. "You are a village maiden on her way to return the donkey to the castle stable. Nay, you belong somehow to the castle, for I see that your mount is of quality stock. Come, tell me," he coaxed. "I desire to learn of you."

But the maid had no intention to learn of him, and stared ahead as though oblivious of the game he was playing. The flare of indignation she had first felt at his comparison of her to a village maid simmered somewhat as she evaluated her rumpled appearance. Sitting astride Cenook, with her skirt stretched across his back, was none too flattering. Her hair was mussed, she wore no jewels or ornaments to distinguish her from the common folk, and a faint devaluating smell of fish was growing more intense about her. In fairness, she could not reproach him for this assumption.

He delighted in her resistance, and her silent aloofness stimulated his masculine pride and aroused his need for conquest.

"You are fair, indeed," he said, lifting himself in his saddle and straining for a better look into her face. "And that ankle," he said, looking down at a bareness Aleen had thoughtlessly allowed. "It is as fine an ankle as I have ever seen," he said with a teasing grin. "I should like to see you again, maiden. I can read poetry quite well, and many say my playing of the lute is beyond the ordinary."

The arrogant, prideful ... He intends somehow to woo me. A deep sigh of relief escaped her as they turned into the gate and headed for the stables.

"You feel safe now? Come. Before I lose you, tell me where I might find you again. Do not make me roam the country in search of you." Her silence amused him, and he smiled as he dismounted quickly to assist her. With a slapping aside of her skirt and a stern look toward him, she slipped off with ease. But he was not intimidated, and with a practiced eye surveyed the whole of her form as her leg crossed Cenook's back. Silently, and with a nod of appreciation, she gave Thorkil the donkey's rope and briskly walked away.

"Maiden, you shall not lose me so easily," Cestus called as he ran after her and grabbed her wrist.

Aleen turned to face him fully and glared her hatred at him. Summoning her strength, she tightened her lips and struggled against his hold.

" 'Tis a noble, lovely face you have, maiden," he said, looking down on her. "Smile for me so that I may see your charms."

His self-confidence and conceit were more than she could bear, and rearing back her other hand, she swung it sharply at him. The blow did not land, for his other hand raised swiftly to stop it.

"A frisky wench you are," he said, laughing as he held both wrists high.

What a noise he is making, she thought desperately, but from the corner of her eye she saw a figure approaching—someone to free me from this beast, she thought gratefully.

"Edmund," she heard Cestus saying as she struggled against his hold. "Come see what I have found on the village road."

It cannot be, she thought desperately as she turned. But it was indeed Edmund, who had just left the smokehouse after depositing the products of the morning hunt. Blood was on his tunic, and he was wiping water from his bare arms that had just been cleansed. A slight grin of amusement crossed his face that only added to her confusion and embarrassment.

She, the Lady of Lauxburgh, being held in such an undignified manner—and being caught in such a snare by her husband, who smiled. She once more struggled unsuccessfully to free herself. In desperation and without realizing what she was about, she kicked her restrainer soundly in the shins.

Cestus grimaced. "See, Edmund, the wench attacks me. Now, maiden, you can attack me no more, for, see, the Lord Edmund is witness to your actions. Is she not comely, Edmund?" he asked pridefully.

"Yes, she is most fair."

"Tell me, Edmund, do you know her name or where she lives? I desire to see more of her, but, as you see, she tells me naught of herself."

"You may see her often," Edmund said lightly. "The maiden lives in the castle."

"Ah," Cestus said with delight, "such convenience."

"You have not been formally presented, Cestus, but the maiden is the Lady Aleen, my wife."

Cestus was peering lustily into eyes that glared up into his, but immediately he opened his fingers wide, allowing her arms their freedom. He placed his hands on his hips and looked deprecatingly to the heavens. He was as a hare who had been caught in many a trap but who was wily enough to free himself by the employment of many ruses. Aleen stepped back to watch with interest how he would untangle himself from this latest snare.

Turning to Edmund, he raised his shoulders playfully, held out his arms beseechingly, raised his eyebrows questioningly, and smiled. "A harmless mistake, my brother?"

Always willing to relieve the discomfort of others, Edmund slapped his brother on the arm and laughed. "Aye, a harmless mistake. Is it not, Aleen?" he asked, turning to her.

She continued her critical scrutiny. Eventually she replied tersely, "No, my lord, it was not a harmless mistake, for he shamed me much by his actions."

"You are fortunate, Edmund," Cestus replied, "to have a wife so comely yet possessing such spirit." He bowed exaggeratedly. "I sincerely beg forgiveness, my lady."

No condescending words of pardon were heard, but her look of disdain conveyed silent meaning that both men understood.

"Good day, my lord," she said to Edmund, and with a flip of her head to Cestus, she strode toward the castle doors.

Their laughter reached her ears as she passed the outside kitchens. She turned swiftly, gave them an icy stare that reduced their laughter to awkward smiles, and turned again to leave. How dare they find amusement in my embarrassment, she thought irritably. With a scowl on her face and stinging rage burning within, she stomped up the steps to her room to tend her wounded pride and to fear for Lauxburgh and the safety of its hapless maidens.

## ◅ XXVI ►

ALEEN HAD just entered the great hall when Cestus excused himself from his group and approached her with the cunning smile she had despised the day before.

"My lady," he said mockingly as he greeted her with outstretched arms. Her recoil was slight, but as quickly as a cat leaping upon a sunning lizard, he reached for her hand and pulled it through his bent arm. "It pleases me greatly that you are now willing to dine with us, and I am indeed honored to escort you to your place." The words were stingingly baited. Another kick in the shins was what he needed for such presumptions, she thought. But with the assembly witnessing their actions, she permitted him to guide her. Somehow she managed a smile, though she was seething inwardly.

"As you see, we have waited for you. Here," he said, slipping ahead of her on the bench, "you must sit between Edmund and me."

You have waited for me indeed, she thought, glancing sharply at Cestus, so close upon her elbow. Edmund's huge chair on her left was unoccupied, as was also the place opposite, and searching among the people still standing, she saw Wilfreda and Edmund gesturing on some matter as they walked toward their places.

"Aleen," Cestus whispered, taking advantage of the few remaining moments of privacy left them, "we are related now. Might not we also be friends?"

The words, had they been spoken by anyone else, would have brought an immediate response. But there was a leering lilt to his words, and instead of being placated, she felt goaded, as though he pinched and pricked to see how quickly and brilliantly the blood of her spirit would spurt forth.

I shall not be tormented by this jester, she determined. I shall smile and be pleasant, and perhaps, if he has the head to notice such things, he will find I am not disturbed by his goading. Perhaps then he will let me be.

Because of Wilfreda, who was now sitting down, and because of the ladies and men already at table, Aleen forced a smile. Edmund, settling down to table, was surprised and pleased to see her sitting so serenely beside Cestus, and assumed by the smile of each that an amnesty had been agreed to.

Knowing full well that many a maiden envied her position, Aleen sat proudly between the handsome brothers, pleased with the realization that she was becomingly attired. She was proud of her crimson dress and the red enameled girdle that enhanced it so beautifully. The twists of her hair, entwined by a matching red cording, topped her head as would a diadem. She held herself proudly, as should the Lady of Lauxburgh. He shall not mistake me again for a servant girl, she thought with a glance toward Cestus, who was selecting a portion of raisin-stuffed venison.

The meal went well, with Aleen eating sparingly of spiced eggs, corn, and bread, but as it was drawing to a close she realized dishearteningly that no mention of Cesus' business at Lauxburgh would be discussed, nor how or why he happened to return. There was only boring talk of the approaching winter, the condition and volume of the granaries, the storage of corn, hay—no mention at all of Edmund's speculative return to Tankenham.

I should have remained in my room, Aleen thought unhappily, for I have learned naught of his plans. Clutching the little book of verses she had brought with her, she left the table with the others. The meal had not been as awkward as she had at first suspected, and now, at its conclusion, she was grateful that Edmund's attentions had been attracted elsewhere and she had not been drawn into serious topics. Not the least of her gratifications was that Cestus, dissuaded by the tone of the discussions, had not baited and taunted her, as was his pleasure.

Arranging herself on a bench against the wall, she stroked Edmund's dogs, which had come up, listlessly wagging their tails. With the exception of Edmund and the few children in the castle, Aleen was the only one who seemed interested in them. Satisfied with her attentions, they settled down by her feet and drifted into the sleep of the contentedly well-fed. For a moment Aleen watched the rise and fall of their breathing, then picked up her book and pretended interest in it, but it was the voices of the group nearby that she yearned to hear. The weeks following Lelia's death had forced sieges of loneliness upon her which she had endured as a deserved punishment for her unwitting part in Lelia's death, but then, after a time, her lonliness proved intolerable, and the companionship of others was a basic instinct that required—demanded—fulfillment. Besides, she had observed that since the arrival of Cestus, the whole tenor of the evening hours had been enlivened, and she was curious to see the sport that drew such laughter and gaiety.

She looked tenderly after Edmund, who had been detained at the door by some of his councillors. If only I could attract and win your attentions so easily, she thought wistfully. Resting her head against the wall, she sighed. Edmund, if only you would come sit beside me, how happy I would be.

Aleen's eyes widened in astonishment, and with a start she flipped a page. "You answered not my question, dear lady," Cestus was saying teasingly.

Aleen glared up at him as he stood for a moment before her. Then, stepping carefully over the dogs, he sat down at a position Aleen considered too proximate for the respect due her. Comfortably seated, he continued in persuasive tones, "Answer me, dear Aleen. Will we be friends? You know full well that yesterday I knew not who you were. Had I known, I would have treated you with deference." His words were as perfumed rivulets surging deviously and smoothing pleasantly the trampled sands of her sensibilities. "Come now, Aleen," he whispered, "smile at me and be my friend. I shall not leave your side till you do. Come, now."

So beguiling were his tones, so uncomfortable and unwavering his gaze, so titillating his physical nearness, that in spite of her fierce determination to hate him completely, eternally, a sparkle lit her eyes, the harsh lines of her resolute face softened, and her mouth arched into an affable though begrudging smile. He had a way with women, Aleen conceded, and she was no different from others who had surrendered to his charms. Yet, he was a rascal, and one who would not tolerate being on the dark side of any lady, especially one who was pretty and possessed an appealingly provocative spirit.

" 'Tis very well," he said, touching her hand lightly. " 'Tis well indeed." His hand brushed against the book in her lap, and he picked it up, held back the wooden cover, and flipped through the thick pages with interest. "So, my lady enjoys poetry. This is one of my favorites," and unmindful of the servants who were noisily dismantling the planks and trestles of the tables, he began to read aloud. The natural urge to watch as he recited gave her the excuse she needed to study him closely. He was handsome indeed, more so than Edmund, but so confident was he of himself and his physical appeal that the trait tinged on the pretentious and made Edmund, by contrast, the more desirable. Cestus had reason to be proud of his physical appeal, Aleen allowed. His body was strong, well-muscled, and grandly formed. His chestnut hair had traces of golden strands, and his eyes, even when not employed in flirting or mocking, were fascinating in their speckled brownness, and gentle in their glance when he wished them to be. Perhaps he was not as naughty as she had supposed. Anyone who could appreciate verses must have depth and sensitivities.

His voice fluctuated musically, as though he was accustomed to reading aloud, and Aleen knew he did not lack in practice. "The words are lovely, are they not?" he asked of Aleen, who had dropped her eyes reflectively.

"Very lovely," her words drawled in answer.

Cestus was silent for a moment. "You do indeed appreciate the words," he declared disbelievingly.

"Yes, the words are most lovely."

"You can read, dear sister, but can you also write?"

"Yes."

Cestus sighed deeply and leaned back. "It is refreshing to find a woman who has taken time to learn writing and reading, and more refreshing is it to find one who appreciates verses. Most women listen politely, but care not for the meaning." The words hung in the air, and his eyes opened wide at the unintentional implication.

Aleen bestowed a sly understanding smile on him. So glad

was she for the pleasant company, and so enjoyable was the reading, that she urged him on.

"Read more to me, my lord," and gladly did he oblige.

The brothers were seen everywhere together, with Edmund constantly whispering instructions to Cestus, who repeatedly nodded his head in comprehension. There was the tour of the kitchens, keep, stables, smokehouse, as Edmund explained the required supervision and management of each. A tour of the castle was conducted just as thoroughly and with as many instructions. So intense were these sessions, and so absorbed was Cestus in them, that Aleen was forced to accede that these were no mere tours to reacquaint a returning brother to his home and holdings, but were indeed a preparation for his assumption of responsibility.

Her deductions were confirmed the day she passed through the hall by Edmund's office. Villagers and peasants were sitting on stools and benches or leaning against the walls drowsily awaiting their turn to present their problems to Edmund. As she passed the slightly open door, Edmund's voice reached her. A quick glance inside, and she saw a dusty peasant nervously fingering his hat in an attitude of condemnation. His excuses had been heard, and his sentence was now being considered. A momentary pause, and she knew Edmund had taken Cestus out of the peasant's hearing to consult with him on a proper disposition of the matter.

"No, Cestus, you must not be harsh. The man would not have taken the sheep had not his wife needed its milk for the restoration of her health. A fine would not be proper. Indeed, how could he pay it, when his own infirmity prevents him from toiling? I would recommend that he be gently admonished. Do not shame him, mind you, and order that five of our sheep be given him."

"But, Edmund," Cestus' voice rose in indignation, "you mean to give a thief of our supply?"

"Yes. Remember, you must temper justice with mercy and charity."

"But should we do this to each of the needy, our own supply would be depleted."

"Nay, my brother, for God rewards charity in extraordinary ways. Trust in your creator, keep his holy words in mind, and you shall not go awry. Now, let me see how kindly you tell him."

Aleen continued down the hall in a daze, the words lingering in her mind as in a dream. Edmund was indeed preparing to relinquish his duties, and the thought pained her heart as cruelly as if a savage beast had torn it from her breast. Why did he not leave when I despised him so? Why must he leave now, when I have grown to love him so dearly?

The thought of Edmund's departure tormented her night and day, and she took more to the chapel, seeking strength, and to the great hall, pursuing levity and distraction from her thoughts.

The usual dullness that had prevailed in the great hall after evening meals was dispersed from the day Cestus arrived. His likable personality and his jovial manner illuminated the room as surely as did the wax candles and bracketed torches that burned late into the night. A group was always assembled around him as he told the riddles that had become so popular and which he was so adept at remembering and so skilled at telling. There were evenings when he was pressed to play the lute, and he would begin by composing a tune and fashioning words to accompany it. His clear voice resounded to the enjoyment and admiration of all. Then, when his composition was completed, the lute was passed from one to another, each trying his skill at improvising and singing.

Not an evening passed that Cestus did not stop to speak with Aleen. She was a sad figure sitting alone, although she tried to hide her loneliness by pretending interest in her books or toying distractedly with embroidery. She looked forward to these moments of kindly interest, and ultimately became aware of another dimension of Cestus' personality. He was a rascal, yes, but he also had the capacity to become a lasting friend, and she found herself wanting to confide in him. He was delightful to be with, and she needed a friend so desperately. As for Cestus, he had found her company enjoyable and most interesting, especially when he was successful in luring her into explaining facets of Viking culture or telling of Viking legends.

The time Cestus spent with her did not go unnoticed by Wilfreda, who watched the innocent communions with haughty displeasure, nor was the friendship unnoticed by the other women, whose interest in the two became intense as the innocent conversations became more regular and increasingly lengthy.

Cestus seemed oblivious of their attitudes until the evening Aleen suggested a discontinuance of their meetings. "The ladies stare at us. I think they question our conduct."

"It is they who have evil on their minds," he retorted, and he turned to them with such a look of scornful reproach that they felt themselves duly reprimanded, at least for the moment. In actuality, fuel had been added to the consuming fire of their dislike for the Viking maid, and their jealousy of her intensified with the continued diversion of Cestus' attentions. There were maidens waiting to be wooed and wed, and their conniving mothers despaired of the talents he wasted on the Danish nonentity. True it was that he lingered among the ladies, at times teasing and whetting his masculine vanity with their blushes and flutterings, but nothing definite was formulated—no particular maiden selected for his special attentions, save Aleen.

While the conduct of the two was beyond reproach and their conversations witnessed from a respectable distance, it was caustically surmised that while Aleen had failed to ensnare Edmund in spite of their marriage, she had turned her wiles to a more likely and more willing victim. It was bitterly remembered how rarely Aleen had lingered in the hall before Cestus' return, and her attire was likewise critically assessed. Her appearance, which had become casually simple following Lelia's death, was now more carefully planned. Her hair was tied and twisted in becoming ways, and more often entwined with golden cords and silken ribbons. Even the embroidery in which she evinced absorption was notably improved. Instead of the linen square and gaudy woolen threads she had initially worked, she had advanced to small liturgical garments with golden designs.

Edmund at first appeared pleased with the friendship that had developed between his virginal wife and his brother, but even he, too, took to lingering in the hall after the evening meals. Sitting on his huge chair, he alternately engaged in talking with his councilmen, steward, and officers and looking at the pair through slanting, curious eyes. One would think him pleased with the pair, so often was his smile cast their way, but only the perceptive could see in his alert attitude the unmistakable glint of jealousy.

Cestus lazily leaned back and crossed one leg atop the other. Picking up the embroidery from Aleen's hands, he looked casually at it and traced with his fingers the clusters of grapes and shafts of wheat enriched with threads of gold.

"Please, Cestus," Aleen was pleading. "Please go speak with them. They are waiting for you. Truly, you must not spend your time here beside me. You are young and unmarried. Please go to them."

Cestus handed back the cloth and looked placidly into her eyes. "And does marriage make of you an older woman? *I* am older than *you*, dear lady, yet you speak as though you were the elder."

"You know full well what I mean. You should amuse yourself with the unmarried ladies, as is natural for a young unmarried man."

"Amuse myself? You jest with me." Cestus shifted his position uneasily. "They bore me." He brushed lint from his sleeve and then surveyed the gathering. "Let us see . . ." He began counting on his fingers. "There is Eadburh, whose face resembles my steed." Aleen gasped at the brutality of his words. "In all honesty, it is thus she appears to me," he said in defense. "Leoba hangs her head when I speak, and does naught but smile foolishly. Her head is empty." He rubbed his nose and sneered. "Eanswith's face is weak, too plain for my liking. Aelthelswith," he said, indicating the count on his fingers, "Aelthelswith speaks incessantly of her travels, her ancestral lineage. Ah"—and he shook his head despairingly—"they bore me. Their heads are empty and their spirits are dead. You wish to condemn me to such company?" He looked closely at Aleen's downcast eyes.

She was flattered that he found her presence to his liking. It was a tribute she cherished and warmly appreciated.

A frown wrinkled Cestus' brow. "I think you wish to be rid of me."

"No, Cestus, truly that is not my desire."

"Then what might it be?" He uncrossed his legs and sat erect and alert for her explanation.

"It is only . . ."

"Yes."

"It is only that I feel compelled to tell you things of which I should not speak. I have never shared these thoughts with another, and if you were elsewhere, I should be prevented from disclosing them now."

His attitude changed. "But you should feel free to tell me all."

"I fear you will speak of my confidence to another."

"Aleen," he snapped in exasperation, "I have spent these many evenings with you, and yet you know me not?"

Her knowledge of him had indeed grown in the days since their acquaintance had turned favorably from a contest of wits to a pleasantly fulfilling friendship. She could trust him, but how else could she prepare him for the disclosure of her soul's secrets and her heart's fears? "I should speak of your brother," she said at last. "I am weighted by a burden I can no longer support by myself."

"Then speak of it. I make solemn oath that Edmund shall never hear of it from my lips. I swear."

She hesitated, then struggled for the proper words. "Tell me first, Cestus, when does Edmund leave?"

"I know not, but I think soon. I should think he even tarries needlessly."

"And his destination? It is rumored he will return to Tankenham."

"That I know not. He has prepared me for his duties, but he tells me naught of his plans. In truth, I know not where he goes, but I think his journey will be a brief one. Why should he leave you? A husband does not leave so lovely a wife to join religious life." He smiled incredulously and flipped a hand, as if to brush aside an issue that was too ridiculous for consideration.

"There is naught to keep him here. We are not truly man and wife," and her words tumbled forth as she told him everything concerning her life at Lauxburgh.

Cestus had heard rumors in the monasteries and castles he had visited, relating to Edmund and Aleen's unusually strange association, but he had dismissed them as being imaginative. What man, except a priest or a monk, was foolish enough to make a vow, and what man, after making such a foolish vow, was yet stupid enough to observe it? But then Aleen was declaring the rumors to be factual.

"In truth, he has not touched you?"

Aleen's silence was confirmation enough.

Cestus' eyes vacantly scanned the distant wall and the empty galleries, reflecting as he did so on what had been told him. Then, placing his hand hard on his leg, he sighed as he shook his head. "My brother possesses control that borders on the heroic."

"I love him, Cestus. I love him dearly, and I shall die if he leaves me. And, Cestus, you swore you would never reveal this confidence. Swear again."

"Aleen, you trust me not. By God above, I swear I shall never speak of this."

So engrossed were they in their intimate exchange that they were unaware that the torches were being lit and that Edmund was nearby observing a chess game. But Edmund's interest in the studied moves were not wholly fixed on the game, but were also upon the couple so completely absorbed in each other. Each was acutely interested in the remarks of the other, and when Cestus placed his hand upon the small clenched hands Aleen held so demurely in her lap, Edmund ran his hand hard against his thick leather belt. His eyes tensed, his steps toward the door were long and deliberate, and he grumbled between clenched teeth, "In truth, my brother goes too far."

The monks continued the chanting of vespers as the abbot walked noiselessly from the chapel to answer the pounding at the door. He gratefully acknowledged receipt of a missive, closed the door against early-autumn winds, opened the parchment, and read its contents. Reflectively he walked through the hall, lightly tapping the parchment to his chin. Edmund was soon to visit—the first since the unhappy day he was summoned from his cell to learn of his father's death and his enforced relinquishment of monastic life. The cell had been reserved for his use since that day, as the abbot had promised. Edmund's robes still hung there; his books still lay on the desk. His visit was welcomed and long overdue. But what had Edmund written? He might find it necessary to take advantage of my friendship with the new pontiff? He begs me to prepare for a journey to Rome? He further bids me to keep silence concerning this. The abbot frowned, tucked the parchment into his cincture, and automatically responded to the Latin antiphon as he rejoined his brethren.

At Lauxburgh, Edmund sat in his chamber, moodily looking past the burning candle to the darkness beyond. He was certain the abbot had received his message, and he was beginning to feel nostalgic about his imminent visit to the monastery of his youth. Reaching toward a drawer of his desk, Edmund opened it, fumbled for a moment, and withdrew a brooch—Aleen's brooch that she had given him for the treasury when Judith had questioned its origins. He could not bring himself to dispose of it. He rubbed his fingers around the gold-embossed circles and the interlocking geometric squares and angles. With a jerk he clutched it in his hand and then slipped it into his traveling pouch.

His plan had been carefully made. When the young Reverend Hewald had returned with a negative decision from the council of the dying pope, Edmund had formulated strategy and waited for either the pope's recovery or his death. The pope had since died and most fortunately was replaced by a former schoolmate of the abbot of Tankenham. Edmund had often heard the abbot extol his saintly friend who had risen in the ranks until he was an aide and then confessor of the late pope. How could the new pontiff refuse the plea of Edmund kneeling at his feet begging for a dispensation while his abbot friend pleaded on behalf of his spiritual son? A favorable decision was assured—there was only the journey to Rome to contend with.

The abbot Dunstan was advancing in age, but was not too old to endure such a journey. It would take time, however. There would be wintry storms at sea to wait out. Frigid, wet weather throughout most of France would suspend their trek at times, and the Alps would likely be impassable with winter snows by the time of their arrival there. Another sea voyage would be necessary to circumvent the Alps, and depending upon the weather, they would either travel the length of Italy, relying upon the hospitality of the monasteries along the way, or continue by ship to Rome, braving on their voyage the storms they would inevitably encounter. It would be an uncomfortable and difficult journey, but there was no doubting but that the abbot would unhesitatingly undertake it for Edmund's sake.

King Alfred was not likely to object to Edmund's absence, since Cestus was now of age, and his overseeing would be a temporary situation. Alfred would know that by Edmund's failure to secure approval for the transference of responsibility that Edmund's absence was not of a permanent nature. There would be no problem with Alfred. As it was, the Vikings were no longer a serious threat—their more enthusiastic endeavors being thankfully exercised elsewhere—yet it would be best to keep his departure from the country a secret, lest perhaps the outlaw bands take advantage of his absence to seek sport, though this was unlikely.

The plans were indeed secret, for Edmund confided them to no one. How could he face Aleen and the people, should they learn the purpose of his journey? What would they say if his petition was again denied? How shall I face them, should I receive my release, only to find the friendship of Cestus and Aleen developing into more deeper meaning? I shall be as a fool. They will know only that I am visiting Tankenham. I must choose my words well when telling of my departure.

Yellow, brown, and crimson leaves were falling from the trees and tumbling about in autumnal drifts. The days were more often overcast and gray now, and the salty air from the sea bore unwelcome chills. Woolen coverlets were being unpacked, bearskins were being placed on cold stone floors, workmen were busily barring windows with wooden blinds and tapestries, and heavy mantles and fur capes were being brushed and aired for use. Lauxburgh was bracing for the bitter assaults of winter.

All knew that the day was fast approaching when Edmund would bid farewell. Aleen lived in constant dread of that day, and each dawning brought added uneasiness. The air was thick with foreboding, especially so this day.

Servants were busy in her room with the preparations of autumn. Wood was being stacked by the fireplace, and tapestries were being hung before the windows. The activity, mixed with her inner uneasiness, unnerved her. Reaching for a mantle, she threw it over her shoulders and hurried to the chapel. It was the only place wherein she could find peace and a measure of contentment. Thankfully, it was empty. The cloudiness outside had not only darkened the interior, but confined within the stone walls the dankness, the odors of burning wax, and the faint scent of incense. A stool had been placed before the statue of the Blessed Virgin, and Aleen silently thanked the worshiper who had placed it there. Perhaps it was the change in the weather that made her so jittery. She sat down and huddled in the scant warmth of her mantle. She could almost feel the statue's stony gaze, and she stared up into the rigid face of the Virgin, who had also known earthly heartbreak and trials. Aleen had found transitory peace before this statue after Lelia's death, and it was here she prayed when the frustrations of life seemed unbearable.

Gradually she relaxed. The prayers she conveyed to the heavenly mother added to her peacefulness, but a sudden noise at the back door brought back all her former furor. Someone entered, and the heavy steps grew louder. When they stopped, she needed no glance, no word, to tell her of Edmund's overwhelming presence.

Presently he was kneeling beside her, and in respect for the sacred species in the tabernacle, he whispered softly, "I am here to bid you farewell, Aleen. Cestus told me some days ago that you suspected I would be leaving. I go to Tankenham for a time. It will be only a visit, but I know not the exact day of my return. Will you pray for me, Aleen?"

He waited in vain for a reply. There was only a drooping of her head. For several moments he affectionately gazed at the brown of her long shiny hair, the slender shoulders, the delicate ear. Then, placing his hand atop hers in the manner of his brother, he whispered again, "It is only a visit, Aleen. I shall be coming back. I charge you to take the greatest care of your health and to pray fervently for my intentions."

Aleen looked at the burly, hairy hand that covered her own. How tenderly warm it felt. He loves me, I know he loves me, she moaned inwardly. But the hand that touched her so gently had at the same time stirred her thoughts into a tempest, and the conditions of the marriage contract flung themselves at her, until her head became dizzy from the assault. He had secured peace for his land by the marriage, and now that Cestus was able to assume responsibilities, there was nothing to keep him from his heart's desire. She had been pitted against his long-standing dream and had lost miserably.

"Pray for me, Aleen," he said in farewell, and after pressing her hands, he rose, walked toward the altar, dropped to one knee, bowed his head, and prayed. From the corner of her eye Aleen could see him, but she could not look directly. The drumming of her heart deafened her, and unreality once again closed in upon her. She was being condemned to a satanic pit of despair. There would be only the heartache of loneliness, the memory of their brief intimacies, the torment of what might have been. There would follow a lifetime of long, dreary, empty, unhappy days. Tears streamed down her face. "Mary, Mary . . ." she prayed as she looked upon the chiseled face. His footsteps echoed through the chapel, and she sat as though she herself were made of stone. She could hear his steps as they went down the hall, until the sound of many voices snatched them away. Edmund was leaving. The life-giving sun was being withdrawn, she thought desperately. I shall be condemned to darkness. I cannot let him go. I must stop him. I must tell him how dearly I love him. He cannot leave knowing this. I shall die if he leaves.

Her hurried footsteps slapped through the stillness, and her mantle billowed as she raced the length of the chapel, through the empty corridors to the door that opened onto the courtyard. But suddenly she was being restrained. A hand went brutally over her mouth, and she fought against the arms that held her fast.

"Control yourself," Cestus was ordering. "He is leaving now. You cannot make of yourself a fool by running wildly after him." He shook her rudely, until she gasped for air. Then, weakened by frustration, she fell against him and permitted the support of his encircling arms. Gently he led her away from the door. "I would have told him," he whispered. "I meant to many a time, but I swore to you. I gave my word I would not tell him of your love. It cost me much, but I kept my word, as I swore. I see now I erred. He should have been told."

Aleen shook her head weakly. "No, no. It is best he was

not told, for now I know for certain he does not love me. He never loved me."

"You are wrong, Aleen," Cestus whispered into her ear. "It is not that he never loved you, for truly he holds you dear, but methinks he loves religion more."

AN EARLY winter was heralded by a tempest that hurled its fury at Kent. The inveterate believers of ancient myths and legends attributed the turbulence to a disgruntled dragon who abided beyond the horizon in nebulous regions. With a vengeance he had dug his terrible claws into moisture-laden clouds and with fearful strength shook loose the pelting rains. The violent flappings of his batlike wings created the thunder and propelled the furious winds that battered trees into shuddering bows of submission. His grumbling snorts caused lightning to snap and crackle from his repulsive mouth, and his scaly tail stirred the sea, creating agitated currents that sent tumbling waves crashing in maddening sprays against rocky cliffs and boulder-strewn beaches. The ferocity of hell had visited Kent and Lauxburgh, and many a soul grown lax of devotion was stimulated to retaliatory prayer.

It was believed by superstitious folk that it was Edmund's absence from Lauxburgh that so aroused the spirits, and it was recalled with dread that such a storm had brought about Lelia's premature birth and her mother's untimely death. Such ill winds could portend only adversity, and many who had given apathetic consent to Edmund's leavetaking now regretted that they had not strenuously opposed his departure as many others had done. Yet Tankenham lay within the border of Kent, and this alone placated them. The distance was small enough if serious consultations were necessary or a return was mandatory, but to Aleen the distance could have been the length to eternity.

The winds whistled about the windows of Lauxburgh, causing noisy disturbances and weird soundings at night. The rooms were sanctuaries for penetrating dampness, and the only relief to be found against the chill was before the open fire. Aleen pulled at the coverlet she had thrown upon her makeshift bed before her fireplace, rolled on her side, and stared into the flames that furnished such splendid warmth. But her comfort was not total, for the furry skins she was lying on did little to relieve the hardness of the floor.

Aleen had her own theories about the howling storm. In her melancholy subjectivity, she envisioned it destroying her world as surely as other causes had destroyed those she loved. Father, mother, cousin, beloved child, servant—all were in frigid graves. There was still Alcuin, but of what use was a brother when he was never present to comfort or counsel? He might be as dead as the rest of those she loved, for he had not been heard from in months, and his perilous journey to the uncharted new lands to the west was fraught with hardships and dangers that made her tremble in concern for his well-being. And Edmund. The slithering serpent of fate, bent on further cruelties to her life, had attacked and claimed him victim as well. His absence was as conclusive as death, and as morbidly sad. True, he had said his journey to Tankenham was but a visit, but a visit would not necessitate entrusting his duties to Cestus. Wilfreda and Godfrey could have assumed his responsibilities, as they often did during his inspections of manors and shires. Perhaps he would return to Lauxburgh to assure himself that all was going well without him, but he would return to Tankenham; he was born for the life. Aleen cursed fate and the circumstances that had prevented them from sharing their love. Life was harsh, and in her self-pity she wished the storm would complete its mission and destroy the last remnants of her life as well.

Contrary to opinion, the storm abated. The sun once again gained dominance over the land and warmed the sharp edges of the breezes that continually slid across the sea to the land. The fields were denuded of moisture, and commerce and travel were resumed. Cold, dampness, and lively drafts lingered throughout Lauxburgh, but at Tankenham they were not as easily avoided before hearths as was possible in the castle, for the monastic accommodations for warmth were few. Penance was a necessary part of the monk's life, and coldness was to be endured as satisfaction for sins and utilized to steel the soul to the avoidance of temptation. Additional clothing was, however, thankfully provided, and Edmund, who had donned monastic robes at the abbot's recommendation to prevent the conspicuousness of his presence, drew some warmth from a woolen mantle and the cowl that covered his head.

His return to Tankenham was a sentimental one, and during the first period of recreation after his arrival the monks had all enthusiastically welcomed him. The cell he had left a few years before was still vacant, and it was there that he was immediately quartered. Once again he participated in the chanting of the Divine Office; once again he arose in the darkness for holy mass; once again he ate simple fare in the company of his silent companions. It was the life he had once regretted leaving and the life he had yearned to rejoin, but now that he *had* returned, he knew his fervor and dedication could never be completely reclaimed. With a gnawing certainty he knew Tankenham was no longer meant to be his. Since his absence from it, he had met someone who had changed his life—a young woman who often appeared in wafting visions before him, dancing happily, as she had done to the music of the flutes, a beautiful girl who smiled coyly as she trailed her silky veil about him, as she had once done to Lelia. He had remembered the monastic instructions of earlier days: how to struggle to vanquish distractions; how to avoid dwelling on transitory matters and instead to set one's mind and heart upon eternal truths. Yet each time he traversed the halls, head inclined, arms crossed before him, his hands tucked inside the sleeves in proper monastic decorum, he somehow expected to see Aleen around every turn and was disappointed that he did not. Each time he entered the chapel, he glanced about expecting to see Aleen, who surely would be there kneeling as he had so often found her in the chapel at Lauxburgh, especially during the days following Lelia's death, when her visits there became more numerous. Each evening during recreation, while the monks indulged in their only session for joviality and relaxation, he expected to find her sitting on a bench against the wall, learning to play the lute or sewing while Cestus read to her. Cestus. How dearly Edmund loved his brother, yet how restless he became at the thought of him.

The day following his return to Tankenham, he had disclosed his secret longings to the abbot, who was not shocked at the disclosure, as Edmund had expected him to be. The abbot had listened with interest to the man who he had thought possessed exemplary qualities for the contemplative life, as he learned of Edmund's love for his young wife. Careful reflection was given the matter, and a time of prayer was recommended to test if this development was but a wily trick of the devil to prevent Edmund's total commitment to the religious life that was now possible for him. Many consultations were held, many questions asked, many prayers offered for enlightenment, but the tempest of his inner turmoil continued to rage. The time had now arrived for a resolution of the matter. When at dusk the abbot joined Edmund in the gloom of his cell, he found Edmund standing prayerfully before a hanging cross behind which curved a brittle palm branch.

"I have disciplined my flesh," he began in answer to the priest's question. "I have mortified my senses, I have spent long hours in prayer ..." He hesitated as he grasped for words, but the abbot, with years of experience in discerning the minds and hearts of his spiritual sons, did not require words to know the disposition of Edmund's heart.

"Edmund, I too have prayed hard for enlightenment in this matter. I have besieged heaven for guidance in directing you," and raising a hand to Edmund's broad shoulder, he squeezed so hard that Edmund looked quizzically at the lined face so handsomely enhanced by a halo of gray-streaked hair. A smile crept over the abbot's face. "Prepare yourself, Edmund," he said. "Tomorrow we embark for Rome."

Two letters were forwarded to Lauxburgh from Tankenham, and both bore Cestus' name. No message or greeting, no word at all for Aleen except what Cestus conveyed to her. The arrival of the first letter had been discussed in detail, and a deeper sadness settled over Aleen when she was told that Edmund had donned his old religious robes and occupied his former cell. He seemed contented except for his concern for Aleen. "I charge you, Cestus, to shield her from all unpleasantness and to provide her with all that will comfort her." "He does care for you, Aleen," Cestus offered. "He would not be so taken with your well-being and contentment if he were not. Find satisfaction in these words." If Edmund truly loved me, she thought bitterly, he would see to my happiness himself.

The second letter arrived a week later, on the feast day of Saint Guthlac, a day when work was suspended, special services were held in chapel, board games of all sorts were played, cockfights were held, bears were baited, and much to the distress of the womenfolk, lots were cast and wine casks emptied.

The missive arrived in late afternoon. Cestus was busy with the celebrations of the day and was difficult to locate, but when at last Aleen found him, her insistent questions forced him to reveal the contents of the latest communication. "If the letter contains unwelcome news, I must learn of it. I must know what of he writes."

"The letter is in my chamber. You may read it when you wish," he said crisply, hoping to dispell her intenseness by a flippant reference to the missive. "It was similar to the first," he continued casually. "He again expressed concern for you. He asks that I be most deligent in providing comfort for you, and desires that all your wishes be fulfilled as best as we are able. That is all." Cestus had said all that he cared to, and smilingly indicated his desire to return to the games.

"Continue," she demanded as he started to move away. Restraining him with a light hand on his arm, she continued, "There is more. I can see there is more you wish not to share with me. Tell me," she ordered, raising her voice so that the men playing a chess game nearby looked up.

Taking her by the arm, he led her away and continued. "Yes, there is more," he said, crossing his arms and sighing resignedly. "Since you insist on knowing—he instructed me not to write until once more I hear from him. He expressed the opinion it would be some time before the next letter arrives. He orders that I administer as best I can during that time, and that I deter anyone who might wish to journey there to visit with him. There. That is all the missive contained."

Aleen would not have been so disturbed had not the message contained a hidden meaning. Her intuition was stimulated, and she again demanded, "Well, then, explain this to me." Her features were strained and hard. "Must I journey to

Tankenham to learn of this myself? I will do this in spite of the restriction."

"It means, dear lady, that he is going into retreat. I have seen this before."

Aleen's frown indicated her ignorance of such conduct, and he hastened to explain. "The monks who feel themselves called to a more serious commitment to the religious life take up residence in a hut on the monastery grounds. They dwell there for long periods in prayer and solitude. When they feel themselves ready, they either make extraordinary vows, venture out to preach in remote areas, or move from the monastery to become hermits."

Aleen's mouth parted as she envisioned the hermit she had first seen the day of the hunt, when they came upon him gathering berries for his frugal meal, the same hermit who had prayed beside Lelia's deathbed. "You are wrong, Cestus. It cannot be so."

"Then why would visitors be restricted?"

Her slender hand stroked the smoothness of her throat. "It cannot be," she said disbelievingly. "He will come back. You will see. He will come back. Nay . . . he *must* come back."

"I have seen many monks do this thing, yet I have never seen one leave the life after retreat."

"But he is not yet a monk with vows. . . ."

"Then perhaps he means to become one." His voice was somber, as though he had been forced to face the harshness of reality. Cestus had been willing enough to temporarily replace his brother, but now the permanence of his position was a matter he could not reconcile, and it was evident that could he have chosen a permanent domicile, Lauxburgh would not have been his selection. "There is no life here," he had often told Aleen. "The women have narrow minds, the maidens are plain and uninteresting." All his criticisms recalled themselves to Aleen's mind as she left him and walked toward the courtyard. She felt pity for the fun-loving, dashing, arrogant young man whose life was now wholly readjusted.

Sitting upon a bench beneath a barren elm, she watched a young soldier who, oblivious of her presence, whispered into the delicate ear of a giggling maiden. Life was carefree for some, but for her there was the impact of Edmund's letter.

Dusk was settling over the land, and as Aleen looked after the departing couple, wetness glistened in her eyes. The chilling pall of evening was gently falling over all. The day, like her youth, was dying, vanishing. The courtyard was deserted. She was alone, as alone as she would be for the rest of her life. She stood in the chilling gloom, faced the wind, and wept as would one who had been condemned to a loveless world.

Wilfreda was supremely happy with Edmund's vocation. It provided a measure of prestige to have a son who forsook all things for God's sake, and it reflected admirably on her religious influence. She had successfully snatched him from Aleen's wily schemes, and he was now even more completely hers, for mothers were always welcome to visit at Tankenham, more so than wives who had been rejected in favor of religion. Her joy was short-lived, however, as her selfish maternal instincts were alerted to yet another danger to one of her sons.

It had been whispered to her how intimate Cestus' conversations with Aleen had become, how it appeared Cestus waited for Aleen to pass his chamber to join her in the long walk to the chapel or hall, how solicitous he was of her needs at table, how accommodating in pleasuring her with his readings, how closely he sat beside her when teaching her the lute, when she should know full well how to play by now. Wilfreda need not have been told, and she was annoyed each time Aleen's seeming ploys were mentioned to her. Her talebearers were only adding emphasis to what was observed by all, and were goading her to act in resolving the problem.

Because of the Viking maiden, whose presence was becoming increasingly resented and more unwelcome, new problems increased Wilfreda's distrust. Whether or not to speak to Cestus about Aleen's unsuccessful enticements of Edmund taunted Wilfreda's judicious reasoning. There was the danger of giving undesired emphasis to the situation by speaking of it to her younger son, yet, if the situation went unchecked, who could tell what trap he would fall captive to? If only there were some way of ridding Lauxburgh of Aleen. Wilfreda bitterly resented, all the more, that the peace of the district rested entirely on the Viking princess's residence there. The

Viking raids had been discontinued since her arrival, just as they had during Marion's stay, and except for scattered rumors of stock stealing and the pilfering of remote farms, and the Norsemen's hunting in Kentish forests, there was peace and no slaughter, as in former days.

If it were not that peace were incumbent on Aleen's presence in the land, Wilfreda would exert her authority and send her promptly back to Wermouth. As it was, Wilfreda not only resented Aleen but also begrudged her occupancy of a major chamber in the family sector. If it were possible, she would have Aleen moved to the servants' quarters—to an insignificant room in the less prestigious part of the castle—but then Cestus would object, and it would not do to have him on Aleen's side and against his mother in any matter. She was thus singularly limited to showing her contempt for Aleen, and this she continued vigorously and with regularity.

Wilfreda and the women were not the only persons disturbed by Cestus' misdirected attentions. Aleen had also sensed, with growing discomfort, the tender gleam in his gaze, how his words softened when she drew near, how his whole attitude changed when she was beside him. She had seen such behavior before in the young men at Wermouth when she toyed and teased their adolescent love, but this was far different. Cestus was a man rapidly falling in love with a brother's virginal wife. There was no sport to be made of this. Aleen felt pity for him, for it was as though Cestus, overwhelmed with the monotony and permanence of his position and the absence of enticing maidens to flatter him, was grasping for her as he would were he a drowning man thrashing about for the only timber on a restless sea.

She could avoid him by remaining in her chamber, but memories abounded there. The chapel alone afforded her peace and escape. In the chapel's silence, life was stilled for more careful scrutiny, and earthly cares diminished in importance, thus permitting a comforting peace to invade her soul. With the physical presence of Christ and with the support of his teachings, Lelia seemed not so far away, nor lost to her forever. Even Edmund seemed closer as she shared the company of the Creator, for whom he forsook the world and all creatures.

During her frequent visits there her thoughts became less

complicated, and with the newfound calmness of spirit, a plan gradually formed—a plan that would offer not only an escape from Lauxburgh and the heart-rending memories there but also a resolution of the awkward situation that was developing with Cestus' increasing interest in her. There was only one place on earth where peace of mind could be hers. Only one place on earth where she would be kindly received and respected. All reasonings and arguments radiated toward one central theme, until her course was determined and her only concern was how and when to tell Cestus of her decision to seek lodging in a convent.

This was the only solution to her problems. Many convents throughout the country secured needed funds by serving as hostels for women of nobility and means. Perhaps one could be persuaded to accept a Viking as a resident. One thing Aleen knew unquestioningly: she must leave Lauxburgh. Now that Edmund was gone, she could sense that her presence was even less tolerated than before. She seemed an intruder trespassing on forbidden territory. Besides, she must leave Lauxburgh before Cestus' affections went beyond acceptable bounds. There was nowhere else to go. Her father's kingdom had been seized by a neighboring rival unknown to her, and a return there might well result in her capture and death. And having left Gruntvig as a child, her relatives there were unfamiliar and could not be expected to welcome a young girl of whom they knew little.

At Chatham, if they accepted her as a boarder, and if she could somehow arrange to pay for her lodging, she could start afresh. Edmund's mind would be eased by knowing her spiritual and bodily cares were being kindly tended. It was this reason which sealed her resolution. It would be an affront to Edmund and Lauxburgh were she to leave for any other purpose or destination, but to quit her present home for a closer contact to religious life would be highly regarded and accepted. That lodging in religious houses had never appealed to her was of little consequence. She could learn to endure whatever hardships she encountered. If Edmund's mind would be at ease concerning her, and if thereby he would feel free to follow the course he decided upon after retreat, any difficulty could be endured in the name of love.

With her plan firmly established in her heart, her soul was

uplifted and her mind put at rest. It would solve all problems, and she lost no time in dispatching a messenger to Chatham with a missive begging the abbess to accept her as a lodger. With a swiftness that amazed her, the courier returned, knocked on her chamber door, and handed her a rolled parchment, which she took with trembling hand.

Seating herself in the warm arc before the fire, she clutched the missive, afraid to read its contents. What if the abbess, like her sister, Wilfreda, wanted no part of her? What if the nun dreaded the prospect of having a Viking maiden in the community as a constant reminder of what the Vikings had done to them many months before? She would understand completely if the nuns refused her request. When at last she hesitantly unrolled the parchment, there was but one word printed in a delicate hand: "Come."

She felt curiously saddened, yet there was the assurance of escape. She was as free as the haddock and mackerel that, finding a tear in a restraining net, wiggle into the freedom of vast waters. Here was a safe retreat into a life in which charity was dutifully practiced. The nuns were gentle people—so she had heard it whispered after their sad stay at Lauxburgh—and she remembered it was told that there were young nuns in the group, and that the abbess was a kind woman and very much unlike her domineering sister, Wilfreda. It would work out well, but how was she to tell Cestus? She dreaded to face him with this, but the sooner she confronted him, the less anxiety she would experience.

Throwing a mantle over her shoulders, she entered the hallway and paused beside Lelia's door, which now guarded an empty chamber shrouded in melancholy gloom. No more will I feel saddened by my passage here, she thought. And as she approached Edmund's door: And no more will I feel abandoned. She walked quickly through the chilled halls to Edmund's office. Cestus had been visiting in the village, but Wulfric had just been informed of his return and invited her to wait. He took a poker, reactivated the fire, and placed new kindling on it. Returning to the adjoining scribe's room, he took up a quill and began scratching noisily against paper.

Turning her back to the warmth of the fireplace, Aleen examined the room. It was as though Edmund were still about, and she smiled at the memory of her second visit to the room, how she waited her turn for the audience beside the peasants in the hall, how she boldly walked before Edmund and announced her intention of taking Lelia from the milk nurse. Edmund had been amused by her boldness. There had been hard times at Lauxburgh, but there were some pleasant memories as well. She reached for a large bow hanging on the wall and aimlessly ran her fingers against the string. It was made for battle and was far too strong and heavy for sport. As she caressed the smoothness of the wood, her mind raced back to the day of the fair, when, to the surprise of all, she had displayed her skill with a smaller bow and won the contest with ease. How regally she had worn the sweet olive crown, and how proud Edmund seemed to have been with her accomplishment.

There was the approaching shuffling and scraping of feet, and Aleen quickly replaced the bow and turned to face Cestus, who was removing his gloves as he entered. He looked upon Aleen, and the weary look on his face brightened into a pleasurable smile.

"I regret that I have kept you waiting, my dear lady, but I am pleased you remained." He was busy unbuckling his mantle, but Aleen felt his studied assessment of her appearance and she was grateful that Edith had arranged and approved her clothing.

Cestus closed the door to the hallway, crossed the room to close the door to the scribe's office and, returning to their seclusion, cast his cloak upon a table and sank into a chair in exaggerated weariness. "Come, sit beside me, Aleen. You are as sunshine beaming warmth upon this cold body of mine."

Aleen approached and stood before him. "If you mind not, I shall remain standing, for I have a matter of importance to discuss with you."

Cestus smiled, and his eyes sparkled wickedly.

His attitude was all wrong, Aleen thought in desperation. He expects me to speak of a trivial matter to which I have added undue importance. And she cringed from the task before her.

"Come, Aleen," he was saying pleasantly, "tell me what it is you wish."

"I have come to tell you that I am to leave Lauxburgh. I have made arrangements."

He was silent for a moment, then said with a smile, "And where, dear lady, are you to visit?"

Aleen looked down upon the folded parchment in her hand. "I shall go to Chatham."

Again a silence followed her words. Then, to her surprise, pleasant words sounded. "A very good choice, Aleen. There is nothing like a visit to a convent to refresh the spirit. A visit there will do you much good. You have never left here, have you?" He rose from the chair and made his way to the desk.

"You understand not, Cestus. I mean not to visit there, but to live there."

Cestus spun around. "You know not what you are saying. Your mind has been bewitched. You would do well to permit the physician to minister to you."

"I have thought well on this, Cestus. I have set my mind firmly on this course, and I have received permission to abide there."

With an abrupt movement he reached for the paper she had been fingering and unrolled it. "Is this all my dear aunt wrote to you? 'Come'? She should have written, 'Hasten. Come with all speed,'" and he carelessly tossed the paper onto the desk.

"Why, my lord?"

"Why?" he shouted. "Because the prestige of Chatham will be enhanced by the presence of the Lady of Lauxburgh. Their numbers will be increased, because many young girls will be inspired to advance one step further and not remain just as boarders, but as candidates for entrance into the order. My dear aunt sees many advantages in accepting you."

"Please, Cestus. Do not make it difficult for me to leave."

"Not make it difficult?" he mimicked. "I shall make it impossible. You shall not leave here. I forbid it. You shall not run off in imitation of Edmund. You shall not hide yourself at Chatham to brood over him."

Before she knew it, he was standing before her with both hands grasping her shoulders. "Listen to me, Aleen. I was waiting only to hear of Edmund's final plans before asking you to seek an annulment of your marriage. If Edmund wants you not, I do. You shall marry me, and I promise I will not avoid your bed as Edmund so foolishly did. You will have no need to mourn for Lelia. I will give you children of your own. Many children to keep you busy and happy. I shall make you forget Edmund. I shall purge your mind of him."

Suddenly his arms slipped around her, and with a fierceness that frightened her, he was arching her back as he bent over her. Weakly she struggled against the hold. This was not tender love, but voracious lust, and she struggled more in resistance to his hold. There were no tender sensations, no feeling of warmth and excitement as when Edmund had held her that stormy evening in the tower, only coldness and revulsion. Dissuaded by her struggles, he released her, and she fell against the desk and looked at him with frightened eyes.

He had not meant to act so cruelly, and he sensed her disappointment in him. An apology was called for, but not uttered. Instead, he turned from her and looked upon the parchment.

With her fury and resentment subsiding, she looked at the handsome figure, the thick golden waves of hair, the broad shoulders, the well-formed body that moved with such elegant manliness. Marriage to him would be exciting and fulfilling, but inevitably, after the birth of one or two babes, when her figure thickened and her attentions were more directed to her children, his devotion would lessen and his interest would wander, until he would be whispering flatteries into another's ears. Cestus meant well, but it was not in his nature to be entrapped by one woman alone. With Edmund, if circumstances had been different, there would have been a lifetime of devotion and love. How dearly Edmund would have loved their children, how tender he would have been to her. With Edmund there would have been security in love—if only God had not interfered. If I cannot have Edmund, I will have no other, she thought.

When at last Cestus spoke, his words were weighted with sullenness. "You have no calling for the life, Aleen."

"What say you, Cestus?"

"You have no calling. God would have made you ugly and formless if he had meant you to hide yourself behind veils and unflattering robes."

"My lord," Aleen replied incredulously, "I am not going

to become a nun, but to board there, as many ladies do on occasion."

"I shall hear no more. You will remember what I have spoken here, and you will not leave. If necessary, I shall place guards by your door."

"That you would not do." Aleen smiled.

"And why not?"

"Because then everyone will laugh at how foolishly you behave."

"They will have more cause to be amused, for surely, if you leave here, I will journey to Chatham and seize you bodily. I shall not lose you, Aleen, not to any man, nor to God himself."

It was still dark when Aleen arose and dressed. After placing three letters on her desk, one for Edith, one for Bertha, and one for Cestus, she reached for the bag she had packed and made her way quietly through the frigid hall, passing alternately into the circles of light cast from bracketed torches. Soft snoring sounds penetrated the doors she passed so cautiously, and as she traveled darkened stairways and halls to the outside, she regretted not having told Edith and Bertha of her plans, but then, this was better than prolonged farewells or their useless arguments against her decision. And Wilfreda! Perhaps she should have been informed, but then, Aleen thought bitterly, she tells me naught of her plans. How shocked and pleased she will be in getting free of me.

With ease she made her way into the courtyard, crept past the kitchens, smokehouse, and well, and slipped between the doors of the stable. Before long Cenook was saddled, and with pieces of sack securely wrapped about each hoof to muffle his steps, she walked him to the outer gate and carefully opened it. Reaching her foot high onto the stirrup, she mounted, and, straining her eyes into the darkness, guided him to the grass beside the road. It would not do to have crunching gravel awaken the slumbering guards, who had long ago grown lax of duty.

When a safe distance was reached, she reined in, dismounted, and freed Cenook's hooves from their coverings. She was compelled to turn for one final look at Lauxburgh, still slumbering in a starry darkness. Of a sudden, the sadness of reality broke upon her. She was leaving behind what little she had of Edmund. She would have no mementos to remind her of him; she would not be there if he ever returned for the promised visit; she would never look upon his face again. Perhaps Cestus was correct. Perhaps this is all a mistake. But when cold breezes began to stir, she mounted, flipped the reins, and guided Cenook to the fork in the road. For a moment Aleen looked upon the cathedral in the distance and the graves that consecrated its soil; then, with burdened heart, she chose the southeasterly route that led directly to Chatham.

# ⌒ XXVIII ⌒

THE CONVENT seemed forlorn and deserted. Rain clouds shielded the morning sun, and droplets mixed with sleet fell softly and steadily. Such was the gloom that had settled upon the countryside, and the convent in particular, that Aleen felt reluctant to approach the gate of so desolate and saddened a place. But approach she must, for shelter and a change of clothing were mandatory. Moisture had penetrated her hooded cloak and seeped through to her tunic, until it clung distressingly to her body. Her hair was matted, and she shivered and blinked repeatedly against the stinging wetness that fell upon her face.

Cenook carried her away from the main road onto a worn dirt path and stopped beside the stone wall that encircled the convent grounds. Aleen leaned far in the saddle, reached for the bell chain that hung beside the grilled gate, and rang it vigorously. The portress was slow in coming, and as Aleen sat huddled against the rain and chill, the faraway sound of chanting mingled with the soft patter of drizzle. Then, joined to these sounds, came the familiar crashing of waves against the steep cliffs in the distance. The sea could not be seen, but its presence there brought welcome relief to Aleen's spirit, as it did to all Viking souls.

The bars in the gate offered an interrupted view of the vast grounds, but Aleen could see that the buildings were larger than she had expected. Many additions had been made to the original two-story building, forcing it to reach angularly in many directions. There were separate buildings to the rear, all undistinguishable except for the barn. The view of the largest addition to the main building was obstructed by the stretch of stone wall, but it was from there Aleen heard footsteps plopping across the saturated ground.

A small figure appeared, and from under a black mantle came a smiling face and large brown eyes that looked up compassionately at the pitiful rider. Then, inserting a long-shanked key in the lock, the nun opened the creaking gate for Aleen's entry. With a grating bang the gate was reclosed, and the nun, still smiling as though enjoying the drenching, motioned for Aleen to follow. Their path traced the curve of the wall, and Aleen, still upon Cenook, was aware that with each step of her mount, mud splattered against the hem of the nun's black robes. When they reached the end of the building, Cenook was quickly tethered and the nun reached up to assist Aleen in dismounting.

Once inside, the nun shook her head over the wet garments that posed such a threat to her guest's health. "I beg pardon for not bringing you to the main entrance, but this is the closest shelter. Please follow me," she said, reaching for Aleen's bag. "We must get you immediately to your quarters."

Through workrooms, down corridors, around corners, the little nun scurried, unaware of Aleen's struggle to keep pace. The convent seemed even colder than the weather outside, and Aleen was more than grateful when she was shown to a room where the little nun worked at lighting a fire in a small hearth. "You must change now," she said softly. "Reverend Mother will greet you as soon as services are completed." With an angelic smile, the nun turned and left.

Once in dry clothes, Aleen relaxed in the warmth of the small fireplace and listened to the rhythm of the chant that echoed through the halls. The voices were pure, and undulated in celestial tones. It was a fascinating sound, a soothing sound, the one tone accommodating the Latin words at once rapidly and then slowly, caressing each final syllable until its almost inaudible ending. A few coughs and the noise of leather sandals on the floor indicated the conclusion of the service, and Aleen sat nervously, expectantly awaiting the arrival of Wilfreda's sister, who was not long in coming.

She was thinner and older than Wilfreda, and decidedly different, as Aleen quickly learned. No sooner had she knocked and entered on Aleen's invitation than she crossed the room, smiling happily, and caressed Aleen affectionately. A kiss was gently pressed on Aleen's cheek, and a sincere "Welcome" fell comfortingly on her ear.

She knows not who I am, Aleen thought. She would not

greet me so if she knew. "I am Aleen, Reverend Mother," Aleen heard herself saying in a faltering voice. "I am the Danish wife of Edmund, the ealdorman."

"Yes, I know," said the nun, continuing her warm smile.

"But I said nothing to the sister portress . . ."

"You had no need to identify yourself. I expected no one but you, so you see, it had to be the Aleen who expressed so ardent a desire to join us." Her eyes twinkled, and her smile was genuinely sincere.

"Reverend Mother," Aleen said timidly, "I am a Viking— you do not mind?"

The smile deepened. "No, my dear. We are God's children. We are all Christians. You will find that no other distinctions are recognized here."

Aleen showed visible signs of relief as the nun continued, "Tell me, Aleen, how is Lauxburgh? My sister, is she well?"

"Yes, Reverend Mother. She is well," Aleen said matter-of-factly, and she lowered her eyes to avoid having the nun read anything untoward in them.

"Did she oppose your coming?"

"No, Reverend Mother, she did not, because I did not confide in her. I told no one except Cestus, who governs Lauxburgh now." Aleen looked into the nun's clear blue eyes. "You were told of Edmund's return to Tankenham?"

"Yes," the nun replied with a nod. "I have been well-informed. It is strange, is it not, how God works his wonders in the human soul? First he chooses Edmund, and then directs you to us. Many will be edified by your decision to live here, and many will be inspired to a life of virtue by your sacrifice of position and luxury." The nun was glowing with pride, and to Aleen's chagrin, she noted that the nun had no misgivings, no doubts, but that it was God who was responsible for Aleen's appearance there.

"I know you are anxious to join us, Aleen, but we must follow the rules set forth by our founder . . ."

My God, Aleen thought, she has misunderstood my request. She assumes I requested admittance into her order. How could she have been so mistaken? I requested only that I be permitted to live here, as would a wayfarer, a guest who shared the accommodations and prayed with them as so many ladies have done for months—years—at a time.

She was shocked, confused by the nun's assumption. What if I should correct her? I might well be refused. She would be disappointed in me and might request that I return to Lauxburgh. But at Lauxburgh there was Cestus and the ridicule of the women. I cannot go back. . . . The nun's voice went on and on. I shall wait and correct the nun at another time.

"Our order requires a short period of adjustment," the nun was saying. "You will be a guest here for a time, and we will have many little talks before your acceptance. We must be certain you will be happy in this life. It is a difficult one, as you know. Our founder, the holy Saint Benedict, when he set forth the details of our rule and way of life, decreed that manual work be virtuously undertaken as a disciplinary force against the weaknesses of human nature. However, because of your nobility, you will be exempt from the menial tasks."

"No," Aleen almost shouted in interruption. "No, Reverend Mother. Should I remain here, I would wish to be regarded as the others, with no exemptions from the customary practices."

The nun was pleased with the reaction. "Very well," she added; then, more animatedly, "We will have time enough to speak of this. You must be tired and hungry from your journey. I will see that food is brought immediately."

The fragile figure turned to leave, but then agilely turned again. "If you desire anything, you may ring this bell for sister," and she indicated a small hand bell on a table near the fireplace. A smile brightened her face again as she added, "But, please, dear Aleen, do not ring it when the nuns are in chapel. It will disturb their recollection." Her eyes twinkled. "I will see you later." But before leaving the room, she paused and then slowly faced Aleen once more. "Tell me, Aleen," the nun said softly, "you arrived here so early in the day, was there a reason for your early departure from Lauxburgh?"

"Yes," Aleen answered reluctantly. "I must tell you that Cestus opposed my coming here. I was forced to leave early to prevent difficulties." Aleen regretted having to expose so unattractive an element of Cestus' personality to so serene and sheltered a personage as the Reverend Mother, but she must be forewarned of the possible fulfillment of his threat.

"He told me that should I leave, he would journey here and take me back with him."

"Indeed," the little nun said pleasantly. "Then I shall be most anxious to visit with him." It was Aleen's turn to evaluate the nun's reaction, and it seemed to her that the nun was more than anxious to activate a long-standing plan to counsel her young nephew, whose conduct in the past had not always met with her approval.

"The Lord God must be very pleased that you overcame so many obstacles to come to him," she said as she closed the door behind her.

The words disturbed Aleen's conscience. It was not because of God that I came here, but because of Edmund, dear, dear Edmund. As she walked to a small, high window, she felt a gnawing dread that she had acted unwisely. She had forsaken the life to which she had become accustomed, unhappy though it was, for a strange unknown life with unusual and difficult customs.

The drizzle was still falling as she looked out upon a bleak meadow. The sky was thick with gray clouds, and a gloomy day was promised. By now Cestus had read the letter she had left for him, a letter in which she had begged him to understand, to be calm, and to be assured that she would return to Lauxburgh if the place was not to her liking. She had begged him to respect Edmund's wishes for seclusion and to inform him of her departure only after he was heard from once more. Perhaps Cestus would be placated and would respect all her wishes.

Had it not been for the clicking of dishes, Aleen would not have known that anyone had entered the room. The small nun arranged the plates attractively, assessed the hearth, added a fresh log, scooped up the damp clothing, and smiled pleasantly. "I will return these later," she said sweetly, and with a swish of her robes she hurried away.

Aleen examined the boiled eggs, cheese, and brown bread, and began eating near the warmth of the fire. The nuns are congenial, she thought. Perhaps the life here can be endured, after all.

Cestus did not journey to Chatham as he had threatened, and one slow, uneventful day followed another. Aleen was permitted to visit the rooms in the wayfarers' sector, the parlor, the barn where Cenook was stabled, and the chapel, but she was not as yet permitted to associate with the sisters except those assigned to care for the pilgrims who stopped there for brief visits. Since there were no guests, the time went slowly, until Aleen found herself anticipating the visits of the nun Hreda, the directress of postulants, who instructed Aleen each day on the various aspects of religious life.

It was an ideal situation, this association with the sisters. She was free to do as she pleased, with nothing expected of her, and she was pleasantly cared for. But after the passage of some weeks, a pressure began building as Hreda began to plan for the first of Aleen's acceptances into the community. The days of leisure were numbered, and many troubles disturbed her, of which money was the primary concern. The only resources she had brought with her were the jewels and articles of gold that had once belonged to her mother. From time to time a brooch, a ring, or a jewel was given the nuns in payment for her lodging and Cenook's feed, but this could not go on. The remaining cache would comprise an adequate dowry should she enter the order, and since no financial arrangements had been made at Lauxburgh prior to her leaving and since no overture for help could be graciously initiated now, the dowry must be entrusted to the convent before necessities diminished its value.

If only the Lauxburgh treasury would come to her aid, as truly it was obliged to do for Edmund's wife, but Wilfreda, no doubt, was offended by the manner of her leave-taking and perhaps opposed the payment of Lauxburgh's money for a Viking she had always despised. And as for Cestus, perhaps it was he who withheld the moneys. No doubt he reasoned that with the depletion of her funds she would be forced to return. Perhaps that was why he did not journey to get her as he had threatened. He had only to wait.

Aleen found herself in another strange situation, of which the matter of the dowry was only one aspect. She had observed the nuns at contemplation and cheerful labor. She had been awakened each morning long before dawn for the chanting of matins and lauds and had learned enough of the rules from the nun Hreda to know that it would be against her nature and inclination to embark on such a life, yet she could not leave. She could not bring herself to return to Lauxburgh and beg sustenance there. She could not brave the expected ridicule of the residents at her failure to fulfill her commitment. She could not face Cestus and have him speak again of annulment and marriage to him. Then, there were the primary reasons for which she had come to Chatham. There was the desire to obtain peace of soul and mind, available from the support and encouragement of holy religion, and her wish to remove herself from Edmund's care, so as to afford him a clear path to follow the dictates of his calling.

Not the least of her cares was Cenook, her only link to the past, a sentimental attachment to happier days, when he had been given to her by her father. She could no longer pay for his keep, yet, if she were a member of the community, the nuns would be pleased to feed him in return for his services as a courier's mount. Besides, he could be used by the guests in pleasant weather for rides about convent grounds.

The course of her life had been planned, it would seem, by the whims of fate, and if she had no attraction to the life, she would nevertheless plunge into it, determinedly meet its trials, and steadfastly conquer them all.

When next the nun came to her chamber, the day for Aleen's acceptance into the community was decided upon.

It was a day not unlike that of her arrival at Chatham. A steady drizzle, mingled with sleet, fell steadily and spattered against the shutters as Reverend Mother entered Aleen's room carrying across her arms the black robe into which Aleen must change before her appearance in chapel for the ceremony.

It was a traumatic experience, discarding a fine yellow linen tunic and silk shawl for a coarse black woolen robe that felt too large and bulky for comfort. A thick belt was buckled loosely around the waist, and her soft leather shoes were exchanged for sandals that exposed much of her feet to the cold.

"You must wear your hair in this manner during your postulancy," Reverend Mother was saying as she twisted Aleen's hair and pinned it into an unattractive knot at the back of her head. "In a few months, when you become a novice, it will be cut short and will thus spare you much concern for its care."

Together they walked to the chapel, where the warmth and the glow of myriad candles belied the cold and bleakness of the weather. The priest who had arrived for the ceremony and the celebration of the holy mass was arrayed in magnificent white silk vestments and stood before the stone altar, where he awaited the arrival of the abbess and her new spiritual child. While the sisters sang triumphant hymns, their voices rising to angelic heights, the priest pronounced the Latin prayers for the blessing of a religious veil and swayed the censer about it before handing the veil to the abbess for placement on the head of the postulant.

It was a brief ceremony. The abbess led her new charge to a place before the choir for the hearing of mass, and when that was completed, she was led to a nearby room, where each of the ten nuns embraced her dearly, congratulated her, and welcomed her warmly into their midst. It was something of a surprise, this meeting with the cloistered nuns, and it was amusing to see the ones who had always silently moved about with downcast eyes now behaving so cheerfully. They were a joyful group, and not at all stern and depressed, as she had expected, especially after the shameful ordeal they had experienced at the hands of the Viking intruders. They were genuinely delighted to meet her, and exchanged heartfelt amenities and offered her their most sage advice. "The life is difficult, my child, but the good God rewards us, even in this life, with contentment and the joy of knowing we do his will." "Pray for perseverance, my dear child, and the good God will assist you in your trials." It was a brief relaxation of the normal routine, and Aleen was much pleased that no reference to her nationality had been made. Before long there was the ringing of a small hand bell, and immediately there was silence and a resumption of prayerful attitudes.

"We will henceforth call you Sister Aleen," the abbess said softly after the nuns had left the room. "Sister Hreda and I have determined that you will have a dual function here. You will join the cloistered nuns in choir for the chanting of the office whenever your duties permit, and you will also assist the extern nuns in caring for our wayfaring guests who afford us with our main source of income. Look to Sister Hreda for all answers to your questions. She will at times place you in the care of other nuns, but she will be your main guide in all matters."

She was led to the second floor of the main building to the new room she would occupy. It was a narrow room, which the nun called a cell. Its furnishings were simple and much like her former room in the guests' sector, with the exception of a straw mat placed on a wooden bed frame. The only other furnishings consisted of a chair and a small table. There was no fireplace, and only a window and a plain wooden crucifix to break the monotony of the walls.

"Today you will be exempt from the rules. You will want to adjust yourself to your new surroundings," Sister Hreda was advising as she tested the mat with her hands. "You may visit the chapel as you wish," she added. "Tomorrow you will begin your training." She placed her cheek against Aleen's. "We are pleased to have you, my dear."

Aleen was left alone in the cold room with the sleet pattering against the window. This would be her new world—this foreign place with its crude furnishings, its dented washbasin, its cracked plaster walls. This was the way poverty was practiced and endured. With her immediate surroundings carefully assessed, she walked to her lone window to view the segment of the world her eyes would look upon so often. She opened the window and looked upon the grotesque barrenness of orchard trees and wet dormant fields. A cold blast of air slapped against her face, and as she latched the window, her long swaying sleeve captured her attention. It could not be her slender arm protruding from so unattractive a garment, and she looked down at the bulky skirt that fell from her waist. Both hands went to her head and traced the veil that covered the ears and tied behind the neck. It was all unreal—it could not be. Tears blurred her vision before she closed her eyes against the bleakness around her.

Edmund, Edmund, her heart cried in agony. I am as one dead to this world. You need have no further care of me. In spite of all the gentleness and kindness here, I am as though buried. And she turned and pressed her face against the coldness of the plastered wall.

Convent life was a bewildering, perplexing, busy, ordered life accented during the night and day by prayers beginning at the second hour, when all were awakened for the recitation of the Office. The days were crowded with interspersed chores that seemed to multiply in variety. The nuns had acquiesced to Aleen's wishes that her royalty be disregarded during the assignment of chores, and as a result, she was never quite certain where she would be found—in the kitchen washing plates, in the refectory either preparing the table for meals or clearing the table following the brief and simple collations. There were many hallways to sweep, vegetables to clean and cut, icy water to be drawn from the well, and sheltered sheep and livestock to be fed. The burdens were always shared with another nun, but the required silence made the activities boring and tedious. The evening recreation was eagerly anticipated, and Aleen watched with interest and delight as each nun, so silently contemplative during prayer and untiringly active during working times, was transformed into a blithe soul ready and eager to amuse and be amused.

In all, it was a lonely life. True, there was silent companionship at every turn, yet the nuns, by their profession of vows, were members of a fraternity to which Aleen, as a postulant, was excluded. There were no novices preparing for vows and no other postulants to relieve Aleen's feelings of isolation. Since the tragedy of the Viking intrusion, mothers were reluctant to permit their daughters to enter Chatham, a condition to which the abbess sought a remedy in Aleen's presence among them.

Gratefully, time passed quickly, and the round of continuous activities permitted little time for reminiscing. Each evening, Aleen exhaustedly retired to her cell, muscles aching and mind sleepy and dazed from the prayerful interruptions to her sleep the night before. She was grateful that sleep came so easily and prevented memories from haunting her, for a situation occurred in the refectory a few days after her entrance that made her resolve to guard against such thoughts and to be more attentive to the fulfillment of duty.

She had carried bowls of boiled potatoes and stewed mutton to the table, when she noticed one of the sisters, the youngest of the group, disengage herself from the others who silently filed in for the midday meal. The nun had approached a sideboard located at the end of the long narrow room and had withdrawn from its interior a crown of thorns. After placing it carefully on her veiled head, she fumbled with a linen bag she had extracted from the same place. Dutifully Aleen had withdrawn her attention and had turned her back to the table for the prayers that preceded the meal, but when once again she faced the nuns, she was shocked to see the young nun holding in both hands a human skull, which she kissed as the rest of the nuns seated themselves. While the nuns all sat with downcast eyes, hands placed in their laps with religious decorum, the young nun began reciting aloud for all to hear: "Mindful of the fleetness of time, the nearness of eternity, and the punishment due weaknesses of the flesh and spirit, I do confess that I have indulged in memories of the pleasures of the world. For this fault I humbly beg pardon of the Lord and the members of this community."

All eyes were downcast save those of the abbess, who nodded forgiveness for the fault, and those of Aleen, who sat gaping at the nun as she again kissed the skull before replacing it and the crown inside the cabinet. Only when the young nun took her place across from Aleen did the sisters begin to serve themselves.

Never will I do anything that will make it necessary for me to do such penance, Aleen resolved. Nor shall I permit my conscience to convince me that such a confession is necessary for my peace of soul.

The abbess summoned Aleen to her office some weeks later. There were kind words of encouragement and recognition of assignments dutifully performed, but the reason for the consultation concerned not Aleen, but the matter of Cenook. "He is of no use to the community. Were he able to help with the plowing, we might consider keeping him, but he requires much feed and attention, which had best be spent elsewhere. I have deliberated carefully on this matter, and since neither you nor our order has need of him, I ask for authority to sell him."

The proposal was as a blow to Aleen's rationality. The very thought of Cenook being harnessed for the plow was outrageous, as was the thought of losing him. How could she feed the sheep and cattle and not have Cenook there to pet?

Cenook, her constant friend and only link to the past. Sell Cenook and have another claim the noble steed as his own? The thought pained her. Cenook was her last possession in the world, and without him she would be destitute; yet, if she meant to stay at Chatham—and indeed, how could she do otherwise?—it would not do to have the abbess frown at her reluctance to part with wordly goods and attachments.

Her mind raced about for solutions to the problem. "Reverend Mother, could he not serve the community as a courier's mount?"

"No, Aleen, our courier has his own animal."

"Then could he be used as a pleasure horse for our guests to ride about the convent grounds?"

The abbess smiled understandingly. "My dear, our guests are travelers, wearied from riding. They have little inclination for pleasure riding."

Aleen looked at the thin nun sitting so erect behind her large desk. "Then do as you wish with him."

The abbess was pleased that Aleen had forsaken worldly goods so easily. "Then I shall send him back to Lauxburgh. He is a nobleman's mount, and they would be eager, I would think, to buy him."

Aleen nodded, her placid appearance concealing the sorrow of heartbreak. There was consolation in knowing he would be at Lauxburgh, in knowing he would be cared for by Thorkil and the crippled Aethelwed, but he could be claimed by anyone, ridden by anyone. . . .

She was never informed of the value the convent placed on Cenook. It was the morning following this meeting that he was taken away. Aleen and the nuns were in their places in the choir chanting the hour of terce when a rider was heard rounding the building and making his way to the barn. Moments later the sound of two horses was heard retracing the route and fading into the distance.

Later that day, when Aleen walked along the frozen path to the barn to feed the sheep and cattle, as was her duty, her soul ached at the sight of Cenook's tethering post and the sheep that now clustered around it. All her worldly loves were lost to her, and there remained to fill the void only the nuns of Chatham and the good God himself.

There were designated times for instructions, and each afternoon during the time the sisters had free to pursue studies, sewing, or personal interests, Aleen made her way to Hreda's cell, where she sat on a stool while the soft-spoken nun explained the customs of the order and the rules to which Aleen would be bound. Such times were distracting for Aleen. Sister Hreda reminded her of the cobbler's wife. Both were of equal girth and merry disposition, and Aleen could not help feeling that if Hreda had remained in the world, she, too, would be surrounded by children and would be as devoted to her family's happiness as was Bertha.

Today the period of instruction would be different. Today she would report instead to the cell of the abbess.

As befitted her rank in the religious family, the cell of the abbess was larger than the others, although the furnishings were as crudely simple. She was waiting, and when Aleen knocked and gave the greeting which all the sisters shared: "Praised be the Lord Jesus," and the abbess answered: "Forever be he praised," she motioned Aleen to the only chair, while she remained standing, her arms tucked into the fullness of her sleeves. She was happily anticipating embarking on a matter that was of obvious delight to her.

Hreda has asked me to speak to you of a counsel which has inspired me through my religious life and which has assisted many nuns to greater confidence in the Lord God. But first, Aleen, you must tell me of your association with your father."

Somewhat taken aback by the request, Aleen knew not how to speak of the Viking king whose errant subjects had inflicted much punishment on the innocent souls she now claimed as her sisters in religion. "I loved him dearly," Aleen said falteringly. "He was kind to me." She looked up at the nun, pleading with distressed eyes for help in proceeding further.

"Was he generous to you?"

"He was most generous."

"Did you feel he protected you from all that was harmful and evil?"

"Yes."

"Did he console you when you grieved? Did you feel he

knew the solution to all your problems, that he knew better than anyone how to correct all that was wrong or hurtful?"

"Yes. Yes."

"Did you feel he was stronger than all other men? Could he be relied upon and trusted to fulfill his promises? Did you feel he wanted you to be contented and would do anything to ensure your happiness?"

"Yes," Aleen repeated, her cheeks dimpling. "That is my father exactly."

"Then you shall fully appreciate my lesson." She walked a few steps toward a wall opposite her pallet and reached up for a piece of dark wood hanging there and took it down with pride. "This sign I have cherished since my youth," she said, and she blew dust from it with care. Turning it, Aleen saw scratched on its splintery surface the faded letters that had once been traced in paint. "These words are taken from a psalm written by David the prophet and contain a treasury of meanings. It says"—and she turned the sign slightly to facilitate her reading of it—"Delight in the Lord, trust also in him, and he will give thee the desires of thy heart.'* I can offer you no better counsel than this," and she repeated the phrase.

"Now, to delight in the Lord you must love him as we all do. Did you know that the good God is called 'Father' more frequently in the Holy Bible than any other name? Therefore, delight in your father in heaven in much the same way as you delighted in your earthly father. Know that he can do all things for you. Trust in him and know that he wishes you happiness. He knows the secrets and the desires of your heart, and he, above all others, can fulfill them. He knows your problems, and can offer the solutions for them, if you but delight in him and trust in him. Be as contented and loving with the Lord as you were to your earthly father, and know that your heavenly father is more powerful and even more concerned for your welfare and happiness than was your earthly parent. I can testify to the wisdom of this saying. I have had many years to put it into practice, and I boast not, mind you. I tell you this only to emphasize this teaching. Early in my religious life I was introduced to these words. I

---

*Psalm 36:4. In some books, 37:4.

delighted in the Lord and loved him, and I begged him as the desire of my heart that this love would increase. He has fulfilled this wish, as he has fulfilled all my desires, and as a result, I burn with love for him, his teachings, and his children. During the past year he has granted all my heart requested. I asked that Cestus would return to Lauxburgh more inclined to mature behavior, and now, as you know, he governs Lauxburgh fairly and wisely. I asked that the nuns be spared the scourge of the plague, and although a few took ill, all survived. I asked that the membership of our convent be increased, and the good God sent us you, and because of your entrance, others have asked to be admitted."

Aleen looked surprised. "Yes, Aleen, two others have come here seeking God. They will join us in the spring. Since I established this convent many years ago, I begged God that my sisters would be spared hunger, and we have yet to miss a meal. It has always been this way." She inclined her head and added humbly, "It is so because I delight in the Lord. I tell you this, Aleen, in the spirit of humility, that you may know the saying is true." She looked up meekly. "Now, in my old age, I desire that when I die God will take me to heaven, and I know he will do this as well. Take this sign with you, hang it as I have done, and meditate often on its meaning."

Aleen took hold of the rough wood held out to her. The abbess placed both hands on Aleen's arms. "These words are consoling, Aleen. I know you love the Lord, and I know full well he will likewise give you the desires of your heart."

Aleen returned to her room at the other end of the dim corridor and placed the sign on her table. She would hang it later, as the abbess suggested. She was confused, disturbed, for the words did not console her as the abbess claimed they would. The desires of my heart are not like those of her heart, Aleen thought. If I be honest, I would know what my heart desires—the life to which God first led me. I would desire a happy marriage, many children, and Edmund ... yes, Edmund above all else. The thoughts were disconcerting. If I continue these thoughts, I shall find myself wearing the thorns and kissing the skull. . . .

Aleen sat down upon the mat, the straw crunching beneath her weight. She would take all into account and reassemble her thoughts. Edmund was now the Lord's property, and she could not covet what belonged to God. She would simplify the whole matter, and with a wave of relief she felt the burden of inordinate desires fall from her shoulders. She would delight in the Lord and desire those things which God desired for her. She would trust in his judgment. She would confide all to him as she had done with her Viking father. She would be content knowing God was wise and just, and that those they both loved were safe in his care. "I desire what God desires," she repeated aloud, and she immediately rose from the mat in answer to the bell that summoned her to prayer.

## ~✦ XXIX ✦~

CHRISTMAS WAS approaching. Meditations and readings all lent themselves to the theme of the season. The anticipated climax of preparatory fasts and penances was eagerly awaited. Special hymns were practiced, tall tapers and holiday vestments were taken from storage, and in the cozy warmth and savory air of the kitchens the cooks prepared in advance succulent treats and sweetmeats. The holy serenity of Chatham was not destined to prevail, however. Several days before the great feast, after the sisters had retired to their cells for the night, riders approached the convent gate, rang the bell demandingly, and accompanied by a great clatter and many laughing voices, finally made their way to the guests' quarters. Judging from the voices, they were all women, perhaps four or five. The sister portress would be busy indeed tending to their needs, and after repeated and incessant ringing of hand bells demanding service, the peace of the night at last settled upon Chatham.

It was after daybreak that Aleen learned the identity of the travelers. She had entered the barn to feed the restless animals when she saw the three palfreys, and partially hidden by a plank wall, none other than Cenook. It was the unbelievable return of a lost friend. Aleen hugged and patted the arched neck, tearfully spoke endearments, and finally saw to it that feed was amply supplied. The visitors had to be from Lauxburgh, and Aleen quickly whispered a prayer that the abbess would assign her to other tasks far from the critical eyes and wagging tongues of the visitors.

The guests slept late, and it was well after the recitation of tierce and the nuns' morning collation that the hand bells were reactivated. A breathless Sister Odilia spurred Aleen to action, handing her a basin of steaming water for delivery to the first guest room. "But, sister . . ." Aleen faltered, blushing furiously at her expected humiliation.

"Yes?" The nun turned quickly, her veil floating on the breeze she created. Aleen could not answer. The nun had much to do, and there was no time to explain the quandary into which she had been placed. Aleen shook her head in negation and balanced the bowl and shifting water as best she could as she proceeded to the room. She must learn to bear humiliation—and now, while a postulant—for there would be times aplenty for patience and endurance throughout religious life. The women will not disturb my peace of mind, Aleen determined. No, I shall treat them as I would any other guests—sweetly, cordially, obediently. I shall impress them with my willingness to be of assistance, and if my appearance amuses them, I shall be indifferent to their comments. I must learn to bear all for God, and now will be the time to begin.

She entered the dim room and set the basin on a table near the hearth. The guest was still loitering in bed, and Aleen did not trouble to glance her way. The fire had not caught properly, and mindful of her instructions to provide a warmth which the guests would appreciate, she poked at the logs until satisfied that the fire would burn steadily. As she arose and turned to leave, a familiar mocking voice sounded from the bed. "Why, it is Aleen." Turning at the sound, Aleen saw Judith's smiling face peering from beneath the woolen covers. "I did not think the abbess would permit you, the Lady of Lauxburgh, to do such menial tasks."

"I am a postulant here," Aleen said with forced sweetness. "I rise early with the nuns and do all manner of chores, as I am directed."

Judith sneered as she critically considered Aleen's woolen robe and the veil that concealed her hair. "I would not think so distinguished a personage as yourself would permit even God to reduce you to a lowly rank equal to that of servitude."

"I do not only permit it—I requested it." Then, attempting to distract Judith to other matters, Aleen asked, "Will your journey be a long one?"

"We are not wayfarers. We came to join the nuns for the feast."

"Oh," Aleen uttered weakly with a hint of disappointment.

"Wilfreda wished to be with her sister for the celebration of Christmas, and we came along as her companions."

At the mention of Wilfreda's name, Aleen blanched, and would have bolted through the door had not religious dignity prevented it. "Indeed," Aleen said, straining to render her voice normal and controlled. "I am certain our abbess is delighted to have Wilfreda here. I must go now, Judith. I have much to do," and before Judith could object, Aleen slipped away.

Good God, Aleen screamed inwardly, how can I face Wilfreda and those women? I thought never to look upon their faces again. And she cringed at the thought of the sarcastic remarks that would be directed toward her appearance and her presumed unworthiness for the religious life.

Slipping past the kitchen into a workroom where broken furniture and an assortment of tools lay about, she paced back and forth. I must think ... I must think. How can I face them and serve them? If only Reverend Mother would assign me to other chores, but she will only indicate that such service denotes my willingness for humility and obedience. I must find the true religious solution to this. Surely they did not come here in the frigid weather to seek me out and make sport of me. No. I shall not ask for other assignments, for certainly Reverend Mother will lament my weakness. I will be obedient and do as I have been directed. Her rapid breathing slowed as the solution gradually emerged, and her eyes shone in satisfaction with her decision. They will expect me to be long of face, to be discontented with the strictness of the life, to be ashamed of my poor garments. I shall surprise them. I cannot have them return to Lauxburgh and begin rumors that I am unhappy here. If Cestus and Edmund must hear rumors of me, they must hear that I am happy and contented with the life. I shall smile though it hurts, and I shall serve with apparent pleasure. With her plan set determinedly in mind, she went forth.

Wilfreda was standing near the fire, huddled in the woolen coverlet from her bed, when Aleen entered with a tray of food. Wilfreda turned to her but did not speak. Her eyes slowly wandered over Aleen's garments before she again turned to the fire as though bored with what she saw.

"You look well, Wilfreda," Aleen said, as though unaware

of her attitude. "Here, please eat while the food is warm," and she arranged the plates on the table for the convenience of the diner. "If there is anything you desire, ring your bell. I shall be pleased to provide whatever will assure your comfort."

Wilfreda sustained her aloof silence as Aleen left. May God forgive my hypocrisy, Aleen prayed as she shivered, not so much from the cold of the hallways as from the attitude of her supercilious guest.

The ladies were seldom in chapel, and preferred to spend their time in Wilfreda's room, which was large and had a round table, where they enjoyed their meals together. Bits of conversation garnered from these meals indicated all Aleen needed to know of Edmund and Cestus. Edmund was still at Tankenham, and Cestus was still in command of Lauxburgh. If her interpretation of the remarks was correct, Cestus had not only forgotten his romantic interest in her, but had found a new recipient for his attentions in a maiden of the village. During the few times that Wilfreda was absent from the room, it was even conjectured aloud that little of his time would be spent at Lauxburgh during his mother's absence. There was always much tittering and laughing following their observations, to which Aleen showed not the least trace of awareness. Her duty was to serve the food and to remove soiled plates as the meals progressed, and this task she assiduously performed.

Their remarks were inevitably directed to Aleen. "Black is such an unbecoming color," Judith said aloud while Aleen was placing the plates and goblets on a huge tray. "It makes one look old and haggard. Tell me, Aleen, are you not depressed with the color?"

"Oh, no," Aleen snapped back. "Since we all wear the same robes, we are not in competition with one another. We are spared the concern about which color flatters us most, and we are untroubled that it is not becoming to us, since not our persons but our spiritual attractiveness merits our attentions. We find our garments a great convenience, and most adequately warm."

"You must wait until the summer sun bears down." Judith laughed. "You will see then how much comfort they provide."

Aleen smiled as though amused by the remark. "I am told

that in the summer we wear black linen robes that are most cooling."

Judith smiled in contradiction. "You expect us to believe such bulky robes are cooling?"

"I recall once speaking with seamen from a most arid country," Aleen explained. "They told me their people wear mantles and capes in the heat of the desert sun to keep the hotness from their bodies. They assured me the heat is thwarted in this manner. Next summer, Judith, when I wear such robes, I will let you know if it is so."

Judith was visibly taken aback. "Then you mean to stay here?"

"Oh, yes. Here I have found contentment. I have all I need. I am pleased to exert my energies for the Lord, and I am blessed with the company of happy and friendly people." Struggling with the weight of the tray, Aleen left them with this allusion to their own attitudes.

The guests were selfishly demanding and would permit themselves no discomfort or inconvenience. The bells frequently rang during prayer times, demanding attentions which could well have waited. Their requests for assistance in dressing, in the combing and arranging of their hair, was beyond what should have been expected from nuns or postulants, and it was not uncommon to see either the nun or Aleen scurrying back to the kitchen with plates of food to be reheated or prepared with more spices to please the guests' discriminating tastes.

It was only when their patience was sorely tried and their faces long and strained that the abbess left the company of the cloistered nuns to inspect for herself what transpired in the guests' quarters. After observing the nun straining with an armful of clothing to be aired and brushed, and after seeing Aleen hurrying to and fro with goblets of warm milk and sewing implements for the alteration of a guest's tunic, did the abbess intercept them along the way. Directing her remarks to Aleen, she began, "And I thought it would be a joy for you to be with those you knew from Lauxburgh. They have abused our hospitality," she pronounced with righteous indignation.

The guests packed the next day, and their displeasure was clearly evident. They were indignant and humiliated at the abbess's plea that they use discretion in requesting services, and they had promptly resolved to leave. Each planned to decrease the stipend they would offer on their departure, and each vowed she would never return.

The steady rain that had fallen throughout the morning had stopped, leaving huge icy puddles on the frozen ground, and it was with care that Aleen and the nuns carried the bags across the lawn to the barn. Two soldiers were waiting there to relieve them of their burdens, and with quiet precision quickly arranged the traveling bags on two donkeys they had brought with them.

The guests were slow in coming, but eventually, with skirts held delicately to prevent their least contact with the moistened ground, they joined the nuns, who huddled in woolen mantles waiting to bid them a courteous farewell. Judith, Wilfreda, and the ladies were silently aloof, but finally Wilfreda could no longer contain her indignation and gave forth with a tirade that caused the soldiers to move away in embarrassment and the nuns to stare disbelievingly at the display of hatred and envy. Wilfreda's sharply edged words slashed hard. ". . . and to think my own sister would turn against me—you, who teach of charity and virtue. You need not deny it, dear sister, that it was she, that devilish Viking, who is behind this, for I know her conduct full well. She plots against me and is even now deceitfully endeavoring to malign me with you, even as she attempted to estrange me from my sons."

Aleen might well have become sickened by the depth of her shame had not her keen perception found in the irrational behavior of the screaming woman a trace, an undeniable indication of insidious madness.

"Hush, Wilfreda," the abbess hissed, and to the amazement of all, Wilfreda quieted. The words next uttered were controlled, placating: "Wilfreda, do not be unreasonable. This is a house of prayer. We must have order, silence, a spirit of contemplation. We cannot maintain this atmosphere with the unreasonable demands of guests. Please understand we did not request that you leave—that has been your decision. As for the child, she said nothing to me. Her conduct has been exemplary. Do not judge her so harshly." The rest of the words were inaudible as Wilfreda listened contemptuously to her sister.

The wind was picking up strength, making the skirts and mantles sway and causing pinkness to color the noses and cheeks of all.

"Here," Wilfreda said at last, thrusting out a hand toward her sister. "This is our offering. You will find it far exceeds the worth of the services rendered."

The words were so bitingly sarcastic that Aleen—if not all of the nuns who had acceded to her constant demands—was enraged. That such words were uttered after all the petty complaints had been endured, all the unnecessary errands were run, all their energies expended on the guests' behalf, was unthinkable. At another place or time, sweet revenge would have been demanded, but even this must be patiently endured.

When Cenook was brought forth and Judith pridefully cocked her head and made her way toward him, there stirred in Aleen emotions which she could barely control. It was Judith's whole attitude, her insolent glancing about to catch Aleen's reaction to her acquisition of Cenook, the haughty lift of her eyebrows, the proud carriage, the swaggering of her body as she passed the escorts, that riled Aleen until she was flushed with anger and the compulsion for retaliation.

It was while the abbess was directing the sisters away from the horses and the splattering of mud that would follow the imminent mounting of the riders that a whistle creased the air. Cenook immediately responded to a latent urge and nervously stepped about in the mud, much to Judith's annoyance, since she was forced to step back in the slush to avoid contact. Another whistle sounded, and Cenook reared up, twisted his body, and came down, his hooves landing in a puddle, spraying muddy water on Judith, Wilfreda, and their companions.

The nuns turned in time to see the ladies gasping in shock, with mud spotting not only their mantles, but their faces as well. This was the final indignity, and they disdainfully refused attention, wiped their faces with their gloved hands, mounted quickly, and with all deliberate urgency quit the convent without further delay.

The nuns were aghast at the events that had transpired,

with the exception of Aleen, who, smiling to herself, preceded them into the building.

As the nuns were silently entering the refectory for the evening meal, Aleen walked to the cupboard, removed the crown of thorns, and placed it with all exactness atop her head, then took up the skull, which she held with as much care as she would have held the treasures of the realm. When the benediction was completed and the nuns sat down, Aleen began the formula she had repeatedly heard. "Mindful of the fleetness of time, the nearness of eternity, and the punishment due weaknesses of the flesh and spirit, I do confess that I willfully endeavored to humiliate our departing guests by whistling to my former steed, who reared up in response to the signal I had often practiced with him. I confess that I deliberately did this, knowing he would step in water and splatter soil on our distinguished visitors. For this fault . . ." Aleen hesitated, self-satisfied and amused by what she had related, and reflected hard on the words of contrition that would follow. She did not feel contrite, and would certainly repeat her actions if she were able. With her head tilted saucily, she continued, but the words were so rapidly slurred that the sisters were alert in their surprise. ". . . for this fault I humbly beg pardon of the Lord and the members of this community."

Sister Hreda's hand went to her mouth to suppress a smile, Sister Fristan's eyes opened wide in shock, and the faces of most, save the abbess's, were softened at the humor of the unusual confession.

It was a small price to pay for sparing the Lord the trouble of dispensing justifiable punishment, Aleen reasoned, and as she completed the ritual and kissed the skull, it was as though she kissed sweet contentment itself.

# ⌒∨ XXX ∿

HOLDING HER skirts to prevent their dragging in the snow that had drifted down in peaceful profusion throughout the night, Aleen carefully made her way from the barn to the kitchen with a bucket of fresh goat milk. The rope handle pressed painfully into her hands, and the milk sloshed over with each ill-placed step. It was an unpleasant chore, this gathering of milk in the early-morning cold, but each nun had her assignment, and whether or not it was to her liking was of little consequence. All tasks were to be performed docilely and willingly, as though Christ had assigned them through the person of the abbess. There were mornings when she wished she had retracted her decision to be regarded as the rest and to be relieved of all unpleasant duties that were poorly reconciled to her social position, but at least she could be grateful that she would endure them only for a time and that others in turn would be asked to perform them as well.

The view that met her gaze as she walked along was breathtaking, and after a moment's hesitation she set the bucket down and, shielding her eyes from the slanting rays of the early-morning sun, gazed at the stretch of sparkling white. The snow lay smooth and undisturbed upon the meadows, the fields, the barren trees, the Roman wall that encircled the convent grounds, the gentle hills that gradually undulated into the forests beyond. Everything she looked upon was graced by snowy purity.

A frigid breeze passed her, and remembering her mission, she reached down for the bucket, but crunching sounds in the distance echoed across the stillness, and in instant reaction she looked up once more and saw upon the hills four horsemen riding in steady rhythm. With each stride, sprays of crystals flew up, while the riders' cloaks billowed with each rocking motion.

With twinges of melancholia she yearned to be beside

329

them, riding free and easy. Oh, to be a man and go about as one pleased.

An uneasiness settled over her, and once again her hand was raised to shield her eyes from the glare. After straining into the distance for a moment, perplexity claimed her face. Two of the riders were soldiers; their shields and erect lances confirmed their profession. The identity of one rider was unknown, but the other ... the other rider could be no one but Edmund. The form, the broad shoulders, the thickly strapped legs, the shock of dark hair, the very way he sat upon the horse—all betrayed his identity. But it could not be Edmund. Edmund was in the cloister of Tankenham. Besides, were it Edmund, his escorts would be more numerous, and he would not be traveling from the seaport to the east. There were ministers and aides to conduct such business. But if it were not Edmund, it was someone who closely resembled him, and as she watched the riders scale the hill and ride off to meet the horizon, yearnings of the heart railed about her as variously as the breezes that startled her to action. Quickly she picked up her pail and made her way to the kitchen with its warmth and the smells of newly baked bread.

The embers of her love had been stirred to wakefulness by the vision of the rider, until gentle flames, fanned by a lover's longing, grew into their former intensity, warmth, and brilliance. The days following were disturbed by the rekindled and redoubled memories of unfulfilled love, and try and struggle though she might to dispel them, they refused release and flashed persistently, annoyingly, urgently, upon her mind. Her sleepless nights were tormented as the rider rode across her memory in slow, ghostly motions, her heart drumming in cadence with his mount. Through waves of vision, distorted by hot tears, the splintery sign the abbess had lent her came to view. The markings, illuminated by the moon, conveyed meanings that further unsettled her: "Delight in the Lord, trust also in him, and he will give thee the desires of thy heart."

"Delight in the Lord, trust also in him," she said, fondling each word. What would the holy abbess think of me if she knew the desires of my heart? If she knew that all I want is to be near my love, to sit beside him and to look into his face whenever I wish? Yes, to be able to touch his hand as though it were not sinful to do so. And, my God, what would she think if she knew how I yearn to be pressed to his heart, to have his dear arms around me, shielding me against harshness and all that is unpleasant?

Aleen rolled to one side, drew up her legs, and slid her hand beneath her pillow. Tears sped swiftly across her cheek, leaving shimmering silvery traces. If only I could be near him and to know he loves me as I do him. But then, she thought, he does not love me. It will never be, never, never, never. She rolled on her back and clasped her hands against her breast. "Oh, God," she whispered, "relieve me of these desires and give me, in their stead, new ones. Give me new desires for my heart. Help me to forget him and to desire only to do your will. Give me an earnest desire for this life," she implored pitifully.

Her torment lasted until the rays of the moon shifted away from the faded letters of the sign and abandoned her to the darkness of the night.

The rider Aleen had eventually convinced herself could not have been Edmund, was in fact he. The secrecy that had shrouded his leave-taking from Kent again concealed his return. The use of the port to the east instead of a Kentish port was a ruse which further concealed his activities. If the Vikings knew of his absence from the land, they did not take advantage of it, nor the inexperience of his replacement. The groups of Viking foragers who stealthily roamed the forests, and the rebel seamen whose long boats occasionally sliced the water of the horizon, made no attacks, and peace continued to grace the land during his absence and blessedly greeted his return.

After a rest from the arduous journey, Edmund thanked the abbot for his companionship on their successful trip, and with the papal dispensation securely tucked inside his jerkin, made off for Lauxburgh. It was midmorning when Edmund dismounted inside the stable and gave the reins over to Thorkil, whose smile reflected the joy of his returning master. Pausing at a nearby stall, Edmund patted Cenook's bobbing head and hastily left. With long strides he crossed the courtyard, paused midway to survey the castle, whose octagonal towers rose so sturdily before him; then, taking a long breath, he smiled and bounded up the steps.

Cestus had located the letter Aleen had written to him before her departure—the letter in which she pleaded with Cestus that he send no one to fetch her, the letter in which she begged him to respect her wishes for privacy and seclusion. Edmund had been given the letter, and had read it repeatedly. Additionally, he had spoken to Wilfreda and Judith about their visit to Chatham, and they, fearful that Edmund might attempt to recall Aleen to the castle, were eager to assure him of the security of Aleen's vocation. In convincing tones they had related how joyously she had performed her most menial tasks, how happy she had appeared to be with her new position in life, and how determined Aleen was to persevere in her calling. Each time Edmund thought to visit Chatham, Wilfreda's and Judith's words came to mind, and the letter with its pleadings compelled him to cancel his plans. But then, perhaps in time Aleen might grow weary of convent life, she might change her mind about remaining there, and she might return. . . .

Weeks had passed since Edmund's return, and ideal hunting weather was of passive interest to him. His utter desolation at the loss of Aleen made him remorseful and sometimes bitter. The castle seemed lonely and devoid of life without Aleen, and each day he expected to hear horses approaching and to see Aleen dismounting and running happily to him, proclaiming her mistake and wanting not the convent life, but him. Each night he retired anticipating the morrow and the fulfillment of his longings. He was too much the sentimentalist not to take frequent refuge in such consoling hopes. But his expectations were realized in a far different manner one morning, when a farm boy, pressed into service as a courier, rode up to the castle.

"A messenger from Chatham," Wulfric announced as he summoned the disheveled boy into the office.

Edmund did not stir in his chair, but watched keenly as the shuffling boy approached and nervously thrust a roll of parchment into the huge hand that opened to accept it.

"The Reverend Mother said I should wait for your reply," the boy stammered in a practiced monotone. Wide-eyed with amazement, the boy studied the brooding figure before him and nervously fingered his faded cap. It was the first time he had looked upon the face of "the good Lord Edmund," as he was affectionately called. The boy studied the features and memorized every detail of Edmund's attire and every line in his scowling face.

Edmund was indeed worried as he unfolded the parchment, for he expected words that conveyed unwelcome news concerning Aleen's health. Convent life was difficult, what with arising hours before the sun stirred beyond the horizon, the tiring duties, the hours of prayers, which he knew filled every moment of a nun's day. The regimen was enough to subject Aleen to exhaustion and a breakdown of health, and he fully expected word that Aleen was abed with weakness or disease.

But he was unprepared for the carefully written words he hastily read: "To Edmund, Ealdorman of Lauxburgh and the district of Kent. May the peace of Almighty God be with you. Reverend Mother humbly begs pardon for this intrusion, but she finds it necessary to write to you of a matter concerning the Lady Aleen. The lady is nearing the completion of her postulancy, and she has, of her free will, expressed the desire to enter our novitiate, which is a year of intense prayer and spiritual formation. Before we can allow her to take this most serious advancement in our religious life, we must have in our possession a document written in your hand in which you surrender all rights to your marriage contract and give your consent for her further commitment to our holy order. This document is required by church law and the directives of the founders of our religious order. You may entrust your paper to our courier, who will convey it speedily to us. Our community prays that the heavenly father will bestow upon you his most abundant blessings for your continued good health." Signed: the abbess Grimbald.

His hand fell heavily on the desk, and he stared at the yellow paper as though struck dumb. He looked up, shook his head, and once more glanced at the paper: ". . . of her free will she has expressed the desire to enter our novitiate . . ." It cannot be, he thought. She should know by now that it was not God's plan that she become a nun. She should be racing back to me on the swiftest of horses. Surely her love for me could not die with the donning of religious robes.

His mind went swiftly over the times and circumstances when she had shown her love, when he had read it in her actions and in her eyes. Even though she had not said the words, his instincts could not be wrong. His interpretation of oft-repeated memories *had* to be correct, and he emphasized his thought with a pounding of his fist. The farm boy started at the unexpected movement. Edmund had forgotten him standing there, and with a wave of his hand ordered him to wait outside. He must have time and privacy to clarify and separate his tumbling thoughts.

Again he read the words: ". . . surrender all rights to your marriage contract." How could this nun, his aunt, who he knew possessed laudable sanctity—how could she ask him to surrender all rights to his wife, when, after difficult struggles with himself, and a dangerous and difficult voyage to Rome, he had at last gained permission to claim the rights of that contract?

Walking to the window where, without Aleen's knowledge, he had often observed her activities on the meadow, he examined the panorama before him: the meadow across which she had often ridden Cenook, the place where she had picked wildflowers with Lelia, the grove of oaks under whose cooling shadow she had napped with the child, the slope and the beach where they had waded in the surf and played in the sand. All seemed drained of interest now, especially the lofty tower where, that stormy night, they had indulged in loving embrace.

Just as Aleen, after Lelia's funeral, could not envision a life without the child, so Edmund could not foresee a life without his wife beside him. But then his selfish desires retreated and made way for his Christian ideals. God could not be denied. Perhaps the Lord God did want her at Chatham, and perhaps there was the faint possibility that Aleen did want that life. Edmund could not stand in the way if this were so. Walking toward his desk, he sat down and took quill in hand, dipped it, and touched it to paper, but he could not gather the courage to put into words a surrender he was still reluctant to make. Neither rubbing his forehead nor tunneling fingered waves through his hair provided the impetus, and he at last crashed the quill against the scarred desk. Cracking the splintered feather in his hand, he said with conviction, "I must be assured that Aleen is determined to pursue this course."

Lunging for the door, he opened it and glared down at the farm boy. "Tell the abbess that I will deliver the document myself." Then he added crisply, "Now, be off quickly."

The boy ran down the hall, deliriously happy with the importance of his new errand, and in a few moments his horse was heard galloping away as fast as its common breeding permitted.

Walking toward Wulfric, Edmund immediately informed him of the journey that would commence as soon as escorts were hastily assembled.

Aleen was throwing pails of dirty dishwater on the ground where no one would walk, when the gate bell began clanging. Walking with quick steps, she returned to the kitchen to summon the portress. No time could be lost, for she had not only to alert the sister to a visitor who wished admittance to the convent grounds, but also had to hurry to join all the other nuns, who had already left for the choir and the singing of vespers. But the portress was already in the chapel. "Please be so kind as to answer the ring," the cook encouraged as she rolled down her sleeves and shook her black skirt free of flour. "I will tell sister you have admitted our visitor."

After reaching for the long-shanked key that hung beside the outside kitchen door, Aleen hurried along beside the wall to the gate, where the impatient visitor was again clanging the bell. When at last she reached the gate, she was breathing hard from the fast walk, and with a breathy "Greetings in the name of the Lord Jesus," she inserted the key in the lock. With a hospitable smile, she glanced up through the bars toward the rider, but then she could not move, for there was Edmund sitting upon Boltar as nobly as a god. For a long moment their eyes met before Aleen's were slowly lowered. At once she was flushed with confusion. Already short of breath, her heart pounded within her until she thought she would faint from its exertion. So overcome was she with the shock of seeing Edmund that she could not think, and she tightened her grip on the iron bar for support. He was waiting for her. She could feel his gaze hard upon her. She made a weak effort to turn the key, but it resisted, until Edmund dismounted, put his arms through the bars, and himself took the key and turned it. There was the grating and scraping of metal, and then, with an easy movement, he unlocked it and gave it to Aleen to hold open for him. She could not bring herself to look up as he mounted and rode through. She was grateful that she did not have to direct him to the main entrance where the abbess would meet with him. He was familiar with the building, and besides, the rule prohibited their speaking without the consent of the abbess. He said not a word as Boltar carried him across the convent grounds.

The world seemed still and quietly alert except for the thud of Boltar's hooves, but then the voices of the choir were heard drifting on the air. Aleen closed the gate with a clank, and as though dependent on it for support, she held fast to its bars. I thought I would never look upon his face again, she thought, fighting back tears. The singing placed an urgency on her. She must join the nuns without delay. Removing the key from the lock, she made her way back to the kitchen, denying herself the pleasure of looking upon the rider who was now nearing the main entrance.

With careful steps and restrained movements she made her way as inconspicuously as possible through the chapel toward her place beside the nuns. They did not glance up as she passed by, but continued their chant as Aleen hastily found her place in the breviary. Her thoughts, however, were not on the verses of the psalms which alternated in recitation from one group to the other, but on the realization that Edmund was there within the convent walls, where she had never expected him to be.

Reverend Mother had said she was contacting him about a needed document. Perhaps he meant to deliver it himself. But why would he leave the monastery for that reason? Perhaps, she thought with numbing dread, perhaps he meant to ease his mind about his taking of vows by seeing for himself that I am contented here. My God, my God, why did he have to come? Why did I have to see him? It will only make his leave-taking the harder, and the memory of him will linger long on my mind.

Aleen glanced toward the nun who sat by her side and at

the hand that held the page in readiness for turning. Red patches and large veins stood out prominently on the aged hand, and Aleen glanced from them to her own white slender ones. Oh, my God, to be like these women, so dedicated to your service. And then the words she had oft repeated during restless nights resounded in her soul: "My God, I wish to delight in you, even as do these holy women. I trust in you. Please give me new desires for my heart. . . . But I cannot be held in guilt, Lord," she prayed, diverting from the prayer, "for thoughts which taunt me cruelly. I cannot be held guilty for the love I have for one of your favored sons. My God, my heart shall burst asunder. Nevertheless, I shall trust in your judgments, Lord, for you alone know what is best for us. My God, I trust in you . . . I trust in you. . . ."

Edmund listened to the monotonously undulating strains of the chant that wafted through the cool dim halls and looked dejectedly at the furnishings in the room to which he had been brought. Two simple chairs stood at either end of a long table, and except for a huge crucifix hanging between two windows, the room was devoid of ornaments. A fitting reception room for a convent, Edmund thought. A faint whish of woolen robes, and he turned toward his aunt, who advanced and bowed with an agility that belied her age. Edmund, remembering the last time they had met in that room, embraced the small figure tenderly. Amenities were exchanged and inquiries made concerning the health of her sister before they settled to the purpose of Edmund's visit.

"I cannot provide the document you requested until I am convinced the Lady Aleen is meant for this life," Edmund declared as he turned about nervously. "You say she requested admittance to the novitiate? Was she unduly influenced? Was pressure put upon her?"

The nun was appalled by the insinuation. "Edmund," she said scoldingly, "do you truly believe we would attempt to keep the lady here against her will? She is not bound to vows, and may leave at any time. Knowing this, she has never expressed a wish to leave. Instead, she has insisted on continuing in this life, and we feel inclined to permit her to do so. She accepts the life willingly. She works well, she prays well."

Edmund was visibly distressed. For want of better exercise

to vent his agitation, he alternately ran his fingers through his hair and folded his arms. He said nothing, and the little nun felt compelled to relieve his mind by proving the genuineness of Aleen's calling.

"The lady embraces the life completely," the nun continued. "She insists on sharing the responsibilities with the others. Furthermore, she shows not the least revulsion for the lowliest tasks. I must admit, Edmund, her postulancy has not been without its difficulties. In the beginning, we were concerned about her and the validity of her vocation. She was remote and preoccupied with dreams. She took little part in our recreations, but eventually she overcame these troublesome thoughts that took her mind so far from us, and now, except for brief times when she slips back into these engrossing inattentions, she pleases us completely in all things. She will become a most satisfactory religious."

The abbess had presented her conclusions, and it fell to Edmund to direct the course of the conversation. His mind, though, was apparently occupied with the conjunction of ceiling to wall, and for a time he kept silent. "And her health?" Edmund asked at last, endeavoring to gain more time for his considerations.

The abbess smiled, relieved somewhat that the subject had been shifted to less serious matters. "You need not worry about Lady Aleen's health. She has sufficient strength and energy. She is very well indeed."

The chanting was heard again as they stood silently, awkwardly, not knowing what to say. Since no further questions were forthcoming, the abbess recalled the purpose of his visit. "Shall I have the sister bring you an ink pot and a quill and paper?"

"Reverend Mother," Edmund said, causing her to halt, "I cannot give this consent until I have seen for myself that this is what Aleen wishes."

"You wish to speak with her?"

"Yes. I need further convincing."

"But I do not recommend this. It is not proper that you speak with her, for she has rejected you for religion. I do not condone this. She must forget you and the past."

"Nevertheless, Reverend Mother, if you wish your document, I must speak to her. I demand to."

The request did not lie comfortably on the abbess' mind, but without further argument she replied, "I shall see if she consents to a conference with you." Her veil curled in the breeze she created with her rapid departure. A moment later, the little nun who had brought him to this room entered with all that was needed for writing, and Edmund frowned as he looked at the blank piece of parchment.

In the chapel, breviaries were closed and the nuns rose to leave. When Aleen passed into the hall with the others, the abbess touched her gently on the arm and drew her from the line. "The Lord Edmund wishes to speak with you," she whispered.

"But, Reverend Mother, I cannot," Aleen said with alarm.

"He said you must speak with him or he refuses to furnish us with his consent for your novitiate."

Reverend Mother permitted her some moments for reflection. I cannot speak with him, Aleen thought in distress, without shouting my love for him. I cannot. But why would he request this if he did not wish to ease his mind, to see for himself that I am happy here? His mind must be at rest concerning me before he embraces his vows. If the religious life is what he so desperately craves, then the same life must be for me. I must give him what he dearly loves. Somehow I must assure him that I am contented here and that he need have no further concern for me.

"Will you consent to speak with him?"

Aleen nodded agreement.

Edmund had slumped casually in the chair. His heavy frame seemed drained of its vital forces, his expression appeared devoid of hope. He was a man who for only a short time had held the expectation of a lifetime of happiness with a woman he had grown to love deeply. Now his hopes had been reduced to this: a cool, bare convent room and a nun requesting that he surrender his marital privileges for the sake of his wife's vocation.

The movement at the door attracted his attention, and he glanced up to see the abbess precede Aleen into the room. Aleen looked briefly at him and then lowered her head in religious modesty, for the sight of the man she loved so completely sent warm, thrilling sensations throughout her body.

Having escorted Aleen to the room, the abbess turned to

leave, but Aleen, suddenly aware that she would be denied the support of her companionship, caught the nun's arm and held tightly. "Please," she said imploringly. Her resolutions would crumble if she did not have the abbess's strength on which to depend.

The abbess accepted the tilt of Edmund's chin as a signal for her to leave, and after grasping Aleen's hands reassuringly, she closed the door slowly behind her, while Aleen desperately watched the moving door seal the privacy of the room.

The silence pressed alarmingly against her, and her heart raced within her. She must gather her emotions, she thought, and place them under the strictest guard. She quickly relaxed her face. Edmund must not read any of the emotions that tormented her soul. She must appear as a contented nun, and she crossed her arms and tucked her hands inside her sleeves in proper convent demeanor.

"Aleen," he said at last, the sound of his voice sending new rushes of sensations throughout her being.

Composing herself, she turned slowly to face him. He did not rise from his place, but sullenly studied her as his interlaced fingers rubbed against his lips.

Aleen suffered during his scrutiny. She had not wanted him to see her in her coarse robes. Black was not flattering to her. She had wanted him to remember her in her pretty gowns and soft veils. She felt terribly ugly and ridiculous, like a child in make-believe clothes. Something akin to fear gripped at her as he stood up and walked slowly toward her. Panic-stricken, she did not know how to guard herself from the excitement of his advancement. But as he approached, she quickly moved to the opposite side of the long table and stood beneath the crucifix. She would draw strength and courage from the symbol of the Lord's passion. Rebuked by her sudden movement away from him, he paused and then moved to where she was standing. He stood quietly as he studied the fibers in the folds of her veil and the slender shoulders so leisurely draped by it.

"Aleen," he said softly, as though confiding the word to delicate ears. "Aleen, you must know that word of your coming here surprised me greatly. Never had I thought this life would please you. Was it after I left for Tankenham that you decided on this?"

She shook her head negatively.

"Before I left?"

"It is difficult to say when the thought came to me."

He was displeased with the answer. He had thought, with a degree of masculine vanity, that her decision was made during his absence, when she had perhaps longed for him. Surely she had not rejected him by deciding on this when they were together at Lauxburgh. Not knowing what else to say, he asked, "Are you happy here?"

Aware of the crucifix so close to her, and feeling a compulsion for honesty, she answered, "I am as happy as it is possible to be in this world. One can be truly happy only in the next existence. I am contented, for the most part." Her words were indifferent, impersonal.

"If you are not wholly contented here, perhaps the life will become tedious and you will feel the need to abandon it. Surely you must think at times that you might return to secular life."

"I expect to stay here, my lord, until the day I die."

The finality of the answer brought a frown to his face. He took her gently by the shoulders and against her will turned her slowly and forcibly around. "Look at me," he demanded.

Her final answer steeled her courage, and she looked with expressionless eyes into his. He studied the slender face, the body he had once tenderly caressed. He would now lovingly embrace her again, but the religious garb forbade such a liberty. He could read nothing but determination in her face, and dropping his hands, permitted her to return to her former position.

With her back protectively hiding her reactions, she closed her eyes with an inaudible sigh of relief. She had hidden her emotions well. She had convinced him.

Edmund moved backward and leaned against the side of the table. How could he tell her that he had obtained the annulment of his vow? After such an exchange, how could he tell her that she should leave with him, that they should be happy together with the sanction of the church? She seemed unwavering in her resolves, and too unconcerned and uninterested in him. He could not tell her of the annulment. He would only shame her by so intimate a disclosure. And since she was truly so emphatic about her decision, she would not care that he had journeyed long and far for papal dispensation. If this was what she wanted, there was only one thing required, the formal statement of consent, and he moved toward the end of the table, sank into the chair, and took quill in hand. Glancing once again at the slender figure standing so resolutely before the crucifix, he finally put quill to paper with an air of resignation.

The scratching quill, had it been a dagger, could not have stabbed at her heart more painfully or drained it so completely of its life's blood. He was signing away her life, and she was painfully aware that she could accept the sacrifice only because of her love for him. Now he could return to Tankenham with a peaceful mind and a clear conscience. She was well cared for, and more importantly, by her resolution, she was no longer an obstacle hindering his vocation. She was still his wife, a position which no other woman could take from her, and she was content that at least the invisible bond that united them on earth was also recognized as a bond in heaven.

What Edmund could not pour forth in audible words he confided to the intimacy of the paper, and at length the scratching stopped, the pen was laid aside, and the paper folded. He stood up with difficulty, walked in her direction once more, and stood behind her. How could he bring himself to bid her farewell? The words were entirely inadequate when this would, in all probability, be their last meeting on earth. Perhaps a silent farewell was more appropriate, and after a moment he walked hastily to the door, his mantle billowing behind him.

With his abrupt departure her strength of will dissipated, and she wanted desperately to call for him. How could she let him go? No, come back, she wanted to scream. It is all a terrible, dreadful mistake. I love you. I love you dearly.

Covering her face with her hands, she began crying. "Oh, God, come to my assistance," she prayed in the words of David the prophet. "Oh, God, make haste to help me." The closing of the outer door forced open the gates of her emotions, and she sank to her knees and cried helplessly. "I will never see him again," she sobbed. "I love him so, and I shall never see him again."

The voices outside the door made her rise to her feet. No one must see her so debased. They must not know she was crying, and drawing nearer the crucifix in an attitude of prayer, she turned her head to conceal her reddened eyes. From the softness of the steps, it could only be the abbess who was making her way to where Edmund had placed the folded parchment. The crackling of paper sounded, and for many minutes the abbess read from it.

I shall rot in this place so long as Edmund is happy at Tankenham. I can endure this sacrifice for him—as long as he is happy.

"Lady Aleen," the nun said, holding out the paper as she brought it to her, "you must read this."

Aleen turned to accept it. "Lady Aleen, you have cried."

Without further comment or acknowledgment, Aleen took the paper, blinked and wiped the moisture from her eyes, and read the familiar script: "Reverend Mother, I willingly entrust to the care of Holy Mother Church and the Order of Saint Benedict my dear wife, Aleen, and give my consent for her to be accepted as a member of your religious order. Although I have received from the Holy Apostolic See the dispensation of a vow of continence I made some years before, I willingly surrender all the rights permitted by the Sacrament of Holy Matrimony. This sacrifice I humbly ask Almighty God to accept, and beg him thereby to bestow choice blessings on my dear wife, in both this world and the next. With this document I return to the Creator my love, the joy of my life, who was lent me for so brief a time."

It was embarrassing to read such a tender outpouring of a man's heart. Aleen frowned uncomprehendingly. This was not the declaration of a man who was to make religious vows. She looked up questioningly at the nun. Why, he loves me, she thought, and she read again: "I have received from the Holy Apostolic See the dispensation . . . my love, the joy of my life . . ."

She looked again at the smiling nun, who had closely watched Aleen's reaction to the contents of the document. With the intuition of one who had been the confidante of many troubled souls, the little nun understood all completely.

It had been a mistake, a terrible misunderstanding, and she confided to Aleen, "Edmund has left Tankenham. He stays now at Lauxburgh." With a mischievous smile, the nun added, "It will take too long to saddle a horse. Go—run after him. You can catch him if you but hurry."

Aleen looked blankly at her. Run after him? Her mind repeated. She means me to leave the convent—to leave the life of sacrifice to which I have resigned myself. But it cannot be. . . .

"He has just passed through the gate," the nun said, turning from the window. "Hurry," she whispered urgently.

Aleen looked at the crucifix for reassurance. "It is right that you should leave," the abbess was saying. "Go now, hurry."

"But, Reverend Mother . . ." Aleen said in confused protest.

"Go." The abbess smiled. "Go, follow after him."

It was like a dream, this realization of her fondest hopes, and she turned to leave. Then, facing the abbess once more, she bent down, grabbed her hand, and kissed it hard. She first walked, then hurried from the building, her skirts swinging about her in unaccustomed motions.

Refreshed by the cool evening breezes, she ran across the convent grounds as patches of fog, driven in from the sea, drifted by like giant puffs of flying cotton.

Edmund's horse was plodding in the distance, but a long stretch of pasture separated them, and a flock of sheep collecting near the gate threatened to block her way. She ran ahead, stumbling on the uneven turf and the rocks that speckled the ground. She panted hard, and her legs ached from the exertion, but she continued wildly, desperately. At last she reached the sheep, who bleated rebukingly as she sidestepped and pushed her way among their heavy, woolly bodies.

Only a stretch of meadow separated her from Edmund, who had been joined by his three soldier escorts. She continued running hard, and her veil, loosened by her running motions, was promptly snatched by a gust of wind and flung to the ground. From the corner of her eye she saw it tumbling furiously in the wind. The hair clasps that had held her hair so tightly to her head also weakened and fell from her, permitting her hair to cascade down her back and to fly in disarray about her head.

Breathlessly Aleen halted by the gate. In her excitement she had been unaware that she still held in her hand the parchment on which Edmund had written his declaration of love, and as she reached to open the gate, the parchment crackled noisily. With renewed determination and a desperate gasp for air, she resumed her run.

The day was coming to a rapid close, the fog was gaining in thickness and speed, and the winds hissed noisily by. "Edmund," she shouted as she ran through the gate, but the winds dispersed the sound. Duty suddenly startled her as the bleating sheep spilled through the gate into the open, unprotected meadow. But there was no time to shepherd them into the safety of the enclosed convent grounds. She must hurry, and she called again into the wind, "Edmund, Edmund . . ."

Soon her energies would be spent, and Edmund, if the wind persisted in impeding her call, would ride off into the distance, leaving her to the darkness that was fast settling upon the land. Once more she cried, "Edmund, Edmund . . ." This time the racing wind permitted the name to reach the rider, who quickly reined in his horse. "Edmund!" He heard it again. It was not a fantasy, nor an imaginary voice. Jerking his horse around, he looked at the black-draped figure tripping in the distance. Nudging his horse into a canter, he rode to meet the woman whose skirts were beating hard against her legs, preventing her from moving farther.

Dismounting a short distance from her, he stood watching as she brushed hair from her face and clutched a piece of parchment to her breast. As Edmund walked slowly to meet her, she held the crumpled paper toward him and looked beseechingly at him. Were his words true? Was his declaration real? His arms opened, and in a moment he was gathering her close. For long moments they stood there disbelieving reality—Edmund holding his beloved tightly, his face pressed firmly against her slender neck, and Aleen, against his heart, shedding tears of relief and joy.

One thing could not be denied—they were together. Forever. And as though to confirm it, the finger of God seemed to stir the winds to encircle them in blessed and invisible bonds.

It was too much to comprehend, so many emotions tumbling about for dominance. But then something struggled for recognition. As though a small voice pleaded to be heard—as though it writhed and squeezed through the affections, demanding sound. Then, after the first rush of emotions, when the breeze cooled the tears upon her cheeks, and her soul quieted for a moment, a small voice fell lovingly, caressingly upon her recollection, conveying aged words borne on the breath of time: "Delight in the Lord, trust also in him, and he will give thee the desires of thy heart."